Ragtime Dudes at the World's Fair

Ragtime Dudes at the World's Fair

Richard Gartee

Lake and Emerald Publications

Books by Richard Gartee
—Fiction—
Lancelot's Grail
Lancelot's Disciple
Ragtime Dudes at the World's Fair
Ragtime Dudes in a Thin Place
Ragtime Dudes Meet a Paris Flapper
—Poetry—
Mountain Breathing
Watching Waves
Canyon Falls
—Non-Fiction—
Skating on Skim Ice

A complete list of currently available titles by the author can be found at www.gartee.com

Published by Lake & Emerald Publications, LLC
Gainesville, FL
www.lepublications.com

Library of Congress Control Number: 2020919919

ISBN 978-0-9895104-0-0

This is a work of fiction. Names, characters, places, and incidents either are the product of the author's imagination or are historical references used fictitiously, and any other resemblance to living persons, or actual businesses, companies, or events is entirely coincidental.

Typesetting services by BOOKOW.COM

CHAPTER 1

"Good. They won't get us in here." Julius slid into an empty chair next to Mo, who was enjoying a leisurely brunch with their best friend, Bryce, in the cavernous dining room of the Fifth Avenue Hotel.

Bryce held up a finger to signal their waiter. "Who won't?"

"The Micks. The Tammany Hall men."

Bryce screwed up his face. "Why would they come here?"

"They couldn't," Mo said. "They'd never get past the doorman. Hell, I can't even get in unless I'm with Bryce. By the way, Julius, how'd you manage it? Come in over the transom?"

"I told him I was meeting you two in the restaurant. Bryce's name opens doors."

Lucky for him that it did. The white marble Fifth Avenue Hotel spanned a full block between Twenty-third and Twenty-fourth streets. Its vaulted dining room was the social, cultural, and political hub of New York City elite and a favorite watering hole of Bryce's father, Senator Holloway. Unlike Bryce, he and Mo were peons.

A waiter in a tux appeared and poured coffee into Julius's cup. "Orange juice, sir?"

Julius nodded, and a pitcher of juice appeared from behind the waiter's back. He poured. "Anything else, sir?"

Julius studied the cornucopia of cheeses, meats, fish, and breads arrayed on the table. "No, thank you. There's more than enough here."

Bryce plucked a bottle of champagne from an ice bucket. "Forget the juice, have a little bubbly."

The waiter reappeared. "Allow me, sir." He deftly retrieved the bottle from Bryce and filled a fluted glass for Julius. He topped off Bryce and Mo's glasses and nestled the bottle back into the ice.

"We can pour," Bryce said.

The waiter gave him a stiff smile. "I'm sure you're capable, sir, but I would lose my situation."

Julius shook his head. Bryce knew better and ought to tip the man a little extra for his faux pas.

"My apologies," Bryce said.

"Think nothing of it, sir." The waiter gave a curt nod and removed himself.

Mo turned to Julius. "So, what's this about some Irishmen?"

"You remember that cute little colleen from Brooklyn?"

"Bridget." Mo smiled. "She was a wild one."

"The most repressed always are," Bryce said.

Julius needed to bring the discussion back to the problem at hand. "And apparently a virgin before she met us."

Bryce grinned. "I can testify that she was not."

"Well, her family believes she was, and that we corrupted her."

"We did no such thing," Mo said. "She had big eyes for the big city and an appetite for bohemian artists long before she ever met us. I learned a thing or two from her."

"Mo's right," Bryce said. "We saw her around the Village pretty often before she started partying with us. But so what? Bridget's a grown woman with the same right as a man to love whom she wants, when she wants."

Julius agreed. It was their duty to love any woman who wanted to be loved by them, married or unmarried. Of course, a lot of society branded them libertines for that, and their philosophy didn't find favor with spouses or parents. Especially traditional Irish families who ran Brooklyn, as evident in the situation with Bridget.

"Her family doesn't know about those other times," Julius said. "Only that she was with us."

"If she's pregnant, it wasn't us. I'm always careful," Bryce said. "Aren't you?"

Julius glanced at Mo and nodded. "No one says she's with child. They're just pissed she lost her virginity to some New York dandies."

Mo tugged his ear lobe. "I wonder how her family found out."

Julius shrugged. "What difference does that make? Word is, there are a couple of hulking Irishmen asking around the neighborhood bars if anyone knows where we live."

"How do you know it's about Bridget?"

"They mentioned her by name. Asked which men she'd been seen with and where they lived."

"Who are these guys?"

"I don't know. Brothers. Maybe cousins?"

Bryce laughed. "Close as some of those families are, they could be one and the same."

"I'm not sure you should be laughing, Bryce. They were asking about you, too."

"I'll have my dad talk to the Tammany Hall leader, Big Tim Sullivan. He used to be in the state senate with Dad back in aught-two."

Mo passed Julius a magazine opened to a feature article on the upcoming Louisiana Purchase Exposition. "Have you read this? We were talking about it before you came."

Julius stared at the magazine. He and his friends had Irish thugs on their trail, and they were talking about the Exposition?

Mo tapped the magazine with his finger. "Read this."

Julius studied the special eight page supplement to Collier's Magazine. "I've been hearing a lot about it. Supposed to be twice the size of the one they held in Chicago when we were kids."

Mo reached over, flipped the page, and pointed to a list of featured exhibits. "Look at this. Twelve palaces filled with things we love."

"Horticulture?"

"Not my first love, no. But look at these others: science, electricity, engineering, art, literature, music—"

"Ragtime," Bryce said. "Scott Joplin lives in St. Louis. We should go."

Julius skimmed the rest of the article, nodding as he read. "A palace of electricity? Sounds great. When?"

"Anytime really," Mo said. "When can you take a vacation?"

"I'll ask." Julius, handy with tools and interested in the rush of scientific discoveries of the new century, worked as an assistant to an engineer who crafted special items for various science departments at Columbia University. Whenever a professor dreamed up an experiment to measure some reaction, or test some new theory, Julius's boss was the one who built the contraption according to the professor's design. It let Julius get involved in a lot of the latest scientific theories. But he'd rather get in on the work Edison and Tesla were doing.

"The fair opens April thirtieth," Mo said, "but it'll stay open until December."

"It'd be nice to get out of the city during the summer heat," Bryce said.

Julius furrowed his brow. "The city may get hotter sooner than that, if Bridget's family finds out where we live."

"I told you, don't worry about them," Bryce said. "When a Catholic girl gets in trouble, the Irish lock her in a convent and chain her cell with a Rosary."

Julius hung his head, embarrassed for Bryce, who didn't have the sense to be. "Sometimes you push wit too far."

Bryce grinned. "Just trying to keep everyone amused."

"I didn't say the girl was in trouble. I said we are."

Bryce waved the problem away. "Julius, stop fretting. If she's not pregnant, that's even better. These things blow over."

The person he really felt sorry for was Bridget. Julius grew up in a Catholic neighborhood and understood full-well why she'd ventured away from it, and the likely outcome now she'd been found out. The convent was a real possibility.

CHAPTER 2

Finn and Bird worked their way through Greenwich Village, downing pints and questioning patrons of neighborhood taverns. Both men were boxers, former stars in their respective weight classes. Finn was a bantamweight whose pinpoint accuracy left many an opponent battered and defeated. Bird had once been the heavyweight champion. His eighty-four inch reach and powerhouse punch scored numerous knockouts.

Bird wasn't his name in the ring. He'd acquired that moniker after breaking his nose so many times that it whistled when he exhaled. To avoid ridicule, he tended to breathe through his mouth. This, combined with the fact that he'd withstood far too many blow to the head, gave the impression of mental dullness. Punchy though he was, Bird had Finn as his protector. A six-foot-one giant guarded by a scrappy five-foot-seven rooster might seem like a vaudeville act, but one sharp look from Finn stopped any laughter.

Finn, hardened by the numerous street fights of his youth, had made an honest living the only way he knew how—with his fists. Fortunately, he'd left the sport before he ended up like Bird. His shoulders sloped more that Bird's, but the muscles banding his arms still commanded respect. He lacked Bird's long reach, so he'd made his reputation by getting in close with quick, fast jabs.

The tavern owner came over to where Finn and Bird were talking with some of his regulars. "You Pinkertons?"

Finn's dark eyes darted to the man, and he stepped protectively in front of Bird. "Do we look like detectives?"

"None I ever saw, but word in the neighborhood is you been asking a lot of questions. I won't have you bothering my customers."

Bird fumbled in his jacket pocket and brought out a folded newspaper clipping. "Cousin's daughter. . . marry. . . must." A tremor in his hand caused the paper to shake.

Finn pulled out a chair. "Here, Bird, sit down before you fall down."

"Is he drunk?" the owner said.

"No, sometimes his legs get weak. Too many years in the ring."

The tavern owner apprised Bird. "I recognize him from somewhere."

"You do. This is Goliath McGuigan."

Bird wiped perspiration from the bald parts of his steeply receded hairline.

"But you just called him Bird—"

"His friends can call him Bird. You call him Champ."

"Right. Champ. But you still haven't explained what you're doing here."

Finn took the newspaper clipping from Bird and showed it around. "We're looking for these three dandies. They probably have a reputation for dallying with 'good' girls."

One of the patrons pointed to Bridget. "I've seen her. She used to come around the Village. Haven't seen much of her lately."

Finn closed on him. Old habit. "What about the men? Was she with them?"

"Sometimes, but more often with others."

Bird stood and grabbed the man's shirt, nearly lifting him off the gournd. "You?"

"Hey, you pugs, none of that in here," the owner said.

"Sure, sure." Finn pried Bird's fingers from the man's shirt.

Bird exhaled forcefully through his nose. It made a sharp tweet.

Several of the men sniggered. Finn whirled around, ready to clock any one of them.

"Not me," the man said, tucking his shirt back into his pants. "She fancied dandies like them in the picture."

Finn pulled a silver dollar from his pocket and handed it to the owner. "We're the good guys, just trying to help Bird's cousin. A round of beers for the table, please."

That brought smiles from the patrons.

"So, you've seen these guys around," Finn said. "Anyone know their names or where they live?"

"Two of them live somewhere in the Village." The man pointed to the picture. "This one standing next to your cousin lives uptown with the richies."

"But you'll find him playing ragtime in any joint with a piano," offered another.

"Now, see?" Finn said. "That's helpful."

Three days since the meeting at her parents' home in Brooklyn, three days searching every pub in Manhattan, and finally they'd found their first clue.

At that meeting, Bridget's mother had greeted them at the door and hugged Bird. "Thank you both for coming. My husband's in the parlor. Please come through." She was a tiny woman, the top of her head barely reaching Bird's armpit, but Finn could sense the steel in her spine.

A distinguished looking man in a charcoal-gray suit stood and shook their hands. "I'm Bridget's father, John."

"Patrick Finnegan, but just call me Finn. I'm Bird's best mate, sort of his protector when he gets confused."

"This is my cousin, M-Mar. . ." Bird faltered.

"I'm Mary Elizabeth," the woman said. "Nice to meet you, Mr. Finnegan." She handed Bird a newspaper clipping. "These are the libertines who dallied with our Bridget. John spotted it in his evening paper."

8

Bird stared at it dumbly. Finn took it from his hand. It was a picture of three dandies with their arms around three women. The caption read: "Theater goers celebrate opening of new Broadway show."

Mary Elizabeth pointed to one of the women. "That's our Bridget."

"The caption doesn't give any names," Finn said.

"Thank God for that," her father said.

"Can we talk to her?" Finn said. "Find out their names and other places they took her?"

"Won't do any good," her father said. "She clammed up."

"Besides," her mother said, "she's sequestered now."

"The nuns promised not to let a man near her, not even family."

"If we find them," Finn said, "what do you want us to do?"

"Make one of them marry her and thrash the other two." He handed Bird two double-eagles.

Bird turned the coins over in his palm and stared at them. When it dawned on him what he had, Bird said, "You don't have to pay us. . . M-mary Elizabeth is family." Sometimes he could speak pretty clearly. Other times, not so much.

"That's kind," her father said, "but you'll have to search Manhattan. There'll be expenses. Spend whatever you need to find them. If that money runs out, come back for more."

Bird handed the money to Finn. "Don't worry, Mary Elizabeth . . . we'll . . . regret . . ."

"Bird means we'll find them and make them regret messing with your girl." Finn punched the air with a flurry of short, quick jabs.

"Only two of the men," her father said. "Leave enough of the third for the altar."

Bird bobbed his head. "Marry Bridget."

"But Mr. Finnegan—" her father said.

"Call me Finn, please."

"Finn, one thing we don't want is for her reputation to be sullied any further. While you're making inquiries after these men, please don't suggest that she's lost . . . anything."

"Pure as winter's snow, as far as we know."

"You don't have to go that far, just not . . . less than whole."

"Your wife used the word 'dallied.' Can we say that?"

John glanced at Mary Elizabeth and nodded. "Dalliance will serve." He shook their hands. "The quicker you find them, and she's wed, the sooner the matter will be forgotten."

Outside on the stoop, Finn stared at the picture. Manhattan was a big place, but at least they knew one place they'd been.

"Okay, Bird," he said, "we're going to the theater."

CHAPTER 3

The following evening, Mo returned to the Greenwich Village apartment he shared with Julius. He hung his bowler on the rack and fell onto the divan, exhausted from searching for an agent.

"Julius?"

No answer. Guess he wasn't home yet.

Mo made rent and a little pocket money giving drawing lessons to a small clutch of old ladies who were friends of Bryce's mother. It wasn't the art career he'd dreamed of, but it kept him in bread and butter while he waited for his big break. He preferred oils—impressionism to be exact. His work was good, even if he did say so himself, but wealthy New Yorkers savvy enough to like impressionism were enamored with the Europeans. Galleries he showed his work to all told him he needed an agent first, but finding an agent was as difficult as finding a gallery, and took just as much time.

So in a nod to more traditional art, he painted portraits. A friend of Mrs. Holloway had commissioned him to paint her debutante daughter. He'd posed the girl in the family garden amongst blooming tulips, and painted her upper body, face, and hands as detailed as if he'd used a camera obscura. Then he worked in some modern touches, giving the background and her dress an impressionistic flair, The combination created a striking effect.

Mo had been well paid and received compliments from those who saw the finished painting, but so far it hadn't yielded any other offers. It didn't matter. He didn't intend to make portraiture his profession, anyway. He'd merely accepted the job hoping her family would spread his name around their social circle. For that was the problem, his name. Not because it was Silverstein, but because it was unknown.

Sure, an unspoken current of anti-Semitism ran beneath the surface of the upper set, but they were at least careful with their words. And even though Mo didn't come from a family of bankers or important money, the Protestant descendants of New Amsterdam found the interconnectedness of Jewish families as inscrutable as the interrelatedness of Irish Catholics. So they took no risk offending Jews they had to do business with. No, Mo's problem was simply that those who could afford large oil portraits for their parlor cared mainly that the signature on the painting would make others envious. His name didn't have that level of recognition. Yet.

Two sharp raps on the apartment door brought Mo to his feet. He turned the knob and found Bryce grinning like a cat in the lap of a Broadway showgirl. "Julius home yet?"

Mo shook his head and glanced at the clock. "Soon, though." He stepped aside and waved Bryce in. "Can I fix you a drink?"

"Always." Bryce doffed his hat and set it on a hook next to Mo's.

Julius and Mo's apartment wasn't large. A small living room and smaller kitchen were enough for two bachelors. It only had one bedroom, but there were two beds. A bay window on one wall, advertised as a "study," was used by Mo for his studio. There was plenty of natural light if he kept the windows clean. Their kitchen had a two-burner gas stove, a sink with a cold water tap, and an ice box that fit a standard-size block of ice in the upper part, but the bottom cabinet barely had room for milk, butter, cheese, a hunk of meat, and a pail of beer. Beneath the ice box was a wide shallow drip pan that had to be emptied daily.

He opened the upper door and used an ice pick to chip off enough ice to fill two glasses. A chunk of ice flew off and landed next to his shoe with a splash.

Splash?

The drip pan had overflowed, creating the good size puddle in which he was standing. In the division of labor between roommates, it was Mo's job to empty it. Sometimes, like today, he forgot, and when he did, Julius gave him hell.

Mo set the glasses on the counter and picked up the overfull pan. More water sloshed over the sides. Oh, well, what's a little extra? He emptied the pan in the sink and threw a towel down on the floor. It soaked through instantly. He picked it up and wrung it out over the sink, repeating until the puddle was gone and the floor only slightly damp.

"Mo, did you get lost?" Bryce shouted from the other room.

"No. I'm coming." He filled each glass with a generous pour of whiskey and carried them into the room, swirling the ice. "Sorry. I had to mop up melted water from the ice box. Don't tell Julius."

"You guys need a maid."

"I am the maid."

Bryce held his glass to the light. "So, is this the mop water?"

"Nah, this fine whiskey is imported all the way from Brooklyn. Best quality you can buy for thirty-five cents a quart—guaranteed to be aged at least seven days."

Bryce laughed and took a sip. "Not too shabby."

Mo offered Bryce the divan and took the chair for himself. "Are you as worried as Julius about his angry Irishmen?"

Bryce sat, stretched out his legs, and crossed his feet at the ankles. "Not something to worry about." He sipped a little more whiskey. "Have you and Julius decided when we're going to St. Louis?"

"When, not whether?"

"Oh, we definitely must go. It will be the largest world's fair ever held. We'd kick ourselves for years if we missed it."

Mo couldn't disagree. "Have you figured out what it will cost?"

"What difference does that make? If it took every penny we had, and we came back broke, we'd never regret it."

"Bryce, that's easier to say when you have a trust fund. Julius and I will need a solid estimate to determine if we have enough now, or how long it will take us to raise it."

A metallic clang of a pail struck the door. The knob turned and Julius entered, carrying a pail of beer. "Hi, Bryce. I see you guys started without me."

"Just got here a few minutes ago."

Julius hung up his hat and started for the kitchen. "I'll be right back. I'm going to get a glass of beer and set this in the ice box. Either of you want beer?"

"We'll finish these first," Mo said. "Be careful. The kitchen floor is still damp."

"You mopped?"

"Something like that."

"I'll take a glass of beer," Bryce said.

Mo raised his eyebrows.

Bryce held up his whiskey. "A chaser for the mop water."

"All right," Mo called to the kitchen. "Bring me one, too."

Julius returned with three foamy glasses.

"How was work?" Bryce said.

"Interesting. We're making a mirrored box to measure refracted versus reflected light."

"Did you ask when you could take a vacation?"

"Haven't found the right moment to bring it up."

"Why the hesitation?"

"I don't want to tip off my boss, but I hope one of the professors we make contraptions for will recommend me to Edison's lab. Or Tesla's, for that matter."

"So, you're not planning to stay at Columbia, anyway?"

"Not if I can work where they're inventing practical gadgets instead of scientific ones that only measure the theoretical."

"Then ask your boss tomorrow. Before you arrived, Mo and I were trying to settle on when we should leave for St. Louis."

Mo held up his hand like a cop directing carriage traffic. "Wait a minute, Bryce. We were discussing what it would cost."

"I'm sure we've enough saved," Julius said. "But Bryce, what's the hurry? When you talked to your dad about the Irish, did he suggest we leave town for a while?"

"Um . . . he's in Albany this week. I'll bring it up when he comes home next weekend. Don't worry about the Irish situation. I promise my dad will resolve it to everyone's satisfaction."

"Then what's the rush?" Julius said. "I thought we talked about summertime."

"Yeah," Bryce said, "but the Fair opens April thirtieth. Wouldn't it be great to be there on opening day?"

Mo rubbed his jaw. "That's really soon. We still need to find out what train fare, admission, and hotel rooms will cost."

"We could share a hotel room," Julius said. "That'd save us something."

"Yes. We'll get a suite," Bryce said. "Let's go back through those magazine articles and make a list of exhibits we'd like to see. That'll help us figure how long we'll want to stay."

Mo handed round several magazines and newspapers containing articles about the Fair that they'd saved, and the men began to peruse them. He fetched a large drawing pad and drew a vertical line down the center. One column he labeled "Things to see," and the other "Things to do before we leave." In the second column he wrote: "train tickets, hotel reservation, pay rent (how many weeks?)"

He turned to Bryce. "I've got drawing lessons to give tomorrow, and Julius has work. Why don't you find out what round trip train fare will be?"

"I'll have Jenkins do it first thing in the morning."

Jenkins was the Holloways' long-time butler, who generally radiated wordless disapproval whenever he and Julius visited Bryce. He wondered how Jenkins would react when tasked to arrange their journey.

"Ask him to see what the hotel options are, too," Julius said.

"Sure, but keep an eye out. Some of these articles may recommend certain hotels."

"This is going to require another beer," Julius said. "Anyone else need a refill?"

They all did.

CHAPTER 4

In the upscale New Jersey borough of Florham Park, Mr. Jones entered the foyer of his mansion, removed his silk hat, and handed it to his butler. He pulled out his gold pocket watch, noted the time, and slid it back into his waistcoat. "Mrs. Jones!" he called down the polished hardwood hallway.

She appeared from a doorway at the other end. "Yes, Mr. Jones."

"Please join me in the parlor and ask the maid to set out some sherry. I've a wonderful idea I wish to discuss with you."

Mrs. Jones, wearing a floor-length forest-green skirt looped up like drapery above a tangerine serge underskirt into which a white pleated blouse was tucked, came toward him. She called over her shoulder, "Nan, sherry in the parlor, *tout de suite, s'il vous plaît.*"

Mr. Jones smiled. His wife, an ordinary girl from a good Philadelphia family twenty-five years ago, now tossed foreign phrases about like breadcrumbs to pigeons. Who was she trying to impress? Not him. He'd made a fortune mining precious metals in places he'd never even seen. It seemed unnecessary to traipse about the globe when all those governments wanted were investments. His strategy had profited handsomely.

What had not paid off was the move to Florham Park. After years of struggling to make inroads with elite social circles in New York, Mrs. Jones persuaded him to leave the snobs of the city and build a grand home in the Garden State. She had selected a parcel of land neighboring the estates of Dr. Leslie Ward, one of the founders of the Prudential Insurance Company, and of Mrs. Hamilton Twombly, granddaughter of Cornelius Vanderbilt.

The move, an attempt to outflank the Astors and their ilk and gain entry to their ranks, failed. It seemed no matter how much wealth he piled in the vault, they were destined to be seen as nouveau riche by those who looked down their puny Puritan noses at the Joneses of New Jersey. As a father of three unmarried grown daughters, this worried him, and his wife even more.

Six years ago, witnessing the way even old Knickerbocker families fawned over visiting nobility, Mrs. Jones decided on a new tack. She explained to him that numerous Americans of means, just like them, had wed their daughters to titled Europeans, instantly making the girls Duchess this and Countess that. Moreover, these titles were hereditary, so his grandsons would be Lords of the realm. Let Cornelius Vanderbilt put that in his pipe and smoke it.

With his blessing, Mrs. Jones hired a governess to prepare their girls for marriages into noble houses. Mrs. Coggeshall was American, but she spoke with an English accent acquired from several years spent in her ancestral village of Essex, England. Her fluency extended to French, Italian, and Portuguese, all of which she taught his daughters. When his youngest turned eighteen, Mrs. Coggeshall declared her task finished and departed his employ.

Mr. Jones's daughters were now in their early twenties and ripe for the altar, but he had for some time balked at packing them off to Europe like baubles sent to catch some Baron's fancy. To his eye, his girls were sparkling jewels, and to his thinking, let the manor born come to him. But the upper class weren't calling on Florham Park, thirty miles from Manhattan. As of late, Mrs. Jones had been pressing him to take the family abroad.

Ah, but no need for that now.

Mrs. Jones preceded him into the parlor, took her place on the brocade divan, and smoothed her skirt.

The maid brought a silver tray bearing a cut-glass decanter of sherry and two matching glasses. She poured, handed them each a glass, and said, "Will there be anything else, ma'am?"

"No. You can go," Mr. Jones said.

Nan left and closed the French-pane parlor doors behind her.

Mr. Jones touched the rim of his glass to his wife's. "To you, my dear." He took a sip.

"And to you, sir." She likewise drank. "Now, what is the cause for this celebration?"

"The Louisiana Purchase Exposition," he said.

She smiled. "Oh? Are we going?"

"Not us, our daughters."

"Why not the whole family?"

"We would only get in the way."

"Of what?"

"Your scheme, my dear. I read today that over fifty countries are sending exhibits to the Fair. Kings, queens, emperors, and all manner of aristocrats are expected to attend. Then it hit me. Why suffer a long voyage to lands where we won't understand half of what they're saying, when the very people we want our daughters to meet are coming to America?"

He saw her eyes twinkle as she embraced the idea. But he beheld reservation there, too. He waited.

"I like it," she said. "But I don't care for the notion of sending them without us. What kind of message does that give prospective suitors?"

"That they are capable and ready to leave their parents for any castle or kingdom that is lucky enough to have them."

She bit her lip. "I do wish we still had Mrs. Coggeshall. She'd be an excellent chaperone for this venture."

"Mrs. Jones, they're not school girls in need of a governess. Lily will be sufficient chaperone for the younger two. She has a firm head on her and will bring them through all right."

"Nevertheless, Lily is not Mrs. Coggeshall."

Mr. Jones laughed. "I'm sure Lily would be delighted to know that."

Lily, hovering outside the parlor door, shushed her sisters. The St. Louis World's Fair? Alone? Oh, my!

As for Mother's comparison, Lily would be proud to be considered half the free-thinker her governess had been. Mrs. Coggeshall proved far more the modern woman than Mother had known when she hired her. Mother had focused on the fact that she came from Newport, Rhode Island, now the most desirable of places to the New York set. It didn't hurt that her ancestor, John Coggeshall, was one of the founders of Newport, and in colonial times, Rhode Island's President.

Had Mother known that Mrs. Coggeshall was also a supporter of women's suffrage and Victoria Woodhull's writings on free love, she'd have never hired her. In addition to teaching etiquette, posture, dress, and romance languages, Mrs. Coggeshall slipped in lessons on anatomy and reproductive biology. She taught them that a walnut-size sponge soaked in a solution of iron sulfate acted as an effective spermicide that could be put in place before they went out.

With this knowledge, Lily and her sisters had loved as they pleased, with nary a pregnancy to show for it.

And now they were to go to St. Louis unchaperoned? Were they ready?

Oh, yes they were. And God bless Mrs. Coggeshall.

CHAPTER 5

A week before the Fair was to open, the doorman of the Holloways' Park Avenue apartment building called upstairs to say Julius and Mo were in the lobby. Jenkins came down to receive them, but once inside the apartment he left them standing in the foyer while he went to find Bryce.

"What the hell, Jenkins?" Bryce said when he saw who it was. "You've known these guys since I was in sixth grade. You could have seated them in the parlor."

"Sorry, sir."

"Well, bring us some drinks."

Jenkins pulled out his pocket watch, showed him the hour, and frowned.

God, Jenkins was worse than a nanny. Bryce shrugged and gave him a goofy grin that made his friends laugh.

Jenkins left.

His mother's large calico cat sauntered in and sat in the middle of the room surveying his visitors.

Julius and Mo looked troubled. Bryce hoped they weren't here to back out of the trip. Bryce pointed to the pet. "That's Mother's new cat, Lam. She says it's short for Lambert, but he thinks it stands for lord and master."

Jenkins returned with a silver tray containing glasses and a decanter of sherry. Lam held his ground, forcing the butler to step around him. Jenkins served the men and discreetly departed.

Lam leaped onto the arm of the divan and studied Mo.

"Lam! Get down from there. Leave Mo alone."

The cat stepped on Mo's leg, walked across him, and stood on Julius. He rubbed his chin against both Julius's lapels and settled onto his lap.

"Egyptians worshiped cats as gods," Bryce said, "and Lam still holds that truth to be self-evident."

Julius absent-mindedly ran his hand along the cat's silky back with a smile on his face, either from the joke or the cat. Then the smile disappeared. "Hasn't your dad talked to Big Tim Sullivan yet?"

Bryce swallowed hard and looked at the floor. Bringing up complications from his wild nights to Father was a matter that required finesse. He hadn't quite worked up to it. "You know Big Tim was elected to the US Senate last year, so he's not in Albany anymore."

"So, the answer is no," Mo said.

"Well . . . I'm certain Dad will, first time Big Tim's home from Washington."

"I know your family has a telephone. Don't they have those in the US Senate, too?"

"What's the hurry?"

Julius drained his tiny thimble of sherry and refilled his glass. This disturbed the cat, who promptly left. "Some old Irish boxers have been nosing around our neighborhood."

"It's probably nothing."

"They asked about you, too. Wanted to know where the three dandies who dallied with 'good girls' lived."

"That's not the half of it," Mo said. "Someone said Bridget's uncle is the bishop of the Brooklyn diocese."

Bryce whistled. "No wonder she came to Manhattan looking for a little fun."

Julius made a face. "Yes, but unless your dad's got a Cardinal in his pocket, Big Tim's influence may not be enough."

"I'm sure a suitable donation to the diocese can buy a bishop's indulgence. I'll talk to Dad."

Refilling his sherry for the third time, Julius said. "You promised you'd do that before. We're beginning to think your idea about going to St. Louis for opening day is a good one."

Mo nodded. "Get us out of town while your father works his magic."

"I changed my mind," Bryce said. "I forgot we had tickets to see *Beau Brummell* at the New Amsterdam Theater this week. It took a month to get them."

"Better to miss a play than get caught there by some Irish thugs," Julius said.

"Oh, those Micks would never look for us at the theater. I doubt if an Irish pugilist can even spell Broadway."

"Since those tickets are so hard to come by," Mo said, "I'm sure we could sell them and put the money toward our trip."

"And opening day at the Fair was *your* idea," Julius said.

Bryce stroked his mustache. "You have a point." Since he'd never mentioned the Irish matter, his father hadn't begun to fix it. But he'd honestly thought it would go away on its own. Obviously, he'd been wrong. Staying out of sight for a few weeks seemed prudent. It was too early in the season to go to the Hamptons, and still too cold in the Catskills. St. Louis seemed perfect.

Julius reached for the decanter and then took his hand away. "Let's go out. I can't sit here drinking sherry like I drink beer or I'll be flat on my ass. If we're leaving this week, we've got a lot to discuss."

Bryce jumped up. Yes! They could see a play anytime. Opening day only happened once. "Right you are, Julius. Let's go make some plans."

CHAPTER 6

Tuesday evening, Julius and Mo were packing their suitcases when they heard drunken, belligerent voices in the street below their open window. "I know they're living somewhere around here. I can smell the lecherous thoughts in their brains leaking out their ear holes."

Julius went to the bay window and peeked through a crack in the curtains. That was too close to suit him. "Mo, we can't come back to this place after the Fair."

"You're overreacting. Bryce promised—"

"Yeah, Bryce promised. He's a great guy to be around and funny as hell, but he's about as reliable as a doped racehorse." Julius surveyed the living room and Mo's studio. They rented the apartment furnished, so leaving the furniture behind wouldn't be a problem. But both of them were avid readers and their bookshelves were crammed. In addition, Mo had a stack of back issues of *The Studio* and other art magazines he'd never give up.

As if reading his mind, Mo said, "If we're skipping out, where are we going to store this stuff until we get back?"

Mo was an only child whose parents were deceased. The rest of his orthodox family shunned him because he favored liberal arts over rabbinical studies and preferred the company of gentiles—especially shiksas. So Mo's relatives weren't going to help out.

Julius scratched his head. "Nowhere I can think of. We'll have to take everything with us."

"We can't fit all this in two suitcases."

Julius snapped his fingers. "Mother's brother has a couple of large steamer trunks in his attic. My cousins and I used to hide in them, playing hide-and-seek."

Wednesday morning, Julius waited until he saw the landlord leave and then hoofed it to his aunt and uncle's house across town. His uncle was at work, but his aunt said he could keep the darn trunks for all she cared.

"Thanks, but we won't need them long."

Now, how to get two big trunks to their apartment? He'd need help.

He kissed her on the cheek. "I'll be back for them shortly."

In a market area a few blocks from her house, Julius located a teamster unloading goods in an alley behind the shops. After a brief haggle, they agreed on a price for the man to drive him back to his uncle's, help load the trunks on the wagon, and deliver them to Greenwich Village. An unexpected expense? Yes, but the quickest means of getting the trunks home.

* * *

Over on Park Avenue, Jenkins was packing Bryce's suitcase for him while Bryce looked in a full-length mirror, shifting stacks of gold coins and silver dollars from one pocket to the other and judging their effect on the cut of his clothes.

Jenkins left the room and returned with a roll of white adhesive tape used for bandages. He tore off two strips about three feet long and laid them, adhesive side up, on the bed. "Excuse me, sir. You're inviting robbery that way. May I suggest an alternative?"

At Jenkins' instructions, Bryce laid his ten- and twenty-dollar gold pieces on the tape. He held back a double-eagle for unexpected expenses and a half-eagle for mad money. Jenkins laid the second strip over the first, sealing the gaps between coins with his thumb and forefinger. "If you'll pull up your shirt, sir . . ." Jenkins wrapped the homemade money belt around Bryce's waist and started to tape it in place.

"Wait!"

"Sir?"

"I see what to do. But not yet. I'll want to bathe before I leave. No bathtubs on a train, you know."

"Of course, sir."

He also wanted to say goodbye to a Broadway chorus girl he'd been seeing lately. And who knows? His shirt might be coming off—if he was lucky.

"If you're going to be carrying this kind of money," Jenkins said, "I suggest you have a tailor make you a money belt."

Good idea, but there wasn't time now. He'd barely made it to the bank before they closed, the bulk of his day having been squandered in a lengthy row with his parents over the trip. Mother had also read about the Fair and worried that St. Louis was too wild. "Why, they're going to keep Philippine savages and American Indians right inside the Exposition grounds!"

"Mother, they are perfectly pacified—part of the scientific anthropology exhibits. There will also be grand palaces of European art and music. It's an opportunity not to be missed."

"Yes, but why the sudden rush?" his father said. "Are you in some kind of trouble?"

Bryce considered telling him, but he was already meeting opposition to the trip. Bringing up Bridget would not help. "No, sir. Saturday's opening day. President Roosevelt is going to open the Exposition, and Secretary Taft is scheduled to speak. Sure, we could go anytime, but opening day only happens once."

Senator Holloway's tone softened. "Roosevelt, huh? I thought he inaugurated the Exposition a year ago."

Bryce shrugged. "Perhaps he's coming back."

Mrs. Holloway wrung her hands. "But St. Louis is so far."

"Only two or three days by train," Bryce said.

"But what kind of people will be on those trains?"

"Oh, for Heaven's sake," her husband said. "I ride the train back and forth to Albany all the time."

"First class. Have you forgotten when he ran away from school to join Roosevelt in Tampa? Where did the army put him? In third class with impoverished immigrants."

"I'm not going alone. Mo and Julius are coming, too."

The look she gave him said she wasn't impressed.

"Mother, think of the prestige. The Louisiana Purchase Exposition is going to be the biggest thing to happen in years. People will remember it for decades to come. You'll be the only one of your friends whose son was there for the opening."

She turned to her husband. "All right, but he needs a first-class ticket. And a berth in a Pullman. I don't want him sleeping on a bench like a . . . hobo."

"Hobos ride in freight cars," Bryce said.

Her eyes welled up.

Oh, why hadn't he kept his mouth shut? He'd been winning 'til he said that.

The senator pulled out his watch and looked at the time. "Fine. First class and a Pullman. I'm going to miss my own train if I don't leave now. Jenkins! Call down to the doorman and tell him to hail me a hansom." He shook Bryce's hand. "Travel safe, son. And stay out of trouble."

Bryce walked him to the door. He'd landed his first victory. Strike while the iron was hot. "There's another matter, sir. If I could have a word in private."

"What? Not now. I told you I'm late. We'll talk when you get back. And Bryce, you're twenty-two. It's time you started a career instead of gadding about. This is your last trip until you settle down."

Before Bryce could respond, his father was out the door.

Oh, well, onward to St. Louis. Mo and Julius wouldn't be pleased about the expensive tickets, of course, but they had to sleep too, didn't they?

One bit of information he'd withheld was his secret hope that in St. Louis he'd meet his musical idol, Scott Joplin. Bryce loved ragtime—playing it energized his whole being. His mother disdained it. If she'd known Joplin was in St. Louis, she'd have nixed the trip right off.

* * *

While Julius went to see about the trunks, Mo carried his finished canvases up the street to a friend. She, like him, was also a struggling artist trying mightily to land a gallery exhibition. The paintings were the only fragile things he owned. The rest of their belongings—books and clothes—could be crammed in any which way. She promised to keep his artwork safe until he and Julius found a new apartment.

Transferring all his paintings to her place required a number of trips. In the process, he decided to leave his easel with her, too. After all, he couldn't very well stuff it in a trunk, could he? He held onto his paints and brushes, though. He might see something in St. Louis he wanted to paint, and he could always improvise an easel from a chair.

By the time he had his art moved, and had thoroughly kissed his friend goodbye, his roommate was back.

Julius and a sweaty teamster carried in two steamer trunks and deposited them in the center of the living room. Julius paid the man and asked him to return in a few hours to haul the trunks to the railroad terminal. The teamster pocketed the money and said he'd be back at three o'clock. Julius shook his hand, and the man left.

Mo inspected the trunks. They were plastered with old cobwebs, but seemed sturdy and serviceable. He unbuckled two leather straps on the nearest trunk, unfastened a hasp that held it closed, and raised the lid. Inside, he found a tray the length and width of the interior, and about six-inches deep. He lifted it out and set it aside. Surprisingly, the trunk's paper lining was pristine. These would do nicely.

Meanwhile, Julius had opened the other trunk and was stacking his books and back issues of *Popular Science Monthly* in the bottom.

"You're taking those old magazines with you?" Mo said.

"I'm not leaving them for the landlord."

"Yeah, but to St. Louis?"

"Don't think of it that way. We're moving to a new apartment when we get back. What would you move down the street, and what would you throw away?"

Mo nodded. "I hadn't thought of it that way." Julius was right. Mo surveyed the room with fresh eyes. What did he still want to have when this was all over? He gathered his copies of *Studio International* and put them in the trunk. Definitely those. Next, the books—an autographed copy of *Sister Carrie*, Dreiser's novel, which censors had tried to ban. Theodore was a decade older than Mo and his friends but frequently returned to the Village for brief stays.

Julius collected Mark Twain, owning practically every book the man ever wrote, including the voluminous *Following the Equator*. As he carefully packed these in his trunk, Mo handed him a copy of *Life on the Mississippi*. "Don't forget this one."

"Never. When we go to St. Louis, I'll finally get to see the river. Maybe ride a steamboat."

Mo laughed. "They still have those?"

"I hope so."

For years after their high school class read *Life on the Mississippi*, Julius had the wild idea that he'd follow in Twain's footsteps and become a riverboat captain. Not a very practical aspiration for a New York City boy, and Julius eventually found new interests in his work at Columbia.

"What the hell," Mo said. "If they still run paddle-wheelers out of St. Louis, you should ride one, just to say you did."

Packing continued with painful decisions of what to take and what to discard. Julius suggested they put the clothes they would wear on the train and at the Fair in their suitcases so they wouldn't need to waste time in St. Louis unpacking their trunks. Mo agreed it made sense.

At precisely three, the teamster knocked on the door and conveyed them and their worldly possessions to the New York Central's depot. Porters at the terminal unloaded the teamster's wagon onto baggage carts and led the men to a platform swarming with passengers. It took several minutes to locate Bryce standing in front of a dark green Pullman car, waving his hat at them. "Mo, Julius, over here!"

Julius gave a low whistle. "Wow, Bryce. First class?"

Mo furrowed his brow. "Shouldn't we have saved our money to spend at the Fair?"

Bryce handed them their tickets. "Mother insisted. Father paid."

Julius and Mo gave their tickets to the baggage handlers, who copied the information on tags they then attached to the trunks.

Bryce noticed the trunks. "My God, we're only going for a couple of weeks. What in the world are you bringing?"

"Pretty much everything we own." Mo took back their tickets and tipped the men, who then raced their carts toward the baggage car as the train whistle sounded.

Bryce rolled his eyes. "Why?"

"Roaming Irishmen," Julius said, grabbing his suitcase and handing Mo his. "Let's board before it leaves without us."

A Negro porter wearing a blue jacket with brass buttons and a smart cap stood next to the Pullman steps. "I'll take those aboard for you."

Three well-dressed women in their early twenties dashed up, breathing hard. The guys stepped back, doffed their hats, and let the ladies board.

"Thank you," the oldest one said, batting her eyelashes.

CHAPTER 7

Julius's jaw dropped as he, Bryce, and Mo followed the porter through a vestibule at one end of the car into something straight out of the Gilded Age. The interior of the car was magnificent, with a curved empire ceiling, a richly carpeted floor, and carved mahogany everywhere. And he'd resigned himself to sleeping in his seat with his hat over his eyes for the next two days.

On each side of the center aisle were six passenger seating sections, twelve in all. A section consisted of a pair of high-back, sofa-style seats upholstered in dark green brocade. One seat faced forward, the other toward the rear of the train, and the arrangement comfortably sat four.

So this is how people like the Holloways traveled.

The porter helped the ladies unpack first. He hung their clothing in the wardrobe, and pointed out the location of the toilet and lavatories. "The drawing room and smoking room are at the opposite end of the car," he said.

Next, he turned his attention to Mo and Julius, seating them in the section across the aisle from the ladies. He relieved them of their suitcases and hung up their clothes.

It dawned on Julius they were going to be sleeping only a few feet from these women. He hoped he wouldn't snore. At home, Mo sometimes accused him of that, unfairly, no doubt.

Bryce sat down next to Julius.

"Excuse me, sir," the porter said. "Your seat is the next one forward."

"I know," Bryce said. "Put my things there, but I'm going to sit with my friends for now."

That didn't make any sense to Julius. "What's going on, Bryce?"

"These seats convert into the lower berth." Bryce pointed overhead. "A second berth unfolds from the ceiling. That's two beds. There are three of us. I knew you and Mo wouldn't like having to share a bed, so I had Jenkins book the adjoining section to give us a third bed."

Julius nodded. Damn considerate. Good to travel with someone as experienced as Bryce. He and Mo would have never anticipated the situation until they found themselves rump to rump in a Pullman bed.

The porter finished hanging Bryce's clothes and returned. Touching the bill of his cap, he said, "Just call on me if you ladies or gentlemen should need anything."

A cold beer would be nice. "Is it possible to get drinks?" Julius said.

"Yes, sir. This train has both a club car and a dining car. You can get drinks in either." He pulled out a nickel-plated pocket watch and glanced at the time. "The dining car won't open for another half-hour, but the club car is offering service now."

Julius elbowed Bryce in the ribs. "Let's go."

Bryce stood just as the train lurched forward, and he fell into the facing seat, landing in Mo's lap. The three ladies across the aisle laughed.

Julius steadied himself and offered Bryce his hand. Bryce stood and Mo followed.

Bryce turned to the women. "Would you care to join us?"

The women's eyes danced among them. The youngest giggled, but the older said, "Thank you, not just yet. Perhaps we could sup together?"

Bryce beamed at her like one of Edison's new electric lights, raising the full wattage of his smile. "We'd be delighted. By the way, I'm Bryce Holloway. These are my friends, Julius Hornsby and Mo Silverstein."

"Lily Jones," said the older one. "These are my sisters, Rose and Violet. Of the New Jersey Joneses."

"Any relation to Pussy Jones?" Bryce said.

The sisters exchanged confused looks.

"The author?" Bryce added.

They shook their heads.

"Oh, she's friends with my parents. I thought if you were related, maybe we had a social connection."

"No matter," Julius said as he, Mo, and Bryce in turn took each lady's hand and murmured something complementary.

Bryce caught the porter's eye, and the man came at once.

"Sir?"

"George, please reserve us a table for six, for supper." He looked to Lily. "Would seven p.m. be satisfactory?"

She nodded.

"Book it for seven o'clock."

"Certainly, sir."

When he'd left, Mo said, "You know the porter?"

Bryce waved the question away. "All Pullman porters are called George."

Rose looked at her sister. "Lily, did you know that?"

Lily gave a quick shake of her head.

"Stick with us," Bryce said. "You may learn many new things before this trip is over."

A little ham-handed, but a clear invitation.

"Is that so?" Lily said.

And . . . the invitation was accepted. This might prove to be an interesting trip.

Bryce grinned. "We'll do our best."

"Where are you gentlemen headed?" Violet said.

"St. Louis. We're going to opening day of the World's Fair."

Violet giggled. "So are we."

"How fortunate for us to have a bouquet of three lovely flowers for company."

God, Bryce was laying it on thick. Still, the opportunity seemed too good to pass up. Julius cleared his throat. "The porter said the dining car serves alcohol. Shall we postpone our drinks until supper?"

Mo raised his eyebrows and gave him a look that said, *Who are you, and what have you done with my friend?* Julius smiled back and turned to the problem at hand. Each section of Pullman seats accommodated four passengers, but there were six of them. Julius waited for someone to come up with a solution.

Bryce did not disappoint. He held out his hand to Lily. "If you would consent to exchange seats with my friends, we could all become better acquainted before dinner without having to shout across the aisle."

Lily looked to her sisters, who nodded eagerly. She accepted Bryce's hand and stepped across the aisle into the seat Mo had previously occupied. Bryce took the seat across from her, leaving it to Mo and Julius to decide which sister to sit beside.

But it was the sisters who made the decision. Interesting.

Rose, seated by the window, patted the seat next to her. "Julius, please join me."

Violet slid over and smiled up at Mo, who settled beside her.

Julius sat down next to Rose, but Violet, sitting across from him, fluttered her eyelashes at him. "I've always found tall men so attractive. How tall are you?"

Julius stood a good five inches taller than Bryce and Mo. "Six foot one."

Not to be out done by her sister's flirtation, Rose said, "Mo, that's an unusual name."

"Short for Mordecai."

"Oh, a Biblical name, you must be from a very Christian family."

Julian coughed.

Before Mo could correct her, she rambled on. "As you perceived, we're all named for flowers. Good thing Mother only had girls. I don't know what Father would have named a boy."

"Basil?" Mo said.

Violet wrinkled her nose. "That's an herb, not a flower."

"Bud?" Julius said.

Rose patted his hand. "Best not to let men name babies."

She withdrew her hand quickly and blushed.

Julius studied Violet's dark blue eyes, and said to Rose, "Your mother certainly chose an accurate name for your sister. In a certain angle of light her eyes almost look violet."

Rose prickled. "What about me?"

Julius smiled at her. "To quote Shakespeare, 'A rose by any other name would smell as sweet.'"

"That's better," she said.

He pivoted a quarter turn in his seat and gave Rose his full attention. "I only noticed the shift of your sister's eye color because of a recent experiment with light at Columbia. I make instrumentation for the—"

"Oh, enough about her."

Julius chewed his lip, searching for a safe subject. These girls were . . . very sure of their own minds. "Are you as excited by the Fair as we are?"

"Giddy with anticipation."

As Rose launched into a fervent narration, Julius studied the sisters. Rose, he guessed to be the middle sister. Constantly striving to be like big sister, Lily, while chafing at the attention heaped on Violet, the youngest. He could sympathize with Rose, but if he'd divined their ages correctly, Violet would be most like him, for he too was the youngest in his family.

The sisters appeared to be about the same age as he and his friends, but the absence of engagement or wedding rings on their hands told him all three were single. It was more common for men in their twenties to be unmarried than women—in his own family, he was the only unwed sibling. Despite strong hints and outright urging of his family, he didn't figure on marrying before he was thirty.

Rose continued to talk without need for further prompting from Julius and without letting Violet or Mo get a word in. "Now, Father had the devil of a time finding us a room. Every hotel is booked, you know. And Mother said, even with three of us chaperoning each other, she wouldn't let us go until he secured us safe accommodations in St. Louis."

Of course St. Louis was booked up for opening day. Thank goodness Bryce had taken care of that for them. Or had he?

"Excuse me a moment," Julius said.

Rose stopped midstream, not pleased at the interruption.

Across the aisle, Bryce and Lily were laughing, probably at something Bryce had said.

"Bryce?"

"Yes, Julius?"

"Rose tells me the hotels in St. Louis are filled up. You remembered to make us a reservation, didn't you?"

Bryce gave him a sheepish grin that told him everything he needed to know. Great.

"Well, where are we going to stay?"

"Don't panic guys. There's a brand new hotel, The Jefferson, it hasn't even opened. So, it can't very well be sold out."

"If it's not open yet, I don't see what good that does us."

"It's supposed to open April twenty-ninth, the day we arrive. How perfect is that? We'll be their first guests."

Julius looked at Mo, who shook his head. "Bryce, people do book rooms in advance, you know, even in hotels that aren't opened yet."

"All right, all right," Bryce said. "I'll do it now."

"How? We're on a moving train."

"It makes stops. They have telegraphs."

The porter came to inform them their tables were ready in the dining car. Julius stood and offered his arm to Rose. Mo did the same for Violet, and Bryce for Lily.

"George," Bryce said loud enough for Mo and Julius to hear, "Please send a wire from me to the Hotel Jefferson, St. Louis, Missouri. Instruct them to reserve a suite in my name for three New Yorkers arriving Friday."

"Yes, sir."

"And bring me the Western Union receipt."

"Of course, sir."

Bryce patted Julius's shoulder. "Everyone satisfied? Let's dispense with business and offer these ladies pleasant dinner company. The dining car awaits."

CHAPTER 8

Mo traversed the clattering metal floor that covered the train couplers and then held the door for the ladies. Pullman cars had vestibules at both ends allowing passengers to cross safely between cars without being exposed to the elements. The sisters lifted their floor-length skirts and sauntered across with a casual grace, followed by Julius and Bryce.

They found themselves in another sleeper car whose aisles were congested with returning diners. Next, they came to the club car, thick with cigarette, cigar, and pipe smoke, and loud with inebriated laughter.

Finally, the dining car. Mo was stunned to find it lit by overhead electric lights, supplemented by Pintsch gaslight sconces. White linen tablecloths, china place settings, and a formal array of fine silverware graced every table. Waiters in white jackets moved efficiently among the patrons. With lace curtains and finely carved woodwork, this rolling restaurant easily rivaled New York's finest.

What they hadn't predicted, was that dining car seating was arranged in two rows of four person banquets with an aisle down the center. Bryce's reservation for six people only garnered them two tables across the aisle, not one combined table. Once again, one of the couples had to sit apart from the others. Mo waited to see how it would play out.

Bryce and Lily took seats across from each other next to the window. Rose sat beside her sister.

It was obvious he and Violet were being pushed aside. He turned to seat Violet at the opposite table when Rose said, "Mo, please join me."

He looked at Julius, who shrugged and accepted Violet as his dinner companion. Mo wasn't sure what just happened, but he felt like he'd been horse traded. Obviously the sisters were in control.

A waiter brought menus, and Bryce immediately ordered champagne. Julius asked for a Pabst.

They perused the menu, discussing the different choices: baked whitefish with tartar sauce, or chicken croquettes, mushrooms in wine sauce with pineapple fritters, prime roast beef, or roast turkey with cranberry sauce. Every entrée came with boiled potatoes, green peas, string beans, or cauliflower. To finish the meal, numerous deserts were listed, as well as a fruit plate with select cheeses.

Mo glanced at the bottom of the page. "*All Meals, One Dollar.*" He swallowed hard. They'd just set out and already down six bucks. Then he looked at the beverage list on the facing page and realized Bryce had blown $3.50 on champagne. At least Julius's beer only cost twenty cents. Back home they could buy a whole pail of beer for a nickel.

The waiter returned with the champagne, served it, and took their dinner orders.

"Bryce tells me you're an artist," Lily said.

Rose lifted the corners of her bow-like mouth and smiled at him. "Are you famous?"

"Not yet," Bryce said. "But he will be soon. Mo is at the forefront of a new style."

"Oh?" Rose said.

Leave it to Bryce to give him an opening.

"Impressionism," Mo said. "Painting the light of a scene without constraining yourself to the details. Capturing the feeling of them. It's popular in Europe among artists like Monet, Pissarro, Renoir, and many others. Now, it's come to America, too."

She wrinkled her forehead. "Aren't you worried that you've chosen a dying profession? Won't photographers eventually put you out of business? I mean, will people sit for days to have their portrait painted when a few minutes in front of a camera will yield a more accurate image?"

Mo shook his head. "Photographers can have the portrait business, for all I care. Stern, mutton-chopped men standing stiffly beside rigid dour-faced matrons? It's more vanity than art. Monet's art speaks not in intellectual terms but in the language of the emotions. That is its meaning. That's what I want to do."

Lily took a sip of champagne and set her glass down. "Our father owns a lot of paintings. But he mainly likes pictures of Jefferson writing the Declaration of Independence, or Custer signing a treaty with Geronimo—"

"Custer didn't fight Geronimo," Bryce said.

"Don't interrupt, sweetie. My point is, to succeed, an artist must choose subjects that please the buyer."

Mo bristled. "That is exactly what art is not. That's commerce. Impression-ism communicates to another person the feeling the artist had at the time of creation. That's art's higher purpose."

"I've seen pictures of work by the Frenchmen you're talking about. They seem . . . technically inept. Something a five-year-old with a watercolor set could do."

"If that's what you see, you are missing out. You have to view them with your heart, not your intellect. True art is an expression of the soul."

Rose touched her glass to his. "Well, I think that's a lovely sentiment." She turned to her sister. "Lily, don't be unkind to our new friends."

"You're right, Rose. Mo, I'm sorry, I didn't mean to offend. Elizabeth Stan-ton taught us to speak our minds, and I just got a little carried away."

"Are you suffragettes?" Bryce said.

Lily winked. "Yes, and more."

Bryce smiled. "What a coincidence, we are, too."

"Mrs. Stanton believed we should not only have a vote in the government under which we live, but should have equality in pay and social life. We have the right to freedom of our minds. And our bodies."

"And from all forms of bondage and oppression," Rose added.

Bryce held up his glass. "Here, here. Are you also familiar with the opinions of women's rights activist Victoria Woodhull on the subject of—"

"Free love?" Lily said. "Very."

"Sisters," Violet said from across the aisle, "other diners can hear you."

"Let them," Bryce said. "It might do them good."

Violet looked nervously at her sisters. "You forget Papa's purpose in financing our trip."

"Oh, don't bring that up, now," Rose said. "Let us have our fun first."

Their meals arrived. The waiter served them and refilled their wine glasses. Julius ordered another beer. Mo mentally added twenty-cents to what they'd spent.

"As an artist, you must be excited about seeing the Palace of Art," Rose said.

"I am. And . . . well, everything, really. We've been pouring over articles about the exhibits and have made a list so we won't miss anything."

The overhead electric lights made her hair shimmer as she bobbed her head. "We have, too. We should compare lists."

Mo liked this woman more and more. "Let's do that as soon as we get back to our car."

"Do you ladies like ragtime?" Julius asked.

"It's kind of wild," Rose said.

"I like wild," Violet said.

"Bryce plays ragtime," Julius said.

Lily smiled at Bryce. "Is that so?"

Bryce puffed out his chest. "Love it."

She winked at him. "Me, too."

Mo had seen Lily do that earlier, too. How closely did the Jones sisters adhere to Woodhull's freethinking? Among his acquaintances in New York City, many young people embraced the turn of the century with a new, freer morality. He didn't know if the trend extended into New Jersey. The possibility of discovering the answer seemed remote. They were, after all, on a crowded train hurling forty-five miles an hour.

He looked forward to comparing his list with Rose's, to see which exhibits they'd both chosen to explore. Everyone seemed to like each other well enough. Perhaps they'd all tour the Fair together, or meet up on the Pike in the evenings when the Palaces closed.

Bryce lifted the empty champagne bottle in the air, looking for the waiter.

Mo pushed his arm back down. "Look out the window. It's dark already. Let's continue our conversation back in our car."

Too late. The waiter appeared at Mo's elbow. "Another bottle, sir?"

"No, thank you. I think we're ready for dessert."

The man cleared the dirty dishes and returned with desserts and the bill. Mo paid it all. He didn't want the women to witness them trying to divvy up the tab—it'd seem cheap. But my God, they'd just spent a week's rent on one dinner.

Over dessert, Julius and Violet listened from across the aisle as Bryce recounted an experience with the Rough Riders.

"He served in the war against Spain?" Violet said. "I'd never have guessed he was that old."

"He's not," Julius said. "He lied about his age and joined up at sixteen."

"Were you and Mo with him?"

"Nah, we were all still in school. Bryce ran away for the summer, but the whole war only lasted six weeks, and he was home before school started in the fall."

She reached across the table and took his hand. "I'm glad you didn't go, and happy that Bryce made it back. Our father was against it. He'd lost his father at Appomattox, and that turned him pacifist for life."

Julius gave her hand a squeeze. "I'm sorry you lost your grandfather."

"Well, we never knew him. Papa grew up fatherless, as Grandma never remarried."

"Then, I feel sorry for him, too."

"You do? You don't even know him."

"But I know you."

She blushed, let go of his hand, picked up her spoon and toyed with her tapioca. Damn, he hadn't intended to embarrass her.

Violet put a small bite of pudding to her delicate mouth and Julius felt his manhood respond to imagining how her lips would taste. And feel. He cleared his throat and turned to listen to Bryce. Few things calmed him down more quickly.

"By the time I reached Florida, Roosevelt had assembled nearly thirty thousand troops. That's not even counting the sailors from the warships in Tampa Bay. Most of the troops dressed in blue uniforms, but not the Rough Riders. We wore brown. Our camp was on a sand flat without a tree for shade. Tampa was very hot, but thankfully there were no mosquitoes. Unlike Cuba when we got there."

Lily laughed. "Unlike New Jersey."

"You should have seen us, a heroic assemblage of Western cowboys, frontiersmen, Eastern athletes, and—" He gave a humble nod. "—sons of prominent citizens. Many more people applied and were recommended than ever could be accepted. I was lucky I got in."

Violet looked appalled. "Lucky? To go to war?"

Julius smiled at her. "His father is not like yours. He's a difficult man for Bryce to please."

"You've known each other a long time?"

"We've been friends since grade school."

Bryce put his elbows on the table and leaned in. "The day we were to board our ship to Cuba, chaos reigned. We raced to the track where the train for the dock was to meet us. We arrived on time, but the train did not. They told us to go to a different track, but there was no train there, either. Our orders said that men who were not dockside at the designated hour would be left behind. Roosevelt couldn't let that happen, so he commandeered an empty coal train, and we rode to the dock in that."

"You must have been filthy," Rose said.

"Blacker than you can imagine," Bryce said. "But that foul train got us there before the deadline. When we arrived, ten thousand men were milling about in confusion. Roosevelt went to sort it out and returned with the unfortunate news that our transport ship, the *Yucatan*, had been mistakenly assigned two additional infantry groups. He told us the vessel couldn't fit that many men. We needed to run to where the *Yucatan* was docked and take possession of her before the other units knew what was happening. And that's what we did. When Roosevelt said, 'charge,' you charged, no questions asked."

Bryce stopped for a sip of champagne, but his glass was empty. Lily handed him what was left of hers and he finished it.

"Thank you. I wish I'd had a drop of that aboard ship. We were packed like sardines, and the heat was stifling. Moreover, the Navy suspected that Spanish vessels were in nearby waters and wouldn't let our ship out of the harbor."

"Oh, you poor men," Rose said.

"The experience put me off ocean voyages ever since. Anyway, we finally got to Cuba, and almost immediately—well, the next day, actually—we had our first run-in with the Spanish. They ambushed us. At first, we couldn't even tell where they were firing from because they were using smokeless gunpowder. Once we figured out where they were hiding, we returned fire and they fled."

Violet looked at Julius. "This is amazing. And familiar. I feel like I've read this somewhere, before."

"I'm sure you have," Julius said quickly. "It was reported in all the newspapers and magazines."

"Eight days later, we were advancing on the San Juan River when a Spanish shell exploded overhead, showering us with shrapnel."

"Were you injured?" Lily said.

"Nothing to write home about. A piece of shrapnel struck my wrist and raised a hefty lump, but it didn't break the skin. However, the next day I watched my captain die."

Violet shivered involuntarily. Julius reached across the table and took her hand again. Her eyes gave him a look of thanks.

Bryce sat up straighter. "Captain William O'Neil was from Prescott, Arizona. He founded the Volunteer Cavalry that became Roosevelt's Rough Riders, and commanded Troop A, my troop. Roosevelt and the other officers called him Bucky. We called him Sir. Anyway, he was strolling up and down in front of us, smoking cigarettes—he was habitually addicted. I begged him to lie down, but he had a theory that an officer should never take cover. Our sergeant warned him, 'Captain, a bullet is sure to hit you.' Captain O'Neill took his cigarette out of his mouth, blew out a cloud of smoke, laughed and said, 'Sergeant, the Spanish bullet isn't made that will kill me.'"

Bryce made as if to wipe a tear from his eye, as he usually did at this point in the story. "A little later he and one of the other officers were trying to see which direction the Spanish fire was coming from. As he turned on his heel to leave, a bullet struck him in the mouth and came out at the back of his head."

There was a sharp intake of breath from the Jones sisters.

Mo patted Bryce's arm. "That's enough war for tonight. Let's finish our desserts and return to our car."

Violet pushed her tapioca away. "I don't think I care for any more pudding."

Julius exhaled loudly. Bryce! Always the center of attention. Too bad he was never quite aware enough of his audience to know how far was too far.

"Don't misunderstand," Violet said. "It has nothing to do with Bryce's story. I'm just full. In fact, I'm sure Roosevelt wrote that very same account in Scribner's Magazine a couple of years ago."

Bryce looked over at her and smiled. "Of course he did, because that's exactly how the dreadful thing happened. Bucky used to say, 'A cavalry man's death isn't peaceful, it comes with saber holes.' Or, in this case, bullet holes."

Julius could only see one way to stop Bryce. He stood up and offered Violet his hand.

CHAPTER 9

Bryce and Lily brought up the rear of the parade as Julius and Violet led them back the way they'd come. When they entered the sleeper car before theirs, it was only faintly lit. Julius stopped short, causing Mo and Rose, just behind him, to almost run into them. Bryce grabbed Lily's arm to keep her from bumping into her sister.

Giddy from champagne, the sisters giggled.

"They've put out the lights and made up the beds," Julius said.

The facing seats had been converted into beds, and upper berths lowered from the ceiling. Curtains along both sides of the aisle afforded privacy.

Bryce turned to Lily. "We could go to the club car if nobody's tired."

"Shush," came a voice from behind a curtain.

Violet hooked her elbow around Julius's arm and urged him toward their car. The others followed.

When they reached the vestibule of their car Violet said, "Rose, I'm going to use the water closet."

Lily whispered, "The rest of you go ahead, I'll wait here until Violet comes out."

Julius, Mo, and Rose made their way down the aisle, mindful not to wake sleeping travelers. Violet stepped into the lavatory and latched the door. Bryce hung back with Lily, slipping his hand into hers.

The train crossed a switch between two tracks and their car lurched, knocking Lily into him. He put his hands on her upper arms to support her. "Careful, I bite."

Lily checked the empty aisle, then leaned into him and gently grazed his earlobe with her teeth. "I don't bite," she whispered, "but I might nibble."

Well. This trip was turning interesting from the very beginning.

The sound of the latch on the lavatory door caused Lily to step away from him. "Later," she said.

"A man can only hope."

Violet came out and Lily traded places. "Stay away from this one," Lily said.

Bryce wasn't sure if she was talking to her sister or to him. But he wasn't leaving until Lily came out.

Violet walked softly down the carpeted aisle and returned with Rose, a toiletry case, and an armful of nightgowns. When Lily opened the door, her sisters were waiting, and they all crowded in to change together.

Now, what should he do? It'd been his experience that when a covey of women convened in a lavatory, romantic possibilities for the evening evaporated. At least that's the way things worked on Broadway.

Whispers and giggles seeped from the lavatory door until the latch clicked. Lily came out first. "Good. You're still here."

He gave her his most charming smile.

She grabbed his collar and hurriedly whispered in his ear her sister's plans for the rest of the evening. Rose was going to make sure the porter couldn't see them. If he could, she'd distract him with some errand. Bryce would then send Mo to Rose's bed, freeing Julius's compartment for Violet. As soon as Mo and Violet made the switch, she'd join Bryce behind his curtain, and Rose could then return to her own bed with none the wiser. "Will Mo and Julius play along?"

"Without a doubt." Bryce loved the way these women thought.

Lily tapped the lavatory door softly with her fingernails. Rose and Violet stepped out, and Rose quietly strolled past all twelve sleeping sections. When she reached the door of the drawing room, she blocked it by leaning back against it and gestured for them to come forward.

Bryce led the way. He poked his head between the curtains. "Mo?"

"Up here."

"Whisper. We don't want to wake anybody. Or give anything away. It's our lucky night. Rose wants you to slip across the aisle and wait for her. Julius, you're about to get a visitor, too. But for God's sake keep things quiet. This could get all six of us kicked off the train."

Mo swung off the top berth, bumping Bryce's head with his foot.

"Ow!"

"I thought you said to be quiet," Julius whispered.

"I did. Sorry, I didn't see Mo coming down."

"What about the porter?" Mo hissed.

"Rose is standing watch. Get out of here. Violet's waiting for you to leave."

"Well, step aside."

Mo tiptoed over to the girls' section and slipped behind the curtain.

Bryce motioned to Lily and Violet, then stepped into his own section. The seats were made into a bed, but the upper berth had not been lowered, customary when a single passenger occupied a section. This also afforded more headroom. He offered a prayer of thanks, that he'd booked an extra bed without knowing they'd meet three freethinking sisters.

The curtain moved behind him, and Lily pressed herself against him. He hadn't even started to undress yet, so she helped him. This obviously wasn't her first time.

They fell into bed and into passion. He freed her from her nightgown and they made gentle love, merging their rhythms with the swaying of the train and sounds of its wheels. Afterward, they nestled, whispering, punctuated with soft kisses.

At some point he reached over and lifted the edge of the window shade. Moonlit countryside raced by. "Aren't you worried we'll be found out in the morning when the porter makes up the bed?"

"Don't worry. Rose has a plan."

"Quite the clever girl, your sister."

"Yes, but also the only sister who is in the bed she belongs in, so it had to be her."

He kissed her. "I think you're in the bed where you belong."

She nuzzled his neck. "For a little while longer."

Later, Rose's voice spoke softly through the curtain. "Lily, the porter's asleep."

Lily kissed him on the mouth. "See you at breakfast."

And then she was gone. Bryce ran his hand over the warm hollow she'd left in his bed. Lily was exactly the kind of woman he liked—smart, freethinking, and independent. She was all for living life instead of looking for a husband with money. He hoped Julius and Mo wouldn't mind if he spent most of their days at the Fair with Lily instead of them.

Unless, of course, after one night with her sisters, they felt the way about them that he did about Lily, then, problem solved—they'd all tour the Fair together.

He lay back and, just before he drifted off, he smiled. They all owed so much to those two Irish pugilists.

Violet lay enveloped in a satisfied afterglow. Julius was every bit the wondrous lover she'd hoped he would be. He'd brought her to that thrilling state—twice. The only thing more she could have asked of him was that he stay awake afterward.

She poked him gently in the ribs. He roused only to the extent of dropping his arm over her before returning to his slumber. Well, she'd take what she could get. She pulled his arm around her and wiggled closer, glad she'd chosen him. What a very nice man.

How her sisters had fared? Sisters talk, and Violet knew she hadn't as many lovers as Lily and Rose did. After all, being older than her, they'd started earlier.

God bless Mrs. Coggeshall for advocating women's rights in every aspect of life. She once told Violet, "You can love many men, as Victoria Woodhull did, but be more careful about your reputations than she was. Men like to brag. Choose discreet lovers, preferably from distant cities."

Violet took her advice and waited until the year the Jones family summered in Newport. The boy was from Maine. That seemed a safe distance from Florham Park.

What Mrs. Coggeshall's lessons had failed to convey was the effect kissing and petting produced in her physiology. One evening, she and the boy strolled in the moonlight to an out-of-way spot and began testing the depths of their yearning. She suddenly felt certain her monthly cycle was starting. Why now? She was mortified. If she allowed him to go further, he'd uncover the truth. She begged to be excused and fled the scene.

Back at the hotel she discovered it wasn't her time at all. Later, when Lily and Rose returned, they laughed at her confusion, explained the mysteries of her body, and encouraged her to try again.

She wasn't sure how she'd explain her abrupt departure the previous night, but she quickly learned that men weren't easily discouraged. He was amenable the moment she suggested another moonlight walk. Unfortunately, once they reclined in a dark grove, he knew less of what to do than she did. Violet found herself having to take charge. She led them through the initiation to the mystery guided mainly by her recollection of Mrs. Coggeshall's hand drawn sketches. It was all very fumbling and awkward, and she was relieved when it was over.

Since then, she'd enjoyed more experienced men from other places. She still hadn't caught up with Lily and Rose, but here they all were, far, far from home on a train with three handsome men. That seemed the very definition of discretion.

Julius's sleeping breath blew softly against her hair. They still had one more night on the train. Certainly, tomorrow night he would make love to her again. What would happen when they reached St. Louis? She could already hear Lily exhorting them to put on a virgin demeanor to accomplish Father's purpose. Undoubtedly that meant goodbye Julius.

"Pssst . . . Julius," Mo whispered through the curtain, "Is Violet awake? Rose says it's time."

Gently lifting Julius's arm out of the way, she kissed the side of his face, and slipped on her dressing gown. Outside the curtain, she ran into Mo. He slid by her and entered his section. Violet tiptoed to the lavatory. There, she felt between her legs for the silk thread fastened to her sponge. Giving it a smooth, even tug, she drew the sponge out. She washed it under running water before returning to her section and storing it in her toiletry case.

Now in their own beds, Violet and her sisters giggled and compared notes in furtive whispers. It turned out they had all had enjoyable evenings. The train rolled hundreds of miles nearer its destination before they finally slumbered.

CHAPTER 10

"Can I help you, sir?" the porter said to Mo who was hovering outside the ladies' curtain.

"No. I was just going to see if the Jones sisters wanted to breakfast with us."

Lily's voice came from behind the curtain. "Who is it?"

"Mo. Good morning Miss Jones. My friends and I were wondering if you and your sisters would care to have breakfast with us."

There was a flurry of whispers, then, "Thank you, but no. We'd like to take our time getting dressed. We'll look forward to seeing you later on."

The three New Yorkers proceeded to the dining car where they ate heartily. Pullman offered a choice of meat—steak, lamb chop, ham, bacon, or sausage—and eggs, cooked any way you liked. While their order was being prepared, fresh fruit was served. Corn muffins, hot rolls, toast, and griddle cakes came next, along with tea or coffee. All three men chose coffee and lingered after the meal, drinking numerous refills.

True gentlemen, they refrained from sharing intimate details about their bedmates, but all admitted to being pleasantly surprised by the sisters' forwardness.

"And what about Rose's tactical skill at pulling it off?" Mo said.

"Kudos to her," Bryce said. "Roosevelt would be proud."

Julius rubbed his face. "I think I'm going to shave when we go back to our car."

Bryce paid the bill, and they left the dining car.

The porter had the beds and curtains put away and the seats restored by the time they got there. The Jones sisters were dressed, coifed, and had a long narrow table set up between their seats. They were just starting their breakfast meal.

Julius retrieved his toiletry kit and went to the lavatory.

Mo and Bryce attempted to start a conversation with the sisters, but it became plain that the ladies did not want someone hovering over them while they ate. Mo tugged on Bryce's sleeve and they went into the drawing room portion of the car. A husband and wife sat together reading a Bible, which put a damper on any boisterous mood. Bryce pressed onward into the smoking car.

Two businessmen were smoking cigars. Mo was surprised when Bryce didn't strike up a conversation with them. Instead he paced the space like a caged animal. Mo knew Bryce wanted someone to entertain—it was almost as if he didn't exist without an audience, and Bible readers and business travelers weren't going to do it. He was clearly frustrated that the ladies had sent them away.

Bryce started back the way they came. "I could use a shave myself. Let me see if Julius is done in the lavatory, yet."

Mo wasn't fooled. Bryce wanted to see if the ladies were finished eating. They weren't. Bryce retrieved his shaving gear and headed to the lavatory. Mo had his own way of entertaining himself. He took out his drawing pad and pencils and sat in his section where he had a good view of Rose and began to sketch her.

There was no mistaking that the three of them were sisters, but Rose had brown eyes while Violet's and Lily's were blue. Her face was rounder than her siblings, and she had fuller lips.

Mo liked those soft, plush lips, and touched his own, remembering last night.

Mo hadn't quite finished the sketch when the porter returned to clear the sisters' breakfast dishes. He blocked his view, so Mo used the interruption to add some shading. He rubbed his fingertip over the pencil lines in several places, smudging them into soft shadows.

"Would you like me to put away the table, Miss?" the porter said.

Lily shook her head. "No. Leave it. We may play cards to pass the time."

The man touched his cap and left, restoring Mo's unobstructed view of Rose.

Julius returned, freshly shaved and smelling of bay rum, and peeked over Mo's shoulder. "Good job, Mo. Looks just like her."

"What does?" Rose said.

"Your picture," Julius said. "Mo's made a drawing of you."

"Let us see."

"It's just a quick sketch in black and white." Mo turned his tablet toward the sisters. "My color pastels and oil paints are locked in the baggage car, so I've only got a pencil to work with."

"Oh, Rose, it looks just like you," Violet said. "Do me next."

"May I keep it?" Rose said.

"Of course." Mo tore the sheet from his pad and handed it to her. "Perhaps when we get to St. Louis where I can unpack my art supplies, you'll pose for a proper portrait."

She glanced at her sisters. "I-I don't know if there'll be time for that . . . with the Fair and all."

"Right. You said last night at dinner that you had a list of exhibits you wanted to see. We made a list as well. I have ours right here." Mo began flipping through his drawing tablet, looking for the page he'd written their notes on.

"I'm not sure where I put ours. I'll have to find it."

Violet slid out of her seat and sat down across from Mo. "Never mind the list. Draw me." Julius was left standing awkwardly in the aisle.

Lily pointed to the seat Violet had vacated. "Julius, please join us. Do you play whist?"

"Yes, but we need four for whist."

She removed a deck of cards from her handbag and began shuffling them. "I'm sure Bryce will be along soon. I presume he knows the game as well."

Julius nodded. "We all do, though we don't play that often, there being only three of us. We're more a rummy crowd."

Mo smiled at the unintended pun, turned to a fresh page and drew a large oval. Both Violet and Lily had more elongated faces than Rose, and their sapphire eyes were almond-shaped. A Siamese cat came to mind, and he struggled not to let that image creep into the drawing.

Violet looked out the window and Mo watched her eyes change color. Remarkable.

"Julius was right about the unusual chromaticity of your eyes," he said.

She screwed up her face. "The what?"

"The shift in hue. Now I really do wish I had access to my pastels so I could draw you in color."

She smiled.

"Good, keep smiling. It gives you cute dimples."

Her eyes twinkled. "You really think so?"

He nodded and continued working.

Her eyes flicked toward the aisle behind him.

Bryce returned, put away his shaving kit, and slid into the seat next to Julius without waiting to be asked. "What are we doing this morning?"

Lily smiled. "Waiting for you. We're about to play whist, but we needed a fourth." She stopped shuffling and set the deck in the center of the table. Each person drew a card to determine who would be partners. Rose drew a five and Julius an eight. Bryce drew a ten. Lily drew last—an ace, making her and Bryce partners.

If they'd been at a proper card table, the partners would have sat opposite each other, but the sofa-style train seating put partners diagonal from each other and opponents next to each other. It'd be all right. Mo knew Bryce and Julius would never look in each other's hand. That'd be cheating. He presumed Rose and Lily wouldn't either.

Mo paused to sharpen his pencil with a small sharpener he carried in his pocket. As the blade shaved the wood to a fresh point, a long continuous curl fell onto his pant leg.

Violet leaned across, snatched it up, and began toying with it as he resumed drawing. "Mo, can I ask you something personal?"

His hand jerked, snapping the point off his pencil and marring the drawing. "Uh, sure. I've got nothing to hide."

She glanced across the aisle at the card game. "Do you play whist?"

"Yes, I do." Mo fished a gum eraser from his jacket pocket and removed the black mark from the page. He laughed. "That's not a personal question."

She hung her head and studied the wood shaving in her hand.

Mo resharpened his pencil and resumed drawing. "Lift your chin, please. I wasn't finished drawing your eyes."

Violet raised her face. Her eyes darted to Rose, then back to him. "Um . . . my sister learned something surprising about you last night."

Ah. Now the real personal question. "And she shared that information with you two?"

Violet blushed. "We *are* sisters."

Well, Rose wasn't the first woman who didn't know he was Jewish until they were in bed, but he'd had the impression she'd been comfortable with the idea. Maybe not.

He glanced at Rose and then back to Violet. "Is she upset that we're different religions?"

"Not at all. She likes you. Said you were . . . a good person."

"And what do her sisters think?"

"Oh, Mo, I just feel so bad that you grew up without Christmas. It's the best holiday of the year. I can't imagine not knowing the excitement of Christmas morning."

"Who says I don't?"

"What? I understood Jews don't celebrate Christmas."

"We don't, but Julius is Christian. One year when we were kids, Julius invited me to spend Christmas Eve at his house. My parents didn't even realize it was Christmas—Chanukah started in November that year and was long over. They just weren't thinking about holidays anymore—wouldn't have let me go if they had been. So, I packed a little overnight bag and traipsed through the snow to Julius's."

She clasped her hands together. "Oh, I'm so glad. That must have been wonderful."

"Frankly, the whole thing seemed pretty peculiar." Mo continued to sketch her as he talked. "The evening started off normal, a big dinner with candles and wine. Not unlike our Shabbat dinners. After we'd eaten, everyone got ready to go to midnight mass. I'd never been to a church, so I ask Julius's sister what I should expect. She explained that they were going to celebrate the birth of Jesus with songs and scripture readings, and then at the end of the service everyone would drink his blood." Mo shook his head. "A thing like that must give kids nightmares."

Violet laughed. "Oh, that's Catholics. Presbyterians don't serve communion on Christmas. Did you go anyway?"

"No. His parents understood my family wouldn't approve and let me stay home."

"You didn't miss much. The real fun is Christmas morning—that's so exciting. At least ours always is."

"Well . . . I don't know if theirs was typical. When I got up the next morning, they'd put a dead tree in their parlor, and covered it with burning candles. Then we all sat around it eating oranges someone had stuffed in our socks. It was the strangest thing I'd ever done."

Violet laughed so loud the card players turned to look at them.

Just then, the porter came through the car announcing lunch would be served shortly and offering to make passengers' table reservations. It seemed to Mo like the sisters had just finished breakfast.

Bryce spoke for the group, without asking. "Yes, six, please."

"Make it a late seating," Lily said. "We're tied at two games apiece. We need time to play another."

Mo put the final touches on Violet's portrait and gave it to her. While she admired it, he started sketching the inside of the rail car.

"Who are you drawing now?"

"No one in particular. This is the first time I've ridden in a Pullman, and I wanted to capture a memory of it."

Violet slid over next to the window. "Come and sit next to me, so I can watch what you're doing."

Mo did, but having changed point of view, turned the page and started afresh.

Violet watched as he gave shape and dimension to the sides of the car, windows, and seating. "How do you make it so realistic using only a pencil?" she said.

"It's called perspective drawing."

"Teach me."

He held out his pencil at arm's length. "From where we're sitting, this looks about seven inches long, because it is. But if someone at the end of the car held this up, it wouldn't appear big at all. So, one trick is to draw objects in the distance smaller than they really are."

Violet nodded.

"The other thing with perspective is this. We know the walls of this car are perfectly straight. But notice that I drew the lines representing them at an angle instead of square."

Violet smiled. "I hadn't even noticed, but I see that now. Drawing the walls at an angle made them shorter at the other end than up by us."

"It's easy to do that with things that have straight edges." In a blank corner of the page he drew a long horizontal line. Beneath it he drew a tall, narrow capital A, then added additional cross lines over it. "Voila! A train track."

"Wow! But you've ruined your picture."

"It isn't anything important. Just a reminder of what the inside of a Pullman looks like."

The card game ended and Rose immediately came over and sat opposite them. "What are you two up to?"

"Watching Mo draw." She held up her portrait. "Look!"

Rose took the paper, gave it a once over, and handed it back. "Mine's better."

Mo didn't want any part of sibling jealousy. He stood up.

Rose quickly grabbed his hand. "Mo, I didn't mean any offense."

"None taken."

"You're a very skilled portraitist. I just meant that I thought the drawing you did of me showed a greater connection between the artist and the subject."

He gave her hand a little squeeze. "I haven't forgotten last night."

"Good. Our journey's not over. We won't get to St. Louis until tomorrow."

Had she hinted they'd spend another night together? He wouldn't object.

The door at the end of the car opened, and the porter entered. Rose let go of his hand. Mo turned to Julius. "Who won?"

"Bryce and Lily, of course."

Behind his back he heard Rose whisper to Violet, "Don't get any ideas. We're not trading."

"I never said I wanted to," Violet said just loud enough for Julius to take notice.

Julius turned to Mo and gave him an inquiring look. Mo silently mouthed the words, "I'll explain later."

Mo smiled to himself. Apparently all three sisters planned a recurrence. It'd be interesting to see how they finagled the porter tonight.

The porter approached and touched the bill of his cap. "Ladies, gentlemen, they're ready for you in the dining car."

CHAPTER 11

It wasn't until Thursday that Finn and Bird finally pinned down where two of the dandies lived. Finn was on his knees peeping through the keyhole of a second-floor apartment while Bird stood with his back to him, blocking anyone from seeing what he was doing. That wasn't difficult. Bird had such a dominating physical presence he was often the only thing people noticed.

A balding man about Finn's height, wearing a starched shirt and dress pants but no suit coat, came charging up the steps. "You there, can I help you?"

Bird breathed through his mouth.

"We're looking for someone."

The man tilted his head up at Bird. "How'd you say that without moving your lips? Are you one of those vaudeville ventriloquists? Our landlord doesn't rent to show people. Anyway, the best way to find out if someone's home is to knock, not hulk in doorways."

Bird banged the back of his head against the doorframe hard enough to make the faded Currier and Ives print on the wall tremble.

"Hey! I can't see anything with that banging."

"Don't blame me," the man said. "I didn't tell you to use your head."

"Bird, show him the newspaper."

The man studied Bird's face. "You're good, I'll give you that. But you're scaring the female tenants. Tell me what you want here. And stop calling me bird."

Finn got up off his knees and came from behind. "He's Bird. I'm Finn." He offered his hand. "And we're not show people."

"Oh, you're . . . I see." The man shook his hand. "I live in the apartment below. Are you looking to rent this place? I'll give you the landlord's address."

"No, we live in Brooklyn, and like it." Finn reached into Bird's coat pocket, retrieved the creased clipping, and showed it to him. "We're looking for the men in this picture, and we heard they live here."

"These two did." He pointed to Mo and Julius. "They don't anymore. Took their belongings and skipped out on the rent, so I heard."

"What about this third man?" Finn said.

"He didn't live here, but he came around often enough. Usually at night."

"Can you tell us their names?"

"Never got to know them. They were night owls, and my wife and I go to bed early. You might check for their names on the mailbox."

"Any idea where they moved?"

"No, but the woman who lives next to us said a teamster came yesterday afternoon and hauled away their trunks."

Finn scratched his head. "A teamster, you say. Was he Irish?"

"I assume so. Aren't they all?"

"But she never said for sure? We should speak to her. Which apartment is hers?"

"Never mind bothering her. She's elderly and fragile. A big lug like him will scare the wits out of her."

That got Finn's dander up. "Don't call him a lug. He's a champ."

The man held up his hands. "No offense, but no one here knows any more than I've told you, and we'd appreciate it if you leave now."

"Don't get your suspenders in a knot. We're going. Come on, Bird, this man's given me an idea."

On the way out, Finn checked the mailbox, but the dandies must have peeled off their names before they left.

The man was right, most New York City teamsters were Irish. Finn and Bird knew a pub where drivers congregated between jobs and after work. They asked around, and a few hours and a few rounds of beer later, they found their man.

"Sure, I remember them like it was yesterday."

"It was yesterday," Finn said. "How many beers have you had?"

"Not enough. Buy me another and I'll tell you everything."

Finn held up three fingers, and the barman set three foaming mugs in front of them. Finn laid a quarter on the bar.

The teamster took a long pull and wiped foam from his upper lip. "Met the tall one over at the market. He paid me to haul two steamer trunks from his aunt's house to an upstairs apartment in Greenwich Village. Helped me carry them, he did, which you don't often see. The first time they weighed almost nothing, but he had me come back in the afternoon and take them to the train station. That time they were heavy as hell, like they'd filled them with books. You know, there's hardly anything heavier than a crate of books. I had a job once, moving the Brooklyn library into their new building. Had a sore back for a week."

"Sounds awful. Tell us about the train station. Did they say where they were going?"

"St. Louis World's Fair. They were real excited about it. Buy me another beer and I'll show you where the aunt lives."

"Won't do any good if they're in St. Louis," Finn said. "Come on Bird, we need to visit your cousin."

When they reported what they had learned to Bridget's father, he said, "It's worth the expense. Go to the Fair and bring them back." He handed Finn a stack of gold coins. "Here's money for train tickets, hotel, and meals. My daughter's wasting away in a nunnery in want of a husband, and those libertines need to be stopped before they ruin some other innocent colleen."

Finn thanked him and they left. Once they were out on the street, he said, "Pack a bag, Bird. Looks like we're going to the fair."

CHAPTER 12

At lunch, Lily praised the drawings Mo had made of her sisters and asked him to draw her, too.

"Of course," he said. If it ingratiated them with the sisters, why not? And it was good practice.

When they returned to their car after eating, she said they were tired of being confined to their seats and suggested their party sit in the car's drawing room.

Everyone agreed.

Mo retrieved his tablet, sat opposite Lily in an upholstered armchair that looked like it belonged in Bryce's mother's parlor, and began to sketch her. She was wearing a white, lacy summer dress. Its high neckline, which covered her almost to her chin, was trimmed in black lace. All the lace was made for an impressionist treatment, capturing its essence without reproducing the details. A wide black belt cinched her waist, giving her a fashionable hourglass shape. Mo assumed she wasn't wearing a corset, given her feelings about rights for women, but he didn't know. Her hair was pulled tightly away from her face, but at the back of her head it hung loose in dark coils.

He erased her chin and tried again. It was sharper than her sisters', but not as pointed as he had made it. Lily's face possessed a maturity her sisters lacked. Something behind the eyes communicated resolve or intention. He puzzled how to best translate that onto paper. Finally, he took his brain out of the equation, relaxed, and let his eyes and his hands do the work.

Bryce hovered over his shoulder, watching every stroke of the pencil.

"Lily," Bryce said, "did I tell you we gave up front row seats to see *Beau Brummel* on Broadway for this trip?"

"Did you?"

Bryce smiled. "It's going to be worth it, don't you think?"

"You mean the Fair?"

"That, too. I can hardly wait to see all the exhibits with you. Mo has a list."

Lily nodded. "He's mentioned that list several times. Living in the city, I imagine you see a lot of Broadway shows."

"Try not to move," Mo said.

She put her eyes back on Mo.

"Oh, sure," Bryce said. "We go to Broadway all the time."

"Father seldom takes us to the City."

"Well, then, allow me. New Jersey's just across the river. When we get back home, I'll get us tickets, and we'll all go. After the show, I'll introduce you to the cast, and you can hear me play ragtime at a little club where the theater crowd gathers."

She bit her lip and looked down.

"Head up, please," Lily's eyebrows were narrower than either sister. Unusual, but not unexplainable. They weren't triplets, after all.

Bryce began to pace. "Do you ladies like to dance? St. Louis is the home of ragtime. I'll bet there are a lot of places where we could go dancing while we're there."

Lily shrugged, then resumed her pose. "Certainly we know how to dance, but I don't want to plan our evenings before we even get there. The Fair's the thing, wouldn't you agree, Mo?"

"I do. And it's huge. No telling what we'll be able to do there."

"Sure, sure," Bryce said. "But I'm just suggesting how we can have a little fun."

"Bryce, quit distracting Lily while I'm trying to draw her."

"Oh, I'm not interfering. I'm just making conversation."

Mo jerked his thumb toward where the others were sitting. "Well, converse over there."

Bryce started away and then turned back. "Lily, I've never even told Mo and Julius this, but last Christmas the minister at Mother's church came up with the idea of an entirely musical service. From organ prelude to benediction, every part of it would be played on instruments or sung. A sort of opera service."

"Bryce's father is a state senator and his mother is Mrs. la-de-da of the social register," Mo said. "I'm surprised he hasn't mentioned it."

Lily raised her eyebrows.

Bryce pretended to play an invisible piano. "And I'm their musical prodigy. So Mother pressed me into service—vassal to their reverend's will. I scored the whole program, slipping a little syncopation into the instrumental interludes—something to wake the sleepers in the back. When the good reverend heard the rehearsals, he threw a fit. The way he told it, I'd practically invited the devil to dance on his dais."

Lily laughed. "Didn't go well with your parents?"

"The worst sin you can commit in the Holloway family is to embarrass them publicly."

She turned toward him. "That's not the only way to upset my father, but it's one of them."

Mo cleared his throat. . She turned back to him and resumed her pose.

"Bryce," he said, "why don't you play cards while I finish."

"How can I? You've got my partner."

Lily pulled the deck of cards from her hand bag and held it out to him without moving her head. "I'm sure Rose will be your partner."

Bryce stared at the deck. "Yeah, but you and I are the winning team."

Mo took the cards from Lily and put them in Bryce's hand. "Go."

"Oh, drat!" Violet said.

Bryce stood his ground. "See? Violet doesn't want to play."

"It's not that," Violet said. "The clasp on my necklace just broke."

"Let me see it," Julius said. "I'll bet I can fix it for you."

Mo waved Bryce away. "Go watch Julius for a while."

Bryce reluctantly made his way to the other side of the drawing room, glancing back at Mo and Lily as he went.

Twenty minutes later, Mo finished Lily's portrait, tore off the page, and handed it to her. She studied it admiringly and gave him a warm smile. "Thank you. My first souvenir from the trip."

"You're welcome." He stood and offered her his hand. "Shall we join the others? I see they never started that card game."

Julius, using his pocket knife, had put the clasp on Violet's necklace back in working order. She leaned forward and invited him to fasten the chain around her neck. The scooped neckline of her dress revealed a generous view of her firm, shapely breasts.

She sat upright and gave the necklace a little tug, testing his workmanship. She let go, and it fell in place just above her cleavage. Her dimples deepened and a warm smile told Mo that Julius was her knight.

Mo offered Lily a seat before taking his own. He flipped through the tablet to the page containing the list he and his friends had made before they left New York. "Rose says she doesn't know where your list is, but I've got ours right here. Why don't we talk about which exhibits sound interesting? After all, the Fair's the reason we've met, and seeing it is our common goal."

Bryce and Julius nodded.

"There are supposed to be fifteen hundred exhibits," Julius said. "I can't imagine how long it could take to see them all."

"A month, at least," Bryce said.

"Oh, we don't have that long," Rose said.

"Neither do we," Julius said. "The University wants me back at work long before then."

"University?" Violet said.

"Julius works at Columbia," Bryce said.

Mo tapped the page on his tablet. "So, what we did was pour over every article we could find about the exposition and winnow out the exhibits we absolutely wanted to see. Others we'll get to if time allows."

Rose smiled at him. "Shall I guess your top pick? The Palace of Arts."

"You're right, of course. But what a wonder! I read that palace alone covers over five acres."

"Five acres! I can't imagine a building that size," Rose said.

"Neither can I," Mo said, "but you'd have to travel the world to see the artwork that will be on display—the latest paintings from Europe have their own wing, another just for the sculpture. And I understand many European artists will be attending. Imagine talking with Renoir about his brushwork. Imagine talking with Renoir. Imagine *meeting* Renoir."

"Imagine meeting the aristocrats who come to see Renoir," Lily said. "Sisters, we should definitely visit the Palace of Arts."

"I assumed you would, anyway," Mo said. "We should meet up there and see it together."

Lily cleared her throat. "No promises. We have a list of people Mother and Father want us to meet."

Bryce's face fell. "I thought you were traveling on your own."

"We are, but that doesn't mean we don't have social obligations."

Bryce gave a bitter laugh. "I know all about those. Story of my life."

"Just ask Bryce if you'd like to get out of them," Julius said. "He's an expert."

CHAPTER 13

Their second evening on the train, the Jones sisters again invited the men into their beds. But getting by the porter wasn't as easy as the previous night. After dinner, the six friends lingered in the drawing room of their car while the porter made up passenger beds. When the rest of their car retired, the porter remained in the drawing room to attend them. Finally, Rose realized he couldn't go to bed until they did.

With hushed undertones, she sent the others to bed, and kept the porter busy by sending him to fetch her a tonic water for "stomach troubles." By the time he returned, her sisters were in the men's beds. She thanked the porter, took a few sips, and went to her own bed where Mo waited.

Sometime after midnight, Rose put on her robe and went to the lavatory, giving her the opportunity to make sure the coast was clear. It was, and everyone returned to their proper beds.

In the morning, the conductor came through the car waking anyone who was still asleep and informing passengers that they would arrive in St. Louis in a few hours. Those who wanted breakfast beforehand should rouse themselves and make their way to the dining car promptly. He wasn't as polite about it as the porter would have been, but he had a schedule to keep.

Lily saw the queue of women waiting for the lavatory and said to the men, "Go ahead to breakfast. Don't wait on us. We'll be awhile."

The men took her advice and had already been served by the time she and her sisters arrived in the dining car. All nearby tables were occupied, so the Jones sisters were seated at the opposite end of the car. It was an anti-climactic ending to a very enjoyable trip. She knew they'd have to part from the men once they got to the fair, but she'd hoped to spend a bit more time with them before then.

When the men finished breakfast, they casually strolled down the aisle to her table and wished everyone a good morning. Lily and Violet smiled. Rose was intently studying a sheet of paper, moving her lips as if memorizing the lines of a play.

Bryce leaned over her shoulder and playfully snatched the paper from her hand, holding it out of her reach. "What do we have here? Is this the long lost list of exhibits?"

"No. Give me that." Rose clawed the air.

Bryce lifted it higher, and laughed. "What will you give me for it?"

"A bad time if you don't give it back." She lunged from her seat and grabbed it out of his hand. She sat back down and tucked it under the napkin on her lap.

That was a mistake. Now, the men's curiosity was really piqued.

"Oh, for goodness' sake, show them," Violet said. "We have to tell them sooner or later." She slipped her hand under Rose's napkin, retrieved the page, and handed it to Julius.

He skimmed it and handed it to Mo. "I don't get it."

Mo read the list aloud as Bryce looked over his shoulder. "Order of importance:

> Prince / Princess
> Duke / Duchess
> Marquess / Marchioness
> Earl (Count) / Countess
> Viscount / Viscountess
> Baron / Baroness
> Baronet / Baronetess
> Sir (knight) / Lady
> Princes and Dukes are addressed with their actual title, but all other ranks as Lord or Lady."

Rose blushed and looked at her lap.

Mo shook his head. "I don't understand."

"I do," Bryce said. "It's a list of possible prizes, in order of value."

Rose jerked her eyes up, boring a hole through Bryce. "We are not gold diggers!"

"So," Mo said, "you never had a list of exhibits?"

"Of course we do," Violet said. "It's in Rose's travel case. I'll show it to you when we go back to our seats."

Lily slid out from her seat, took money from her purse and laid it on the table. She put her hand on Bryce's elbow. "We always intended to tell you, but not here. Let's all adjourn to the drawing room. Rose, fetch our list of exhibits and we'll explain everything."

Awkward silence made for an uncomfortable walk back to their car. Fortunately, the drawing room had no other passengers. The men and women took seats opposite each other, except Rose, who continued on to the sleeper sections. Moments later, she returned with a folded sheet of paper. She sat down next to Violet and handed it to Mo.

He unfolded it and smoothed out the creases. It actually contained a list of foreign pavilions, but Lily had added "Palace of Arts" at the bottom after their discussion yesterday.

Lily straightened her posture and swept her gaze over all three men, fixing their eyes on hers. "First, Rose is right, we are not gold diggers. Our father has more money than any of us could ever need. What he desires is status. The social elite in New York have closed ranks and won't let new money in, but the opposite is true in Europe, where many aristocratic families are in need of precisely that—new money."

Bryce folded his arms across his chest. "So, title hunters rather than gold diggers."

Lily stared him down. "I told you from the start that we had social obligations once we got to the Fair."

"Husband hunting?"

Lily pressed her lips into a thin line and nodded. He was right, but the way he said it made it sound a little sordid.

But it was Julius who raised the serious objection. "I thought you were free-thinking women, beyond all that Victorian horse manure."

Violet's eyes welled up. "We are, about important things like women's rights. But we owe our father. He's given us everything." She looked at Bryce. "Surely, you do things you don't want to do because your parents ask it of you."

Bryce looked chagrined. "Yeah, but . . . but we're not talking about being polite to some gray heads at a tea party. I'd never let them tell me whom to marry or when."

Rose gave Mo a pleading look. "We're not doing anything awful. Everyone gets married sooner or later."

Julius laughed. "I'm rather thinking of later."

"That's the privilege of being a man," Rose said.

"And of choosing my own mate," Bryce said.

"Also the privilege of a man," Lily said.

Violet dabbed her eyes with a lace hankie. "We understand that nothing we can do will make Father a Duke or even a Baronet. But his grandchildren would inherit the title and his daughters would be called Lady."

Julius snorted. "I don't know if I'd go that far."

"Very funny," Violet said. "But as you learned from the list Mo read, any of us who marry aristocracy, become titled by marriage, or so Father says. And that gains the Joneses the respect Mother wants more than anything."

Bryce shook his head. "How is this different from an arranged marriage?"

"It's nothing like arranged," Lily said. "We'll pick our own husbands."

Bryce curled his lip. "And bring them home to Daddy?"

Lily nodded. "That's the idea." She swallowed hard. "Look, it's not like it hasn't been done. There are numerous duchesses and countesses today who came from American industrialist families. We won't be the first, or the last."

"And we're not going to pick men we hate just for our father's sake," Violet said. "We'll find someone we can get along with."

Julius leaned in close and whispered, "But you're not exactly virgin brides."

Lily shrugged. "We'll see how important that really is to a bankrupt Earl. Even free-lovers, Victoria Woodhull and her sister, Tennessee, whom you praised earlier, married Englishmen and resettled to England. It didn't seem to bother their husbands."

"Tennessee became a baroness in England. Lady Cook, I believe," Violet said.

"Also Viscountess of Monserrate," Rose said. "Married well, yet remained her own person. So it can be done."

"Well, I'm appalled by the whole idea," Mo said.

"Don't be that way," Rose said. "The last two days have been a merry frolic for all of us. You can't pretend you didn't enjoy it. Or that you ever intended to make us wives."

"She's got us there, Mo," Julius said.

Mo frowned. "No, but I thought we'd have a fortnight together. I wanted to show you things at the Fair."

Rose took his hand. "That would have been wonderful, but it can't happen. Now that you understand we have an objective, you need to leave us to it."

Mo looked away.

"Mother says it's impolite to talk about money," Lily said, "but since we're telling the truth here, Bryce is the only one among you rich enough to just jump on the train as a lark. You three must have your own reason for dashing off to St. Louis."

Mo wouldn't meet her eyes. She'd been right.

She touched his sleeve, causing him to look at her. "And don't say it was because of us. You didn't know we were going."

Mo winked. "No, but I'm glad we met."

She smiled. "I'm not complaining, either. But before you judge us, tell us the real reason you're spending all your savings going to the Fair?"

"Just because Julius and I aren't as wealthy as the Joneses doesn't mean we can't afford the Fair."

Lily blushed. "I'm sorry, my remark was uncalled for."

Mo dismissed her apology with a wave. "Apology accepted. Truth be told, I'm an artist who hasn't really penetrated the New York art market. I'm hoping to mingle with artists from elsewhere and discover what it takes to break in."

Lily smiled. "Well, we've seen what you can do with just a pencil. With your level of talent, I'm sure you'll succeed."

"His oil paintings are even better," Bryce said.

"I brought paint and canvases with me," Mo said. "I plan to paint some scenes at the Fair. Possibly the three of you could be in one."

Lily's smile tightened. They still didn't understand that she and her sisters had work to do, and that they would be a distraction. "I can't promise that. Perhaps we should have said something sooner, but we've told you everything now. We have a duty to our father. And having three recent lovers hanging about won't be helpful."

"Why don't you forget this whole ridiculous plan?" Bryce said. "I can gain your father entry into my parent's social circle." He snapped his fingers. "Like that."

Lily shook her head. "That won't make us a countess or a Lady, will it?"

Bryce jumped up and stormed off, muttering.

"That's a shock," Rose said. "I didn't think he felt that strongly about anything."

"Surprised me, too," Mo said.

"Bryce has never mentioned it," Julius said slowly, "but I suspect he's gotten some pressure of his own to marry well. Your intentions may have cut a little close to the bone."

Lily stood. "Sisters, we'd better repack our suitcases. I don't think it will be long before we'll arrive in St. Louis."

CHAPTER 14

The conductor, in his navy-blue coat with brass buttons and gold stripes on his cuffs, strutted down the aisle, bellowing, "Saint Louis! Saint Louis!" He paused at the end of the car, turned back toward the happy travelers, and puffed out his chest. "Welcome to Union Station, the largest and busiest railroad station in the world. Upstairs you will pass through Grand Hall, considered one of the most beautiful public lobbies." He touched the bill of his cap. "We thank you for your patronage and wish you a pleasant stay in our great city."

He left them, crossing into the next car, shouting, "Saint Louis! Saint Louis!"

Rose gawked out the windows as the locomotive pulled into the train shed. Tracks on either side of the car wove around them like a cable knit on a sweater. She assumed they had similar complications in New York, but she hadn't been there enough to know. Across the aisle Julius and Mo were similarly absorbed watching their approach to the station. Daylight disappeared as their car rolled beneath a vast roof that covered fifteen platforms.

With a hiss of steam and the squeal of steel, their train came to a halt. The porter hustled suitcases out to the platform and returned for more.

Lily stood and smoothed the wrinkles from her dark brown skirt. She'd been a bit subdued since that little contretemps with Bryce, Rose had noticed. When Lily'd told her about their night together, she hadn't mentioned any clinginess or jealousy on Bryce's part. So perhaps it was just as Julius had said, marriage was a sore spot for Bryce. If so, she didn't blame him. She'd had her doubts about the scheme from the beginning.

Lily slipped a matching jacket over her pleated white blouse and donned a hat trimmed with orange silk poppies.

Bryce stood and grinned at her. "Nice chapeau." Apparently, all was forgiven.

"Reminds me of a painting by Monet," Mo said. "All you need is a parasol."

"We brought parasols," Rose said. "They're in our baggage."

Mo extended his hand to Rose, and she joined him in the aisle.

"Pardon me," the porter said as he continued taking passengers' suitcases out to the platform.

Rose pressed herself against Mo to allow the porter to pass. God bless the man. "I, for one, do hope we meet again at the Fair," she whispered. Once the porter was by, she stepped over next to Lily.

Mo nodded to each of the sisters. "I know I speak for all three of us when I say making your acquaintance was an absolute delight. We hope we'll see you again. But in case we don't, may your time here bring you the greatest joy."

"Yeah, good luck hunting," Bryce said as he followed the porter off the train.

So maybe not everything was forgiven.

"I guess I offended him," Lily said.

Julius put on his hat and handed Mo his. "Oh, don't pay any attention to Bryce. He probably just thinks he's being witty." He reached out for Violet, and she took his hand.

"Thank you, sir." She slid out of her seat and met his eyes. "Whatever happens hereafter, your company has given me the deepest pleasure. Something I shall always remember fondly."

A passenger behind them cleared his throat loudly. "The rest of us would like to get off."

"Oh, sorry," Julius said. "Ladies, we'd best proceed."

The platform was crowded and chaotic. In the crush of people there was no room for romantic farewells.

Bryce was waiting for them, suitcase in hand. "The porter says there are street cars outside on Market Street. I'm going to go find out which line will take us to our hotel."

"Wait, we have trunks in the baggage car," Julius said.

"Right, I forgot. Well, you and Mo locate your trunks and I'll search out a teamster."

Julius looked around, but the Jones sisters had disappeared in the mass of arriving passengers. Well, they had trunks, too. Perhaps he'd run into them wherever the baggage was being unloaded.

Pushing through the mass of disembarking passengers, and asking directions from everyone wearing a railroad uniform, they eventually found their trunks. But no sign of the sisters, who were undoubtedly on their way to their hotel already. And he realized he'd never asked Violet where she was staying.

Bryce arrived with two men pushing baggage carts, who in short order, wheeled their trunks to a freight dock and loaded them on a wagon. Julius, reluctant to let a stranger drive off with all of his and Mo's worldly possessions, climbed up next to the driver.

"All right," Bryce said. "Mo and I'll take the streetcar and meet you there." He turned to the teamster holding the reins. "Take these to the new Hotel Jefferson. You know where it is?"

The driver nodded. "Been carrying people there all morning. Hotel makes us unload large baggage at the back entrance, but there's a hallway inside the hotel that your friend can pass through to meet you in the lobby."

Julius opened a map of St. Louis he'd pulled from a rack in the station. The baggage area of Union Station was on Twentieth Street. The driver pulled out and headed north toward Market Street where he brought the team to a halt. A harried policeman stood in the center of the intersection with arms outstretched, waiving and pointing one driver after another, a silver whistle clamped between his teeth emitting frequent shrieks. Crowds on Market Street were even thicker than inside the terminal. Hordes pouring out the station doors encountered a swell of wagons, hackney carriages, and trolley cars. It was as if half America's population was arriving at once.

While they were stopped, Julius admired the terminal building on his right. Built of Indiana limestone, it stretched the length of the entire block. At the far end were turrets that could have come from a European castle, and a square clock tower taller than a church steeple. Eight gothic dormers along the front reminded him of St. Patrick's cathedral in New York, except the roof shingles were red.

When the cop motioned for them to go, the driver snapped the reins. "I'm not going down through that mess. I know a better way." He looked over at Julius. "They say there's supposed to be two hundred thousand people coming for the opening."

Julius whistled. He hadn't heard that. It seemed like an exaggeration, but given the crowds around him, he couldn't dispute it. The hotel wasn't far, ten or twelve blocks, and had it not been for the heavy traffic they'd have been there in no time. Even with the congested roads, they arrived, un-loaded the trunks and secured them in the hotel storage well before Mo and Bryce made it there by trolley.

Reunited, the three friends stepped up to a dark walnut counter topped with a wide marble slab. A sign hanging on brass chains read: Check-In. A hotel clerk, looking completely frazzled, stepped over to them. "How may I assist you today?"

"We have a reservation," Bryce said. "The name's Holloway."

The young man ran his finger down the columns of a large ledger book. He turned the page and did the same, then tried several more pages. Finally, he looked up with the expression of a man about to tell a boy the family dog was dead. "I'm sorry. We have nothing down for you."

"Oh, surely you missed it. Look again."

The clerk bit his lip and finally nodded. He wet the tip of his finger with his tongue and slowly rechecked the list. When he finished, he shook his head. "Sorry, nothing even close to Holloway."

Bryce took off his hat and laid it on the countertop. "Well, someone has made a mistake, then. But just give us three rooms and we won't worry about who did what."

The clerk's jaw dropped. "Three rooms? We haven't even one left."

"Well, all right, one room with three beds, then. You can manage that."

"No, sir. We're completely filled up—all ten floors."

Bryce scratched his head. "How can that be? You just opened today."

The man shrugged. "The Fair—every room was booked beforehand."

"Including ours. I have a telegram."

"May I see it?"

Bryce rummaged through his pockets. "I don't know where it is at the moment, but I assure you I sent it."

The clerk held out his hands in a gesture of helplessness.

Julius was beginning to have dark suspicions, but he held his temper. "Come on, Bryce, think. Where'd you put it?"

"Did you leave it on the train?" Mo said.

"Of course not. I must have put it in my suitcase."

Julius eyed the crowded lobby. "Can you look? The way this town has filled up, having a place to stay tonight seems pretty important all of a sudden."

"Don't go anywhere," Bryce said to the clerk. "I'll be right back."

The man closed his eyes, as if he was about to take a brief nap standing up. "I'll be right here."

Bryce laid his suitcase on a lobby divan and unbuckled the straps. After poking around in it for a few seconds, he held a yellow Western Union form triumphantly aloft. "Found it!"

The clerk's eyes popped open and Bryce handed it to him. He barely glanced at it and then handed it back. "I'm sorry, sir, this doesn't help. It's only a copy of your request for rooms. I need to see your confirmation from the hotel."

Bryce tried his winning smile. "That's all I've got. But you can see plain as day that I reserved our rooms. Now, what can you do?"

"Nothing. I'm sorry."

Bryce spun around and looked at Julius and Mo.

Julius waited to see what he would do. Bryce was frequently frustrating, but always entertaining and often resourceful.

Bryce turned back to the clerk. "I'd like to see the hotel manager."

"Certainly. I'll get him." He walked into an office behind the counter and returned with a portly gentleman wearing a suit that strained at the seams and a waistcoat whose buttons threatened to escape the buttonholes. His round fleshy face and small dark eyes reminded Julius of a flapjack with two blueberries.

"How may I be of assistance?"

Bryce introduced himself and slid the telegraph receipt across the marble. "We sent you a reservation, but the clerk says you have not reserved our rooms."

"I told them they need a confirmation telegram," the clerk said.

"We never got it," Bryce said. "Sending it's the hotel's responsibility, isn't it?"

The manager nodded. "Let me check to see if we ever received your reservation. I'll just be a moment, if you don't mind waiting."

"We've nowhere else to go."

The office door was open, and Julius watched the man sort through stacks of papers on his desk. Eventually, he returned to the counter with one of them.

"Yes. We did receive the telegram that matches your receipt, and we replied that we were full and couldn't accommodate your party."

"Replied? Where did you send that message?"

He glanced at the form in his hand. "To you, in-care-of the railroad. I believe your reply is waiting at Union Station."

In this situation, Julius would've gotten embarrassed, but Bryce turned on the charm instead. "That doesn't do either of us any good, does it? My father is a senator, and I know full well that hotels always hold a few rooms back for unexpected VIPs. I need for you to give us one of them."

"What you say is true, but this weekend we're already full of important officials. Secretary Taft is delivering the keynote address, and St. Louis is up to our eyeballs in Senators and Congressmen. Those rooms you mention are already gone."

Bryce was still nonplussed. "The fact is, we're here now, standing in your lobby. You need to do something. I don't want to have to contact my father. He's a busy man."

The manager grimaced. "Why don't you gentlemen have a coffee in the café, compliments of the hotel, while I make a few inquiries?"

"Can we leave our suitcases somewhere?" Julius said.

The man turned to his clerk. "Have the bellman hold these gentlemen's bags." He went into his office and closed the door.

Julius, Mo and Bryce located the café and ordered coffee from a wispy waitress in a long skirt and white apron. She returned with three cups and saucers and filled them from a gleaming silver pot. She set cream and sugar on the table, curtsied, and left.

Julius took a sip and inhaled the fragrant steam. Wonderful! In his lab at Columbia, they had a battered enamelware pot full of coffee that sat over a Bunsen burner and slowly turned to sludge as the day progressed. This was real coffee. Too bad, they weren't staying here. He set his cup down. "You certainly managed that manager."

Bryce stiffened. "That's a harsh interpretation. All I did was exchange one verb for another."

"Explain," Mo said.

"If you tell someone you want them to do something, they have an out. What if what they want isn't the same as you want? But if you say, 'Here's what I need you to do,' it has a whole different effect."

"Sounds manipulative," Mo said.

Bryce shrugged. "Needs must. We can't sleep in the street."

"True," Julius said. "But none of this would have come up if you had actually booked us a hotel before we left New York, not at the last minute from the train. You made that poor manager feel like it was his fault."

"Well, if we're pointing fingers, blame Jenkins."

The manager tottered into the café. It was the first time Julius had seen him away from his counter, and what he noticed was a pair of tiny feet that would have better fit a man fifty pounds lighter. Julius felt sorry for them.

"I've secured a place for you in Camp Lewis."

"A camp?" Bryce said.

"Yes, but the tents have wood floors, iron beds, even electric lights. Public showers and baths are nearby. Plus, you'll have direct access to the Fair via horse-drawn omnibuses."

Bryce stood up. "I'm not in the army anymore. I expected you to do better than a cot in a tent."

The man hung his head. "It's absolutely the only thing I could find. I called every lodging that possesses a telephone. Tomorrow is opening day, you know. Now, perhaps some dignitaries are only here for tomorrow's ceremonies. Maybe rooms will become available once they leave. Why don't you stay at Camp Lewis tonight, enjoy the opening of the Fair tomorrow, and then see if you can find a vacancy Sunday or Monday? At least you'll have a bed until then."

Mo and Julius stood, shook the manager's hand, and thanked him.

Mo patted Bryce on the back. "His plan makes sense. We can rough it for a day or two while we search for better accommodations."

The manager looked relieved. "You'll save a lot of money, too. Camp Lewis is only fifty cents a day. That's cheaper than any hotel."

Which was exactly the wrong thing to say to Bryce.

"Look," Bryce said. "If we were worried about money we wouldn't have chosen the Jefferson, would we?"

"No. Of course, I didn't mean to imply—"

"Could I ask you to do us a favor?" Julius said quickly. "The hotel has our steamer trunks locked up in the back. I'd appreciate it if you would hold them here. If a room is going to open up in a day or two, there's no sense hauling them out to the camp and then back again."

The manager rubbed his fleshy jowls and stared at the floor for a moment. "Okay. A day or two wouldn't hurt. I'll need you to sign a liability waiver, though."

"Be glad to," Julius said. "That all right with you Mo?"

Mo nodded. "Much appreciated, sir. Thank you, again."

"I need to send a telegram to my father," Bryce said. "Can you take care of that here, or do I need to go to the Western Union office?"

The manager looked horrified. "Are you still going to do that? I told you I did everything I could to help you."

"Breathe easy, sir. I'm not wiring him to complain about the Jefferson. I'll ask him to use some of his connections to find us a room for tomorrow onward."

Bryce sent his telegram. Julius and Mo signed waivers for the storage of their trunks. The doorman hailed them a hack. The bellman retrieved their suitcases and loaded them in the back of the carriage.

On the way to Camp Lewis, Bryce said, "Don't worry. My father will get us some place great."

Julius hoped that was true, as the carriage took them ever further north from the city and the exhibition grounds, out into the wilds of Missouri. Finally, their misadventure terminated at eighty-five acres of rolling farm land, now overgrown with tents.

Their driver dropped them and their luggage in front of a large wooden building that he said served as the camp reception, bath house, and dining hall. Julius paid him, and his vehicle clattered off. They carried their suit-cases up the steps onto a wide wooden porch and found the camp manager, who collected four-bits each for the night and handed them a sheet of paper containing camp rules and a map of the tents. He'd circled the one he said was theirs.

The men stepped out on the porch and surveyed the rows of white canvas tents. Julius laughed. "Wants and needs, eh, Bryce? Tell a man you *need* ham, and pig's ass is what you get."

Chapter 15

Excitement of opening day wouldn't allow Bryce to linger in bed. He woke the others at dawn, and they were shaved, dressed, and breakfasted by seven-thirty. Even so, they weren't the first. By the time they located the omnibus to the exposition, there was already a lengthy queue ahead of them.

The omnibus, a long, colorfully painted coach drawn by a single pair of horses, pulled to a stop. People began boarding through a door at the rear. Bryce craned his neck to see inside. Nothing fancy, two long benches, one on each side.

When the twelfth passenger boarded, the driver said, "That's enough."

Bryce, still well back in line, scuffed the dirt and shook his head.

A small boy at the foot of the coach howled. The last woman to board leaned out the door. "I'm not leaving my son, sir."

The driver nodded. "If he sits on your lap, he can go."

The boy scrambled aboard.

The driver turned to the waiting line. "Be patient. Another omnibus will be along shortly." He climbed up to the driver's seat, released the brake, and snapped the reins. The horses leaned into their harnesses, and the vehicle rolled away. Its merry passengers began to sing, "Meet Me in St. Louis, Louis."

Bryce looked at Julius and Mo. "If that damn manager at the Jefferson hadn't put us out in the sticks, we'd have been there by now."

"Language, sir," said a man behind them. "There are ladies and children present."

Bryce tipped his hat. "My apologies, sir. Just frustrated. We don't want to miss anything."

Mo touched Bryce's sleeve. "Stop worrying. The fair doesn't officially open until one. We've plenty of time, so just relax."

Bryce nodded.

"But the parade starts at nine," the man behind them said.

"That wasn't helpful," Mo said to him. "Bryce, why don't we go inside and have another cup of coffee while we wait."

"What, and lose our place in line? Never!"

Just then a second omnibus appeared in the distance, coming toward them.

"See?" Bryce said.

Mo nodded. They waited. When it arrived, the line crawled forward as the next dozen boarded.

Julius slapped Bryce on the back. "We'll definitely make the next one."

The wait for the next one was longer. When it finally arrived, it drove past them. The line started to move in centipede fashion after it. The driver saw them and held up his hand. "Go back to where you were. I've got to water these horses and then I'll pull around."

Bryce jumped out of line and paced in a tight circle.

"Too much coffee?" Julius asked.

"No. But if we'd stayed at a hotel, we could have ridden a trolley and been there by now."

"You don't know that. Yesterday, you and Mo took the streetcar, yet my horse-drawn wagon beat your time by a considerable margin."

"Bryce, get back in line," Mo said. "He'll surely be ready to board any moment."

"They can only work these horses four hours a day," the overly-informed man behind them said. "Then the team has to be changed out."

Mo looked at the man. "Interesting fact, but again, not helpful. We're trying to settle his nerves."

Bryce didn't see any reason for Mo to say that. He wasn't nervous, just anxious to get there before everything started. Weren't they all? He just showed it more than the others.

Mo let Julius and Bryce board ahead of him. Mo had just put his foot on the step when the driver held out his arm to block his way. "That's all."

Bryce whirled around inside the carriage. "No, we're not leaving Mo behind."

"Sorry," the driver said. "Twelve to a load. Them's the rules."

Mo watched Bryce slip a coin from his pocket and shake the driver's hand. "Will you double check? You may have miscounted."

The drive glanced at his palm, and then inside the carriage. "You're right, I did. Ma'am, that boy needs to sit on your lap."

The woman picked up her son, and the other passengers slid along the bench to make space.

The driver took Mo's elbow. "Up you go, sir."

"What kind of funny business is going on up there?" said the informed man who'd stood in line behind them.

"Nothing. Just company policy, small children can ride in their parent's lap."

Mo took his seat next to Bryce and nodded to a handsomely dressed couple on the opposite bench.

"My husband and I are from Chicago," the wife said. "What about you?"

"New York City," Mo said, tipping the brim of his bowler. Julius and Bryce followed suit.

"Looks like we'll have lovely weather today," she said.

Mo smiled and nodded.

"My brother helped construct the exposition," she said.

"Is that so?"

"Yes. He wrote that, just ten days ago, St. Louis was hit by a late snow storm, then a quick thaw. He said the workers were sinking up to their ankles in mud."

Bryce frowned. "I hope that doesn't happen again. Jenkins didn't pack my winter coat or galoshes."

"Don't worry," said the husband. "Clear days from here on. David R. Francis won't let it be otherwise."

"Who's that?" Mo said.

"President of the Exposition," the husband said. "I met him when he came to Chicago to study what we did in ninety-three. Persuasive man. He could convince Zeus not to thunder during his parade."

His wife gave him a shriveling glare. "What are you saying? It's not going to rain today."

"That's exactly what I said, no rain."

Through the window behind the couple, Mo caught a glimpse of a white rotunda capping a tall building. He elbowed Bryce, who elbowed Julius. "Will you look at that, fellows?"

A wave of excitement rippled the length of the coach as others took notice. Soon, the omnibus passed an entrance, where a large number of bands were getting positioned for the parade. The driver turned onto Lindell Boulevard and brought them to a great plaza, where he unloaded them.

Into a swell of humanity.

The crowd was worse than Union Station yesterday. It was worse than anything Mo had ever seen in New York—on the streets after a show, midday
on Wall Street, Sundays in the park. Behind them the Wabash Station, St.
Louis Railroad, and Suburban Transit lines disgorged even more passengers, adding to the masses. The collective body muddled forward toward
the entrance turnstiles with all the speed of a snail. On his right, Mo saw a
facade of the Alps behind a tall Austrian-looking building.

They paid the fifty-cent entrance fee and followed the crowd toward the
Plaza of St. Louis, pausing to admire a fifteen-foot tall sculpture of St. Louis
of France astride his horse, sword raised.

A street sign for the road on their left read: "Model City." Mo spotted a
New York City sign atop the first exhibit.

"Hey, Bryce, Julius, look to your left. Home."

Bryce glanced at the building. "Just came from there." He pressed onward.

"I know," Julius said. "But aren't you curious what's in there?"

"Sure, but we know New York. No need to waste time on its exhibit. Let's
see what's up ahead."

They passed two bandstands and Mo saw a tall obelisk monument. A man
hawking *Official Guide to the Louisiana Purchase Exposition* stopped Mo and
launched into his pitch. "The only Official Guide—includes a history of
the Louisiana Purchase and a full account of all features of the exposition."
He waved a copy in Mo's face. "Over two-hundred pages, with nearly a
hundred photos, plus floor plans."

"I'll take one." Mo paid the man, who next turned to Bryce and Julius.
"What about you gents? Conveniently sized, fits right in your pocket."

"No thanks," Julius said. "We're together. We'll share."

The peddler moved on, and Bryce rushed into the "reserved" seats and secured a good spot on one of the hundreds of slatted park benches arranged
in rows around the plaza monument. Seats were already filling up.

Mo opened the guidebook and Julius looked over his shoulder. Bryce stood up on the bench and scanned the grounds in all directions.

By nine o'clock the place was packed. Officials of the Exposition marched into the Plaza of St. Louis, joined by the representatives from foreign governments. A four-mile long parade commenced, the longest Mo had ever seen. The opening day program listed twenty marching bands. When the parade concluded, John Philip Sousa's band remained and was joined by an enormous chorus that Mo estimated had at least 450 singers.

The President of the Exposition, David Francis, called the assemblage to order, and the Reverend Gunsaulus of Chicago offered an opening invocation. Longest prayer Mo had ever heard.

President Francis gave the opening speech and told those assembled that at the appointed hour, President Roosevelt would press a gold key in Washington, D.C., which would electrically transmit a signal that would start the Exposition machinery. During his remarks, Francis said, "At no previous exposition has art received so much recognition and attention."

Julius might like the technology of turning on the exhibits from half a continent away, but the art was exactly what Mo had come for.

Francis' opening address was followed by a choral performance of the Fair's official song, "Hymn of the West." Thereafter came orations by Frederick Skiff, the Director of Exhibits; Congressmen Tawney of Minnesota, some U.S. Senator Mo had never heard of; and finally Edward Harriman, president of the Union Pacific and Southern Pacific Railroads. These were interspersed with songs and appropriate poems.

Bryce seemed even more restless than usual, and Mo was about done-in with speeches, when Secretary of War, William Howard Taft, was introduced to deliver the keynote address. He began his rousing speech and quickly got to the heart of the Exposition's purpose. "From each of the great expositions of the world can be dated the world's familiarity with some marvelous invention so quickly adopted in our life that the change that it effected has almost passed from memory. Take, for instance, the telephone, introduced at the exposition in Philadelphia . . ."

Really? Mo never knew that. Julius probably did. Still, telephones hadn't spread to every village yet.

"Expositions as this shall pass into memory, and every material evidence disappear, the measurement that they make of progress become a benefit to mankind, the value of which cannot be exaggerated."

Mo looked at the magnificent palaces surrounding the plaza and at the quarter-mile long, six-hundred-foot wide Grand Basin of sparkling clear water behind the speaker's platform. It seemed inconceivable that on opening day Taft should speak of a time when all this would no longer be.

Taft spoke of the wonderful strides that are being made in the battle of mind over matter.

Julius took off his hat, wiped his brow, and put it back on. The speeches had been going on for two hours.

Next, Taft moved on to an issue important to the President and to himself as Secretary of War. "We have entered upon another and a different kind of expansion, which involves the solution of other and different problems from those presented in the Louisiana Purchase. They have been forced upon us without seeking, and they must be solved with the same high sense of duty, the same fearlessness and courage with which our ancestors met problems."

Undoubtedly, Taft was referring to territories won in the Spanish-American War. Bryce would be proud, sure, and Cuba might be handy. But what was the U.S. going to do with a bunch of islands in the middle of the Pacific, anyway?

"Without being blind to the difficulties or the dangers, it gives me great happiness to know and to say that the President of the United States, whom I unworthily represent today, is glad to take his stand among those who believe in the capacity of the American people when aroused by the call of duty, to solve any problem of government."

Mo glanced at Bryce, who was practically bursting the buttons on his shirt. Was he about to run up to Taft and tell him about the Rough Riders?

With brief accolades to David Francis and the organizers of the Exposition, Taft concluded. The audience applauded wildly. He held up his hands to quiet the crowd. "President Roosevelt will officially open the Fair from the White House, via a special gold telegraph key installed there for that purpose. However, the President is still in a meeting, so we will delay the opening for fifteen minutes."

Some in the crowd groused.

"He does have a country to run," Taft said.

Mo, Julius, and Bryce stood, stretched, and looked at the surrounding crowd. A few minutes later, Francis announced, "I shall now, by touching a key connecting with the White House in Washington, inform the President of the United States that the hour and the minute have arrived for turning on the power of the universal exposition of 1904."

Mo looked at his watch. It was 1:14.

Presumably, Roosevelt must have pressed the key in Washington, for a second later Mo heard the sounds of pumps and machinery starting up. Francis spread open his arms and cried out, "Open, ye gates; spring wide ye portals; enter in, ye sons of men and behold the achievement of your race; learn the lesson here taught, and gather from it inspiration to still greater achievements."

A cannon salute boomed, flags on every palace unfurled, Sousa's band struck up "The Star-Spangled Banner," and thousands of men and women gathered there began to sing. Mo, Julius, and Bryce joined in. Wasn't this the greatest place in the whole world to be?

As the sweeping chorus of the national anthem continued, water burst from fountains in the Grand Basin behind them. Mo whirled around and saw cascades next to Festival Hall at the far end of the basin begin to flow. Midday sun made the streaming rush of their falling waters glitter.

A stranger next to him grabbed his arm in excitement. "No exhibition has or will ever equal the colossal and delicately wrought beauty of this place. It is glory itself."

Mo couldn't agree more.

Chapter 16

At the foot of the obelisk, cheers erupted from thousands of throats. Julius, awash in the exuberant euphoria around them, couldn't stop grinning.

Then the congregated masses began to move toward the nearest building, the Palace of Varied Industries. But not Bryce. He took off toward the most eye-catching building in sight, Festival Hall, the white columned rotunda at the other end of the Grand Basin.

Julius and Mo hurried to catch up. Julius's long legs easily outpaced Mo, who fell behind. "Bryce! Wait for us," Julius shouted.

Bryce slowed his walk and Mo caught up. "Isn't that the most breathtaking architecture you've ever seen? Mo, you should paint a picture of this view."

"I believe I will. The guidebook says that grand dome is larger than St. Peter's basilica at the Vatican."

They crossed a bridge over a lagoon and proceeded up a walkway beside the Grand Basin, from which fountains were now shooting skyward.

When they reached where the cascades spilled into the basin, they paused to admire the view again. Julius didn't have Mo's artistic eye, but even he marveled at the wealth of statuary and ornamentation on and around the building ahead. Atop the dome gleamed a bronze statue of Victory. It reminded him of the statue of Diana above Madison Square Garden back home, except instead of a bow and arrow, the figure held a laurel wreath aloft.

They crossed yet another bridge and worked their way around a man-made lagoon to the back side of Festival Hall, where there was a colonnade honoring the thirteen states and Indian territory that came out of the Louisiana Purchase.

Bryce pulled on the heavy door to Festival Hall and rushed in. Julius caught the closing door and he and Mo entered, too. Inside they found a large auditorium containing three or four thousand seats and a stage large enough for hundreds of musicians, all empty. He craned his neck and looked up at the dome. It must have been 200 feet in diameter. He'd never been to the Vatican, but his mother's priest had brought back pictures. Julius didn't have a camera, but maybe they sold picture postcards of the Hall. If so, he'd buy her some.

They walked back outside. Eight large exhibit palaces radiated from Festival Hall like a fan around the Grand Basin and lagoons. How to choose where to start?

Directly south of Festival Hall, the Palace of Fine Arts sat on a hill sixty-feet above them. He knew that'd be Mo's choice. "This way, fellows."

They climbed wide granite steps up to the Beaux-Arts style palace. Julius had no architectural training, but it looked to him like a Greek temple and a Roman bath had fornicated and given birth to limestone offspring.

A Corinthian portico fronted the building. Julius stepped back and pointed up. High above, six figures adorned the main portico. "Mo, does the guide-book say what those are?"

Mo opened the guidebook and thumbed through it to the section on the Fine Arts Palace. "They symbolize the six great periods of art, as follows: Egyptian, Classic, Gothic, Oriental, Renaissance, and Modern."

On either side of the main entrance were two statues of seated figures, one representing Sculpture, and the other representing Painting. A nameplate said the second was by Louis Saint-Gaudens. "Hey, look, Mo. That's the guy who made *Diana* for Madison Square Garden."

Mo shook his head. "No, you're thinking of his brother, Augustus. But talent apparently runs in the family."

Julius shrugged. Art was Mo's bailiwick. No doubt he was right.

Bryce approached the door of the Palace of Art and was stopped by a security man in a navy-blue uniform. He turned around and came back down the steps, frowning. "Jefferson Guard says we can't go inside, yet. Won't open until Thursday."

They descended the stairs and leaned against a balustrade overlooking the East Cascade, admiring the dominating feature, a fountain entitled "The Spirit of the Pacific," which was topped by an airy figure of a graceful girl floating in space, attended by an albatross. Below them, water gushed from East, West, and Central fountains four times as tall as Julius. It spread out as it flowed down a long slope of ledges until it took its final plunge into the Grand Basin. He marveled at the size of the pumps that had to be churning somewhere behind the scenes.

All three Cascades were lined from the top of the hill to the basin with more sculptures than Julius could count. Along the edges of the Cascades, powerful vertical and horizontal jets of water shot from various artistic sculptures and fell into the basin. Jets further down the basin shot plumes of water seventy-five feet in the air. Why, the water show alone was worth the admission price. He'd never seen anything like it.

A man further down the railing strolled over and stuck out his hand. "Sam Harris."

Julius shook it. "Julius Hornsby." He shaded his eyes from the blinding afternoon sun shining behind Sam's head. "This is really something, isn't it?"

Sam swept his arm over the vista before them. "I tell you, it's inspiring to feel that the whole world is here. Every nation showing its best products."

"Wasn't that some parade?"

Sam beamed. "All those bands with uniforms as varied and brilliant as the kaleidoscope. And music from every civilized country. It was . . . oh, my."

"I hear there's going to be ragtime," Bryce said.

"I expect you'll find that over on the Pike."

"Sorry, Sam, I should have introduced my friends, Bryce and Mo."

The men shook hands all around.

"Is that where you're going next," Julius said, "the Pike?"

"Not until later. The Pike stays open until eleven at night. The exhibits close at dusk."

"I didn't know that." Julius said.

Mo rubbed his stomach. "Ought we get some lunch?"

Julius nodded. "I could use a beer, too. What about you, Bryce?"

"Sounds good. Sam, care to join us?"

"Thanks, no. I've eaten. There's a fabulous free luncheon being served in the Palace of Varied Industries."

"Darn," Mo said. "We were right near there before we came up here."

Julius turned to Mo. "That must have been where the crowd was headed when Bryce took off."

"How was I supposed to know?" Bryce said. "Let's go there now."

Bryce led them down the half-mile long slope along the Grand Basin beside huge lawns embroidered with rich beds of colorful flowers. Of course, it was his fault they'd missed the luncheon. He hoped the food wasn't all gone by the time they got there. Nothing he'd done so far on this trip had worked out. He'd have to make it up to Mo and Julius.

They arrived back at St. Louis Plaza to find a mob of thousands in front of the place waiting to get in. He thought of suggesting they find somewhere less crowded. But then someone nearby said, "I know that I can buy plenty to eat at the Fair, but I want to eat here, where the crowd is eating. It must be good."

He glanced at Mo and Julius. They shrugged.

Slug-like, the crowd inched forward. Amidst the thousands gathered around them, a rumor circulated that the meal inside excelled any of the restaurant concessions of the Exposition. Maybe they'd made the right decision.

They'd almost reached the entrance when a Jefferson Guard at the door stopped a sandy-haired man in front of them. "I'm sorry," the guard said, "but you need a ticket from the Exposition management."

Oh, no.

The Swede puffed himself up. "I represent two Swedish newspapers, having circulations larger than any other in Europe."

"I can't help that," said the guard. "Stand aside, please."

"But I represent—"

Before he could finish, the Swedish journalist was pushed out of the way by the swarm.

Bryce clawed to get back their place in front. "What's required here?"

"You have to have a ticket for the reserved seating from this morning's ceremonies," said the man next to him.

"I am an exhibitor," said a Frenchman, facing down the guard. "I have come all the way from Paris to participate. May I enter?"

"Not without a ticket," the guard said. "Stand aside, please."

Bryce gathered Julius and Mo close and tried to move past the guard. "We were sitting in the reserve section."

"Show me your tickets."

"I . . . we—"

"Stand aside, please."

"He's telling you the truth," Julius said. "I saw the reserve sign when we sat down."

Bryce held up a half-eagle. "If you let us in, we'll gladly pay for our lunch."

"There are scores of restaurants on the grounds anxious to take your money. Stand aside."

Julius clapped Bryce on the shoulder. "Let's try the Pike. I could use a beer."

Bryce put on a smile. More to make up to them. "Sounds good."

* * *

Bridget's father drove Bird and Finn to Grand Central Terminal in his carriage. He shook their hands and gave Finn the train tickets. "Stay as long as necessary. You need more money, you send me a wire."

"You've given us plenty, sir," Finn said.

Bird picked up both their battered leather grips and waited for Finn to show him where to go.

Finn located the platform, and they boarded, selecting facing seats in coach class. He pointed to an overhead rack, and Bird laid their luggage up there.

Other boarding passengers gave the men a wide berth, and no one asked to share their seats even when the car filled up.

"All aboard," came the conductor's shout from the platform. It was followed shortly by a blast from the whistle, and a jerk as the train lurched forward. Bird tipped his head back and closed his eyes. After years on the boxing circuit, a train ride wasn't anything special.

Finn took two sandwiches from a brown paper bag and kicked Bird's foot. "You hungry?"

"I could eat."

Finn handed him one.

Bird unwrapped the brown butcher paper and took a large bite. With his mouth full, he mumbled something.

"What?"

"How long 'til we get there?"

"Monday."

"What's today?"

"Saturday."

Bird set his sandwich on the paper and counted on his fingers. "So, three days?"

"Two and a half."

Bird resumed eating and let the information jell. Finally, he said, "Do we have enough sandwiches?"

Finn nodded. "Enough for today. We'll buy more as we go."

Bird smiled. "You think of everything." He finished eating, wadded the wrapper into a ball, looked around for where to put it, then shoved it in the crack between his seats.

"Another?" Finn said.

Bird shook his head. "No, save it for later."

Finn rolled the top of the bag closed and ate the rest of his sandwich.

They rode a while without further conversation. The steady clack of the wheels took on the rhythm of a speed bag, and brought up a lifetime of memories.

Finally, Bird said, "I'm glad you're helping me with this."

"Always."

"Do you think it will take us long to find those guys?"

"Why? You got someplace else to be?"

"No. I just thought you might know."

"I don't. But you heard your cousin's husband. We'll stay as long as it takes."

"Bring one home to wed Bridget."

"Damn right. And remind the other two who they messed with."

CHAPTER 17

At the Pike entrance, Bryce, Mo, and Julius were greeted by a sculpture of four mounted cowboys with a look of pure joy on their faces as they fired pistols toward the sky.

"That's us, boys," Bryce said.

"Not likely," Mo said.

The first pavilion they came to was the Irish Village. "I'll bet they have beer in here," Julius said.

Bryce grabbed his sleeve. "Maybe we ought to try somewhere else?"

"Why?"

"You know—"

"Surely, your dad's straightened it out with Bridget's family by now."

"Well . . . uh."

A brunette colleen with freckles, dressed in traditional Irish garb, stood at the entrance. Julius smiled at her. "Can a fellow buy Irish beer in here?"

When she smiled back at him, deep dimples appeared. "Irish whiskey, too."

"You got a table available?"

"Our restaurant holds two thousand." She pointed to a door. "Step right in, someone will seat you."

Bryce hesitated. "What if someone recognizes us?"

"Bryce, do you really think all the Irishmen on the planet know each other? Do you think Bridget's family has a reach that extends halfway across the country? Relax."

When they were seated and their server came, Mo and Julius ordered beers, and the corned beef platter.

Bryce said, "I'll have the corned beef, too, but give me a beer and a bump."

"A what?" the server said.

"He means he'd like a shot of whiskey with his beer," Julius said.

After lunch, they perused souvenir shops selling genuine Irish linens, flags, even replicas of the Blarney Stone. Julius was tempted to buy something for his mother, but decided he'd wait 'til they were ready to go home. He didn't want to lug a bunch of packages around the Fair, especially when they would be pulling up stakes at the tent city soon.

"You ready to go?" Mo said.

"I am. Where's Bryce?"

Mo looked around. "Don't know, he kind of disappeared."

"Maybe he's waiting for us out on the Pike."

They walked out of the Irish Village and looked down the mile-long Pike. Pavilions for Asia, Japan, the Streets of Seville, and Hagenbeck's animal show were nearby. Further along, signs advertised "moving pictures," a Moorish Palace, the House of Mirth, and a Water Chute ride. "This looks exciting," Julius said.

"It does," Mo said. "But we ought to see one or two of the palaces before they close. We can come back here this evening."

Julius pointed. "There he is!"

Bryce walked up and handed them each a white box.

Julius turned it in his hand. Plain pasteboard, well made. "What's this?"

"Open it and see."

Inside, he found a beautiful silver flask, engraved with the words "Louisiana Purchase Exposition, St. Louis, 1904." He was speechless.

Mo's was just like it. "This is a surprise, Bryce."

"My way of apologizing for letting Jenkins screw up our hotel rooms." He reached in his coat and showed them he had one too. "Fits right in your pocket."

"Thank you," Mo said. "Kind of expensive gift, though."

"Oh, pay that no mind. I figure in the long run it will save us money. We can buy a bottle and fill these instead of buying expensive shots."

Mo smiled at him. "Now you're thinking."

"That's not all. I learned we can go to the Fair administration building and buy a month-long pass for five dollars."

"You think we can afford to stay that long?" Mo said.

"I can't," Julius said. "I never told the university I'd be gone a month."

"Even if we only stay a fortnight, it'll save us money," Bryce said. "At fifty cents a day, two week's admission will cost us seven. A five dollar pass is a wonderful economy."

They returned to the Fair and Bryce led them down Administration Avenue. They passed the Palace of Transportation. Julius wanted to go in and see the latest in horseless carriages, but Bryce pressed them to buy their monthly passes. That took longer than expected. First, they had to be photographed, and then wait while the film was developed and the photo printed on the cover.

The clerk handed them their ticket books, and they showed each other their pictures. He would never laugh at someone's photo in the paper again. Outside, Julius started toward the Palace of Transportation. After that, maybe they'd have time to at least peek in the Palace of Electricity and Machinery before closing time.

"No, this way." Bryce crossed Olympian Way and walked to the smallest, most nondescript of all the Palaces.

"Forestry, Fish and Game?" Julius said. "What are we doing here?"

"I'm told there's a licensed distillery in operation south of the palace with a government bonded warehouse selling its production. I figure we'll sample the local swill and buy a couple of bottles to keep our flasks filled."

Again, it made sense. The whiskey wasn't bad, and Olympian Way coursed east past blocks of colorful flowerbeds to the main area of palaces.

Done with following Bryce, Julius took the lead when they reached the colossal Palace of Transportation. Entering through sixty-foot high arches, he found himself in something resembling a gigantic railroad station. Fourteen sets of train tracks ran the entire span of the building. A crowd gathered around the centerpiece exhibit, a 160 ton locomotive mounted with its coal car on a massive revolving turnstile. The crowd was enamored of the machine, but he was amazed that such a large mass could be continuously rotated. What sort of bearings did the setup have, and how many? It ran perfectly smooth. How did they manage such tight clearances on something so heavy?

Pullman had a display of their cars, but the men skipped them, having just ridden in one.

Boats, yachts, steamships, and motorboats surrounded a historical display of navigation along the Mississippi River. There was a speedboat powered by a steam turbine engine that drew his attention, but then he heard a barker at the edge of the automobile section. "One hundred and forty models of cars powered by gasoline, electricity, and steam. See the vehicle that will allow people to travel at speed and at will, an end to the unruly horse."

Haynes-Apperson Company of Kokomo, Indiana, displayed the first successful gasoline-run automobile, created in 1894. The antique had spindly wire-spoke wheels clearly borrowed from bicycles. Things had come a long way in ten years!

France, the world's leading manufacturer of automobiles, had an exhibit almost exclusively devoted to their vehicles. Yet, among the rows of horse-less carriages, were many names Julius never heard of. Ford, Studebaker, Packard, Rambler, and Oldsmobile all displayed their notion of the per-sonal automobile of the future.

The previous December, two brothers from Dayton, Ohio, named Wright had apparently achieved the first fully powered flight. Julius had seen noth-ing about it in the journals, but a visiting physicist from England had shown him an article from the *Illustrated London News*. Julius had kind of hoped to see their airplane here. Perhaps it was a hoax. Displays on powered flight seemed concentrated on ever-popular balloon distance races. According to a colorful poster, T. C. Benbow would be bringing an engine-powered gas-bag airship he had developed.

"You wouldn't get me up in one of those things," Bryce said.

"Oh, I'd go in a heartbeat," Julius said. "Imagine the view from up there."

"Bryce, I thought you were champing at the bit to ride the Observation Wheel," Mo said.

"That's different. It may take us two-hundred-fifty feet in the air, but we'd be standing on something made of iron and connected to solid ground."

"I'm surprised. I've always thought of you as the daredevil type."

Bryce grinned. "More devil than dare."

They wandered the fifteen acre Transportation palace until attendants told them it was closing. They came outside into a phantasm. More electric lights than Mo had ever seen had been turned on.

Back in the Plaza of St. Louis, where they had started the day, the blaze of artificial light on Palace of Electricity reflected its aura in the Grand Basin. Atop its structure, six pyramid towers crowned by a star and copies of the sculpture, *Light Overcomes Darkness*, were radiantly lit. Mo looked around. All the other sculptures were illuminated, too. As the night grew darker, colored lights mounted on Festival Hall turned the cascades into waterfalls of rubies, emeralds, diamonds, and sapphires. It was like sculpting in water and light. Never had there been such a sight.

He could have stayed there until they turned the lights out, but Bryce and Julius wanted to revisit the Pike.

"Come. Let's see what this looks like from the top of the wheel," Julius said.

Returning to the Pike, they walked its mile-long road, reveling in the carnival atmosphere. Unlike the fairgrounds, where the Beaux-Arts palaces, Venetian lagoons, Italian fountains, and flowering terraced gardens worked together to form a breathtaking picture, the Pike was a jumble of architectural styles. Along one side, a hundred-fifty-foot tall Japanese portal stood next to an exhibit of ancient Rome. Further down was a Chinese pagoda, and across from it, Old Cairo. There was a plantation building at Old St. Louis, and a French village opposite it. A clown's head the size of their apartment hung above the Temple of Mirth, but the sad clown didn't look happy to be there.

Julius wanted to stop at Japan to meet the Geishas, but Bryce pressed them onward, searching for the entrance to the big wheel. The Pike road turned south, and they found an attraction advertising an artic adventure trip from New York to the North Pole. Right behind it, the top carriages of the Observation Wheel could be seen, but it didn't seem to be turning.

"Maybe they're stopped for unloading right now," Bryce said. "Let's hurry."

They weren't loading. The Wheel wasn't open for business, yet. Mo was as disappointed as the others. "Where do we want to go?"

"Japan," Julius said emphatically.

It was a bit of a hike back there, but they agreed.

Inside "Japan" was an elaborately carved forty-two foot-tall gate from a Buddhist temple, and ponds full of carp as long as his arm. Forty stores featuring candy-makers, carvers, artists, weavers, and fine jewelry vied for their dollars. There were two teahouses and a restaurant offering traditional fare. It'd been a while since they'd eaten lunch at the Irish place, so they chose the restaurant.

Petite women who barely came up to Mo's shoulder waited on them. Their faces were completely covered in makeup, whiter than a porcelain teacup. Their eyebrows were fine black pencil lines and their mouths red bows. They wore tight floor-length dresses printed with beautiful flowers and walked with small shuffling steps.

Their server took their order and tottered away on tiny feet.

"I thought Geishas would be more like Broadway showgirls," Julius said.

Bryce nodded. "Me, too. These are China dolls."

She returned with a porcelain carafe of sharp-tasting white wine and tiny cups not much bigger that shot glasses. She remained with them, refilling their cups until their meal came, then served their food. It wasn't bad—braised beef, a side of rice, and some peas, which instead of being shucked, were served like green beans.

A little tipsy from all the wine—evidently more powerful than it looked, they exited Japan. Next door was a concession ride. Six-foot tall letters over a wide archway read: Under and Over the Sea.

"This looks interesting," Julius said.

"Ride to Paris in a submarine and fly back to the fairgrounds in a dirigible for just two-bits," a barker called.

They entered a vaulted chamber, paid their fare, and joined the line to enter a submarine docked in a harbor. "Reminds me of illustrations from a Jules Verne book," Mo said.

Julius grinned. "Exactly what I was thinking."

Once inside, the hatches were battened down, and the boat seemed to descend. Through giant seven-foot-tall portholes, they saw varieties of fish swimming in underwater panoramas. Mo didn't know a single soul who had ever been in a submarine. He didn't know that much about fish either.

Suddenly, a sea monster with large tentacles seemed about to attack. Women screamed. Truth be told, he'd jerked back in fright when it first came into view.

Fortunately, they got away, and the sub arrived in Paris. The crowd went ashore and took an elevator up the Eiffel Tower. It was nighttime there and illuminated Paris lay before them like a thousand diamonds.

Patrons were invited to take their time enjoying the view and browsing souvenir stands. Mo bought a miniature pewter Eiffel Tower as a gift for the woman who was keeping his paintings while he was away. In the next room, they entered the front half of a dirigible, apparently tethered to the tower.

Once it cast off, they flew over French countryside, Brussels, Berlin and the night sky of London. Then, while crossing the Atlantic, they got caught in a fierce storm. Rain and lightning rocked the airship.

The sky cleared, and the sun dawned as they reached New York harbor. The Statue of Liberty stood on her island in the distance below them.

"Hey, Bryce, you want to get off here?" Julius said.

"Too late," Mo said, for they were already streaming over farmland and rivers of the eastern half of the United States. Soon, their cabin shook as the airship landed in St. Louis. They exited laughing.

"There, Bryce," Julius said. "You've ridden a balloon, and you swore you never would."

Bryce was all smiles. "And a submarine, too, all without leaving the building. How'd they do that?"

Mo had some ideas—he'd seen vertical rolling canvasses used on Broadway, though never on this scale. Or with this sophistication.

"Let's go again," Bryce said.

Mo looked at a clock on the building across the street. "Do we know what time the omnibus to the camp stops running? It's a long walk back."

"You're right," Julius said. "We've got our passes, now. We'll get an early start tomorrow." He unscrewed the top of his new flask and took a swig.

Bryce handed him the bottle of whiskey. "Drink this up first. I don't want to carry it around. Let's save what's in our flasks for tomorrow."

Julius put his flask away and took a pull from the offered bottle, then handed it to Mo.

Mo drank and passed the bottle back to Bryce, as they exited onto Lindell Boulevard and located the camp omnibus.

"You just made it," the driver said.

In the distance, well away from the Fair, a giant searchlight pierced the night sky.

"Hey, guys, look at that," Mo said. "What do you think it is?"

Julius and Bryce turned in the direction he pointed.

"Why, that's Camp Lewis," the driver said. "Mr. Lewis put a gigantic searchlight on top of the main building for opening day. He claims that light can be seen as far away as Kansas City."

"Isn't that amazing?" Mo said.

Julius nodded. "Everything here's amazing." He stepped aboard the omnibus, followed by Mo and Bryce.

Bryce slid down the bench and passed Mo the bottle. A passenger sitting across the aisle gave them the fish eye.

Julius took the bottle from Mo and offered it to the man across the aisle.

The man turned his head aside. "Not on your life."

Bryce nabbed the bottle from Julius. "Suit yourself, mister."

CHAPTER 18

The silvery beam of the searchlight was still blazing skyward from Camp Lewis when the omnibus pulled up. Julius craned his neck back, following the beam up into the night. "Isn't that something, boys? Cuts a path through the starry sky, straight as a steel rail. You could ride that light beam all the way to Sirius."

They skipped the main building, drawn toward the rows of tents where campers grouped around bonfires played guitars, mandolins, and the occasional harmonica, keeping alive the party atmosphere of the fair. Although it was nearly midnight, no one seemed about to stop. Julius sure wasn't ready to sleep. The excitement of opening day had the place crackling like a Tesla coil.

They joined a lively group, three men playing guitars with a woman on an accordion. Another man in the group rapped two spoons against his leg in a complicated rhythm. All were singing.

The spoon player pointed to a log next to the accordion player. "Pull up a pew."

Bryce immediately sidled up next to the woman and began studying how she fingered her instrument. Mo and Julius joined him.

"Bryce, anything left in that bottle?" Julius said.

Without taking his eyes off the girl, Bryce handed it over.

Julius took a pull and passed the whiskey to Mo.

The song ended and one of the guitar players said, "You better not let Mr. Lewis catch you with that."

"Why not?" Julius said.

"Didn't you read the rules? No alcohol allowed."

Julius took the bottle from Mo. "Better finish it now, then." He drank deep.

"Do it somewhere else," the guitar player said. "We don't want to get kicked out on your account."

"Oh, they wouldn't really do that," Bryce said.

"Well, we're not willing to chance it. Take your liquor and skedaddle."

Julius stood. "Fine. Come on, guys."

Bryce didn't move. "Hang on. I want to see if I can play the accordion. I'll bet I could. The keyboard's like a miniature piano. I was just starting to work out what all those buttons on the other side do."

The guitar player scowled.

Mo tugged Bryce's arm. "I'm sure you'd pick it up in a heartbeat, but we've been asked to leave. Politely, so far."

A reluctant Bryce came along with Mo and joined Julius. "Where to next?"

"I suggest our tent," Mo said.

Julius scanned the campground. People were still up having a lively time, and he wasn't prepared to sleep yet. "Why?"

"To get rid of the evidence. Let's top off our flasks, and then either hide the bottle or finish it off and bury it in the trash. If they kick people out for breaking the rules—"

"We've got nowhere to go," Julius said.

"Exactly."

Bryce shook his head and glanced back at the woman with the accordion. "Bunch of nervous Nellies. No one kicks out paying customers for having a little nip."

Julius put his arm across Bryce's shoulder and steered him toward their tent. "That may be, but there's no reason to flaunt their rules, either. Let's follow Mo's plan. Stow everything in the tent and then go have a good time."

"And drink what, sarsaparilla?"

"If that's what's offered," Mo said. "Trust me, I've met teetotalers. They're less rational than you think."

Julius spotted the night manager waiting outside their tent as they approached. He waved a copy of the camp map they'd been given when they checked in. "The rules are printed right here, plain as day."

Julius quickly tucked the bottle inside his coat.

"A passenger on tonight's omnibus says he saw you bring alcohol into the camp."

Bryce spat. "That bastard."

"No swearing, either," the manager said. "Rule number twelve."

Bryce gave him an evil grin. "It's not swearing if it's true. Have you seen any evidence his parents ever married?"

"That's it. All three of you, pack your belongings. You're out of here."

Mo stepped between them. "Be reasonable, sir. It's midnight. The omnibuses stopped running. There'd be no way for us to accomplish such a thing. Please, show a little Christian charity."

The man chewed his lip for a thoughtful moment. "All right, sleep here tonight, but consider yourselves evicted come morning." He started to leave, but then turned back. "And no more drinking for the rest of the night."

Bryce held out his arms, palms open, like the crucified thief. "You see any hooch? Search me if you want."

Julius tucked the bottle deeper in his coat and took a step back. No way of knowing if the man would take Bryce up on his offer.

The manager shook his head. "If you want breakfast, wake early. You're leaving on the first omnibus." He stalked away toward the main building.

Mo sighed. "Bryce, when we get an angry rooster calmed down, don't tug his tail feathers."

"Well, why did his mother give birth to such a stickler for rules?"

Julius entered the tent and rid himself of the guilty bottle, tucking it into his suitcase. "I agree with both of you. There's not a single reason for a tent city miles from nowhere to have a say in what beverage a man imbibes. On the other hand, Bryce, if he'd taken up your offer to search us, I'd be the one caught with the bottle. Thanks a lot."

Mo shook his head. "My point was, I'd gotten him to concede, then Bryce had to smart off. The man could have easily changed his mind, and right now we'd be walking a dark road, suitcases in hand."

"Who cares about him?" Bryce said. "We're done with tents, anyway. I'm sure my father did his job. By tomorrow night we'll be tucked in tight at the Jefferson."

CHAPTER 19

Morning sun made the white canvas tent cloth glow bright as the frosted globe of a gaslight. Julius shaded his eyes and swallowed several times, trying to produce enough saliva to quench his cotton mouth. He rolled up into a sitting position, placing his feet on the wood floor. The iron rails of the cot pressed into his thighs. He stood up, stretched, pulled his suitcase onto his bed and opened it.

Mo and Bryce were still snoring. "Wake up, guys. Condemned men always get a good meal. Ours awaits."

"Is it morning already?" Mo said.

While Julius dressed and repacked his case, Mo and Bryce got up and did the same. They carried their suitcases to the lavatory in the main building, where they washed their faces and shaved. Braced for the day and smelling of bay rum, they entered the dining hall, ate a large breakfast, and drank copious amounts of coffee.

It was over breakfast they learned the Fair was closed on Sundays.

"Are you sure?" Julius said. "That makes no sense. Have a grand opening on Saturday, then close up the very next day."

Their informant shrugged. "It's the Sabbath. What else can they do?"

"What about all those Asian pavilions?" Mo said. "It's not their Sabbath."

"Well, it should be." The man shrugged. "Doesn't change the fact, the Fair's closed today." He wished them a good day and left the table.

"Probably won't matter to us," Julius said. "It'll likely take us all day to find a hotel and move our trunks there."

"Not necessary," Bryce said. "They're already at the Jefferson. We'll go there, and I'll bet they have us a room."

Julius wasn't ready to put money on it. Then he realized if the Fair was closed today, there might be no omnibuses. He stood, gulped the last swallow of his coffee. "Mo, Bryce, you finished?"

"What's your hurry?" Bryce said.

"Might take us a while to get there."

They walked over to registration. Julius leaned his elbows on the counter and smiled at the matronly clerk on duty.

She smiled back. "How may I help you?"

"We were supposed to leave this morning, but I've just been informed that the Fair is closed today. Do you know how we can get a ride into the city?"

"Why, the omnibus, of course."

"They're running, even though the Fair is closed?"

"Certainly. People have to get to church. Go outside and wait at the regular pickup point. One will be along shortly."

When the omnibus driver asked them what church they wanted to go to, Bryce said, "Whichever is closest the Hotel Jefferson." He had no intention of praising the Lord today.

For a small tip, the driver passed the church and dropped them off right in front of the hotel. When they entered, Bryce spotted the clerk from Friday, who briefly made eye contact, then scurried away.

That didn't bode well. Was he about to be humiliated in front of his friends again?

They waited at check-in as minutes clicked off the clock, but the clerk never returned. Bryce once thought he caught a brief glimpse of someone peeking around the corner. Finally, the door to the office opened, and the manager appeared, startled. He recovered quickly and painted on a broad smile. "I'm sorry. No one told me. Were you waiting for me?"

"Or anyone, really," Bryce said.

The manager glanced in both directions along the counter, then put his attention on Bryce. "How may I help you?"

"You said VIPs that just came for the opening would be checking out today and you'd have a room for us."

The man looked sincerely pained. "I'm sorry. None of our guests have left. We're still completely full."

Bryce stole a quick glance at Mo and Julius. "You surely received instructions from my father."

His face brightened. "Oh, yes. Just a moment." He ducked into his office, returned as quickly as his bulk would allow him, and handed Bryce a note. In well-crafted penmanship, it instructed Bryce to call Elsworth Statler and provided a telephone number.

Bryce handed it back to the manager and asked him to have the hotel switchboard place the call. For some unexplained reason, the man was more impressed that Statler had personally left the message than that Bryce's father was a senator. "Of course, you can use my phone. I'd be honored." He opened a door behind the counter and led Bryce into his office.

After a brief telephone call with Mr. Statler, Bryce hung up, still puzzled about where they were going. But at least his father had secured them an accommodation better than a tent. A dry tent. Apparently, Statler was a restaurateur from Buffalo, New York, who knew and admired Senator Holloway. At present, he owned and operated an inn somewhere nearby that he'd built especially for the Fair. Most important, he was holding a suite for them and said they could have it for as long as they wished.

Okay, now Julius and Mo would see the benefit of having powerful parents. True, it was only an inn, but how small could it be if it had a suite?

The manager sent an employee to locate a teamster with a wagon and direct him to the hotel's freight dock. It took a considerable while, as apparently in St. Louis, even teamsters went to church. By the time church let out and the wagon came, the morning had fled, and it was an hour past midday.

Bryce looked at the scrap of paper on which he'd written: Inside Inn, Oakland Avenue. Not knowing the streets of St. Louis or how to find his way by streetcar, he suggested they ride in the wagon carrying the trunks.

"Fine by me," Julius said. "I planned to anyway."

Once the trunks were loaded, Bryce climbed up beside the driver and handed him the address. Mo and Julius sat in the back with their trunks. The manager of the Jefferson stood on the loading dock with his hands on his hips, looking relieved to be rid of them. Bryce resisted the temptation to tip his hat.

The horse-drawn wagon clattered south on Tucker Boulevard. Women in fancy hats and long dresses strolled along the sidewalk on the arms of beaus wearing their best Sunday suits. Bryce would have preferred a leisurely perambulation with a young lovely than being seen perched beside this sweaty teamster. But needs must.

At an intersection, the driver tugged the reins in his right hand. "Gee, Betsy, gee!" The team turned onto Market Street. More traffic there— buggies, surreys, and open carriages moved in both directions. A set of rails was imbedded in the pavement. From behind him, a trolley bell clanged. The teamster steered the wagon to one side, and a streetcar rumbled past. Bryce wished he was on it.

After what seemed like an eternity of leaden progress, Bryce checked his watch. Yep, an hour squandered, and he doubted they'd traveled more than five miles. The driver had made several turns. He could only hope the man knew where he was going. At the next road he turned again. The street sign said Oakland Avenue. Good, they weren't just wandering St. Louis.

Forest bracketed both sides of the avenue. No more city buildings here. God! He hoped Statler's inn wasn't out in the boonies like Camp Lewis. A little further on, two sets of railroad tracks ran parallel with the road. He relaxed. At least they'd have train service to the Fair.

Suddenly, ahead, on his right, between the trees, he glimpsed a statue of a four-horse chariot high atop a white building. Then it disappeared, his view blocked by more forest. Could it be the Fair?

Other, smaller exhibit buildings began to appear briefly at natural gaps in the woods. Okay! If the inn was this near the Fair, then he and his friends had indeed lucked out.

The forest petered out, leaving his view unimpeded. Their wagon passed a building easily four times the length of his parents' favorite watering hole, the Fifth Avenue Hotel. A quarter mile beyond it, the driver turned into the grounds. A sign read: Cheltenham Entrance. A Jefferson Guard held up his hand. "Exposition's closed today."

"Delivering these three and their baggage to the Inside Inn."

The guard waved them on.

Oh! The Inside Inn, as in inside the Exposition itself. His father had really done well by them. He'd have to find a nice gift to thank him.

The wagon turned onto a long drive bordered by a decorative knee-high white stone wall. The white hotel, trimmed with red brick, was huge.

Julius tapped him on the shoulder. "Bryce, do you realize we're inside the fairgrounds?"

"I do."

"Is that our hotel?"

"It is."

Julius whistled. "It must be four blocks long, if it's an inch."

The driver turned his head toward them. "Newspaper said it's the largest hotel in the world."

"I can believe that," Bryce said.

The Inside Inn wasn't a skyscraper, just four stories tall in the main section and two-stories on each wing, but it stretched horizontally across more land than a New York City hotel could ever afford. Flags flew from two sixty-foot tall towers that defined the entrance. Lush acres of neatly trimmed grass surrounded the building, partially shaded by oak trees. Women with parasols and men in straw boaters sauntered over the park-like lawns.

The driver brought his team to a halt in front of the entrance. A flock of bellboys descended upon them like a murmuration of starlings, taking their suitcases and unloading Julius and Mo's trunks. Bryce paid the driver and climbed down from the wagon.

In the spacious lobby, Bryce strode to the reception counter. "Room for Holloway, I believe it's a suite."

"Do you have a reservation card?"

Oh, no. "A what?"

The clerk held up a card presented by a previous guest. "One of these."

Bryce put his hand over his eyes. Not this reservation business again. "No, I . . . Would you please look again? See if you have room being held for Holloway?"

"It's not listed in my book, sir."

Bryce frowned. Mo and Julius had joined him and could hear the whole conversation. He was experiencing more highs and lows than the observation wheel. "Listen, I spoke with Mr. Statler not over two hours ago and he told us to come here straight away."

"Oh," said the clerk. "Oh, yes." He picked up a note from a stack of papers before him. "My apologies. We have you a two-room suite with private bath on the American Plan, which includes two meals a day and admission to the Fair."

"We've already bought monthly passes," Julius said.

The clerk pursed his lips. "Our rates are set by the Exposition Commission. I'm not authorized to change them. You'd have to talk to Mr. Statler, but he's in a meeting."

"Julius, let's get our room now and worry about that later." Bryce signed the register and asked for three keys.

When they'd entered the lobby, he'd noticed a sign on a stand: Congressional Tour Assembles Here, 3:30. It was worth checking out. He handed Mo and Julius their keys. "Have the bellmen put our luggage in the room. I'll be right behind you."

A few minutes later, Bryce located their suite and found the door unlocked. "How's the room, fellows?"

"Wonderful," Mo said. "The bedroom has two beds, and housekeeping has moved the divan away from the wall and put a third bed behind it."

Julius stood at the window. "Look at the view, Bryce." Bryce walked over. Julius pointed. "That's the Plateau of States right outside our doorstep. Can you see the dome of that exhibit in the distance through those trees? According to Mo's guidebook, that should be the Pennsylvania building."

Bryce was beaming inside and out. "Well, let's go see it."

Julius gave him a sharp look. "Can't. Exposition's closed on Sunday."

Bryce's grin grew wider. "Not to us."

Mo glanced up from unpacking his suitcase. "Oh, Bryce, don't do something that'll get us kicked out, please, I beg. This is a nice suite, and we just moved in."

"No, no, this is perfectly legitimate."

"How?" Mo said.

"The Exposition Commission is giving a private tour to Congress in a few minutes, and I got us included. I told them Senator Holloway couldn't make it, but we three were here on his behalf. They signed us right up."

"But your dad's a state senator," Julius said.

"A detail they failed to obtain, and I didn't volunteer."

"Perfectly legitimate, huh?" Julius said.

"In this world, nothing is perfect. Grab you hats, friends. We're going to the Fair."

CHAPTER 20

Violet, still in her chemise and petticoat, held the pale blue organdy evening gown up to her shoulders and admired it in the mirror. A scallop of purple silk flowers graced the lower skirt. Put there just for her—the dressmaker had only finished it the day before they left, and she had yet to wear it. "Oh, Lily, isn't it the most beautiful thing you ever saw?"

"Gorgeous," Lily said, "But save it for another occasion. It's Sunday, nobody of any consequence will be dining in the restaurant tonight."

"You don't know that. Dukes and princes eat on Sunday, too."

"True, but I assume it. The type of man we're supposed to meet won't be found in a two-thousand seat hotel restaurant. His butler will serve him dinner in his suite."

Just because she was oldest didn't always make her right. If her sister had paid attention to Mrs. Coggeshall, she'd know aristocratic men traveled with valets, not butlers. Violet whirled around in a circle, imagining the floor-length dress stealing yearning glances from men and envy from women.

Lily finished buttoning her shoes and lay the buttonhook aside. "Put that back in the wardrobe and select a different dress. Is Rose ready?"

"Not yet. She's writing a letter to Papa about opening day."

Violet hung the dress back in the wardrobe and put on a green gingham she'd worn dozens of times before. She turned her back to Lily. "Button me up, please."

Lily set to work, calling over her shoulder. "Rose, finish your letter later. We're dressed and waiting on you."

That wasn't true. Violet still had to retouch her mussed hair. Lily! Always bossing them.

"I was ready before either of you," Rose called from the bedroom.

Lily fastened Violet's top button and left to inspect Rose.

A moment later, Violet heard, "Oh, Rose, you're not wearing that, are you?"

"Why not? You just told Violet no one important is going to see us."

"Probably true, but at least make an effort, if just for the sake of habit."

"Why? I'll never outshine you two."

"We're not in competition, and how one sister looks reflects on all of us."

Violet decided she'd better intervene. Too frequently, Lily made Rose feel like the underdog. She grabbed two barrettes and stepped into the fray. "Rose, be a dear and help me with my hair."

Rose put the cap on her fountain pen and threw it on the unfinished letter. "Oh, all right. Take a seat."

Violet winced as Rose pushed the metal clasp beneath her hair and snapped it closed. The cost of being the peacemaker.

"I was surprised we didn't run into Mo and his friends yesterday at the opening ceremonies," Rose said.

Lily hovered nearby. "It would have been a miracle if we had. The St. Louis newspaper reported opening day attendance exceeded 237,000."

Violet nodded. "Biggest crowd I've ever been in."

Rose gripped her head. "Hold still."

Violet pursed her lips and thought of Julius. "I wouldn't have minded . . . seeing them again."

"I, for one, hope we don't," Lily said. "We had our fun, but we're done with that. Rose, change into that nice pink dress with the ribbon sash, and let's go to dinner. When we get back, we need to decide which palace to start with tomorrow."

Rose jammed the second barrette against Violet's scalp, closed it, and left in a huff.

Violet walked over to the mirror and pinched her cheeks until they were pink. Frankly, she was glad Lily was leading the way. She had no idea where to look for a prince, let alone how to win one.

CHAPTER 21

By the time the congressional tour brought the men back to the inn, Julius was starved. He'd missed lunch and wasn't about to skip supper. At the front desk, he asked if the hotel had a restaurant.

"Two," the clerk said. "A buffet and a formal dining restaurant."

"Do we need to reserve a table?"

"I should think not. Our restaurant can accommodate 2,500 diners at a time. Just go right through those doors, and down the hallway."

Julius could smell succulent aromas long before they entered the room. The maître d' efficiently seated them at a table for four, handed them menus, and left.

They unfolded their linen napkins and placed them on their laps as a waiter promptly appeared table side. Julius scanned the room and noted that all the servers were men. No cute waitresses here.

Mo studied the menu.

"Don't worry about price," Bryce said. "We're on the American Plan. Our meal's included."

Julius nodded. He'd figured as much. "I'll have sirloin steak with onions, creamed potatoes, and succotash."

Mo opted for broiled mackerel and German potatoes. Bryce ordered lamb chops.

"And a beer," Julius said.

"Sorry, sir, I can offer you coffee, hot or iced tea."

Julius screwed up his face. "Water, then."

"Same," Mo said.

Bryce ordered hot tea, and the waiter left.

"How come you're drinking tea?" Julius said.

"Habit from Mother, I guess." Bryce discretely slipped his flask out and took a sip. He grinned at them as he slipped in back in his jacket. "Habit from Father."

"Good idea." Julius signaled their waiter. "Changed my mind, I'll have coffee."

"Hot or iced, sir?"

"Hot, of course. Who'd ever drink cold coffee on purpose?"

"Cream and sugar?"

"No, black."

"Coffee for me, too," Mo said. "Hot."

After the waiter served their coffee and departed, Julius retrieved his flask and added whiskey. "Here's to the inventor of Irish coffee." Mo did the same.

Bryce licked his lips. "Now I wished I ordered coffee. Whiskey and tea isn't a happy marriage."

"It's not too late," Julius said. "Tell the waiter to bring you a coffee, too."

"Nah, I'll drink my tea and think of dear old Mother."

Julius took another sip and set his cup on the saucer. "That was quite a tour today. Thanks, Bryce."

Bryce made a dismissive gesture. "I'm glad things are starting to go our way. The last two days felt like everything was going wrong."

"Well, that's behind us," Julius said. "How about that wireless telephone we saw at the Palace of Electricity? Did you catch the expression on that Senator's face when they put the headset on him?"

"The one from Maine?" Bryce laughed. "I doubt his state even has telephones."

"Oh, sure they do," Mo said. "But, Julius, how can a telephone work without wires?"

"Got me, but I'm going to find out. If I had to guess, I'd say it must function similar to Marconi's wireless telegraph. I'm going back there in the morning as soon as the Fair opens and just pester the stuffing out of the presenter."

Julius intended to visit the Palace of Electricity frequently, not just to take in all the inventions, but in hopes of meeting Edison and getting a job in his Camden lab. The Edison Globe Museum inside the palace showcased every type of lamp he'd invented. His latest invention, the Kinescope, was said to show moving pictures. Julius had hoped to see that today, but the VIPs from Washington had crowded him out. It didn't matter. He'd be here for days after they left.

"Maybe we should start with exhibits that the tour skipped," Bryce said.

Mo shook his head. "Now that we understand just how big the exposition is, we should go through the guidebook and make a plan, so we see as much as possible in what time we have."

"I agree," Bryce said. "For instance, right next to our hotel, in the Plateau of the States, they have an exhibit from the Indian Territory. I heard Geronimo is being brought to the Fair. And a congressman told me that New Mexico has a whole tribe of Pueblo Indians at their exhibit." Bryce seemed ready to jump up from the table and break into a ceremonial dance.

"Imagine that," Mo said.

Julius nodded. Mo was right. If they approached the Fair haphazardly, they'd waste too much time walking from one side of the grounds to the other. "But we don't necessarily have to stick together, do we? We have a home base now—thank you, Bryce—and can see what interests us, and when we meet up, let the others know about anything particularly good."

The food came, and it was delicious. Although the meal was included in the price of their room, Julius left the waiter a generous tip. He stood up, and there were the Jones sisters across the room. The perfect end to a wonderful day. He started toward them. May as well say hello.

"Julius," Mo said, "the exit's the other way."

"I know. Follow me, guys."

He caught Violet's eye as he neared their table. Good, they were dining alone, no dukes or earls yet. "What a pleasant surprise, are you staying here, too?"

Lily frowned. "I thought I heard you make reservations at the Hotel Jefferson."

Bryce walked behind Lily and grazed her bare shoulder with the back of his hand. "Plans changed."

She pulled away.

Julius smiled at Violet. "We just moved here today."

Her eyes darted between him and Lily. "How did you know where we were staying?"

"Didn't. Bryce's father knows the inn's owner and secured us a suite."

"Oh."

Violet was acting strange. Lilly, too. He thought they'd parted on good terms.

Mo ambled over next to Rose. "Good thing he did. We spent the last two nights in a tent."

"A tent?" Rose said.

Mo nodded. "A camp run by teetotalers. We'll tell you all about it. May we join you for a coffee?"

Lily started to rise. "Actually, we're about to retire."

"We were?" Rose said.

"Yes." Lily stood and nodded to Violet. "Early day tomorrow, and all."

Julius helped Violet with her chair. A whiff of flowery perfume graced his nose as she passed.

Mo assisted Rose, who turned her back to Lily and mouthed the word, "Sorry."

They watched as the sisters swept past long rows of linen-covered tables, like brides dashing through thrown rice.

"That was awkward," Julius said.

"And unexpected," Mo said.

"Not at all," Bryce said. "I've seen it before. They're on a hunting party and afraid we'll scare away the big game."

Julius looked around the dining room. "Yeah, but everyone in this place is American."

Mo smiled. "Perhaps they just think we'll distract them from the hunt."

CHAPTER 22

The Exposition printed an Official Daily Program listing the day's schedule of events. Mo, Bryce and Julius perused it over breakfast. The Michigan, Pennsylvania, and Ohio buildings were being dedicated that day.

"We should go," Bryce said. "They're practically outside our window." Besides, the Indian Territory building was in the same area, and he hoped to meet real Indians like he'd been reading about for years.

Julius ate the last bite of his pancakes and pushed his plate aside. "Last night, you agreed we'd separate and each see what interested us most and then meet up later."

"Did I? I thought you said it'd be better to start with the nearest exhibits and then proceed onto the next and so forth?" Bryce wanted them with him. After all, neither of them had ever seen an Indian, either, and it was more fun with other people.

"That was Mo's suggestion. What do you want to do, Mo?"

"Quit talking and start walking. The day's wasting." He stood up and dropped his napkin on the table. "Let's begin at the Plateau of States. That's what Bryce wants, and it *is* the closest."

Bryce smiled.

As they left the restaurant, he quickly scanned the tables for Lily and her sisters. They weren't there—probably still primping. They'd come late to breakfast on the train, too. But on the train, she hadn't treated him the way she did last night. Well, her loss. She'd never find a stuffy European who was half the fun he and his friends were.

The Plateau of States was indeed just outside the inn. The backsides of Indiana, Rhode Island, and Nevada were straight across from the hotel. To the east were Utah and the Indian Territory buildings. Bryce felt pulled to them like iron to a magnet. He would have cut across the lawn were it not still wet with dew. Instead he followed Mo, who did the sensible thing and took the gravel roadway .

At Commonwealth Avenue, he yearned to lead his friends to the Indians, but they were intercepted by a bevy of cream-cheeked farm girls steering guests toward Pennsylvania. "This way, down Colonial Avenue. The dedication is about to start."

The Pennsylvania building closely resembled a state capital building, two stories high, with the center of the building surmounted by a huge square dome—the one he'd seen through the trees on their way to the inn. On both ends were spacious colonnade porches supported by white Ionic columns.

The building was on a small hill. They climbed five sets of granite steps and entered a large rotunda. A statute of William Penn stood at the door looking . . . very Quaker. The color scheme of white and gold was enlivened by twelve allegorical paintings in semi-circular arches around the room. In addition to the large open area beneath the rotunda, the first floor consisted of separate rooms for ladies and for gentlemen, a reception room, smoking room, and a room where packages could be checked.

After a series of speeches and songs, the building was declared open to the public and visitors invited to explore the three large art rooms on the second floor. So far this morning, Bryce had been bored. Maybe there was something upstairs. He took the steps two at a time with Mo and Julius on his heels.

Quickly he learned Pennsylvania was as uninteresting as he'd always suspected. Just a collection of portraits of forty-two distinguished past and present Pennsylvanians. Not that interesting, unless you were related to one of them, he supposed. In another room were mural paintings from the Philadelphia Women's School of Design. Bryce waited while Mo took his time with those.

"What do you think?" Bryce said. "Any good?"

"Technically, not bad, but that's the problem. It's all technique. Too realistic, no sense of the artist's emotional reaction to the scene."

Another display consisted of a hundred photographs of monuments erected to Pennsylvania regiments on the field of Gettysburg. He didn't come here for this. "I thought the Liberty Bell was supposed to be here."

"It's not arriving until Independence Day," said a docent standing nearby.

He caught Julius and Mo's eye. "Seen enough of Pennsylvania?"

"Plenty," Julius said. "Let's go to Ohio."

Mo consulted the Daily Program. "Too early."

"Good," Bryce said. "Then there's time to visit the Indian Territory. We passed the building on our way here, situated right behind Utah."

Julius shrugged. "Sure, why not?"

Bryce was soon disappointed. The two-story high Indian Territory building looked like a Southern mansion, not a trading post or Indian camp. Inside were a big lobby and a large assembly hall with a stage at one end. Not an Indian in sight. A pleasant receptionist informed them that the Army was bringing a band of Apache to the Fair, but they would live at the Apache Village over at the Pike.

Bryce turned and left. "Seems like everything worth anything here is over at the Pike."

"Oh, don't be like that," Julius said. "What about the Palaces? There's plenty to see."

Mo, holding a map, said, "Ohio is a few blocks up this avenue. Why don't we stop at a few other states along the way?"

The next building was New Jersey, but that just made him think about Lily. Unlike the majority of buildings in the Plateau of States, New Jersey had forsworn Roman-Greek columns in favor of a colonial style. They were greeted by a pleasant young college student wearing a tricorn hat who informed them the building was designed after Ford's old tavern at Morristown, which for a time during the Revolutionary War was George Washington's headquarters. He invited them to enter.

A woman dressed like Molly Pitcher was giving a tour. "The wallpapers are of a colonial pattern in vogue in revolutionary days. The furniture pieces in various rooms are faithful reproductions. If you will follow me . . ." They squeezed, with a dozen others, into a room off the main lobby and stood around a bed. "Here, we have reproduced the bedchamber used by Washington."

They returned to the main room, and the tour disbanded. Molly went to the entrance to greet the next group of visitors. Bryce walked over to where Mo studied a display of historical relics. He looked up at Bryce. "If we see the Jones sisters, we'll have to tell them about this place."

"Why?"

"On the train, Lily told us her father collected paintings of historical scenes."

Bryce snorted. "Lily."

"Don't be like that, Bryce. How many times have you been with a woman one week and ignored her the next time you saw her."

"Never. A gentleman shows some respect."

"I guess you're right," Mo said. "But let's be cordial if we run into them."

"When am I ever otherwise?"

"Friday, when we got off the train."

"Well, I . . . had to see about our bags on the platform. They didn't stick around either. Off the train, and whoosh—they were vapor."

Julius joined them. "Who?"

"The sisters. Bryce still has his nose out of joint."

"Do not. Incidents like last night slide off me like water off a duck's ass."

Julius flicked the brim of Bryce's hat, knocking it off his head. "Pick up your hat and let's find Ohio."

Bryce scooped up his hat. "Go west, young man."

CHAPTER 23

Violet, dressed and waiting, sat with her hands in her lap.

Lily leaned against the bathroom door, reading the newspaper. "Rose, please hurry your bath."

"Patience, Lily. You want me to smell good for some handsome prince."

"Speaking of which . . ." Lily folded the paper back with a rattle. "I know where one is going to be."

"Really?" Violet rushed to Lily's side.

Lilly showed her the article. "According to this, a Chinese prince is here to dedicate his country's pavilion."

Rose came out of the bathroom, tying the sash of her dressing gown. "Chinese? I thought we were aiming for English aristocracy."

Violet's eyes widened. "But Rose, a prince! That's top on the list."

"So what? We can't speak Chinese."

"I'm sure he speaks English. Hong Kong is British, after all."

"Violet, Hong Kong and China are two different countries."

Well, she knew that, but Hong Kong was full of Chinese. Her sisters always treated her like a know-nothing baby.

Rose crossed her arms. "And I doubt Mother expects us to bring home a Chinaman."

"Not an ordinary Chinaman." Lily read from the article, "His Imperial Highness Prince Pu Lun is next in line to become Emperor."

Violet's shoulders sagged. "Lily, he's probably already promised to some princess."

"It doesn't say that," Lily said.

Rose frowned. "Father has sent us on a fool's errand. We have no idea where to find nobility in crowds of two hundred thousand." She wrung her hands. "Oh, I wish Mrs. Coggeshall were with us."

Truthfully, Violet did too. The old woman would have a better clue than they.

"Well, we know of one prince," Lily said.

"From a place we know nothing about," Rose said.

Lily stood her ground. "Then we need to familiarize ourselves with the prince's culture so we can converse intelligently when we meet him. There's an exhibit of Chinese art and furniture in the Palace of Liberal Arts. We'll go there first thing after breakfast."

They left the inn and strolled down a long avenue. Even though Rose had the map, Lily acted like she was in charge. To their right, a crowd gathered at the Pennsylvania building, but Lily continued headlong on their course. On their left, they passed a building concerned with copper metallurgy and another that purported to be a working coal mine. Next were the pottery and cement exhibits, then some oil well derricks. Not likely to find any dukes or lords there.

On their right were the smaller state buildings, New Hampshire, Vermont, and Michigan. Their street ended in a T-intersection. Rose consulted her map and pointed left. They walked a short block to Government Terrace and turned right. There was a bandstand, but no one was playing at this hour.

The Palace of Mines and metallurgy blocked Rose's view until they were nearly past it, and then, suddenly, there was the Palace of Liberal Arts.

It was one of the most heavily decorated and ornate buildings she'd ever seen, surely the finest looking palace at the Fair. Beautiful sunken gardens spanned the entire front of the building. Three huge Roman triumphal arches were connected by a Doric colonnade. The grand estates back home in Florham Park would look like tenements if put next to this.

Standing before the sunken gardens, Rose craned her neck. Atop the center arch was a sculpture of a four-horse chariot representing triumph, victory and fame. How did they even get that up there?

Lily tugged on her arm. "Come, Rose. Stop gawking."

"Why are you rushing us? When will we ever see anything so magnificent again?"

Inside were long aisles of exhibits by U.S. and foreign companies showing off inventions, musical instruments, photography, and more. A company called Photoscope featured a self-run photo booth that produced souvenir photographs in short order. Violet ran into the booth and took a seat. "Lily, Rose, let's make some pictures for Mother and Father. It only costs twenty-five cents."

As soon as the sisters were in position, Violet dropped a quarter into the slot. Six quick flashes, and then in less than a minute six finished photographs popped out of the machine. They were good likenesses, too. Shame the bright flash had given her the expression of a startled deer.

They walked on, but the gorgeous Underwood Typewriters booth stopped her. Its Art Nouveau design seemed to be styled of typewriter parts. Not that she or her sisters could type, nor would she ever have to learn. Still, Rose admired the motif.

The China exhibit included a magnificent display of woodcarving, intricate furniture, ancient books, and rare objects from Chinese temples. Rose and her sisters ogled a display of 4,000 different hand-painted fans. The fans had beautifully painted flowers, birds, mountains, and other scenes. Their handles were ebony, ivory, bright lacquered wood, silver, or mother-of-pearl. A young woman, in what Rose assumed was traditional dress, demonstrated several flourishing gestures with a fan as she explained that this was the first time China had participated in an international exposition.

They moved along to a display of over one hundred models of different types of boats. A guide informed them that a full-size Chinese boat could be seen moored in one of the Exposition's lagoons.

Elsewhere in the Chinese exhibit was an extensive display of armor and weapons. She was less than interested, but a seven foot long carved ivory elephant tusk intrigued her. Rose studied the intricate carvings, tempted to trace their impressions with her fingernail, but she was stopped by a guard who informed her it was valued at $16,000. Another object that caught her eye was a tree crafted entirely from silver.

If the prince had this kind of wealth, he didn't need an American wife's money, did he? She didn't think any of them would win him over on charm alone.

When they'd thoroughly explored the China exhibit, Rose was left with the impression that their cultures were so different that any potential happy marriage seemed unlikely. "Great Britain has an exhibit at the other end of the palace. Let's go there."

"We could," Lily said, "or we can go to the Pike. There's a Chinese Village there with a restaurant, tea house, artists, and even a place where they worship their various deities."

"You mean they're not Christian?" Violet said.

"Oh, most Chinese must be Christian by now," Lily said. "Our church has supported missionaries there for years. However, we'll learn more about the prince's country if we visit his village before we meet him."

"But we're here right now," Rose said. "Shouldn't we see if there's anyone interesting at Great Britain? At least they'll speak English."

Lily nodded. "You have a point. Besides, there are three of us and only one prince, so we'd best see who else is on offer."

They started toward Great Britain but got waylaid by a waft of sweet fragrances emanating from an exhibit on perfumery. The entire process from beginning to end was being demonstrated. First, a sheet of glass was spread evenly with a layer of lard.

Rose wrinkled her nose.

"I never knew," Violet said.

Rose laughed. "That we were wearing pig fat? Me either."

Flower petals were spread over the gooey mess, and then another pane of glass was laid on top of the first and likewise prepared. This continued until the stack of glass plates was as thick as a book.

"Now, we'll heat the aggregated layers, and distil the oil into the essence of the perfume," said a man running the demonstration.

The essential oils collected in a beaker, into which he stirred alcohol and water. He poured the final product into a lovely cut-glass perfume bottle. "Voila!" He passed the bottle beneath their noses.

She liked the bottle better than the scent.

They moved on to the British section, but it seemed too focused on scientific advancements in chemistry, phosphorescent luminosity, and electric crystals. It was all a lot of stodgy lectures by gray-bearded men, the sort of thing that only Julius might enjoy. Rose realized they were clearly ill-prepared. They had no idea how to ferret a Count from a count-for-nothing. "Lily said earlier we should go to the Pike. She's right. We may as well."

"Oh, it's too early for that," said a man standing next to them. "The Pike is best saved for evening hours when the palaces are closed."

All three sisters turned toward the sound of his clipped British accent like spaniels coming on point.

The man tipped his hat. "Pardon my interruption. I couldn't help overhearing." He pulled three white calling cards from his vest pocket. "Sir Guy Ford." He handed them each a card.

Lily gave a small half-curtsey. "Lily Jones. May I present my sisters, Rose and Violet."

He briefly touched each girl's offered hand.

Rose ran her thumb over the raised engraved lettering on the high quality cardstock. "Sir Guy. Is that like a lord?"

He smiled. "Not quite, but most Americans' grasp of peerage seems derived from Mark Twain's *Connecticut Yankee in King Arthur's Court.*"

"Not Jane Austen?" Rose said.

Sir Guy tugged one corner of his mustache.

Violet giggled. "We know the difference. Rose was pulling your leg."

"My leg? I didn't feel anything."

"Sorry," Violet said. "It's a colloquialism. It means—"

Sir Guy laughed. "I know what it means. It was my turn to have one on you."

"So," Lily said, "are you a visitor like us, or are you with the British exhibit in some official capacity?"

"Both, really. I presented a paper on liquidation of gasses earlier this morning. But now I'm free as a bird. I was just going for a spot of tea when I overheard you say you were leaving. Would you care to join me?"

"That would be lovely," Lily said. "Thank you."

They began to stroll through the exhibits. Rose let Lily and Violet take the lead positions on either side of His Lordship.

"I suppose all this science seems too academic," he said, "when there is a wondrous Fair right outside these walls."

"Not at all," Violet said. "My uh . . . An acquaintance works in the science department at Columbia University. He's shared some of his enthusiasm for the latest discoveries."

"Well, Columbia's no Cambridge, but I've heard of it." He held the door for them, and they stepped out into the sun. "We have a laboratory behind the palace. There's a restaurant next to it where one can get a decent cup of tea, if you don't mind the walk."

"We don't mind." Lily said, "*Sir* Guy."

"Please, just call me Guy." He offered her his arm.

Lily accepted. "Tell me, Guy, are there many English Lords at the Fair?"

"Yes, but I'd be careful. Some of my peers haven't come for the wonders, merely to find a rich wife who will save their impecunious estates."

Rose caught Lily suppressing a smile. So, it turned out it was as easy as that.

Chapter 24

Bryce saw no reason to waste more time visiting state exhibits. But they continued down Commonwealth Avenue, poking their heads into Iowa, Minnesota, and Massachusetts, never lingering. To Bryce, the buildings felt like clubhouses where visitors from that state could meet. In most cases, the real achievements for a state were on display elsewhere—in the Palace of Manufacturers, or Mines, or Agriculture, depending on whatever that state was known for. Some, like Pennsylvania, had exhibits in several different palaces.

When they reached Ohio, there were more speeches. Bryce had thought Taft might speak at the dedication since he was from Cincinnati, but Taft wasn't there. After the ceremony, a bevy of young women carrying baskets of smooth, round nuts passed through the crowd handing them out. Bryce studied his. "What's this?"

"Don't know," Julius said.

"It's a buckeye," the girl said. "Like the state."

Bryce turned it around in his hand. It resembled a shiny, dark brown golf ball, except for a beige spot on top. It reminded him of a chestnut. He put it between his teeth and tested its hardness.

The girl grabbed his hand. "No you don't eat 'em."

"Why not?"

"It's poisonous."

"Then why are you giving them out?"

"It's a souvenir. Carry it in your pocket for good luck."

He held his out to Julius. "She says these are lucky. If it was rounder, I could use it for golf."

"When did you ever play golf?" Mo said.

Bryce shrugged. "I played once. With my dad at Hastings-on-Hudson."

Mo looked at his watch and consulted the Daily Program. "We've plenty of time before Michigan's dedication. Why don't we walk over to New Mexico? I'll bet that's interesting."

When he saw the Spanish pueblo-style building, Bryce's hope that he'd meet Indians soared.

A supervisor watching workers put the final touches on the exhibit told them, "We won't open until Saturday. But if you're interested in New Mexico, we have exhibits in the Palaces of Education, Mines and Metallurgy, Anthropology, Agriculture, and Horticulture." He pointed across the street. "Over there, we're going to have a working exhibition of turquoise mining, and lapidary. It'll show how stones are cut, polished, and made into Native jewelry."

"Will there be Indians?" Bryce said.

"Apache and Pueblo tribes," the man said.

At least he had something to look forward to.

Next to New Mexico was a lunch pagoda. "I could do with a sandwich and a beer," Julius said.

Bryce tossed the buckeye away. "May as well, can't eat these."

* * *

Bird and Finn arrived in St. Louis on the noon train. They'd ridden in coach, and slept sitting up, which left Bird a little grumpy and not so sweet smelling. But they were days behind and didn't have time to waste. As soon as they stepped onto the platform, they began to question every porter they met. Well, Finn did the questioning. Bird mostly walked next to him, looking intimidating. It helped get answers.

Fifteen platforms, jammed with arriving or departing passengers, kept the porters too busy to stop and talk. So Finn and Bird walked alongside them, flapping the newspaper photo in their faces and asking if they recognized the men in the picture. Although Bird cut a wide swath through the crowd, Union Station was now the largest, busiest terminal in the world. Talking to the porters proved fruitless. No one remembered who arrived an hour ago, let alone last Friday.

Not original thinkers, the boxers tried what worked before. They went to the loading docks to ask teamsters. Luck of the Irish, they found a man who recognized Julius in the photo.

"Him, I drove to the Hotel Jefferson. I remember, because he insisted on riding with me like he thought I was going to steal their trunks. Kind of offensive, now that I think about it."

"Yeah," Bird said. "These are bad men."

"Well, I wouldn't say 'bad.' He gave me a nice tip. It was a little insulting, being mistrusted by an Easterner like that. Folks in Missouri are plain honest."

"I'm sure that's true," Finn said. "Hotel Jefferson, you said. What would you charge to drive us there?"

"I wouldn't. I told you; around here we don't cheat people."

"You're not. I'm offering to pay. We've just arrived and have no idea how to find this Hotel Jefferson."

"No, no, I won't take your money 'cause the ones in that picture aren't there."

"How do you know?"

"My friend Charlie drives a hack. He told me he picked them up later that day and drove them out to Camp Lewis. That's where they're staying."

Finn broke into a broad grin. "Now we're getting somewhere. How much will it cost for a ride to Camp Lewis?"

"Aw, I'd have to charge too much. The camp is way north of the city. It'd be cheaper for you to take the trolley out to the fairgrounds, where you can catch the camp's omnibus."

"Honest to a fault," Finn said. "But you've helped us more than you know, so we'd like to repay our debt by giving you the fare."

"If that's what you want," the teamster said. "I'll give you a piece of advice, though. I don't know what your business with these men is, but if you're planning to stick around, ask the camp manager if he has a vacancy. Every hotel in town is full and you won't find another place to stay."

CHAPTER 25

The cold beer tasted good. Julius wiped a bit of foam from his mustache. "Where's Michigan?"

Mo consulted the guidebook. "Across from the fisheries, by the U.S. Government building."

"Figures," Bryce said. "Michigan is spending good money to promote themselves and what are people going to remember about the state? Some guy holding a stringer of fish."

"I'm not sure about that," Julius said. "Several of the automobile companies in the Palace of Transportation were from Michigan. They may be building an industry there."

Bryce shook his head. "I don't see the automobile ever becoming anything more than a rich man's toy. Sure, some snob on Park Avenue will buy one to impress the neighbors, but he won't go all the way to Michigan to get it when the Pierce-Arrow factory is practically next door in Buffalo."

Mo finished the last of his sandwich. "Do either of you care if we skip the Michigan dedication?"

"Not me," Julius said.

"Me either," Bryce said.

"The palaces have a lot more exhibits than these state buildings." Mo showed them the map. "The Palace of Liberal Arts is not that far, just behind the U.S. building."

"Liberal Arts?" Of course, Mo would choose that.

Mo opened the guidebook. "It has something for all of us—a whole section of musical instruments for Bryce. And Julius, they have telescopes."

Julius stood. "Let's go there."

Once he saw the Palace of Liberal Arts, Julius remembered just how much its beauty had exceeded all other palaces on Sunday's tour. It was grander than any building in New York and topped with a sculpture so large he'd seen it from Oakland Avenue on their way to the inn.

The palace's quadrangle design had eight entrances. How to choose? Just pick one.

Inside was a four-hundred-seat restaurant. Too bad they'd already eaten. Now where were the telescopes? This place was huge. "My God, we need a map just for this building."

Mo handed him the guidebook. "We're in luck. The back pages have floor plans for every palace."

Julius smiled. "Money well spent."

To their left was the exhibit from Great Britain. He quickly learned that, while they were giving lectures on scientific subjects in the palace auditorium, actual experiments with gasses were performed in a separate laboratory building behind the palace. After a morning of speeches, he doubted Mo and Bryce were ready to sit through a lecture. Better that they should just browse the exhibits and let themselves be surprised by what they find.

They found the Regina Music Box company, which exhibited a wide variety of cylinder music boxes, some in fine furniture cabinets. Their tinkling little tunes sounded like chimes in a Swiss clock. Further on, a multitude was gathered listening to a large orchestra. He stood on his toes but couldn't see the performers. Then Bryce said, "I've never heard an orchestra like that," and pushed past, cutting a swath through the crowd. He and Mo followed. Reaching the front, they found no musicians, just a mahogany cabinet with a large silver horn riding the grooves of a black shellac platter rotating on a spring-powered lazy Susan. It sounded marvelous.

When the song ended, a man tilted the horn away from the platter. A sharp needle was mounted on the narrow end of the horn. The man exchanged the disk for another, gave a crank on the side several sharp turns, and set the needle on the outer edge of the spinning platter. Sousa's band marched out of the horn—every instrument distinct and clear.

He turned to Bryce. "Wow!"

Bryce grinned. "This is the future, guys."

Sure, Edison sold cylinder phonographs that played a minute or two of sound. But these devices played longer, with a larger horn and a clearer sound. And the platters? Much easier to store and sort than cylinders–it was the difference between books and scrolls.

"What's this called?" he asked the man who changed the platters.

"Gramophone. An advancement in every respect. These disks hold more music than cylinders, have better fidelity, and can be pressed from a master rather than cut individually, lowering production costs."

They listened to several more songs before walking on. Ragtime was coming from a piano exhibit up ahead. Bryce dashed off. "Come on! That's Joplin's style. I'd know it anywhere. Maybe he's performing."

Julius and Mo caught up. A man in a brown suit sat on a piano bench, pumping two pedals that looked like they belonged on a church pump organ. The man's hands rested on his knees while the piano keys moved completely on their own. Julius couldn't believe it. Where the sheet music normally stood, a roll of paper punched with holes steadily moved across some mechanism.

Julius elbowed Bryce in the ribs. "You should worry. You can now be replaced by any rube with two left feet."

"Fooled me," Bryce said. "I thought sure Scott Joplin had a new composition."

"He has," the piano salesman said. "It's called 'The Cascades.' He composed it just for the World's Fair."

"Play it again," Bryce said.

"Sure, just have to rewind the scroll. Joe, this fellow wants to hear that song again."

The mechanical piano replayed the tune flawlessly.

"Again," Bryce said when it ended.

"We have other scrolls," the man said.

"I've almost got it. Just once more, please."

The man nodded. "Give it another go, Joe."

When it ended, Julius said, "Let's see something else, Bryce."

They walked on and came to a twenty-two foot high fountain topped with the statue of a fairy blowing out thousands of bubbles a minute. Foam billowed around the fountain. A woman, cute as a nymph, was handing out free booklets.

"What's this?" Julius said.

The nymph handed him a booklet. "Fairbank Company, Gold Dust and Fairy Soap cleaning products."

Julius gave her a once over. They could have used her as a model for the bubble fairy.

"We also make a new type of cooking oil. Here are recipes you can have your wife try."

He handed it back. "Thanks, but for that I'd need a wife."

"Oh, that's a shame. Every man should have one."

"I notice you're not wearing a ring. If you'd like to try one of your recipes on me, I'm free Sunday."

She blushed. "I live at home."

"In St. Louis?"

"With my mother."

"Mothers love me."

She bit her lip.

He waited. Mo and Bryce had walked ahead.

"Tell you what," she said, "come back here later in the week, and I'll give you an answer."

"I'll do that. But what's your name?"

"Catherine."

He tipped his hat. "Julius."

She turned away and resumed passing out recipe books.

He found Mo at the Baldwin piano exhibit watching Bryce play Joplin's "The Cascades," without benefit of sheet music. He had to give Bryce credit. The man had an ear.

Julius was well pleased with the palaces. Unlike the state buildings they'd visited that morning, which admittedly didn't have that much to offer, the palaces were overloaded with mind-boggling things. Each palace could take days, and there were a dozen palaces. Even so, they left the Palace of Liberal Arts long before he was ready because, as Bryce said, it was near enough to the inn that they could return anytime.

They exited a side door and crossed the Plaza of Orleans to the Palace of Manufacturers, where a pair of huge Greek Sphinxes on block pedestals guarded the entrance. Inside, the palace was a jaw-dropping twelve acres under one roof, with aisles so wide they had street names.

Welch's Grape Company was handing out free juice. Mo sipped his slowly. Julius accepted a glass and tossed it down quickly. A little cloying, but not bad. The Bissell Sweepers exhibit was unique. Its roof resembled a carpet sweeper. Looking up from inside the exhibit, Julius could see giant rollers and brushes that would have swept him up like a piece of lint.

A box company showcased a machine that cut and formed corrugated cardboard boxes. That was interesting. But most exhibitors weren't showing manufacturing processes, just selling their wares. One exhibitor told him, "We're calling this place the shopping center of the Fair." And that was about right. Scattered throughout the building were bazaars and arcades of small booths where peddlers sold souvenir watch fobs, teaspoons, postcards, cigars, and porcelain figurines. More than one booth sold Stereoscopes and Stereoscope cards. Bryce bought several packages of scenes to take home to his mother.

The Singer Sewing Machine Company's display was two stories high. Inside, women operating treadle sewing machines sewed corsets which were naturally being offered for sale. Like he or any of the women he went out with had any use for those.

Austria had a large array of watches and clocks. Another exhibitor had numerous statues of partially clad females for sale. Just what the well-heeled highbrow needed to decorate a parlor or foyer. Mexico sold sombreros for only a dollar each.

Bryce tried one on. "What do you think fellows? Should I get it?"

Julius shook his head. "Stick with your bowler."

He started to skip France, which featured a display of elegant gowns, but they also had a blue diamond on display that was said to be worth a hundred thousand dollars. Imagine that. Next to it was another jewel that they claimed was the world's only pink diamond. He glanced around at the crowd. If the Jones sisters were here, this is where they'd be found.

CHAPTER 26

After tea, Lily allowed Sir Guy to show her and her sisters Britain's Liquid Air Laboratory. On the way there, they paused at a public lavatory where she and her sisters freshened up.

The laboratory exhibited equipment for separating and compressing the lighter gases, hydrogen and helium. "At cold enough temperatures these normally invisible vapors became liquid," Sir Guy said. She didn't care much for the subject matter, but his British accent kept her intrigued. Everything he said sounded brilliantly intellectual—although given that he was a scientist, it probably was.

At one workbench, a technician in a long white coat placed a lit match over an apparently empty test tube and the air above it exploded with a loud harmless pop.

"What you and your fellows are doing is truly remarkable," Lily said. Actually, she couldn't care less, but Violet seemed genuinely interested.

He wanted them to go back to the Palace of Liberal Arts, where there were more lectures. She agreed, having seen enough liquefied gas. Once there, Sir Guy continued to dominate the sisters' afternoon, promising to accompany them to the Pike that evening.

After what she considered more than enough time listening to the wonders of Great Britain's science, she gently suggested they see the other 135 exhibits the palace had on display.

Sir Guy was gracious about it and moved along with their party, but he wasn't what Lily was looking for. Not high enough in rank, and he had his own money and didn't need their father's. On the other hand, he knew the British contingent and could make introductions. And as he reminded Violet, "Throughout history, lords and scientists were often one and the same, at least in my country. Sir Francis Bacon was First Viscount of St. Alban. Sir Humphry Davy and James Clerk Maxwell were baronets."

Violet nodded, though Lily knew her sister had only the vaguest idea who those gentlemen were.

They continued to explore the Palace of Liberal Arts, where exhibits were grouped by country, with the United States being dominant. Austria, Germany, Italy, and France also occupied sizeable portions of the palace. They spent hours ogling the marvels offered by each land. But the afternoon waned, and Lily grew anxious for them to proceed to the Pike. They needed to be well prepared before meeting the prince.

Once again, Sir Guy acquiesced, but he suggested they bring two of his fellows from Great Britain to fill out their party. That was fine with Lily.

Soon they were on the Pike. They located the Chinese Village and began at the Tea House. The tea was too weak for Sir Guy and his friends, so they moved on to the restaurant for dinner. She'd anticipated that the food would be similar to Chinatown in Newark—not that she'd eaten there often. But it wasn't. That gave her pause. If she married a foreign prince would she have to eat his country's traditional fare? Or would the wife have domain over the cooks and menus? Now that she thought of it, the question applied no matter what country their prospective husbands came from. Best to choose a man from a land where the food was good.

* * *

At six o'clock the palaces closed, and the men made their way to the Pike. It'd been hours since Julius ate that sandwich for lunch, and it seemed to him dinner should be the first order of business. They'd already tried Ireland and Japan. Ahead was a Chinese village with a restaurant, but across from it was Streets of Cairo. A belly dancer with a bare midriff beckoned. Her hips undulated as she tapped tiny cymbals. No question, this was the place for them. Admission was twenty-five cents, but it seemed worth it.

They entered the restaurant and were offered their choice of a western style table and chairs or cushions around a low table on an ornate carpet. Julius looked to his friends for a decision.

"When in Cairo . . ." Mo said.

"I agree," Bryce said.

Soon they were seated on the rug at a long table with a half-dozen strangers. Egyptian-born servers brought them silver cups of wine. More belly dancers arrived, whirling around the diners—no corsets here. Two large platters of rice cooked with bits of carrots and raisins were set on the table. Another man brought a whole shank of cooked lamb, from which he sliced portions for each guest. Julius kept his eye on the dancers. For dessert they were served a sweet pastry filled with walnuts and honey, and tiny cups of strong black coffee.

A man dressed in a long robe and a fez hat came to their table while the dishes were being cleared. "Was your meal satisfactory? Would you care for anything else?"

"Delicious," Julius said. A sliver of walnut stuck between his teeth. He looked for a toothpick but didn't see any. He pried it loose with his pinky nail.

They left the restaurant and merged into a crowd being entertained by singing gypsies and street musicians. Further on, a man was playing a flute to a large snake rising from a basket. Julius gave him a wide birth.

Bryce was stopped by a barker attempting to induce him into riding a camel. The camel, a huge shaggy thing, spit at them, barely missing Bryce. "No thanks. I'll stick to hansoms."

A gathering of women their age were watching a man put trained monkeys through their paces. The men joined them, laughing at the monkey's antics.

A blond next to Julius kept glancing at him out of the corner of her eye. "They're like miniature people, aren't they?"

"I've seen men less well-behaved," he said.

She laughed. "So have I." She had fine even teeth and bright eyes.

Julius doffed his hat. "Julius Hornsby."

She extended her hand. "Emily Stoud."

He touched her hand to his lips, briefly. "Are you here on your own?"

"With friends." She cocked her head toward two women on her right.

"Why, so am I." He nudged Mo. "This is Emily. Emily, these are my friends Mo and Bryce."

Bryce turned his head at the sound of his name. "Eh? What?"

"Emily, meet Bryce."

Bryce and Mo tipped their hats. Just then one of the monkeys yelped and began chasing the other. The trainer shouted some foreign words that didn't sound like endearments. Maybe Egyptian?

The crowd howled with laughter.

The trainer snatched the monkeys and put them in cages. The show was apparently over.

Emily introduced her friends and the six of them strolled through various booths selling Egyptian goods. A man peddling hookah pipes sat puffing, producing clouds of smoke. He offered them a hose, but the women held their noses and walked on. The men declined and hurried to catch up.

While Emily's girlfriends were inspecting a selection of colorful scarfs, she fingered the material of Julius's jacket sleeve. "Nice work. Where are you from?"

"New York City, and you?"

"Right here in St. Louis."

"You must be very proud of your city."

"Everyone is."

"Which palace do you like best?"

"They're all so beautiful, especially with the lights. Are they like that every night?"

Julius scratched his head. "I think so. It's only been open two nights, so I can't say. Mo has a guidebook. It may tell. Which exhibits took your fancy?"

She looked at her hands. "Truth be told, we've only seen their outsides. We work downtown, and just came out to the Pike for the evening. We peeked into the fairgrounds and saw everything lit up. I'd like to really see it all some time, but Sunday is my only day off, and the Fair's closed."

Julius nodded. "We were disappointed about that, too. Where do you work?"

"The new Hotel Jefferson."

"No kidding? We very nearly stayed there, but our reservations were screw —confused and we couldn't get in. If I'd have known you then, you probably could have helped."

"I don't think so. All three of us work in the restaurant—breakfast and lunch service."

"So you're free in the evenings?"

She batted her eyelashes. "We are . . . some evenings."

"Well, if you'd like, I could meet you here again tomorrow."

"I'll have to see what my girlfriends are doing. A girl can't just come out here alone, you know."

"Of course not. A gentleman could come into town on Sunday though, if you like."

"It'd be my pleasure. Why don't I meet you at the Jefferson at one o'clock?"

"Excuse me," Bryce said. "Julius, the ladies want to go on the water chute ride. Let's go with them."

Julius looked at Emily. "Is that all right with you?"

"Yes. We can sit together."

Emily took his arm and the three couples strolled past the Chinese Village, Alaska, and a ride called the Magic Whirlpool. They came to a massive tower. A sign at the top read: Shoot the Chutes.

While many attractions on the Pike used barkers to draw in customers, this one relied on moving pictures of a prizefight to entice people to enter. Boxing wasn't a sport Julius or either of his companions cared for—they preferred Broadway follies to pugilism, any day. But he was fascinated by the mechanics of projecting moving images and paused to watch. Emily pulled him inside the concession.

Entrance to the attraction was free, but riding a boat down the chute cost ten cents. To reach the ticket sellers they first had to run a gauntlet of stalls selling souvenirs. The entire concession area and the ride were covered with thousands of brilliant electric lights, more than any other building on the Pike. One of Emily's girlfriend cried out, "It's like a fairyland!"

Julius's brow furrowed. Fairyland brought to mind Catherine the soap fairy. It dawned on him that he'd accidentally made plans with two girls for Sunday. How big was St. Louis, and what if she and Emily knew each other?

Signs in the attraction touted that the ticket sellers for the Chutes were the four most beautiful women in St. Louis. He wondered how that made Emily and her friends feel. He paid the saleswoman for their tickets and admitted that she was gorgeous, but really not so much better than his date. Should he say as much to Emily, or would that seem like flattery?

They climbed a couple hundred stairs until they reached a landing where wooden, flat-bottom boats were hooked to the dock. An attendant helped them board. Four bench seats each held two passengers sitting abreast, perfect for couples. Julius and Emily took the front seat, Bryce and his girl behind them, then Mo and the third girl. A couple whom none of them knew was seated at the stern.

When the attendant unhooked their craft, a strong current swept them toward the center of the tower. Their boat turned into the chute, and suddenly they were plunging down a massive, 350 foot long slide. Emily gripped the side of the boat with one hand and his leg with her other hand. He wrapped his arm around her, pulled her close, and braced his right hand on the bow. Emily's fingers dug into his thigh as she squealed.

In less than a minute their vessel splashed into a lake, spraying them with water. Emily let go of him and wiped droplets from her cheeks. "Let's go again," she cried.

"Yes!" Bryce shouted in his ear. "Again!"

CHAPTER 27

"Gone, and good riddance." The manager at Camp Lewis handed Finn back the newspaper clipping. "This may be a tent camp, but that doesn't mean anything goes. We have rules."

"When was it you tossed them out?" Finn said.

"Saturday night—no, I let them stay until Sunday morning."

"Do you know where they're staying now?"

"Don't know. Don't care."

Bird's legs weakened, and Finn set him on the steps of the wide porch, which spanned the camp reception, bath house, and dining hall building. "The driver who brought us out here said we should ask if you have a vacancy."

"It depends. Are those other New Yorkers your friends?"

"No!" Bird shouted.

The manager took a step back and eyed them. "You look like a couple of rough customers."

Finn deepened his brogue. "Don't hold that against us. We're just a couple of Irish boxers who took a few knocks in the ring."

"Boxers, huh? Are you here for the Olympic Games?"

"We're not competing, if that's what you're asking. Those days are behind us." Finn rested his hand on Bird's shoulder. "But this here is the heavy-weight champion, Goliath McGuigan."

"Former," Bird mumbled.

"A boxing celebrity staying at my camp!" the manager said.

"Two," Bird said.

The manager looked at Bird. "What's that?"

"He means me." Finn threw a few punches in the air. "I won more fights than he did. I just never got a championship bout—through no fault of mine. The reigning bantamweight champ kept ducking a matchup." Finn made a flurry of quick jabs. "He wanted no part of this."

"Coward. Well, I'm a boxing fan," the manager said, "and my wife's Irish." He handed them a map with their tent circled. "Rules are on the back. Follow them and you have a place to stay. That'll be four-bits a day, each."

Finn paid him. "Showers still open?"

"Twenty-four hours a day."

"Come, Bird, let's hit the showers before bed. We'll start searching the Fair tomorrow morning."

They showered and then found their tent. It was white canvas, but it had a wooden floor and two beds with sturdy iron frames and decent mattresses. Certainly better that sleeping on the train. Finn settled in and began to doze.

"Finn?"

"Go to sleep, Bird."

"Can't. Bed's too short. My feet hang off the end."

"Bend your knees and sleep on your side."

The iron bedframe creaked as Bird changed position.

"Finn?"

"What, Bird?"

"It's too narrow. My knees stick off the edge."

Finn sighed, got up, turned on the light, put his pants on, and went outside in his undershirt. Shortly, he returned with two boards. "Stand up, Bird. Pick up the foot of the mattress."

Finn slid the wood underneath the mattress, leaving ten inches of board sticking out the end. "Try it now."

Bird got in bed and lay on his back. His feet rested comfortably on the boards.

Finn climbed back into bed.

"Finn?"

"Now what?"

"The blanket won't reach."

"Stay there." Finn got up and threw his blanket over Bird.

"You're a really good friend, Finn."

Finn fell back in bed. "Kiss my ass."

"We're not *that* good of friends."

* * *

Camp Lewis served a hearty breakfast, and after eating more than their share, Finn and Bird boarded the camp omnibus. Bird's gait was a little uneven, as happened some mornings. The wagon wobbled as he floundered his way down the aisle between the two bench seats.

A young boy sitting between his parents squealed and buried his face in his mother's bosom.

"Make him stop," she said to her husband. "He's shaking the whole omnibus."

"Sir, please be careful," the man said. "You're frightening my wife and child."

Finn laid a steadying hand on Bird's shoulder. "It's okay. He can't help it."

At the fairground, the omnibus let them off in a great plaza bordered by tracks of three or four railroad companies. The boxers were momentarily confused, but the surge of disembarking passengers pressed them toward a row of chrome turnstiles.

"How much?" Finn asked an attendant.

"Fifty cents."

He fished two half-dollars from his pocket, pressed one into Bird's palm, and handed her the other. She dropped it into a slot and waved him forward. As his abdomen met the silver bar it rotated and pushed him through. He marveled at it.

Finn realized Bird wasn't with him and turned around. Bird, just behind him, bumped against the bar, but it wouldn't turn. He stepped back and tried again, with the same result.

"You've got to pay her first."

Bird handed the attendant his coin and slammed his thighs against the turn-stile. "It's not working."

"You have to wait until I put the money in the slot." She deposited the coin and motioned for him to enter. Bird eyed the turnstile with suspicion.

"Come on, Bird, it's good now."

"This thing won't move."

"Yeah, now it will. Just walk toward me."

Bird pushed through the turnstile, glanced back at it with suspicion.

The two boxers proceeded as far as a large statue of Saint Louis Joliet astride his horse, when their mouths fell open. Before them, rushing cascades poured into acres of lagoons that curved around sculpted gardens. In the distance loomed massive palaces, larger and finer than Madison Square Garden.

"It's . . . big," Bird said.

Finn nodded. "Bigger than I expected."

Masses of visitors pressed shoulder to shoulder in the plaza. The congestion barely diminished as visitors peeled off into walkways leading to various palaces, and a constant flow of new arrivals took their place.

"How are we gonna find them?" Bird said. "There's more people here than in New York City."

"There's not. It only feels like it. We'll find 'em. It's like fighting twenty rounds. Don't step out of the ring until you win." Finn stopped a passing vendor and bought a map of the Fair. He unfolded it and showed it to Bird. "The Palace of Liberal Arts sounds like someplace Broadway dandies might hang around. We'll start there, and if we don't find them, we'll just go from building to building, crossing out each one as we finish it."

They made their way to the resplendent nine-acre white building, crossing over several bridges to get there. Below one bridge, gondoliers poled couples in long, skinny boats. Boats shaped like swans and dragons motored beneath another bridge. Ladies in shirtwaist dresses with ruffled skirts and gentlemen wearing summer hats waved as their boats passed by.

The elaborately decorated building initially confused them, having eight different entrances with no clear indication of which one to use. "According to this map there should be a large sunken garden on the front side," Finn said.

Bird pointed. "Like that one?"

"Yes, indeed, Champ."

Manicured gardens and water pools spanned the entire length of the palace, the front of which had three Roman arches. The center arch was the largest, topped with a sculpture of four-horses drawing a chariot. That had to be the main door, so that was where they entered.

They were unprepared for what they found. A hundred exhibitors were neatly arranged in ten or eleven 750-foot-long rows, crisscrossed by aisles that seemed as wide as streets.

"This place is the size of Greenwich Village," Bird said.

"Not hardly, but I get your point," Finn said.

They wandered the aisles, looking for the dandies, but were continually distracted by new-fangled inventions and unique foreign objects. A large harp stood near the entrance to a musical instrument company from Germany. Bird bumped it by accident, and when he grabbed hold to steady it, it made an angelic note. Charmed, Bird plucked one of the strings and smiled at the dulcet tone. So he plucked another and another, and then ran his meaty paw across the breadth of the strings.

The dull dissonance produced a short German man, wringing his hands. "Nein! Please do not play." He put himself between Bird and the harp. "If you want to hear it, Frau Radke will perform at four."

"Don't get your pretzel in a twist," Finn said. "We're going."

Later, they came upon a twenty-two-foot tall fountain of billowing bubbles coming from a sculpture of a fairy at the top. "170,000 bubbles a minute," shouted a barker, "all from just a half-cake of Fairy Soap."

Bird scooped a handful of foam out of the fountain and looked up at the fairy.

"Come along, Bird."

Bird clapped his hands together and watched bubbles float to the floor.

At the end of the row, they heard ragtime piano coming from several aisles over. "Got them!" Finn cried.

"Huh?"

"That tavern owner in Greenwich Village told us one of them played ragtime every time he got near a piano. I'll bet my last pair of clean socks, that's him."

They backtracked and followed the sound to a piano exhibit. Unfortunately, all they found was a plump-bottomed woman on a piano bench pumping two foot pedals like she was waddling home from market. The keys were moving on their own in syncopated time.

Bird was fascinated, Finn frustrated.

"We can't dawdle at every exhibit, Bird, or we'll never find the men who defiled your cousin. We just have to go through these palaces and stay focused on finding those dandies, not get distracted by all there is to see."

Bird thought about this for a moment. "I'm hungry, Finn. And I could use a beer."

Finn checked his watch. "I see why, we've been in this place all day and forgot to eat. They're about to close." He consulted his map and found the Irish Village on the Pike. "I know just the place. How does Irish stew and cold beer sound?"

"Good."

A hundred thousand incandescent lights came on as they made their way to the Pike. Bird and Finn were dazzled. They lingered on a bridge, staring at the Palace of Electricity until hunger won out.

Ireland was not difficult to find, being the first building they came to as they entered the Pike. Bird ate three plates of boiled corn beef and cabbage. Finn ordered boxty and coddle. They each had a few beers.

Finn took out the newspaper photo and showed it to their server, who said she couldn't help them. He stopped other servers as they passed their table on the way to other customers. Finally, one of them said, "Listen, there are thousands of people a day on the Pike. None of us remember any of them."

CHAPTER 28

That morning, Julius and his friends had gone their separate ways. He spent his day in the Palace of Electricity, where most of the exhibits were machines that generated or used electricity. That was fine with him. He started at the Edison exhibit, but the inventor wasn't there. An aide told Julius that Edison would be visiting frequently to ensure his works were being properly presented. All Julius could do was hope the great man came before he left for home.

Bryce said he was going to find the Pueblo Indian village, or maybe the Apaches, Julius wasn't sure which. The man had an obsession with Indians since reading a stack of dime novels. Mo told them he was going back to the Palace of Liberal Arts because they'd left before seeing the foreign exhibits, and China was supposed to be displaying some amazing artistry. Japan, too. "Who in America knows anything of mysterious Japan?" Mo had said.

Mo had a point, but his friends were missing all these electrical discoveries and works of genius. That was what was going to shape the future of America and the world, not some native tribes or pretty porcelain. He'd have to bring them here at least once.

At midday, he walked outside to view the operation of a solar furnace, an assemblage of 40,000 mirrors that harnessed the sun's energy to create temperatures of 10,000 degrees Fahrenheit. Interesting. He'd recently done a different project with mirrors at his work. He wondered if there was any similarity between light and electricity.

That evening, he hurried to the Pike, where he and his friends had agreed to meet for dinner. Mo had questioned if they should be paying for restaurants when their meal at the hotel was included in their room charge. Bryce dismissed the matter, and Julius, thinking about how much time they'd spend running back and forth to the hotel, sided with Bryce. Besides, he hoped Emily and her friends would be there again.

"There you are," Mo said. He and Bryce were leaning against a sign at the Pike entrance. "We're starved."

Julius gave them a sheepish grin. "I had to wait for the lights to come on at the Palace of Electricity. It is the most magnificent thing you've ever seen."

"We saw it Saturday night," Bryce said. "Don't you remember?"

"Yeah, but it amazes me every time." Facing the Grand Basin, and surrounded by lagoons, the palace's spectacular illumination reflected in the water to dramatic effect. "Are the ladies waiting?"

Mo looked puzzled. "Ladies?"

"Emily and her girlfriends. She said they might come again tonight."

Bryce shook his head. "Mo and I walked the length of the Pike and back looking for you, and we didn't run into them."

Julius was mildly disappointed. Bryce and Mo were good company, but . . . "Where do you want to eat?"

"I'm thinking French," Bryce said.

"Maybe we should wait," he said. "They might want to eat with us."

Mo shook his head. "It's well past suppertime. If they were coming, they'd have been here by now."

He knew Mo was right. Besides, he had a sure date with Emily for Sunday. And Catherine. He'd have to give some thought to that.

Julius dug a quarter out of his pocket. To reach Paris, they had to pay twenty-five cents and make their way through a medieval French Village with the usual collection of booths. He'd grown accustomed to vendors at every Pike attraction. Still, there were exotic items for sale at the Fair that you couldn't buy in New York. Here, it was fine linens, French perfumes, even champagne. Bryce bought two bottles.

Inside, they had to decide between two restaurants. Café Chantant was an Art Nouveau-style dinner theater. The other choice, Cabaret Bruant, advertised its "celebrated" Champagne Dancers. They weren't celebrated enough for Julius to have heard of them, but it seemed a place they'd like.

After a decent meal and a dozen beautiful dancers, the men wandered through the rest of the attraction. There was a reproduction of the Bastille, complete with a guillotine. Another building featured "transparent mirrors," illusions that suggested mirrors but were not. Julius couldn't figure how the illusion worked, but boy, hadn't this been his day for mirrors!

They strolled along the Pike without destination or purpose, open to what caught their fancy. He still kept an eye out for Emily but knew, at this hour, there was no hope.

A barker called, "Come one, come all, see Beautiful Jim Key, a horse that can spell and do arithmetic. Only fifteen cents. The show is about to start."

"That must be a damn smart horse," Bryce said. "I'd like to see that."

"Me, too," Mo said.

They paid the fee and entered. An Arabian horse stood, surrounded on three sides by doubters. A black man with a gray beard standing next to him introduced himself as Dr. William Key, a veterinarian, and Beautiful Jim's owner.

"This horse has been called the Marvel of the Twentieth Century. He can read, write, spell, add, sort mail, tell time, use a cash register, and even cite the Bible."

"Don't tell us, show us," a heckler called out.

"Patience, friend, before you leave here you will be slack-jawed. When our recently departed president, William McKinley, saw Beautiful Jim Key perform a few years ago in Tennessee, he declared, 'This is the most astonishing and entertaining exhibition I have ever witnessed.' I vow you will say the same."

Behind Jim were three racks. Two of them held white tin cards printed with the letters of the alphabet and the numerals one through thirty. The third rack was empty.

"Beautiful Jim, can you show the folks your name?" Dr. Key said.

The horse turned to the rack of letters and pulled off the letter J with his mouth. He set it on the top shelf of the empty rack. He then repeated the feat, choosing I, M, K, E, and Y, placing them in the correct order. The crowd applauded.

A man on the other side of the room said in a clipped, British accent, "Even a blind horse can smell an apple. That doesn't prove he can spell anyone else's name."

"The lovely lady on your arm, would you kindly tell Jim Key her name, sir?"

"Miss Lily Jones."

Julius's head swiveled. There they were, all three of them.

The horse deftly put Lily's name on the rack. The audience applauded wildly. The horse didn't seem bothered by the noise.

"And now you, sir?"

"Sir Guy Ford."

Beautiful Jim repeated his feat.

"Where do you hail from?" ask Dr. Key.

"Britain."

Julius was astounded when Beautiful Jim pulled and assembled the correct letters. He knew it had to be a trick, but he was befuddled by how it was done.

Like a proud father, Dr. Key gripped the lapels of his coat. "Beautiful Jim is also proficient in figuring. He can add, multiply, divide or subtract any numbers below thirty."

"Two plus two," a boy in the front called out.

"Too easy," said Dr. Key, but Jim had already picked up the number four.

"Two times two," someone called out.

Dr. Key wagged his finger. "You're trying to trick him." But Jim picked up the four again and held it, nodding his head.

"Three times nine," the boy said. "Even I can't remember that one."

The horse selected two and seven and set them on the rack.

"Beautiful Jim, I think this boy needs to go back to school."

The horse walked over to a school bell and rang it. The audience laughed.

Julius kept watching, not the horse, but the owner. He had to be giving the horse some kind of signal as to what to do. But Julius was damned if he could spot it.

A cash register was brought on stage, and Jim was shown various denominations of money. In each instance he went to the register, and with his nose, rang up the correct amount. For his finale, Dr. Key borrowed a silver dollar from someone in the audience and dropped it into a gallon jar of water. Beautiful Jim put his nose inside the jar and retrieved the coin without drinking the water or spilling a drop.

At the conclusion of the show, they were met by hawkers selling photos, souvenir buttons, postcards, and Beautiful Jim Key pennies. There was even sheet music for a tune called the "Beautiful Jim Key Two-Step." Bryce ran his eyes over it, nodding his head slightly, then bought a copy.

Afterwards, Julius spotted the Jones sisters with three gentlemen escorts. The man who'd identified himself as Sir Guy Ford was buying them gold Jim Key collar pins.

He casually wandered over, unsure if they had noticed him in the audience. Mo and Bryce caught up. Julius tipped his hat. "Quite a horse."

Violet and Rose smiled. Lily's mouth fell open. "Oh."

Okay, she hadn't seen them inside.

* * *

"Guy, please excuse us a moment." Lily pulled her sisters into a tête-à-tête. "Don't flirt with these New Yorkers. Remember, as far as everyone at the Fair is concerned, we're chaste and maidenly. They could expose us and ruin our chances."

"Mo would never do that," Rose said.

"Bryce might." Lily pretended to fuss with the Jim Key pin on her sister's collar and then turned back to Guy. "Sorry, where are my manners? These gentlemen are acquaintances we met on the train. They're from New York City, I believe." She introduced the Brits and the Americans by name, and the men shook hands all around.

Bryce wasn't warm to the foreigners, but she had to admit he had picked up on her signal and was honorable enough to not reveal any previous intimacy between them. In fact, he seemed anxious to get away from them. That was probably for the best.

They were about to go their separate ways when Bryce pointed to the sky. "Look! It's moving."

"You're right," Julius said. "Let's go."

Sir Guy tipped his head toward the stars. "What is?"

"The Observation Wheel," Bryce said. "We've wanted to ride on it for several days, but it wasn't running. Now it is." Bryce tipped his hat. "Nice meeting you. Got to go. Hail and farewell." He took off down the Pike with Mo and Julius on his heels.

"That sounds like a capital idea," Guy said to his friends. "What do you say, ladies? Shall we see what the Fair looks like from above?"

Lily didn't think chasing after the New Yorkers was a good idea at all, but Rose and Violet were already leading their escorts toward the wheel. She shrugged and took Guy's arm. If they took their time, the men might be gone before they got on.

It didn't work out that way, despite her best efforts to hold her party to a leisurely pace. When they arrived at the wheel, there was a queue. While Guy bought their tickets, she scanned the line ahead of them and spotted tall Julius. No doubt the two men next to him were Bryce and Mo. Thirty or forty people separated them from the New Yorkers.

Oh, please put us in separate cars.

Her sisters chatted with Guy's friends, two British anthropologists well-heeled enough to fund their own expeditions. Like Guy, they didn't need Father's money. Unlike Guy, they were married. So, definitely out of the question, but good practice. She gazed up at the slowly revolving wheel. It had spokes like a bicycle wheel, but its thirty-six passenger cars looked to be the size of Pullman train cars.

Guy returned with six tickets. She noted the price—fifty cents each—but he refused her offer to pay for theirs.

"The ticket seller told me each car has chairs for forty people and can hold twenty more standing. If we're fortunate, we'll get the next car."

Lily watched as the wheel stopped to unload passengers and let the next group board. She tried to do a quick head count of the people in front of her, but they were milling around too much. With any luck, it'd fill up before they reached the head of the line.

The queue snaked forward. Closer now, she could see the cars were like long wooden cottages with peaked roofs, tall windows on all sides, and a door at each end. An attendant stood inside the door assisting passengers as they crossed the gap between the platform and the car floor. She saw the New Yorkers board.

The car continued to fill up. She held her breath as they approached, hoping that at any moment the attendant would hold up his hand and say, "Please, wait for the next car."

He didn't.

Lily accepted the offered hand and stepped aboard, following her sisters and their escorts down the aisle to where Guy was saving six chairs. She glanced around quickly, hoping they were at least at the opposite end of the car from the New Yorkers.

Thank God, she couldn't see them. Taking the chair next to Violet, she smoothed her skirt and looked out the window.

The attendant closed the door, and the wheel began to turn, lifting their carriage into the air. Not very far. It paused while the car beneath them was loaded, then moved, and stopped again. But this time they were already above the roofline of nearby buildings. Not quite high enough to catch sight of the fairgrounds, but she could make out the penumbra from palace lights in the distance. As soon as they loaded another car or two, the whole spectacle would be in view.

Violet grabbed her chair and moved it. "Look, Lily, these chairs swivel." Violet spun around and giggled. Her chair came to a stop facing the aisle. "Hi again, isn't this the most fantastic thing you have ever been on?"

"It is. I'm glad you decided to come, too."

Lily recognized the voice—Julius. She cocked an ear, but kept facing out the window.

"Guy decided for us," Violet said. "And I'm glad he did."

Seated next to Lily, Guy turned his chair toward Violet at the mention of his name. "Oh, good sport. We're in the same car."

Lily ignored them.

Violet grabbed Lily's chair and swung it around. "Look who's standing right behind us."

Lily gave him a polite smile. The wheel moved again, and Julius reached up to brace himself.

"Don't you want a chair?" Violet said.

Guy stood and shook hands. "Here, good fellow, take mine."

"That's awfully nice of you," Julius said, "but I prefer to stand so I can see out every window."

Guy moved over next to Julius. "I see what you mean. Lily, I'm going to stand for a bit, as well."

Lily swiveled her and Violet's chairs back toward the window. "Sis, we're missing the view."

Apparently the last car had finally been loaded, for the wheel began to rotate at a slow, steady pace. By now they were high enough to take in the full scope of lighted palaces, cascades, and fountains. Dazzling reflections in the lagoons and Grand Basin mesmerized the passengers, and conversations dwindled to "o-o-o" and "ah."

"How long is this ride?" Rose said.

Lily shrugged.

"Half an hour," Guy answered.

"It makes four revolutions per hour," Julius said. "So, I figure we'll get two full go-rounds."

"Sounds correct," Guy said.

Those two were getting dangerously chummy, but she could do nothing about it until the wheel stopped. Half an hour from now.

When their car reached the top, the lights of St. Louis spread out below them. As it began its decent, everyone on Lily's side swiveled their chairs to see the other section of the fairgrounds. It didn't have as many electric lights, just the Palace of Agriculture and the Pike, but beneath them to the southwest, bonfires dotted the grounds below.

Guy's friends left their seats to join Guy and the New Yorkers. If her sisters had half the wiles this venture was going to require, the men would have never left their sides. They'd have to work on that.

"I'll wager those fires are the Philippine Reservation," Guy said.

"I'd say you're right," said one of anthropologists. The man turned to Bryce. "Have you seen it yet—the Igorote Village?"

"No, but I've visited the American Indians."

The man leaned in conspiratorially. "Not a place to take the ladies. There are three tribes, the Suyoc, the Bontoc, and the Tinguanes. They live in huts and cook outdoors, like I suppose they do on their native island. But the Suyocs refuse to wear clothing, so the Fair had to put up signs warning visitors they might see nudity in the area. That hasn't quite dampened interest in them, at least from some quarters." He glanced at Lily and reddened. "I don't mean the Jones sisters, mind you."

"Of course you didn't," Bryce said. "But I don't know what people expect. I heard many of these tribes were kidnapped and brought here to be exhibited like animals in a zoo. It's a disgrace."

"No, it's educational and enlightening," the man said. "The Fair organizers have brought many wild tribes from the Philippines, Africa, the Amazon, and your Western territories so that scientists and the general public can study races that evolution has left behind."

Bryce grimaced. "That smacks of self-superiority. We fought the Spanish-American war to end colonial oppression, not to make Filipinos sideshow curiosities."

"Visit the Philippine Reservation and judge for yourself. The Bontocs eat dogs, for God's sake. And I assure you, primitives aren't capable of learning."

Julius spoke up. "I doubt that's true of any species of humanity."

Bryce nodded. "Our American Indian tribal schools have proven the fallacy of such assumptions."

The scientist sniffed sharply. "I remind you, sir, this is my field of expertise. Just because Dr. Key taught a horse to count and spell, doesn't make the horse human."

Lily had to jump in before this got out of control. "Turn around, gentlemen. You're missing the whole Fair."

With a final glance at one another, they turned around and went back to enjoying the fair. Lily tried to do the same. The view was beautiful, but she'd be glad when this ride ended and they could go their separate ways.

CHAPTER 29

Wednesday morning, Lily and her sisters made their way to the China pavilion for its official opening ceremony. Located on Administration Avenue between Belgium and Britain, it was a group of four buildings whose Oriental architecture stood in sharp contrast with its neighbors. Their visit to the Chinese Village on the Pike had prepared her somewhat, but the oddest thing was that the roof corners of every structure turned skyward. Where would water go when it rained? Or didn't it rain in China?

They entered through a picturesque pagoda decorated with Chinese characters on dark, central pillars. To her left was an octagonal gazebo. A short stone wall partially enclosed the complex. The scent of roses in bloom wafted from a lovely flower garden. It was early for roses in New Jersey, and she wondered if St. Louis's climate was different or if they'd transplanted them here from a greenhouse.

Standing in the doorway of the large central building, amidst a cluster of his countrymen, was what had to be Crown Prince Pu Lun, nephew of the Chinese emperor and its future ruler. She recognized him from the newspaper photo. Round-faced, wearing a gorgeous, gold silk tunic embroidered with a dragon that Violet would have died to own, he was not, by Lily's standards, a dashing figure.

The prince, she had learned, was twenty-nine years of age. Not so much older than herself as to make marriage one of those May-December matches. The thought of settling with an old coot gave her goose flesh. She just wouldn't do it, regardless of her mother's wishes.

The prince, though of a reasonable age, was short in stature and wore round, wire-rim glasses. Wasn't there an Italian prince, or a Spanish Count to be had?

"What time is the dedication ceremony?" she asked him.

"Not today, Friday," he said in surprisingly clear English.

Lily's face grew hot. "Oh, I'm so sorry. We've made a mistake." She nudged her sisters and started to back away.

"No, please." He gave them each a short bow, repeating, "Welcome, welcome, welcome."

Well, they'd at least make the polite response. Lily and her sisters curtsied, and she introduced them in turn.

Pu Lun made a short speech explaining that, though the structural framework had been constructed by American workers, the ornamental finish had all been applied by skilled artisans brought from his home country. "All of it done by hand. Please, come see." He motioned for them to enter.

It was more colorful than any public building she'd ever seen—scarlet, gold, ebony and blue had made up the palette. In the center was a courtyard with a goldfish pond. Although the prince certainly spoke English better than most of New York's Chinatown—and a few of her father's friends—the staff around him babbled in a confusing cacophony of high-pitched syllables that made her ears hurt.

"Your exhibit is very . . . colorful." She glanced around. Nearly every wooden surface was intricately carved and polished to a shine. "Beautiful woodwork and furniture, too—must have taken a lot of work."

He looked at her, his expression flat. "Six thousand pieces, many workers."

She was at a loss where to go next. Violet stepped up. "Your Highness, we saw many beautiful examples of your country's artistry at the Chinese exhibit in the Palace of Liberal Arts."

He gave Violet a small smile. "You're interested in China?"

Okay, let Violet have this one, and she'd find someone more like Bryce—no, she shouldn't even think of him. No need to have the memory of Bryce in her head at this moment.

"Oh, yes," Violet said. "We visited your village on the Pike. It was remarkable."

His smile broadened. "Not my village. This is where I live."

"I don't think I understand."

"A prince doesn't live in a village." He gestured about him. "This is reproduction of my summer palace." He pointed to his right. "Through that doorway is my bedroom."

Someone in the Prince's entourage cleared his throat.

He paid them no mind. "You can enter if you like to see my bed. It is made from ebony and mother-of-pearl."

Lily saw Violet's eyes widen. "Your bedroom?"

"Yes." The prince turned and spoke to one of his aides, who handed him three envelopes. With a flourish, he presented them to Rose, Lily and Violet. "I am hosting a reception tonight at the Washington Hotel. I hope you will honor me with your presence."

"Is that where you're staying, the Washington Hotel?" Violet said.

"No, I live here, in my palace, while I am at Exposition. I thought I made that clear."

Lily tensed at her sister's faux pas, but the Prince seemed gracious enough. She held up the ornately decorated red envelope. "Thank you for the kind invitation. We look forward to seeing you this evening."

They curtsied again, and he bowed. "Please, look around."

They explored his palace like it was a museum, for in many ways that's what it was. Once she began to look closer, she could appreciate the fine scroll work and inlay that adorned so much of the furniture. Handsome, colorful, intricately patterned porcelains filled the rooms.

"Can you imagine this is all his?" Violet said.

"And this is his summer place," Rose said.

In the bedroom, Lily admitted to herself that the inlay work on his bed was extraordinary. Making sure no one else was in earshot, she laughed and quietly said, "This is my bed and you can sleep in it anytime you want."

Rose picked up on it. "I be in my palace all night."

"Stop it, you two," Violet said.

CHAPTER 30

Finn kept Bird on track Wednesday as they searched two more palaces, barely yielding to the temptation of the wonders on display. Methodically, they paced every row and aisle, examined the face of each man, admired the comely forms of many ladies, and frightened more than a few. Not that they were trying to appear menacing, quite the contrary. But a Goliath with a ham hock at the end of each arm and a nose like a sweet potato wasn't someone refined ladies put on their dance card.

The palaces were so large that finding three fellow New Yorkers was looking harder by the hour. The afternoon waned. After leaving the second palace of the day, Finn studied the map. "There are over fifteen hundred buildings on these grounds. For all we know, right now they could be entering a place we already searched and checked off our map."

"I really like the Fair," Bird said.

"Me, too, but we've got a job to do, and the way we're going about it won't work."

A marching band playing, "Meet Me in St. Louis, Louis," approached. Finn and Bird stepped off onto the grass to let them pass. The tune switched to "Yankee Doodle," and Bird sang out the words.

Once the band was beyond them, Finn said, "Let's quit the Fair for today and see if we can find where they're staying."

"How are we going to do that?"

"We're going to the Hotel Jefferson."

"I don't understand."

"That was our first certain clue to their whereabouts, and we never followed it."

"That man drove us to Camp Lewis said . . . something . . . I don't remember."

"He said he took them to the Hotel Jefferson, but they ended up staying at Camp Lewis. And he was right. The camp manager said they stayed there two nights before he kicked them out. So, where did they go?"

"I don't know."

Finn patted his friend's shoulder. "I know you don't, and neither do I. But I think we ought to check the Jefferson—see if they went back there."

They exited the fairgrounds, found the trolley that would take them into the city, and stopped at the Hotel Jefferson.

As it happened, the check-in clerk on duty at the Jefferson was the one Bryce had given a hard time. A meek man, intimidated by a dandy like Bryce, wasn't about to stand up to a heavyweight champion and his scrappy, street-smart companion. At Finn's first question, the clerk collapsed like a paper hat in the rain. He recognized the men in the photo and spilled the beans about the telephone message his boss had for them from the Inside Inn. Finn pressed him for their names, but the clerk drew a blank.

Meanwhile, a thundering rainstorm had begun.

Emily Stroud, Julius's Sunday date—well, one of them—had finished her shift in the hotel restaurant. Since it was pouring like Noah's flood, instead of going out the kitchen door, she crossed the lobby and exited by the front door. The hotel had no rule against employees leaving that way, and besides, the trolley stopped right there.

Emily waited under the awning until the trolley arrived and then dashed aboard. Two men she'd seen in the lobby boarded last and took the seat next to her. The smaller, muscle-bound specimen said to the behemoth he called Goliath, "That clerk said the New Yorkers were staying at the Inside Inn."

"Funny name," the big one said with a whistle.

The shorter one handed a newspaper clipping to the larger man. "Put this in your coat pocket and I'll show you on the map."

She caught only the briefest glance at the picture before the big fellow folded it with his meaty paws, but it was long enough to recognize Julius and his friends.

* * *

As soon as Lily and her sisters returned to the inn, she asked the concierge to arrange a carriage to convey them to the reception that evening. They repaired to their room to bathe and dress for the occasion. Violet finally would get to wear her new gown.

The sky outside their windows darkened. Lily turned on the lights and studied the careful calligraphy on the stiff ivory card that had been wrapped like a present in the red paper envelope decorated with gold filigree. Its brief few lines were the sum total of information concerning the event. She imagined nothing too intimate, perhaps forty or fifty dignitaries, possibly some representing foreign countries. Would there be other nobles—a duke or marquis ripe for the picking? She let out a sigh of relief. They'd stumbled along, not knowing where the right people might be found. Yet, thanks to Violet's naïve charm and a cordial Chinese prince, they were about to wind up in a room full of prospects.

When they were ready, they went to the lobby and waited as a fierce rainstorm descended on the Fair. Good thing she hadn't ordered an open carriage.

Outside, the fairground was dark, and the buildings were shadowy hulks.

"Someone told me they turned off the lights to save money," Bryce said.

Lily whirled around.

Bryce raised his eyebrows. "You're not going out in this weather, are you?"

Lily gave him a polite nod and walked toward the door. Her sisters hesitated, and Lily snapped, "Rose, Violet, the coach is here."

"We're going to a reception for Prince Pu Lun," Violet said, hurrying after Lily.

The doorman held an umbrella over them as they boarded the coach.

When they arrived at the Washington Hotel, another doorman helped them from the carriage. They entered the hotel ballroom. What? She hadn't expected a reception for 1,400. Trying to sniff out an impoverished aristocrat in this mob was not going to be an easy task.

The first hour was spent in a receiving line to greet their host. Surely everyone here had already met him, or they never would have been invited. Still, protocol was protocol, so she waited, making polite conversation with those in front and behind them as the line inched slowly forward.

However, the experience was enlightening.

"He's so unpretentious," said a woman wearing a white hat decorated with a band of peacock feathers. "Why, Saturday, at the Exposition luncheon in the Palace of Varied Industries, his Imperial Highness stood beside the rank and file of great Americans and ate the same food served to the rest of us."

"Did you see his wife anywhere?" said the woman's companion. "I wonder what she looks like."

"Wife?" Lily said.

"No," said the peacock hat. "I suspect he left her back in China. But you know these foreign potentates all have consorts."

Lily leaned over and whispered in Violet's ear. "Forget this prince, he's married."

Violet turned. "I never thought otherwise. Any heir to a throne is married off young, or betrothed at least. If you'd paid attention to Mrs. Coggeshall, you'd have known that. If you want to marry a prince, he'll have to be a widower."

Lily frowned. Translation: old, definitely old.

Oh well, there was always the crowd to mine.

CHAPTER 31

Bryce watched the downpour and wondered if the Jones sisters going to the reception without escorts meant they'd dumped the racist Brits they'd been with yesterday.

Julius clapped him on the shoulder. "Pike's closed, too. We'll have to make our own fun here."

Not one to dwell on rejection, Bryce said, "Sure, a party." He led his friends into a spacious parlor adjoining the lobby and opened a bag containing several bottles of Piesporter wine he'd bought at a German wine exhibit. "May as well see if this is any good. Julius, you have a corkscrew on your pocket knife. Open one of these. Mo, ask a waiter to bring a tray of glasses. We'll gather a congenial group of hotel guests and have our own princely reception."

The light, white German wine slid down easily, and others joined the party. Bryce managed to keep the conversation and conviviality flowing. Everyone pitched in, contributing bottles of their own, until hours later, the table was littered with empty wine bottles.

Bryce paused, mid-story, to tip each of the empty bottles over his glass, collecting a few drops from each. He was feeling mighty good, at home in his element. When there were no more bottles to test, he resumed his tale. "So the first genuine Indian I've ever met comes hobbling down the street toward me on crutches. Then he sees me, stops, stands on one foot, flaps his crutches like wings, and caws like a crow."

Bryce paused again, scanning his audience's reactions. That's when he overheard Lily and her sisters passing nearby.

"The language barrier would be too great, anyway," Rose said.

"He speaks perfect English," Violet said.

Rose shook her head. "You're forgetting the thousands of people around him who don't. You'd have to learn the language to know what was being said about you. Not to mention asking for breakfast."

Bryce jumped to his feet. "Ladies, join us for a glass."

Lily hesitated, but Rose and Violet approached.

"Julius, open another bottle," he said.

"Can't. You've cleaned out our supply."

"Well, something else then. Don't we have a bottle of champagne left in our room?"

"Gone," Mo said.

"That's all right," Lily said, "I'm afraid we can't stay."

Bryce wobbled a little. Julius steadied him. "I'm sure you could if you tried."

Lily took Violet's hand and turned to leave. "Sorry."

Rose lingered, stepping over to Mo. "She doesn't speak for all of us, you know. I might have a drink with you some other time . . . Just don't ask while she's around."

"Rose!" Lily called over her shoulder.

"Coming."

Bryce laughed it off. "Well, Mo, it looks like you're the only dandy to win a fair maid."

Mo smiled and pointed at the table full of desiccated bottles. "Maybe we should call it a night."

Now, that was a terrible idea. He'd had their whole party laughing until Lily showed up. She hadn't been such a damp squib on the train.

Most of his audience began to leave.

"Don't go. The night's young."

Mo clapped him on the shoulder. "No, it's not. The Palace of Fine Art opens tomorrow, and I intend to be there first thing."

"How about you, Julius? You're never one to quit a party."

"Mo's right." Julius got on one side, Mo on the other, and began to lead him toward their room. "We don't have much time here. I don't want to waste it sleeping off a hangover."

"Those girls are taking this business of finding a title for their father too seriously," Bryce said. "We can have titles. No reason to go foreign for that."

"What are you talking about?" Mo said.

"Julius can be the Baron of Bed-Stuy."

Julius laughed. "That's Bedford-Stuyvesant, if you please."

"And Mo, you'll be the Earl of East Side."

"What about you?" Julius said.

"Oh, just call me the Prince of Tin Pan Alley."

CHAPTER 32

Thursday morning Rose woke before her sisters. No sign of daylight through the drapes. Her sense of time had been messed up ever since she'd gotten here. She rolled over, buried her face in the pillow, and told herself to go back to sleep.

It didn't work. Fifteen minutes later, she slipped from the bed and tiptoed into the bathroom, trying not to wake her sisters. Rose closed the door and began filling the bathtub. Meanwhile, she pinned the braids she'd slept in up on her head, and wrapped a towel around her hair. When the tub was full, she doffed her nightgown and slid into the warm water, lying back until she was immersed up to her neck.

The steamy bathwater caused her muscles to let go, every part of her falling into tranquility. As she slipped farther under, tiny wavelets of water lapped at the hairs on the nape of her neck. She pressed her feet against the bottom of the tub and pushed herself a bit higher. She didn't want to get her hair wet.

The encounters with Mo and his friends last night and the night before entered her thoughts. Lily wasn't treating them right. The men had been adventurous yet attentive lovers on the ride to St. Louis. Now, her sister treated them the way the snobs in New York did Mother and Father. Would Sir Guy and his friends—their titles too low in rank to be inheritable— suffer the same fate? Would Lily demand they cast them aside as she pressed on toward quarry of higher station?

Rose scooped up a handful of bathwater and watched it spill over her fingers like the cascades at the Fair. Had Prince Pu Lun and his unseen wife faced the same onerous duty—forced by family to choose a mate by rank?

At least princesses and countesses were raised in a society that taught them how to seek their own kind. She and her sisters had no such training. Any foreigner who could afford to come to America was probably rich enough to not need their money. They were on a foolish mission that rubbed against the grain of everything they believed. America's founding fathers brooked no monarchy, no aristocratic titles. Yet, a hundred-twenty years later the wealthy were grasping at hollow titles like they meant something. And wouldn't feminist leaders like Susan Anthony, Elizabeth Stanton, and Victoria Woodhull say they were setting the women's movement back forty years?

Okay, so Woodhull and her sister had married lords. That didn't mean Rose had to. She'd embrace their free love doctrine and reject their defection to the aristocracy.

In a bright spot where the bathroom light reflected in the bathwater, Mo's face swam into view. She moved her leg, and the image disappeared with the ripples. The water settled, and tall Julius appeared in the reflection. She blocked the light with her hand, but when she removed it, the mirage morphed into grinning Bryce. God, she was a randy wench. But, she noted, not once had the likeness been of the Brits.

Rose sighed. She loved her father deeply and hated the thought of disappointing him. But trying to hornswoggle a foreign lord into a marriage she didn't want in the first place seemed like selling herself for a title. She had no desire to be Lady Rose, anyway.

The water had cooled, and so had her enthusiasm for phantasms in her tub. But she'd relished the time away from the demands of her sisters. Being the middle child felt like Lily and Violet were constantly yanking on opposite arms.

She pulled the plug, stood up, and dried herself. Stealthily opening the door, she peeked into the room. A sliver of dawn slipped through the edge of the drapes, but her sisters still slept. She dressed quickly and quietly. As an afterthought, she took paper and pencil into the bathroom and left them a note on the mirror that she'd gone downstairs for coffee and would wait for them in the dining room.

* * *

At the opposite end of the inn, Mo, too, lay awake in excitement, much like he'd felt as a boy on Passover morning. The aroma of his mother preparing the meal, knowing he'd soon eat sweet charoset, and even children could drink wine. He'd lie in his bed anticipating the search for the afikomen with his cousins, the winner getting a prize. But this day his reward would be more than a mere coin. Today the Palace of Fine Arts would finally open, and within it, perhaps the greatest assemblage of art in one place the world had ever known.

Mo could lie in bed no longer. He threw off his covers and went to wash and shave while Bryce and Julius snored. When he was dressed, he looked at his watch. Too early, especially after Bryce's party last night. The guys would be pissed if he woke them. Bryce had done most of the drinking, but Julius had done his best to keep up. No telling how late they'd sleep it off.

He slipped from the room and proceeded to the inn's buffet, where he helped himself to coffee and a sweet roll. The room was sparely populated. He took a table by the window and watched the dawn arrive.

After refilling his coffee twice, he realized he couldn't keep drinking coffee, or he'd be jumpy as a cat on a trolley track. He stood and crossed the lobby, passing the restaurant. A few early souls like him were in there, and he considered whether a hearty breakfast would soak up the coffee sloshing around in his stomach. He decided to go for a walk outside instead.

The lawn and shrubs sang with verdant joy after last night's rain, but everywhere dew was heavy, so he stayed on the path. Patches of morning haze hovered between him and the distant palaces. The air was crisp and a little damp on his face. He was tempted to go back to his room for paints and a canvas to capture the scene. But light was a fleeting thing to paint. By the time he returned, the sun would have burned off the mist, and everything would look different.

The fairgrounds didn't open for hours, so he confined his perambulations to the inn property. Ahead, a woman with a shapely derriere strolled, holding a parasol. From the rear, she seemed familiar, but when she reversed course and started toward him, he realized he'd been mistaken. He tipped his hat as she passed, and she nodded.

It'd been over a week since he'd last put brush to canvas. His creative juices were like an artesian well, and when he didn't express them, pressure built up. Sure, he'd sketched Rose and her sisters on the train, but that was just doodling. And he'd done nothing since. Several more times he was tempted to retrieve his art supplies and do some work, but he didn't.

But today, he was going to see the great works awaiting them in the Palace of Fine Arts. Perhaps it was best to wait for that burst of inspiration.

For an hour he wandered the acreage around the inn. Grass, where partially shaded by oak trees, was still wet when he decided to rouse Bryce and Julius, their ire be damned. He entered the hotel, glanced in the restaurant, which was fuller now, and proceeded to their room.

Mo threw open the door. "Rise and shine, the day awaits!"

Julius, lathered in shaving soap, stuck his head out of the bathroom. "Already up."

"Bryce?"

"Over here." Bryce, buttoning his shirt collar, looked none the worse for last night. "Where have you been?"

"Went for a walk."

"Have you eaten?" Bryce said.

"No, I waited for you guys."

"Good. I'm starving," Julius said.

Bryce stood up and put on his coat. "Well, hurry up, Julius. We're waiting on you."

CHAPTER 33

Mo took the wide granite steps two at a time up to the Corinthian portico that fronted the Palace of Fine Arts. He, Julius, and Bryce, first to arrive, found their way blocked by a ribbon stretched across the entrance. Soon a crowd gathered, and after the usual speechifying, the ribbon was cut and he surged forward.

It was everything he hoped it would be.

The three-story palace was a large nave with additional pavilions east and west. Skylights provided abundant light. Unlike the state buildings they'd visited Monday, where artwork had been displayed on upper floors, all of this palace's exhibits were on one floor. No stairs to climb. Good thing, because according to what he'd read, the Palace covered five acres, and housed 11,000 works in 134 galleries. He could spend a week here.

The American section wasn't open yet, but the European sections were, and that was more than enough for Mo. Oil paintings were so numerous, they hung two and three high, covering nearly every surface of the walls. The galleries were covered with burlap and jute cloth to ensure the paintings a neutral background. He'd have to remember that trick if he ever mounted a show of his own.

Like the Palace of Liberal Arts, the exhibits here were arranged by countries. Mo headed into the west pavilion where the French artists were allotted nineteen galleries. Alcoves flanking the corridor displayed exhibits of architectural and sculptural ornament. Julius paused to study them. Mo waited for him, but he was dying to get to the French Impressionists.

Paintings in the galleries were grouped as contemporary—works produced within the past twelve years—or retrospective—pictures painted prior to that. Mo breezed past the retrospective, but then his eye caught a familiar brushwork. And it was "Odalisque," a painting by Pierre-Auguste Renoir. He stood gazing in wonder at the reclining oriental beauty for the longest time—the colors, the suggestive brushwork of the lace, the arabesques of the clothing, the drape of the hair. Finally, remembering his companions, he glanced at Julius and Bryce to see if they were growing bored, but they were equally entranced.

"These are really master artists," Mo said to Bryce.

"They are indeed," said a stranger standing next to him. The man stuck out his hand. "Joseph Henry Sharp."

Mo shook it and introduced his friends. Sharp looked to be at least twice their age. He had gray hair, with a trim mustache and goatee. Neatly dressed, he wore round wire-rimmed glasses.

"You admire Impressionism?" Sharp said.

Mo smiled and nodded.

"Mo's an artist," Julius said. "Worships the Impressionists."

"Is that right? So am I."

"Are you? What do you paint?"

"Well, not to brag, but I currently have a commission from President Roosevelt."

"Do you know Roosevelt personally?" Julius said.

"I do. I had an exhibition in Washington of scenes I'd painted of native life in Montana. He saw it and asked me to paint portraits of the 200 Sioux and Cheyenne warriors who survived the Battle of the Little Big Horn."

"Bryce was in the Spanish-American war with him," Mo said.

"Well, not *with* him, personally," Bryce said. "But tell me more about Indians. New Mexico is supposed to have a Pueblo tribe here on Saturday."

"Is that so?" Sharp said. "I wonder if I know any of them. I've been to Taos and painted several of the Pueblo people. Fascinating culture."

"You have?" Bryce said. "I'd love to hear more about them. Perhaps we can discuss it over dinner. We're staying at the Inside Inn."

"I'm downtown, at the Jefferson. But we can meet some evening. I'd like to talk to Mo about Impressionism, too. Not tonight, though. I came here to see where they hung my paintings, and I'm disappointed to learn that they didn't get the American section open yet." Sharp pulled out a calling card. "I have a meeting right now, but call me at the Jefferson and we'll set a day for dinner."

Sharp excused himself and left.

Mo stared at the card. "That was amazing," he said, "meeting an artist the first day the palace opened."

"If you can tear yourself away from the lady . . ." Bryce nodded at the Renoir. "I'd like to see what's in the other wings."

Mo realized it'd take days to see everything here. "I agree. Let's take a quick stroll through the rest of the place, just to get a sense of what is where."

The east pavilion housed paintings from Germany and Great Britain. They breezed through it, just a quick survey. Mo noted Britain featured a sizeable number of Pre-Raphelite and Neo-Classical oils. A crowd around Sir Edward Burne-Jones's "The Dream of Lancelot at the Chapel of the San Grael" caused him to pause, but the colors were too dark and muted for his taste.

At the south end of the Palace, five large rooms showcased priceless Japanese prints, carved gems, embroideries, enamel work and wrought metal. The Japanese style was so unique, so light, so exquisitely balanced, he'd have lingered there, too, but Julius and Bryce were already heading for the fourth building of the palace quadrangle, the International Sculpture Court.

It was worth it, as well. The enclosed space was laid out as a garden, with fountains, live plants, and shrubbery. Marble and bronze figures dotted the garden and filled the galleries.

The French sculptors had their own section of the exhibit, and here he found Julius staring at a bronze nude male figure of heroic size sitting on a rock with his chin resting on one hand as though deep in thought. "This is really something, Mo."

"I'm glad you like this palace, even if the exhibits don't whirl around and shoot out sparks."

Julius laughed. "Just because science interests me, doesn't mean I don't like art."

"Bryce, what do you think?" Mo said.

"Love it. This fellow is pondering some deep thoughts. No, wait, he looks like Julius on the john."

Julius knocked Bryce's hat off.

"Hey, guys," Mo said, "a little decorum, please."

Bryce scooped up his hat and put it back on. "Let's look at some goddesses and muses. I think they're in the next gallery."

The Jones sisters appeared from around the corner, dressed to the nines, and on the arms of three gentlemen. Definitely not the ones from the other night. Mo tipped his hat. "Good day, ladies. Isn't this beautiful?"

"Very," Lily said.

Violet introduced them to her companion, Lord Bath, a man easily twice her age. He stiffly introduced the men escorting Lily and Rose as Axel of Denmark and Henry of Gloucester. Having "of" in their names was probably a good sign. Mo noticed Lord Bath spoke without moving his upper lip and wondered if he had an affliction.

Lily attempted to hurry her party away, but Axel didn't want them to leave without discussing the statue before them.

"I remember when Rodin presented a smaller version of this at the Salon des Beaux-Arts in Paris," Axel said.

Violet patted his arm. "How wonderful."

Julius turned to Mo and rolled his eyes.

"Have you gentlemen seen the Anglo-Boer War Concession on the Pike," Henry said.

Mo shook his head.

"We're planning to go this evening. Perhaps you'll join us. It enacts our war with the Afrikaans in a three hour pageant."

"I'm not much for war shows," Bryce said. "Or glorifying killing the natives."

"Bryce was recently in a war," Rose said.

"Good man," said Lord Bath. "But the Afrikaans aren't African tribes, they're the white descendants of the Dutch who decided they owned the damned place. They were the ones mistreating blacks. Our Prime Minister, Lord Salisbury, wasn't going to allow that to go on and sent British troops to give them what for. It was a bloody mess, but in the end we brought the Boers to the peace table."

Mo saw the need to intervene before Bryce got his hackles up. "I thank you for the invitation, but we have other plans tonight. Perhaps we'll see you tomorrow though, at the official opening of the China Pavilion."

"I don't think so," Lily said.

Mo cocked his head. "Oh? Prince Pu Lun is supposed to be there. Don't you ladies know him?"

Lily took Axel's arm. "We do. But one prince is enough. Shall we walk on?" She led her party away from the New Yorkers.

Once they were out of earshot, Bryce said, "If he's Lord Bath, does that make his wife Lady Bathtub?"

Mo laughed. "By god, they've caught an old fish. Haven't they?"

Julius wasn't laughing. He looked up at Rodin's statue. "What do you think, old boy?"

CHAPTER 34

Thursday, Bird and Finn got a late start. Last night, the trolley line they'd ridden from the Jefferson arrived at the fairgrounds after the Fair closed, and the boxers got wet waiting for the camp omnibus. Finally, they hired a hack.

Their morning delay wasn't for lack of dry clothes, but they couldn't leave everything in a soggy pile. So, after breakfast, Finn borrowed some rope and strung clotheslines inside the tent.

The camp omnibus ended on the opposite side of the fairgrounds from the Inside Inn. Finn's map showed an Intramural Railroad around the Fair that would take them right to the Inside Inn. However, when they found the station, a worker told them, "Don't open until Tuesday."

"Jeez," Finn said. "You'd think they wouldn't have opened the place until they got everything running."

Although Bird's legs occasionally got weak, both men had once been conditioned athletes. The long walk to the other side of the Fair was manageable.

The Inside Inn, like everything else at the Fair, was on a grand scale. The white building, trimmed with red brick, covered the equivalent of four city blocks. The men headed down a gravel road that crossed acres of lawn to the main entrance. Bellmen scurried, loading departing guests and luggage into horse-drawn carriages.

"I hope we're not too late," Bird said. "What if they've gone back home?"

"Nah, they wouldn't come all the way out here and only stay a couple days," Finn said. "Give me the photo." He showed the now-ragged clipping to a dozen bellmen without a hint of recognition. Finally, he asked one, "How many of you guys are there?"

"A hundred-fifty-six," the bellman said.

They quit asking bellmen and entered the lobby. It too was vast, housing a drug store, haberdashery, shoe shine parlor, newsstand, barbershop, spacious parlors, reading rooms, reception rooms, and the entrances to two restaurants. Hotel registration was of no help. "If you don't know the guests' names, I can't help you."

"But I have a picture." Bird unfolded it on the counter.

"And I have 2,257 rooms with over five thousand guests," the clerk said.

Stymied, but not discouraged, they showed the photo at each of the shops in the lobby with nil results.

"I'm hungry," Bird said.

"That's right, Bird. They have to eat, too. Let's get an early supper and ask the servers if they've seen them."

Not to be outdone by the scope of the lobby, the restaurant had seating for 2,500 diners. Bird and Finn were stunned. Their table—and every last table —was laid with fine china and linen napkins. The maître d' handed them menus. "Your waiter will be right with you."

Bird read the menu. Twice. Three times. His brow furrowed. "Help me, Finn."

"You have to order each item separate, meat, vegetable, potatoes."

"What's tongue sandwich?"

"Probably just what it sounds like. You don't want that. They have pork chops. You like those."

"Yeah."

"Fried potatoes okay?"

Bird nodded.

"Green beans, stewed tomatoes, or green peas?"

"Do I like peas?"

"You used to. Now I think you have a little trouble keeping them on your fork."

"My hands shake."

"I know. Not your fault. Why don't you order green beans?"

The waiter came, and Finn ordered for both of them. When he brought the food—three pork chops for each of them—Finn showed him the photo. He swore he'd never seen the men. "Of course, the hotel staff numbers two thousand. They could eat here every day and I might never see them."

"Ask the other waiters to stop by our table and take a look, please. There will be a nice tip in it for you and one for the man who can name them or tell me their room number."

The offered reward brought numerous waiters to their table. Sadly, none remembered waiting on the men in the photo.

When they finished eating, Finn checked his watch. "The Fair will be closing soon. Let's see if we catch them coming back to their rooms."

The pork chops sat heavily in their stomachs, and as men accustomed to exercise, they elected to perambulate the hotel corridors. "We shall ferret out their rooms ourselves," Finn said.

Ah, but it did not play out as such. The hotel, four stories tall at the center, with two-story tall wings right and left, proved a labyrinth. Even registered hotel guests sometimes required a bellman to help them locate their rooms. Although they frequently got turned around, the boxers roamed the halls showing guests the worn clipping and frightening more than a few just by Bird's size and Finn's bearing.

A helpful bellman stopped to ask if they were lost. They were, but they only wanted to know if he knew the room number of the men in the picture. He did not, but everything about them raised the hairs on the back of his neck.

Finn and Bird took no notice of the effect they were having and continued on their mission.

Another bellman passed them, escorting a middle-age couple to their room. His arms were loaded with luggage and he said he couldn't pause to look at the newspaper they held out. At the far end of the hall, he set the bags down and opened the door. A few minutes later, he left the room and started back toward the boxers when an elderly woman threw open her door and hissed at him. He stopped in his tracks. "Yes, ma'am?"

"Young man, do you see those two rough looking characters down there? They've been lurking in the halls questioning people. I don't like the cut of them."

The big one looked like he could lay him flat with one blow. His companion might have to take two. The bellman was about to graduate high school and didn't feature spending his summer in the hospital. "What would you have me do, ma'am?"

"Why, take them to the hotel manager, of course."

He glanced down the hall and back to her. "Maybe I'll just have the manager come here."

"That will do equally well." She closed her door and turned the key in the lock.

Bird and Finn took the stairs to the next floor. That's where the manager found them a few minutes later. "This place is huge. It's easy for guests to get lost. I'll help you. May I see your room key?"

"Key?" Bird patted his pockets. "Finn, does the tent need a key?"

Finn screwed up his face. "Wrong thing to say, Champ."

"I take it you're not guests here," the manager said.

Finn showed him the news photo. "No. We're trying to find these guys' rooms."

"The Inside Inn is not a Fair exhibit. It is for the exclusive use of our guests, and I've received complaints that your presence is upsetting them. Since you're not registered here, you need to leave the property at once." He led them downstairs to the lobby and out the front door. There, he gathered the head bellman and several others, and pointed to Bird and Finn. "These two are banned from the premises. If you see them here again, call the Guard."

* * *

Friday, with no way to get back into the Inside Inn, they had no recourse, but to watch from across the road. A large portion of the fairgrounds had originally been a forest, and the Fair architects had left a generous number of trees. Finn and Bird arrived that morning on the first omnibus and set up watch under a tall tree across from the hotel driveway. Unfortunately for them, the inn was fronted by acres of lush lawn. The distance made it hard to identify guests exiting the inn until they reached Commonwealth Avenue.

Finn was standing, his back against the tree. Bird sat on the ground, legs splayed, holding something up to his eyes.

"What'cha got there, Bird?"

"Binoculars."

"Where'd you get those?"

"Bought 'em at that kiosk over there while you were in the bathroom."

"You bought them?"

"Yeah. Since we can't get in closer, I thought we'd need binoculars."

Somehow, Bird had briefly found the polestar in that vast muddle inside his head and followed it to clarity.

"That's good thinking, Bird. I'm pleased. Sometimes your brain works like its old self."

"I have my days. Do you want to try them?"

Finn did. The faces of women under their parasols and men wearing derbies jumped to him. "These are amazing."

The boxers took turns with the binoculars. Not long after, Bird shouted, "I think I see them!"

"Where?"

He handed Finn the binoculars. "See those three women surrounded by a half-dozen men? Don't the younger three men look like the ones in the paper?"

"Maybe. We'll have to wait until they get closer to be sure." Finn studied each member of the group. "The older men look like foreigners. But the young guys . . . yeah, maybe. Looks like they're flirting with those girls right in front of their escorts."

"That sounds like the kind of dandies that beguiled Bridget."

"Those three look like sisters. The older man might be their father and the others their brothers, maybe."

"Then these ladies will be all right."

"I wouldn't be too sure. The middle woman looks ready to run off with them."

Bird stood up. "They try that and we'll stop them."

"Hang on, hang on, we've got to be smart about this. We don't dare attack while they're surrounded by all those people. If those are really the men we're after, we'll follow them until we get them alone." Finn continued to study the group. "Even with binoculars, I can't tell from here if that's them for sure, but whoever those men are, they're chatting up three fancy looking tarts."

Bird bumped Finn with his shoulder. "Don't call ladies tarts. That's the kind of thing those dandies might call Bridget."

"You're right, Bird. I'm sorry. Hey! They're walking this way. No, wait. It's just the ladies and their escorts. Where'd the other three go?"

Bird took the binoculars from Finn and scanned the hotel grounds. "I don't see them. Do you think they went back in the hotel?"

"Must have forgotten something," Finn said. "They'll come out again."

* * *

The boxers remained vigilant throughout the day, yet never saw the dandies again. They took turns grabbing quick sandwiches at a kiosk two streets over. The Fair closed for the evening and they watched returning hotel guests without success. The ladies and their escorts came back, but the dandies weren't with them.

It was getting too dark to see, even with the binoculars, when two Jefferson Guards braced them. "What are you two up to?"

Finn was frustrated, hungry, and irritable. "Waiting to catch three scoundrels who dallied with the wrong girl."

"What do you plan to do with them?" one of the Guard said.

Finn threw a series of sharp jabs aimed toward the hotel. "Blacken their lecherous eyes, split their lying lips." He made an upper cut toward the sky. "Give them a good crack on the chin."

The guard took out his handcuffs.

Bird stepped between him and Finn. "No. He don't mean that. We're only to take them back to Brooklyn to marry my cousin's daughter."

"A girl can't marry three men. What are you, Mormons?"

Bird, perfectly serious, crossed himself. "Catholic."

The guard reached for Finn. "I find this one's story more likely. Come with us."

Finn came to his senses. "Wait! I was making a joke. Seriously, his innocent cousin is a good girl who waits in a nunnery for us to bring them back for nuptials. She's only marrying the one. The other two are witnesses." He fumbled in Bird's coat pocket and pulled out the clipping. "Here she's the one with them in this picture."

The guard struck a match and looked at it. "Which one is she?"

"The one in the middle between the two men," Bird said.

He blew out the match. "If what you say is true, the why are you out here spying? Why don't you just go inside and speak to them like gentlemen?"

"They're cowards," Bird said. "They disappeared this morning and we're watching for them to come back."

"They're a slippery trio," Finn said. "Have you gentlemen daughters or sisters? If one of them were sitting in a nunnery waiting on a runaway husband, wouldn't you go after him?"

The guards exchanged looks. "We might. But the World's Fair isn't the place for skullduggery. You shouldn't be out here when the Fair is closed unless you're guests at the Inside Inn."

"We're staying at Camp Lewis," Bird said.

"Then get back out there." The guard slapped his baton against the palm of his hand. "And don't let us catch you spying on the Inn again."

The boxers walked briskly back to the plaza and caught the Omnibus back to camp. During the ride back, Finn said, "You know, this morning it didn't seem like those women were meeting the men for the first time. They acted like old friends."

Bird's brief respite of clarity was fading. Perhaps he'd thought enough thoughts for one day. "Women . . . friends?"

"The Guard won't let us stake out the inn again, so we'll have to go back to searching the palaces. But if we spot those women, we follow them. I'll bet they'll lead us right to the dandies."

CHAPTER 35

Julius and Mo were already at breakfast when Bryce trudged into the restaurant looking glum.

"What's the matter with you?" Julius said. "Someone shot your dog?"

"I've learned that the Apache warriors won't arrive until Wednesday."

Mo held up a copy of the *World's Fair Official Daily Guide*. "The New Mexico exhibit opens today. You told us they're going to have a real pueblo tribe there."

Bryce brightened. "Is today Saturday, already?"

Julius nodded. "This week has really flown by."

Bryce jumped up. "Great! Let's go. Maybe that crazy Indian will be there, the one with the crutches. I'll introduce you to him."

Julius cut a bite of sausage and put it to his mouth. "I'd like to finish my breakfast first."

Mo patted Bryce's chair. "Sit down and eat. It's too early. Nothing's open yet."

"I'm too excited to eat." Bryce sat down. "I'll just have coffee."

"That's not going to calm you." Mo signaled for the waiter.

Bryce reached over to Mo's plate with his fork and stole a bite of griddle cake. "Mmmm." Next, he stabbed a link of Julius's sausage and bit into it.

"Hey!" Julius said. "Who gave you grazing rights?"

The waiter arrived. "Sirs?"

"Coffee, please," Bryce said.

"Bring him griddle cakes and sausage, too," Julius said. "And another sausage for me."

New Mexico wasn't a far walk from the inn. They'd been there on Monday, but today it was decked out in red, white, and blue bunting. The Spanish Renaissance building was a modest size compared to the grander state exhibits around it. Inside, the men split up. Mo watched a pottery demonstration while Bryce went to talk to two comely Indian maidens. Julius was reading a placard about a featured exhibit, the oldest bell in the United States. It had been cast in Spain in 1355 and hung at the Cibola mission in New Mexico by a Friar with the Coronado expedition. It certainly did look old and well rung.

A short Indian appeared out of nowhere and stood next to Julius, only coming up to his chest. "Cibola was one of the seven cities of gold."

Julius looked down at the top of the man's head and realized he was on crutches. This must be Bryce's Indian.

The man turned his leather-tan face and deep black eyes up at Julius. "This bell may contain much gold and silver. It was the custom of Spaniards to offer blessings by tossing precious metals into the molten metal during casting."

"Is that right?"

"Coronado attacked our pueblos seeking gold, yet his own people threw the stuff into a damn bell." He lifted one of his crutches and struck the side of the bell to emphasize his point. It made a sharp clang.

Two white men rushed over. "Jesse, stop that. You can't be in here, you know that. Go outside and wait with the others."

Bryce rushed over from the other side of the room while Jesse was being escorted out. "What happened?"

"I think I just met your crazy Indian."

"You did? Where is he?"

"Two men just threw him out."

Bryce started for the door. "Find Mo. He'll want to meet him, too."

Julius found Mo at a pottery exhibit and dragged him away. Outside, a large circle of Pueblo tribe members were just starting a native dance. The women Bryce had been talking with hurried past them and took their places. After a time, Jesse broke through the circle and stood in the middle on one leg, flapping his crutches, just as Bryce had described the other night. Two of his tribesmen left their places, picked him up under his arms and carried him outside the circle.

When they set him down, Jesse waved his crutches at them and made several angry cries, "Caw, caw."

Bryce headed for Jesse. Julius and Mo followed.

"Hello, again," Bryce said. "Do you remember me? These are my friends Mo and Julius."

Jesse stopped cawing and tilted his head like a bird for a long moment. "Bryce! My brother, come, I will show you something."

Julius, Mo, and Bryce followed Jesse around the side of the building to a stone archway designed to look like the entrance to a mine. This was bound to be more interesting than anything going on in the state exhibit. Without hesitating, Jesse hobbled inside and looked back, waiting for them to catch up.

The interior was a working exhibition of turquoise mining and lapidary. "This is a reproduction of the Porterfield Mine, which is reputed to produce the finest turquoise in the world," Jesse said. When the lapidary demonstration finished, he said, "Now, we'll go to the Palace of Mines and Metallurgy down the street. There you will see how these stones are made into Native jewelry." He turned and made for the exit, lifting both feet at once and swinging forward on his crutches in a comical gait.

The men followed him outside. On the way to the palace, Julius asked, "Is Jesse a typical Indian name?"

Jesse spat on the road. "It's a typical *Indian School* name."

"What do you mean?"

"They take young boys from the pueblo and send them to schools to learn to be like white men. Then when Sam McCowan needs tribal dancers for the World's Fair, they put us back in feathers and beads and ship us to St. Louis."

"Who did this?" Bryce said.

"Superintendent of the Chilocco Indian Training School, now director of the St. Louis Indian exhibits." Jesse spat again. "Exhibits, as though human beings were museum objects."

Julius saw Bryce ball up his fists and knew he was about to lose his temper. But by then, they'd arrived at the Palace of Mines and Metallurgy, just as a fifty-six-foot-tall statue of Vulcan was being dedicated.

"This is the largest cast iron statue in the world," said the man with a deep-south drawl leading the ceremony, "and the symbol of Birmingham, Alabama, reflecting its roots in the iron and steel industry."

The giant Vulcan made Julius feel like an ant. He barely came up to its ankles. The Roman god's left hand held a hammer resting on an anvil. In his right hand he held aloft the newly forged tip for a spear. Fierce eyes gazed from his bearded head. On his front, the statue was covered by a blacksmith's apron, but as they walked around him to enter the palace, Julius noticed the buttocks were bare. Only a god would dare to forge iron in the buff.

Inside, Jesse led them to the New Mexico exhibit where they watched turquoise being cut, polished, and set in silver jewelry. Then two men from the tribe approached Jesse. "Hey, Crazy Bird, you need to return to the state pavilion."

Jesse tucked his crutches under his armpits and clasped Bryce's arms. "I am needed elsewhere. Carry on."

The men started to lead him away, when he turned and limped back. From under his shirt he slipped three rectangles of polished turquoise, each about one by two inches in size. He surreptitiously pressed one into each of their palms under the guise of a handshake. "Here, take this."

The men from New Mexico led Jesse from the palace.

Julius opened his palm and glanced at the stone. "Do you think he swiped these from the mine?"

"With Jesse, there's no telling."

"Should we give them back?"

"To whom? We don't even know that they're stolen. Returning his gift might offend him. Just put it in your pocket and be grateful."

Since they were already in a palace they'd not previously visited, they spent a good part of the afternoon exploring the exhibits. Despite its dreary name, the palace was distinguished by a lavish use of color.

Julius found the machinery ingenious, particularly the polishing drum run by a small electric motor. Mo liked the geology showcases exhibiting minerals and semi-precious gemstones. All three of them were impressed with Canada's exhibit of gold dust and nuggets worth over $50,000.

They exhausted Mines and Metallurgy and moved on to Louisiana, which exhibited a sculpture of Lot's wife made from an eight-hundred-fifty-pound block of salt. Julius laughed. "You think they carved that or found her that way out in the desert?"

"If that's really Ado," Mo said, "no wonder Lot left her behind. Even Sampson couldn't tote an eight-hundred-fifty-pound wife on his back."

"Ado?" Julius said.

"Yeah, the name the Rabbi's gave her. That's not in your Bible?"

"I don't know. To tell you the truth, I barely read the Jesus parts."

Elsewhere in the same exhibit, a column of sulfur had been shaped into Mephistopheles. His sharp features and demonic eyes spoke volumes. "I believe Louisiana's trying to send us a warning," Mo said.

Julius nodded. "Yeah, they seem to have a theme going here."

"I never cared much for people trying to push their idea of what's wicked," Bryce said. "How about we head back to New Mexico?"

Exiting the palace, they found themselves on the avenue that led to the Fine Arts Palace and Bryce stopped them. "We've come out the opposite side. New Mexico is south, toward our hotel. Turn here at Germany and we'll cut between those buildings behind it."

Julius and Mo followed him around Germany's pavilion. Bryce turned onto a road that led back to the state pavilions. They passed Oregon and could see Texas ahead, when a sign caught Julius's eye. House of Hoo Hoo? "Wait up, Bryce." He pointed. "We've got to find out what a House of Hoo Hoo is."

Bryce turned in his tracks, impatient, yet intrigued. "I'll bet it's not what you think it is."

"Can't count it out. This fair has everything."

The building resembled a one-story wood house with a row of attic dormers across the front roof. They entered what was essentially a clubhouse with walls of different types of veneer, a large round table, and wicker chairs. A gentleman about forty-five years of age came into the room. "You're not members?"

"Not that we're aware of," Mo said.

"No," Julius said. "We're merely curious. What's a Hoo Hoo?"

Bryce smirked.

"The Concatenated Order of Hoo Hoo, a fraternal organization composed of lumbermen, sawmill men, and lumber newspapermen."

"So, no women?" Bryce said.

"We have one. She joined before we had a rule against it."

Julius didn't care for organizations that excluded females, be they social or political. It was one of his gripes against the Catholic Church. He knew first-hand women were every bit equal to men. Take Lily, for example. He disagreed with her goal, but admired her perseverance.

Julius looked around the room. "But why Hoo Hoo?"

"It comes from the lumberjack's shout."

Julius had never met a lumberjack and didn't know if that was true. "I always thought they shouted 'Tim-berrr!' At least in stories."

The man looked sheepish. "You're right, of course. Hoo Hoo was an expression coined by one of our founders, Bolling Arthur Johnson, to describe a peculiar tuft of hair, greased and twisted to a point, atop the head of a bald man. But it quickly became a catch phrase among lumbermen for anything unusual or out of the ordinary."

Mo laughed. "The first Hoo Hoo's given name was Bolling?"

"Yes, but our first Grand Snark was Charles McCarer, whose hair had inspired Johnson to come up with the phrase Hoo Hoo in the first place."

"Grand what?" Bryce said.

"Snark. Our founders wanted to be unconventional, the very essence of Hoo Hoo. In a spirit of fun, names of our organization's offices were taken from Lewis Carroll's poem, *The Hunting of the Snark*."

Mo winked at Bryce, and said, "Does that mean members hunt the Grand Snark?"

Their informant didn't get the joke. "No, he's appointed by the Supreme Nine."

"Nine?" Bryce said.

"Yes, the Senior Hoo Hoo, the Junior Hoo Hoo, Scrivenoter, Bojum, Jabberwock—that position used to be called the Bandersnatch, but we changed it to Jabberwok."

"Naturally," Mo said. "People might get the wrong idea if you told them you were bandersnatching the Hoo Hoo."

Julius bit his lip, trying not to laugh.

"Oh, *I'm* not the Jabberwock. I'm just a regular member watching the club-house."

Bryce looked at him dead serious. "So, what do we have to do to join?"

"Are you in forestry or lumber?"

Julius couldn't contain himself and burst out laughing.

The man looked unperturbed. "I see you fellows are mocking us. Actually, that's a very Hoo Hoo thing to do."

"Mo, Bryce, I think we ought to get the Hoo Hoo out of here."

The three of them, laughing so hard they staggered, made their way down the road toward New Mexico. By the time they arrived, the Indian dances were over, and there was no sign of Jesse.

Julius looked at his watch. "It's suppertime, and we sailed right through lunch again. Let's go back to the inn and eat."

CHAPTER 36

"Julius, help me move your trunk," Mo said.

"What for?"

"Mine's underneath it." Since their suitcases contained all the clothes they needed for the Fair, they'd told the porters to stack their trunks in the corner. It'd been a good plan until Mo needed his art supplies.

Julius shot the cuffs of his suit coat. "Ask Bryce. I don't want my suit to get wrinkled."

Mo glanced at him. "Pretty dapper. Off to church?"

"Nah, got a date with Emily. You remember, we rode the chutes with her."

Bryce finished tying his tie and turned from the mirror. "You told me it was Catherine, the soap fairy."

"I'm meeting her at six. Her mother is cooking us dinner."

"Well, better not call either one the other's name. You know women hate that."

"I won't."

Bryce gave him a lecherous grin. "Are you trying to hog all the women in St. Louis?"

"Just the ones that want me. Although . . . that does seem to be most of them."

Mo smiled. "Okay. Bryce, help me lift Julius's trunk off from mine."

"Hey, I'm dressed up, too."

"Where are you going?"

"Since it's Sunday, and the Fair is closed, I figured I'd go into St. Louis and see if I can meet Scott Joplin. Do you want to come along?"

"No, I'm going to stay here and paint. Help me get to my trunk before you leave."

Bryce complied without enthusiasm, and as soon as the task was done, brushed imaginary dust from his sleeves and left with Julius.

Mo unbuckled the two leather straps and unfastened the hasp. He raised the lid, lifted out the upper tray and set it aside. In the depths of the trunk he located a blank canvas, and a rucksack containing his palette and tubes of paint. Digging deeper, he found the bundle of his best brushes carefully rolled up in newspaper. He'd left his easel in New York, so he went to the hotel loading dock and cobbled a few strips of wood from a skid into a makeshift tripod. It was kind of hefty, but it would do.

He hung the rucksack strap over his shoulder and tucked the homemade easel under his arm. Grabbing the canvas, he made his way out of the inn, across its property, and slipped into the fairgrounds, unchallenged.

Mo walked northwest toward the cascades. He decided he'd paint a picture of the beautiful Festival Hall and Grand Basin. A smile came to his lips as he passed the Hoo Hoo building. It was closed, as were all the exhibits, and he had the streets to himself.

Unfortunately, when he arrived at the spot he had in mind, he saw that the cascades were not running. Still, the ornate structure reflected in the surrounding pools made a lovely scene. It would do nicely.

He had just gotten set up and squeezed paint onto his palette when two Jefferson Guards approached. "Fair's closed."

"I know. I'm staying at the Inside Inn. I just came over here to paint."

"There's a rule, though, no tripods allowed. It's the exclusive right of the photography concessionaire."

The second officer turned to his partner. "I think that restriction only applies to cameras, not painters."

"I don't make the rules, just enforce them. I can't risk my job splitting hairs over what a tripod's used for."

The second guard turned to Mo. "Look, why don't you go to the Kodak Pavilion tomorrow morning and speak to Mr. Rau. Ask him if the rule only concerns cameras."

Mo showed them his palette. "But I already spread out wet paint."

"That's not our problem," the first guard said. "You're not even supposed to be in here today. Please return to the inn."

Well, luckily he hadn't started the canvas, or he'd have two wet things to carry. He packed his paint and brushes in the rucksack, slung it over his shoulder, collapsed the tripod, and carried everything as best as he could without getting paint on his clothes. The guards followed him at a distance until he turned onto the inn grounds. At the front door, he looked for a porter, but there weren't any.

Rose came out the door, almost bumping into him. "Oh, hi, Mo."

Mo nodded. "Hello, Rose. I'd tip my hat, but my hands are full."

"Let me help you with that." She reached for the palette and canvas.

"Careful, there's wet paint. I wouldn't want you to get any on your dress."

"Okay. I'll carry your easel."

"It might be too heavy."

"Don't be ridiculous." She freed it from under his elbow where he held it pinched against his body, then tried to hide her surprise at how heavy it was.

"Uh, okay, thanks. You're sure it's not too much? I could wait here while you find a bellman."

"No. I've got it. Where's your room?"

"Upstairs, fourth floor. Won't Lily be upset if she sees us together?"

"She's not here. She and Violet have gone on something called a 'trolley party.'"

"With the men we met at the Palace of Fine Arts?"

Rose snorted in a most unladylike manner. "No. It turns out the Lord of Bath currently has a wife, whose name, by coincidence, is also Violet. My sisters have moved on."

"But not you?"

"I was weary of the game before it began."

When they reached his door, Mo struggled to balance the wet paint while trying to fish his key from his pocket.

"Can I help?"

"The key is in my right pocket . . . Let me set these on the floor, while I—"

"Just hold still." Rose leaned the easel again the wall and slid her hand into his pants.

He felt himself swell.

She didn't fumble around, just quickly pulled out the key and put it into the lock. It turned with a click that he was sure echoed down the corridor, but glancing both directions, he saw the hall was empty. He rushed in, laid everything on the credenza, and turned to retrieve the easel.

Rose had brought it in with her. "I see you have a suite, too."

Mo grabbed stuff from his trunk he'd left strewn about and stowed it back inside. "Sorry it's a mess. These trunks are usually stacked out of the way. I just left everything lay when I went out."

"Where are Julius and Bryce?"

"They rode the streetcar into St. Louis for the day."

Rose laughed. "Be funny if they rode the same trolley as my sisters."

Mo turned serious. "We really don't understand what's going on with you three. You know, we had such a congenial time on the train and all of you were so . . . amorous. Yet every time we run into you now, we're treated like muddy dogs about to get dirt on your skirts."

Her eyes welled up. "I don't feel that way."

"Then please . . . What's going on?"

"Lily's afraid one of you will let slip about our free-love beliefs."

"We're the soul of discretion."

"Even Bryce, when he's trying to be funny?"

"Well . . ."

"Lily wants the men we meet here to think we're chaste."

"But you're not."

"No, but we kind of have to be. We don't want to attract foreigners who think American girls are easy. Lily wants them to want us for the right reason."

"Your father's money?"

"Well, yes. Then, ideally, once she's winnowed the field to those who need us, we can choose who we love, or are likely to love."

"You know this plan sounds absolutely absurd."

"Didn't I say I was tired of the game? But it is done all the time these days."

Mo shook his head. "It's just difficult for me to reconcile the lovely person I know you to be with this pandering after rank and title."

Rose stepped forward and hugged him. "You're sweet." She broke their embrace. "I'm glad you don't hate me, but the other thing, the marriage part, you really don't understand. It's different for women. In most states we can't vote. In some we can't open a bank account in our own name."

"And you think it's any different in Europe?"

"It's not worse. And the suffragettes are trying to get voting rights in England."

"They haven't won."

"Not yet," Rose said. "But Lily believes being a duchess or countess commands a lot more respect than being a New Jersey housewife—even a rich one."

"I can't disagree with that."

"And it's not like we never intended to marry. We just want it to be our decision."

Mo turned his head away. "For your father."

Rose put her hand on his face and forced him to look at her. "Father has been wonderful to us. If our choice of husbands enhances his legacy without diminishing our independence, then we are all better for it. The only real purpose of marriage is continuity of family. Women can have love without wedlock, but you cannot carry forward a name or title without it."

Mo pressed his lips together and kept silent.

"But in the meantime." Rose leaned into him and kissed him hard.

Oh, my.

When she let him breathe, he hung a 'do not disturb' sign outside, turned the lock, and shoved his trunk across the door for good measure.

CHAPTER 37

Julius, with Emily on his arm, waited at the trolley stop. A wisp of her blond hair slipped from her bun and strayed down her neck. He reached over and touched it. She pulled away and glanced nervously in both directions.

"A lock of your hair came loose," he said. "That's all."

"Thank you." She tucked the wayward strand under her hat.

Emily's behavior confused him. The woman who brazenly held onto his thigh during their boat ride on the Pike had become Miss Prim in the bright Sunday afternoon.

She stepped closer and hooked her gloved hand in the crook of his elbow. "It's a shame you have to leave so soon."

"I told you, I'll be glad to see you home."

"Thank you, but no. I take this line to and from work every day. It's perfectly safe for a lone woman."

"But a gentleman should see a lady home. It's chivalrous." He'd deliberately cut their date short, so he'd have time to accompany her wherever she lived for whatever she fancied and still get to Catherine's by six. Since she'd declined his offer, he'd have an extra hour to kill. Well, that's the way the whole afternoon had gone.

He'd arrived at the Hotel Jefferson a little before one. Entering the lobby, he glanced at the check-in clerk standing behind the long walnut counter and felt relieved it wasn't the same man on duty as before. Although there was no reason he should feel chagrin—the whole mix up was Bryce's fault.

Emily was primly perched on the lobby divan, wearing a wide-brimmed white hat trimmed with pink flowers. Her gloved hand rested on a matching parasol. Julius gave her a warm smile, and she stood. She was wearing an ankle-length skirt of pink wool and a frilly white V-neck blouse that revealed her creamy skin. An unfortunately large bow hid her cleavage.

Julius tipped his hat. "Good afternoon. You look lovely."

"Thank you." She looked at the large lobby clock. "You're early."

"I didn't want to be late. Shall we go?"

Her blue eyes met his. "What did you have in mind?"

He knew what he had in mind but wasn't about to blurt it out in the middle of the lobby. "I thought I'd take you to lunch, and then we'll decide where to go after that. Is there a restaurant you can recommend?"

"We can eat here, in the hotel restaurant."

"Really? I can't imagine you'd want to spend your day off in the place where you work all week."

"Ah, but our chef is the best of any downtown. Not to mention the boon of not having to clean up the meal afterwards."

Julius considered. Emily might have another reason. Perhaps the staff had quarters here? She'd never said where she lived. "If that's truly what you want."

The maître d' greeted Emily by name and seated them at a nice table in a heavily trafficked part of the restaurant. Over the course of their meal, scores of Emily's coworkers managed to pass by. Julius began to feel like a peacock in a guinea pen.

When the bill came, Emily snatched it and began fumbling with the strings of her purse. "Lunch will be my treat."

"Thank you, but the way I was brought up, the gentleman pays."

"Does the gentleman have an employee discount?"

Julius nodded. "All right, but I'm repaying you as soon as we leave."

If Emily had a room in the hotel, she hadn't taken him there. Perhaps she shared it with the women who had accompanied her to the Pike. So they'd spent the remainder of the afternoon promenading the neighboring avenues and a nearby park with dozens of Sunday strollers.

Mentally, Julius shrugged. The afternoon with Emily hadn't turned out as she'd led him to believe. Oh well, there was still Catherine. But he kept his hopes small. Catherine's mother would be there, after all.

The streetcar rumbled toward them. The driver gave two sharp tugs on the cord and the bell clanged twice. Emily's eyes widened. "Oh, I meant to tell you. The night of the big rainstorm, two men came to the hotel asking about you and your friends."

Julius swallowed his surprise. "We're they Irish?"

"I don't know, but one of them was big as Goliath. That's even what the other man called him. Are they acquaintances of yours?"

Julius managed to feign nonchalance. Damn Bryce. "Nah."

"So, you don't know the men?"

"Never met them," he said truthfully. "I wonder what they wanted."

The streetcar came to a stop. Julius leaned down to see if Emily would allow a kiss. She grabbed his hand, shook it, and turned to board. At the last second, she pulled down the brim on one side of her hat to block the view of others and gave him a peck on the cheek.

Her blue eyes sparked. "Look for me on the Pike some night. I can't say when, but soon."

What'd she expect him to do, go there every night and wait for her?

"Of course," he said.

The bell rang again, and Julius waved goodbye as the streetcar pulled away. Once it was gone, he walked two blocks south to the stop for the line that, according to Catherine's directions, ran past her mother's home.

Had two Irishmen followed them to St. Louis? Well, if they did, they were looking at the wrong hotel. But still, it was disturbing to think they were out there. He would have to have a talk with Bryce.

But not now. Catherine awaited.

* * *

Rose lay on Mo's bed next to him in a puddle of sunlight. A cardinal pecked at his reflection in the windowpane and flew away.

"We forgot to close the drapes," Mo said.

Rose snuggled closer. "It doesn't matter. No one outside can see into rooms on the higher floors."

Her hairpins had come out and her coiffure had fallen apart. She didn't mind. Such was the price of love.

His fingertip idly traced a line down her sternum. "After those . . . calisthenics, should I take you to lunch?"

"I'm not a bit hungry, but if you are . . ."

"Me neither, but I thought it polite to offer."

She rolled onto her back, spread her arms, and gazed at the ceiling. "I'm completely content."

He sighed. "Me, too."

"I would like to see your painting, if you don't mind."

"Painting?"

"The one you were carrying when we ran into each other."

"Oh, that. It's literally nothing—a blank canvas."

"Are you being modest?"

"No. It's actually blank. I hadn't even started before two guards ousted me from the fairgrounds."

"Why'd they do that?"

"Some rule about photographers having exclusive rights to tripods or something. I have to wait until tomorrow to get permission. But today was my day to paint. I don't know when I'll have another chance."

Rose turned on her side and looked at him. "You can paint me."

"You'd pose for me?"

She kissed him on the tip of his nose. "I just said I would."

"I'd be grateful. I planned to paint a scene with Festival Hall in the background, but this will be even better." His eyes glazed over, and she surmised he was already setting the scene in his imagination. "We'll find a spot on the inn lawn where the roof of a palace can be seen in the distance with you in the foreground."

"Not what I had in mind," she said. "After all, if we did that, I'd have to put on clothes."

"Well, wherever I painted you, you'd still have to put—oh."

Rose reached down and pulled the sheet up. "Don't get too excited. I won't let you paint me completely nude, but I'd be willing to pose draped, like those classical goddesses in the Fine Arts Palace."

His eyes widened. "You're serious?"

She nodded. "As long as you promise not to let anyone see it before we leave St. Louis."

He frowned. "Well, Bryce and Julius share this suite. They're bound to notice it."

The thought that they might see a painting of her disrobed created pleasant warmth in her abdomen. "They're okay. I meant not my sisters or the men we're with."

Mo chuckled. "I can't imagine either of your sisters visiting our room."

"I did."

"Point taken. I'll do my best to keep it out of sight. But I can't store it in my trunk until the paint dries, and that takes days."

Rose pulled the sheet from the bed, wrapped it around her and shimmied over to the divan like a Japanese Geisha. There, she stretched out in a pose she'd seen in the French gallery exhibit. She untangled a portion of her hair with her fingers and let it fall over her bare shoulder.

Mo threw on his shirt, quickly set up his easel, grabbed his palette, and began painting with workmanlike concentration.

It was . . . more businesslike than she expected. She watched his eyes study her, turn to the canvas, then to her again. Occasionally, he'd glance at his palette to load more paint on his brush. But he always came back to her. His eyes, tracing the outline of her draped figure, made her feel as if he were seeing through the sheet.

Rose discovered that she quite liked posing in this state of partial undress. She'd never done anything like this before. Oh, a portrait once, with her sisters in décolleté dresses revealing plentiful cleavage. But posing for the oily-haired photographer only excited her when he'd pulled gently on her sleeves and said, "Let's bare a bit more shoulder."

Mo continued to work steadily. No longer her lover, just the artist and his brush, moving as one.

The next time Mo's eyes turned to the canvas, Rose gave a little tug on the edge of the sheet, causing it to slide down and expose her left breast. Let's see what this does to his concentration.

When Mo looked back up, his eyes widened. "Uh . . . your drape has slipped off on that side."

She glanced down. "Has it? Oh, goodness." She slowly pulled the sheet up to where it just covered her nipple and then tucked it in place behind her. "Thank you. Showing my private bits would be too risqué."

"Of course."

The aftereffect gave rise to warm sensual delight spreading upward from her loins to her breasts, and into her heart. She yearned for him to finish painting so they could make love again.

And that was curious. Less than an hour ago they'd lain together, and he'd seen every inch of her. Now, being half-clothed in a sheet aroused her. Or was it being the object of his close observation? Her nipples grew hard and jutted the fabric out. She wondered if he was catching that with his paintbrush.

She moved her leg far enough that it poked out from the bottom of the sheet and exposed a generous amount of her calf.

Mo set down his brush and palette, walked over, and put the sheet back in place. "You have to remain still to keep the folds in the fabric the same. I've almost finished the basic outline, just a few minutes longer."

His touch set her spinning. He returned to his easel, but she grew flush and was about to throw off the sheet entirely and drag him to the bed. When he said they could take a break, that's exactly what she did.

Later, deep in afterglow, she marveled at what the act of showing herself had wrought. Still, a woman had to be careful. "I said it'd be okay if Bryce and Julius saw the painting, but please make them pledge not to tell anybody about it. Especially Bryce. Especially not to my sisters."

"I promise."

Suddenly, a key clicked in the lock, and the door banged into the trunk.

"What the hell?" Bryce said from the hallway.

Rose instinctively pulled the sheet up to her neck.

Mo hurriedly put on his pants, ran to the door, and said through the crack, "Didn't you read the sign hanging on the doorknob? Come back later."

"This place stinks of turpentine. Are you painting?"

"I am. Go downstairs and wait for me."

"Is Julius back?"

"I haven't seen him. Now, go. I'll come down and join you in fifteen minutes." Mo pushed the door shut.

Rose was already getting dressed.

Mo grabbed the sheet she'd left on the divan, spread it across the bed, and drew the cover over the whole works. It wouldn't fool anyone for a minute, but she didn't have time to show him how to make a bed properly. She had to get her hair into some semblance of presentability before she could walk through the hotel corridors.

She found her hat and donned it. That should cover up any hair still amiss.

Mo scooted the trunk away from the door and reached for the doorknob.

"Not yet," she said. "First, I want to see what we've done."

She stepped behind his easel, looked at the canvas, and laughed with relief. He'd started at her feet and worked his way up, giving great attention and detail to every fold and wrinkle in the fabric, but her head was only a vague outline. Certainly there wasn't enough there for anyone to identify the model. "I take back what I said before. It won't matter if anyone sees it."

"If you hadn't wanted to make love a second time, it might have a face."

"Are you complaining?"

"Certainly not." He took her in his arms and kissed her. "Besides, I'll know it's you."

"Then put it by your bed, so you think of me at night."

He kissed her again. "I never fed you lunch. Will you join me and Bryce for dinner? He's waiting downstairs."

She caressed his cheek. "Thank you, but I better not. Lily and Violet are possibly back and looking for me. That could be awkward, and I don't want Lily saying anything to break my mood." She pressed her lips to his and her body melted into him. When their lips parted, she sighed. "This has been my best day at the Fair yet."

CHAPTER 38

Catherine's mother's house was smaller than its Victorian neighbors. Trimmed with a modest amount of gingerbread—just enough to establish that it belonged on that street, with a wide porch spanning the front holding two rocking chairs and a swing hung from the rafters on chains. Two terracotta flowerpots sitting on either side of the door held colorful pansies. A large dog with floppy ears and a gray muzzle lay with his chin on his paws.

Julius put his foot on the bottom step, and the dog opened his droopy eyes but didn't rise.

"It's all right, boy. The ladies are expecting me."

Julius continued up the stairs, and when he reached the porch, he bent down and patted the dog's head. "Sorry, to disturb your Sunday nap."

The dog clambered up on arthritic hips, and, wagging his tail, pushed his head under Julius's palm. Julius scratched behind the dog's ears and knocked on the door.

The door flew inward, as if someone had been waiting with their hand on the knob. Catherine opened the screen door and smiled broadly. "Please, come in."

Julius removed his hat and stepped inside. The dog started to follow, but Catherine pushed him back out and closed the screen door. "Not you, Bowser." She shut the front door, latched it, and leaned back against it, drawing Julius into her embrace. She was much shorter than he, so she laced her fingers in his hair and bent his head down to meet her kiss. His lips softened and melted into hers.

Now this was how he'd hoped his Sunday would turn out.

"I've wanted to do that since we met," she murmured.

"What's your mother going to say?"

Catherine's eyes crinkled as a smile radiated throughout her whole being. "As it happens, Mother was called away suddenly to help deliver a baby. She apologizes for not meeting you, but she has left our dinner prepared. I only need to set it on the table."

Julius cocked his head. "And we're alone?"

"Why not? I'm a grown woman. Who I entertain in my own home is nobody's business."

Julius grinned. "Besides, you have Bowser to protect you."

She laughed. "There's that, too." She kissed him again and let it linger. "Are you very, very hungry?"

"How soon will your mother be back?"

"Oh, I'd imagine not before tomorrow morning. You know how birthing goes."

Actually, he didn't, but he wouldn't argue.

"In that case, we could put off dinner, if you have something you'd rather do first."

As it happened, she did.

* * *

Rose turned the key and entered their room.

"Oh, there you are," Lily said. "I wondered where you'd gone. Have you eaten?"

"No, I . . . waited until you two were back, so we could dine together."

"Good, but let's have a late supper. We need your help first."

Violet said, "Rose, you're positively glowing."

Darn. They knew her too well. "I am? I suppose that's an effect of a day without feeling constantly on the hunt."

"Well, that's what we're here for," Lily said. "Now, I want to come up with a new look for Violet—something that will make her look a bit older. A more grownup hairdo might do the trick. Don't you agree?"

Rose studied Violet for a moment. "What if she wore her hair up instead of wearing it down? It would show off her lovely neck, and maybe a little lower cut dress that lets her jewels stand out."

Lily nodded. "She should wear one of our good necklaces. Which do you think, the emeralds or the sapphire solitaire?"

"Oh, definitely the latter, she's got those lovely violet eyes, and the sapphire will really compliment them."

"You're right. See what you can do with her hair."

Rose unpinned her hat and set it on the table.

Violet's eyebrows shot up. "Rose, whatever happened? Your hair . . ."

"My hat came off. I did the best I could to put it right before I crossed the hotel lobby."

"Were you outside?" Violet said.

"Briefly." She wasn't exactly lying. That's where she'd run into Mo.

"A positive disaster," Lily said. "You'll have to fix your own hair as well as Violet's before we can go to dinner."

Rose shrugged. Why make such a big deal about it? Didn't they fix their hair every day? She picked up a brush and began work on Violet. "So, how was your trolley party? Did it go well?"

"Lily thinks these lords might be the ones," Violet said.

Rose looked to Lily for confirmation, and she nodded. "They didn't tell us that their estates were in desperate straits and we didn't tell them that we're looking for titles, but I think both parties have an idea where the other stands."

Rose set the brush down and began gathering Violet's hair into a tight chignon. "So now we bring out the good jewelry to let them know we have money?"

Violet nodded. "Lily thinks it's time."

Rose gripped her head. "Hold still."

"You'll meet them tomorrow," Lily said. "We're going to the Fair with them. They're bringing somebody for you, too. We don't know who he is or his rank, but I believe he's in that book of peerage Mother bought."

Did she have to? She'd much rather spend the day with Mo and his friends.

Lily selected a dress from the wardrobe and held it up to her in the mirror. "We'll wear our best clothes and our better jewelry. They'll get the message."

* * *

It was nearly nine before Catherine served Julius supper. After dessert, she took his hand. "I wish I could keep you all night, but I don't know how early in the morning Mother will return."

"Are you saying she wouldn't approve?"

"You're kidding, right? This is St. Louis, not Gomorrah."

"Yet she left you alone, knowing a man was coming over."

"I told her you were a very nice man."

"I am."

"Well, there you are, then. Anyhow, she had the whole meal prepared and didn't want me to cancel with you already on your way here."

"I'm glad for that. Please tell her I enjoyed her cooking immensely." He kissed Catherine. "And her daughter doubly so."

Catherine kissed him back. "I wish we had more time, but the final streetcar of the night comes in about ten minutes. If you miss it, it's a long walk to the fairgrounds."

He stood up. She walked him to the door, handed him his hat, and kissed him for a long minute. "Come by and visit me at work one day."

"Gladly. What time is your lunch break? I could take you out somewhere."

"That's a lovely thought, but I only have thirty minutes."

"Oh." Not enough time to take her to his room. "Well, all right, I'll bring box lunches and we can picnic in those gardens in front of the palace."

She kissed him again. "Oh, Julius, you're the man I hoped you would be. Yes, let's do that."

"You haven't told me what time you get lunch."

"Half-past one. Tomorrow?"

"Er . . . I don't know what my friends have planned for tomorrow, but one day this week. It'll be a surprise. You work every day, right?"

"Right. Okay, surprise me. Now, you better hurry. I hear the streetcar rumbling this way."

Julius kissed her again and dashed down the porch steps. Bowser lifted his head and yawned.

CHAPTER 39

Bryce stirred his coffee, watching the black liquid swirl, oblivious to Julius and Mo's discussion of which palaces they'd visit next. Their fortnight was quickly coming to an end, the days cascading away like the waterfalls in front of Festival Hall. He wasn't ready to go home yet and not at all sure if they could. He'd failed to ask his dad to intervene in the Irish matter, though he'd let Mo and Julius think he had. What if they arrived at Grand Central Terminal to a reception committee of Bridget's family?

"I'm going to ask Mr. Statler if he will extend our stay," Bryce said.

Mo closed the guidebook and set it aside. "For how long?"

"I don't know. But we underestimated the size of this Fair. At the rate we're going, we can't possibly see the rest of it in the next five days."

"Actually, six days, if you count today," Mo said.

"Still, not near enough time, wouldn't you agree?"

Mo nodded. "We've barely seen half of the Fine Arts Palace."

Now Bryce just had to convince Julius. "There are eight more palaces we've yet to visit, and they're bringing the Apaches from Fort Sill this week—Geronimo, too."

"I'm not that excited to meet Geronimo," Julius said. "Though I wish I had another week."

Bryce winked. "You mean another weekend?"

Julius grinned in acknowledgement, then grew serious. "Which reminds me, Bryce, Emily told me a strange thing yesterday about two men asking for us at the Hotel Jefferson—one was called Goliath."

"Sharp's staying at the Jefferson," Mo said. "Could be the artists he was going to introduce to us."

Julius cocked his head. "Sharp ever mention an artist named Goliath?"

"That doesn't mean there isn't one," Bryce said. "As Mo pointed out, we haven't seen half of the art palace."

Julius furrowed his brow. "They didn't sound like artists. Bryce, should we be worried that someone followed us here?"

"I'm not," Bryce said. "If I recall my Bible, Goliath wasn't too bright, and David knocked him on his ass."

"Just because David outsmarted him, doesn't mean Goliath wouldn't have hurt David if he could have got his hands on him," Julius said.

"Forget them," Bryce said. "We don't even know if these guys were Irish."

Mo nodded. "Surely, Senator Holloway has taken care of that situation. Right, Bryce? The question on the table is, should we stay here longer?"

Bryce breathed a sigh of relief. *Thank you, Mo.*

"I have a job," Julius said.

Bryce waved dismissively. "Send them a wire. Tell them you'll be back when you get back."

"That's not how it's done, Bryce. A boss gets a message like that, he'll reply not to bother coming back at all."

"Tell them all the scientific stuff you're seeing will help you do your job better."

"That's even almost true." Julius chewed his lip. "Okay, I'll ask if I can stretch it another week."

Well, a week was better than nothing. Give the situation back home time to resolve.

"But can we afford it?" Julius said.

"We'd have to economize." Mo said. "No more dinners on the Pike."

"The Palaces of Agriculture and Horticultural offer free food samples," Bryce said. "We haven't visited either palace yet."

Mo thumbed through the Fair guidebook, stopping on a page. "Minnesota is giving out free baked beans, pickles, and bread and butter for lunch."

Bryce made a face. "We've visited the state exhibits. Except for New Mexico, there wasn't much that interested me."

"I agree," Julius said. "If we're staying longer to see the other palaces, then that's where we should concentrate our efforts. You guys have yet to see the Palace of Electricity. I swear, electricity is the future."

Bryce turned to Mo. "Then we're agreed?"

"Of course, I'd like to see it all before we leave. Talk to Mr. Statler and ask if he'll let us stay on."

Bryce felt the tension leave his body. It didn't solve the Irish problem back home, but it postponed having to ask his father to fix it. And even if men had followed them—and that didn't seem likely—they were asking at the wrong hotel. The Inside Inn was safe.

* * *

The New Yorkers attempted frugality, grazing free samples wherever companies or countries offered them, saving their pocket money. But all did not go as planned. Upon returning to the inn that evening, Bryce went to see Mr. Statler and found the hotel staff distraught. A boy had been killed and Statler scalded when a coffee pot exploded. He was battling for his life and no one could tell Bryce when he might return or who would be in charge of the inn until then.

"Inquire again next week," he was told.

That'd be too late. He'd have to speak to someone in authority tomorrow or Wednesday at the latest. They were supposed to check out on Sunday.

The next morning, Bryce went to the inn's business office and persisted until he got a meeting with the temporary manager. He was a slight man with a worried brow who repeatedly wrung his hands. Good. Bryce could use that.

"I don't know how Mr. Statler was able to get you that suite in the first place," he said, "but I can't extend your stay by even a single day. We are completely sold out, and people who have paid cash deposits in advance are arriving daily."

"But Elsworth Statler and my father are friends." Not exactly, but not quite a lie, either.

"I'm sure that's true. Let me give you the hospital address where your father can send Mr. Statler wishes for a speedy recovery."

Shoot. Bryce pressed further, but the manager, despite his nervousness, was unyielding on the point of delaying their departure. Reluctantly, he returned to their room where Julius and Mo were waiting to leave for the Fair. "Sorry, we can't keep our suite beyond Sunday. I tried. I really did."

Julius patted his shoulder. "I'm sure you gave it your best shot."

"We'll just have to squeeze in as much as we can in the remaining days," Mo said.

"This will help." Julius pointed to the Tuesday Official Daily Guide. "The Intramural Railroad opens today. It runs completely around the perimeter of the grounds, making seventeen stops. One of them is right outside our inn. It'll allow us to get to more exhibits in less time."

"Good thing," Mo said. "I'd been thinking that if we kept walking the length of this place and back every day, I'd need my shoes resoled."

His friends seemed to be taking the news well. Of course, they didn't know they couldn't go home, yet. He kicked himself for not having talked to his father before they left. But that really wasn't his fault, was it? He'd tried at the last minute, but the senator had brushed him off and hurried away.

Now it was too late. Even if he telephoned him long-distance, what could be done? Father was in Albany during the week and wouldn't even be able to call on the bishop until the weekend.

Julius and Mo's trunks caught his eye. They had all their worldly possessions and nowhere to take them. He'd be safe enough on Park Avenue as long as he stayed out of certain neighborhoods. But his friends had to find a new apartment the moment they got back. Probably Mo and Julius could hide out in a hotel for a day or two.

Suddenly, a cloud lifted. Maybe Bridget's family had forgotten them entirely in the time they'd been gone.

"Bryce, stop woolgathering," Julius said. "If we have only a few days to see everything, let's go."

The Intramural Railroad cost money. Bryce didn't care about that, but in the end, it didn't save them any time. It only went twelve miles an hour. The one time they rode it, Lily and her sisters were onboard with three new strangers. He caught her eye and tipped his hat, but didn't approach their group. He didn't have time to waste on women who didn't want him. There were plenty who did.

CHAPTER 40

The Intramural Train steamed along at a pace that Lily easily could have bested with a buggy and a lame horse. She spotted the New Yorkers at the other end of the car. Bryce tipped his hat, but the men stayed where they were. Good. She didn't want a repeat of the scene when they'd run into them on the Observation Wheel.

That reminded her of an article in that day's paper. A huge steel pin had fallen off the Observation Wheel and killed a worker. What if it had happened while she and her sisters we suspended hundreds of feet in the air? She was glad their present conveyance rode steel rails spiked firmly to sturdy ties.

The train slowed as it approached the next station, and when it came to an abrupt halt, she bumped shoulders with the Earl of Thornborough seated beside her.

"Pardon me," he said.

She smiled demurely. "It's not your fault."

The plan was to ride the train once around entirely and thereby see parts of the grounds they had yet to visit or otherwise wouldn't, such as the large forest on her right When they reached the first of three stations in the forest, Bryce and company left the train, and the tension eased out of her shoulders. She had worked hard to find His Lordship, and she didn't want Bryce to blow it up for them.

For a moment she was puzzled by their departure. Bryce hadn't seemed the type to hike in the woods, but as the train started forward, she saw out the opposite window the Palace of Fine Arts and knew where they were going.

She studied her reflection in the window, wondering if she looked aged. She certainly felt aged, though not yet twenty-three. She feared the burden of having to be in charge of her sisters and making their venture to the Fair a success was etching her face with worry lines.

"Lovely, isn't it?" the Earl said. "Reminds me of a rather famous forest in Nottinghamshire."

Lily turned away from her musings. "Is that so? I didn't realize England still had forests."

"Oh, yes, quite a few. Not in large cities like St. Louis, but any baron worth his mettle maintains a good size stand of wood on his estate—for game, you know."

Edward, as he liked to be called, was the seventh Earl of Thornborough and somewhat of a snob, though an impoverished one. The man across from him, Rose's companion, was a marquess and outranked him. But Edward had privately confided to Lily, "Lord Melborne famously told Queen Victoria, 'People were merely made Marquises when it was not wished that they should be made Dukes.'"

The Marquess was a man of the wrong century. He had bushy eyebrows and mutton chops that belonged more in Charles Dickens' time than this one. Lily could tell Rose was not pleased.

In any case, Lily's earl was outranked two to one. Violet's gentleman, though currently only a viscount, was heir apparent to a marquess as soon as his great-aunt died. His given name was Fortescue.

None of them had captured a duke, but despite Lord Melborne's opinion, she thought two marquesses and an earl would be enough to satisfy her parents.

The train stopped near the Palace of Agriculture and a substantial size man with a nose like a flattened eggplant boarded with his shorter friend and took empty seats across the aisle from them. The larger man's nose whistled as he breathed.

"Pugilists," Edward said in her ear.

* * *

At the Palace of Fine Arts, the New Yorkers ran into Joseph Henry Sharp again.

"Have you heard?" Bryce said. "The army is bringing Geronimo."

"I wonder if he'd let me paint him."

"I thought you already had."

"No, I've been in Montana. Fort Sill is in Oklahoma."

"But not only Montana, you said you'd painted some Pueblo tribes."

"Oh, yes, in Taos, New Mexico. Wonderful country for painting. The light in the mountains has an ethereal quality."

"I'd like to hear more about that," Mo said.

"But first," Bryce said. "Tell us if you know an Indian from there named Jesse."

Sharp scratched his head. "Can't recall one by that name."

"Short, hops around on a crutch, caws like a bird," Julius said.

"I'm sure I'd remember such a character," Sharp said. "Listen, fellows, I've got to see a man about when they're going to open the American section of the palace, but as I said last time, I'd welcome the chance to talk further. Dinner tomorrow night?"

"Name the place and we'll be there," Bryce said.

"Faust's Tyrolean Alps restaurant, shall we say six? I've eaten there before and the food is excellent."

"Great," Bryce said. "We look forward to it."

Sharp shook hands all around and hurried off.

"Bryce," Julius said. "I thought we were going to quit eating out."

"I thought the inn would let us extend our stay. Since it's not, I don't think we have to be so tight with our money."

"I, for one, am looking forward to hearing more about Taos," Mo said.

"And the Pueblo peoples," Bryce said.

Julius shrugged. "Well, Bavarians have a reputation for great beer."

* * *

After a pleasant day and a fine supper in the company of three courtly Englishmen, Violet, already in her nightgown, sat on the bed with her legs curled under her, trying to keep out of the row between Lily and Rose.

"So what if he is a marquess," Rose said. "I can't look at him without thinking of Ebenezer Scrooge."

"He's no pinch penny, just the opposite. That's why his estate is so poor."

"So he's willing to spend father's money on me? I don't care, I want nothing more to do with him."

"Rose, be reasonable. You've only spent one day with him."

"It only took us a day to know the Chinese prince was wrong, too." Rose wagged her finger in Lily's face. "I won't have you or anyone else choosing suitors for me."

Lily slapped Rose's hand away. "Then make some effort rather than leaving Violet and me to do all the work while you sit on your high horse saying, 'Not good enough.'"

"I never said he wasn't good enough. I said he looks like he belongs in the last century."

Actually, Violet quite liked her viscount. Fortescue had a rakish charm, and she wondered how he would be in bed. Lily would insist she wait to find out—at least until after he gave her a ring.

"Rose, dear," Violet said. "You have to have someone or our party will be uneven and you'll be a third wheel."

"Or tomorrow, you and Lily could meet them without me. Make him the third wheel."

"Surely you don't want to miss the Fair."

"Who said I would? I'll go on my own."

"No," Lily said. "An unaccompanied woman in this crowd? Mother would never approve."

Rose stamped her foot. "You just told me to find someone to my liking. I can't very well do that with Ebenezer hanging on my arm."

Violet giggled.

"Do you want to trade?" Lily said. "You can have my earl and I'll take your marquess."

"Thanks, but there isn't one of them I'd want for a husband."

Violet brushed her hair and began braiding it for bed. Her viscount would make a very handsome groom, but she'd like to take measure of his prowess before committing. There was no point dragging a prize home to Florham Park, only to discover he was a flop in bed. What kind of family named their son Fortescue? The name did little to engender an image of virility.

"Lily," she said, "Rose brings up a good point. If we're to seriously evaluate these men as potential spouses, we should pair off and see what they're like on their own, away from the others."

"That's the problem, Violet. Rose doesn't choose to be with any of them."

"But I do." As Violet thought of her viscount, a warm flush crept from her bosom up her neck, turning the tips of her ears pink.

Lily smiled. "I see what you have in mind, but don't even think of it. Make him wait for the wedding night."

She looked down and busied herself finishing her braids.

"Violet's right," Rose said.

Violet's head snapped up. An ally in Rose?

"Perhaps tomorrow is too soon, but maybe the following day you two should go out with them separately to learn what they're like out of the pack. So far, they've spent most of their time with us trying to one-up each other. Leave me here tomorrow. You take the earl or my marquess, which ever you prefer, and leave the other without a date for Thursday."

"Oh, Rose, I hate to think of you without a date," Violet said.

Rose gave a quick shake of her head.

Violet got the message, keep silent. Lily looked to be considering the plan.

"Look, I'll find my own man in my own time," Rose said. "You and Violet should be certain these are the nobles you want to invite to meet Father and Mother."

Lily pursed her lips. "You're not wrong. But if we leave you back tomorrow, don't wander the Fair alone. Mother would never forgive me if anything unbecoming happened to you. Several times today I felt like we were being watched."

Rose laughed. "We were. By everyone noticing what an odd pair Ebenezer and I made."

"Rose can hire a Roller Chair," Violet said. They'd seen handsome college men from Princeton and Yale pushing visitors around the fair in wheeled wicker chairs.

"I'd feel like an invalid."

Lily shook her head. "They can be engaged as guides, with or without the chair. That's an excellent solution, Violet."

Violet smiled with pride.

"We just have to plan our day so we don't run into you. It'd be awkward."

Rose nodded.

Lily put on the hat she'd removed earlier. "I'll ask the concierge to arrange for a guide to pick Rose up in the morning." She left, closing the door behind her.

"Maybe your guide will be a Princeton man," Violet said.

"Are you envious?"

"No, I'm quite happy with my viscount . . . or I think I will be. But I'm grateful for you suggesting that we pair off."

"You're a grown woman. Don't listen to Lily. Test the water if you want."

Violet smiled as she pulled back the covers and crawled under them. "Coming to bed, Rose?"

Rose took off her dress and hung it up. "Yes, as soon as I put on my nightgown and brush my teeth."

CHAPTER 41

The Wednesday morning newspaper informed Julius that, in addition to securing the World's Fair for St. Louis, David Francis had also managed to bring the Olympics here. Today, the Olympic Stadium would be opened for competition. That didn't matter much to Julius. He and his friends weren't going to waste their few remaining days here watching men run and jump. But the next paragraph disturbed him greatly. "James Edward Sullivan has arrived from New York City to preside over the games."

The article explained that Sullivan was an American sports official of Irish descent and one of the founders of the Amateur Athletic Union.

Sullivan also undoubtedly knew every boxer back home, including the men who had skulked outside their window before they left.

Julius showed the article to Bryce. "What happened when your father talked to Big Tim Sullivan?"

"He didn't."

"What?" Mo said. "You told us not to worry."

Bryce's eyes darted between them. "No. Julius told me to have my father talk to the bishop. Don't you remember?"

Julius waved his hand dismissively. "So what'd the bishop say?"

"How would I know? I've been here with you guys."

Suddenly the truth became clear to Julius. "That's the reason you wanted us to extend our trip. It's not safe to go back, is it?"

Bryce picked an imaginary piece of lint off his jacket and walked to the wastebasket to deposit it. "It's more complicated than I thought. Bridget's family is larger, more connected, than we anticipated."

Mo's brow furrowed. "You're saying we can't go home again? Ever?"

Bryce laughed it off. "Don't be so melodramatic."

Julius glared at him. "But Mo and I are the ones stuck without an apartment."

"And we can't stay here beyond Sunday," Mo said. "This isn't melodrama. We need a plan."

Bryce grinned. "Well, step one, I suggest we keep the hell away from the Olympics and Mr. James Sullivan."

Julius pulled the change from his pocket and slammed it on the table. "No, I'd say our first step is for you to call your father this morning, before we go to the Fair."

Mo nodded. "Do it, Bryce."

Bryce sighed. "Do you think I haven't already thought of that? But Dad's in Albany all week. It'd be Saturday or Sunday before he can see Bridget's bishop. I just hope we don't have to move back to Camp Lewis."

"They won't take us back," Mo said. "We've burnt that toast."

Bryce clapped his hands together. "Look, fellows, there's no sense spending any more of our morning moaning about the problem. Let's go see if the Apaches arrived."

If their situation looked bleak, it was nothing compared to Bryce's bitter complaints upon learning that Chief Geronimo hadn't come with the rest of the Apaches. An army guard told them he'd be coming later.

Julius felt bad, not for Bryce, but for the poor Apaches whom, he discovered, were in fact prisoners to be kept in a stockade under the watchful eye of cavalry soldiers. He was ready to leave almost as soon as they got there.

"Come away, friends," Julius said with a bow. "Let me show you the wonders of the Palace of Electricity."

Once there, Julius showed them the AT&T exhibit featuring a switchboard that could handle up to 9,600 lines.

"I'm impressed," Bryce said. "That's probably every telephone in New York City."

The company also provided free working telephones throughout the Fair for visitors to use. But who could they call? Only the wealthy had them, and among those, he knew only Bryce's parents.

Suddenly, an idea snapped in place. "Here you go, Bryce. You can call your father, no charge."

"I told you it won't do any good."

"It'll get the ball rolling."

With a friendly shove, he pushed Bryce into a phone booth, closed the glass-paned door, and leaned against it, trapping him inside. Bryce picked up the earpiece and spoke into the mouthpiece.

Then a man in a white lab coat approached them, carrying a device about eighteen inches tall. It resembled a two-arm candelabrum, but with silver earmuffs where the candle holders should have been. Its base was a hollow ring like an embroidery hoop.

"Excuse me, sir. Would you like to try a wonder of the future?"

"You bet." This was the wireless telephone Julius had wanted to get his hands on ever since he'd seen the senator from Maine use it the day of the congressional tour.

"We call it a radiophone."

"Yes, I know. How does it work?"

"Hold it in your hand and raise it up until the earpieces cover your ears."

That was obvious. What he wanted to understand was how it sent and received calls without wires. But this demonstrator probably didn't know. He'd have to figure it out for himself.

"Now, press this button, and when the operator comes on, tell her the party to whom you wish to be connected, just like you would at home."

Home? He and Mo had never had a telephone. "Uh . . . I don't know anyone with a telephone."

"Where are you staying?"

"Inside Inn."

"Ask the operator to connect you to your hotel. You can leave yourself a message with the desk clerk, just to see how it works."

He had a better idea. He pushed the button, and jumped when a woman's voice said in his ear, "Operator, how may I help you?"

He grinned at Mo. "It works!"

"How may I help you?"

"Oh. Yes, can you connect me to the Hotel Jefferson in St. Louis, please?"

He waited. Nothing happened. He pulled it from his ears and handed it back. "It's not working."

The device crackled. "Hotel Jefferson, how may I help you?"

Julius and Mo looked dumbfounded.

"Hello . . . Hello, this is the Hotel Jefferson."

Julius put it back on. "Hello. Can you hear me?"

"Yes, sir. How may I be of assistance?"

"I'd like to leave a message for an employee, Emily Stroud. She works in the dining room."

"All right, go ahead."

"Um . . ." He hadn't thought that far ahead.

"I'm sorry. I must not have heard all of that. Can you repeat the message?"

"Tell her Julius called from the World's Fair to give his regards, and that he'll be leaving for New York this coming Sunday."

"Very good, sir. Will there be anything else?"

"No. Thank you. Goodbye." Julius handed the man the radiophone. "How do I end the call?"

The man listened for a second. "It's already disconnected."

Mo reached for it. "May I?"

"Of course. And you don't have to stand in one place. As you can see, there are no wires. You can walk freely about while you converse."

Mo put the device up to his ears and asked to be connected to the Inside Inn. When the hotel answered, he said, "I'd like to leave a message for a guest, Miss Rose Jones. Tell her Mo telephoned her on a wireless telephone whilst roaming freely in the Palace of Electricity."

By the time Mo finished his call, Bryce stepped out of the telephone booth looking as if a weight had lifted from his shoulders. That could only mean good news—Bryce could ignore things, but he couldn't lie worth a damn. Julius rushed over, but Bryce merely said, "Dad was in a committee meeting and couldn't be reached."

Mo caught up to them. "When is he seeing the bishop?"

"Bryce never spoke to him," Julius said.

"Hey, I tried. He's a busy man. No sense dwelling on it. Let's see what else this palace has to offer."

Mo eyed Bryce with suspicion. Julius had his doubts, too, but what more could they do? He may as well show his friends all that he had found. "Wait until you see what's coming. Electricity will change every facet of our lives. There's electro-therapeutics, electro-magnetism, electro-chemistry—not to mention the new things they're doing with electric motors. Labor saving devices of all sorts, all available to everyone. It's going to be a new world. And it's all on display here."

CHAPTER 42

Wednesday morning, sans Rose, the Jones sisters and their escorts were shocked when they left the hotel and entered the fairgrounds. All the lagoons had been drained. A worker informed the earl that they would remain dry for several days while his crew repaired some leaks. Although the white palaces and colorful flower gardens were just as beautiful, the lack of reflecting pools took some of the grandeur from the Fair's picture.

They had yet to visit the Palace of Electricity, and the Brits were keen for it. Without Rose, the sisters were outnumbered three to two and soon found themselves among thousands of glowing lights. Perhaps the whir of motors would make up for Rose's absence.

As the Jones party made their way through the electrical displays, two lugs behind them made a rather obvious job of trailing them. Stealth was not a skill Bird or Finn possessed.

When the sisters and their escorts left the palace, crossed two more dry lagoons, and entered the Palace of Varied Industries, the boxers followed them in.

Lily and Violet pressed the Englishmen to breeze through the exhibits until they realized it wasn't industrial at all, but filled with many beautiful artistic objects. The west end had exhibits from Great Britain, including a model of King Edward's yacht, gorgeously furnished; a model country house; and English potteries. The aristocrats fell right to bragging.

A pottery display was maybe not the best place for Bird. In certain moments, his legs were susceptible to weakness, making his gait unsteady. Finn got him out of the display and they waited for the women by the west doors.

But instead of exiting the doors closest to Great Britain's exhibits, the sisters' party walked all the way back across the Palace and left by the east entrance. Fortunately, Finn caught a glimpse of them as they headed that way, and he and Bird fell in behind them.

The entourage crossed the Plaza of St. Louis into the Palace of Manufacturers, where they entered Baude's restaurant. Finn and Bird sat behind the Jones party and ordered the Wednesday special, baked chicken pie.

Toward the end of lunch, the Brits urged the sisters to accompany them to the Palace of Transportation, where there was a heroic display of automobiles that greatly aroused their interest. Finn set his dirty plate aside and unfurled his map to see where they were going. Bird ordered a sundae.

At the neighboring table, the men paid and the Jones party left the building. Bird was still eating his ice cream and reluctant to give it up. While he finished, Finn paid the bill.

When Finn and Bird came outside, Lily, Violet, and the three aristocrats were waiting for them with a Jefferson Guard.

"Where are you going?" the guard said.

Finn opened his map and pointed. "The Palace of Transportation."

"What for?" Fortescue said.

"To see the latest automobiles," Finn said, as though the streets of Brooklyn were littered with them.

"Why are you bothering these ladies?" Edward said.

"You've no cause to say that." Finn turned to the guard. "On my word, neither of us has ever met or spoken to these two women."

The guard turned to Violet and Lily. "Ladies, is that true?"

After a moment, the sisters nodded.

"Then why are they following them?" said Rose's marquess, now odd man out. "First in the Palace of Electricity, then Varied Industries, then the restaurant, and now the Palace of Transportation."

"Quite, so," said Fortescue.

"They're not in the . . . Transportation," Bird said.

"Right you are," Finn said. "How can they claim we followed them there, when they are, in fact, standing here?"

"But somehow you knew we were going to be there," said the marquess.

"Constable," Finn said, "I told you we've never had a single conversation with these fine ladies, and they just confirmed that. As for these Englishmen, we wouldn't know them from the king himself. We paid our money to see the Fair, same as them. There are only fifteen palaces. We're bound to be in the same ones some times." Finn folded his arm and took a stance in front of the guard. "This is a free country, isn't it?"

The guard turned to the Brits and shrugged. "It's a free country."

"Let's go," Edward hooked Lily's elbow, and the five of them walked away.

"You two," said the guard. "Tell me your names."

"What for?" Finn said.

"I'm going to write them down in my notebook, so if there are any future complaints, I'll remember you."

* * *

Back in their suite, Lily listened to her sisters' chatter and experienced a moment of fatigue. Rose and Violet clearly had no idea of what she was going through. The burden of having to make their quest for titled husbands a success was overwhelming. While her sisters decided whom they liked or didn't, she too had to find a spouse that didn't rankle her. As for the ideals of female independence and free love, well, those would have to be tucked in a quiet corner of her mind until their positions were secured.

Violet flopped down in a chair. "Rose, how was your day? Tell us all about your Princeton man."

Rose snorted. "He turned out to be a local boy attending Washington University right here in St. Louis."

"So, you didn't like him?"

"I didn't say that. I'll hire him again tomorrow, so you and Lily can keep to the plan of seeing your men separately. How was yours?"

"A lot of technology, electric motors, horseless carriages, and a huge train. Most exciting was when our escorts called on the Jefferson Guard to ward off two lugs who'd been following us everywhere."

Rose's voice went up. "Really?"

"Yes," Lily said. "I saw them the other day on the Intermural Railroad, too. I told you last night I thought we were being followed. Today, I knew it for sure. I'm glad you had an escort."

"Could Mother have hired men to keep an eye on us?" Rose said.

That gave Lily pause. Did their parents not completely trust her? But then she considered the character of the two men. "No. Edward thought they were pugilists. Mother wouldn't hire boxers. I'm sure she wouldn't even know where to find them."

"What did they want?"

"Nothing, apparently," Violet said. "After Edward and Fortescue confronted them, they disappeared and never followed us again. By the way, your antiquated marquess was quite assertive. You ought to give him further consideration."

"No. He's definitely not for me."

"Be that as it may," Lily said, "tomorrow night you need to have a date. The Earl of Thornborough is taking all of us to a formal dinner. If you don't want your dinner companion to be Marquees Muttonchops, you'll have to find someone suitable in a hurry."

Rose grimaced. "Well, it can't be my guide. He's just an American college boy. They'd talk down to him until he wet himself."

"Oh, they're not that stuck-up," Lily said.

"That's your opinion. How about Henry of Gloucester? He's British."

"He's also married and has no title," Violet said.

"Exactly. Lily won't be tempted to make me take him home to Florham Park. But he'll look good in a tuxedo, and he can rehash the Boer war with Lily's earl until they're bloody well satisfied."

Lily sighed. Rose was certainly persistent with her little rebellion. Oh well, the two aristocrats she and Violet had hooked might have to do.

CHAPTER 43

The New Yorkers left the Fair earlier than usual and returned to the inn to change for dinner with Sharp. While they dressed, the unresolved issue of the Irish continued to haunt Julius. "Why are we afraid? Let's just go home Sunday and if her family is still upset we'll just explain that we didn't do anything with her that she hadn't already done with someone else."

"They won't believe that of their darling girl," Bryce said.

"Then we defend her right to choose, at least she'll have us on her side."

"The people we'd be defending her against are part of a tight community. You and Mo just lie low until I fix things."

"Yeah, but when are you going to do it?" Mo said.

"When we get back, I promise I will deal with the matter promptly."

"I don't see why we should wait on you any longer," Julius said. "We're already homeless because we were afraid of a few voices outside our window. If we don't face them now, we may never be able to go home."

"Have you thought that maybe the crisis has already passed," Bryce said. "We don't need to rush out to Brooklyn and stir up trouble."

"How else will we find out?" Mo said.

"I'll ask my father."

"You keep promising that, but nothing happens," Julius said.

"Well, the state assembly is in session. He's not available to chit chat."

Julius nodded. "I accept that, which is why I suggest we go home and take measure of the situation ourselves."

"It's your funeral."

"Let's table this discussion for now," Mo said. "We don't want to keep Sharp waiting."

Mo and his friends entered the Pike from the Plaza of St. Louis and turned left where a hundred-foot-high backdrop of snowcapped mountains over-looked a tall stone tower connected to a large building made to resemble an alpine village. This prestigious affair was Faust's Tyrolean Alps Restaurant. They'd passed it on the Pike every night, but had yet to dine there.

Mo stepped inside and found Sharp waiting for them. He had with him two artists from Europe, Remy Valois and Charles Latour. Mo had met and befriended them earlier in the week at the Palace of Fine Arts, so he handled the introductions. The newcomers were pleased to meet Julius and Bryce.

The vast restaurant seated 2,500 people inside, and another 2,500 outside. The main dining room included a hundred piece orchestra, and Sharp shouted over the music. "I've asked for a table outside where we can con-verse without all the oom-pa-pa. I hope that's all right."

"Good idea," Mo said.

They were seated and given menus that listed 194 items as diverse as roast mallard duck, sirloin steak Béarnaise, filet mignon, green turtle soup, fil-let of sea bass Meunière, saddle of spring lamb Jardinière, and of course, schnitzel. It was going to take them all night to read the menu and decide what to order. The restaurant also offered bottles of 1893 vintage cham-pagne, as well as most German wines and Bavarian beers. Mo also noticed the prices were well beyond even what the finest dining establishment in New York would charge. So much for their plan to economize. But, since they were going home Sunday, why not splurge tonight?

Bryce immediately suggested they order the champagne, but at six bucks a bottle, Mo thought that was going overboard. Sharp suggested instead they order a selection of German wines, and Bryce relented. Julius ordered a lager, which came in a large stein that must have held a quart. While the wine was opened and poured, a second waiter took their dinner orders.

When the waiters left, Mo asked Sharp's friends if they had painted any scenes of the Fair.

"I haven't," Latour said. "But that's an excellent idea."

"What about the Apache?" Bryce said. "Have you seen them yet?"

"Yes," Sharp said. "It's a sad condition where they're keeping them."

"Deplorable," Bryce said. "Exhibited like animals, guarded like villains."

"Yes, even after the Apache surrendered, they've been treated like prisoners of war. It's wrong. The Indian wars ended almost twenty years ago."

"What about the Pueblo Indians?" Julius said. "We met them earlier this week. They seemed a little better treated."

Sharp unconsciously stroked his white goatee. "Oh, very nice people. In Taos, they come and go as they please. They pride themselves on their church, San Geronimo de Taos, which sits handsomely at the entrance to the Pueblo village."

Bryce got so excited he almost spilled his wine. "Geronimo?"

"Oh, not the Apache leader," Sharp said. "San Geronimo is the Spanish name for Saint Jerome." Sharp turned to Mo. "But you should go to Taos to paint. The light in the mountains is indescribable."

"I'm considering a trip there myself," Latour said.

"I recommended it to Ernie Blumenschein and Bert Phillips," Sharp said to Latour, "and they've decided to remain in Taos and start an artist colony. Look them up if you go."

"I'm probably displaying my ignorance," Mo said, "but who are you talking about?"

"Two European-trained American artists we studied with in Paris," Remy said. "You wouldn't know them."

"Impressionists, like yourself," Sharp said. "I'm sure you'd hit it off."

Mo felt the seed of an idea sprout and expand tiny leaves. Suddenly, he experienced an irresistible draw toward a place he had never heard of.

Sharp ordered more wine and waxed on. "Once a few more artists join them, I foresee Taos becoming the cultural oasis of New Mexico."

"Are the Indians there friendly to white men?" Bryce said.

"Exceedingly. Every September they invite the entire town to the pueblo for a day-long celebration."

Bryce smiled and nodded. Apparently he was feeling the pull of Taos, too.

"But isn't New Mexico kind of backwater?" Julius said. "I mean, it isn't even a state yet."

"That's true," Sharp said. "You won't find telephones, electric lights, or streetcars. But I believe Taos has a hunger for culture just waiting for young men such as your selves to assuage it. Not just art. Bryce, Mo says you're a great pianist. Taos needs the latest music and literature, too."

Now Mo could see Bryce really liked the idea. All he needed was to bring Julius around. "It doesn't matter if you live back east or out west, no one has an inkling of what's coming except those of us who have seen the wondrous innovations displayed here."

Julius nodded. "Wireless telephony, electric vehicles, moving pictures—I barely believe half of what I've seen myself."

"You should open an emporium," Sharp said. "An enterprise that blends art, music, literature, and science in one place."

Dear God. An emporium? The idea seemed to Mo as brilliant as the Edison lights around them.

"A grand emporium," Bryce said. "Our store will combine the culture of New York with the marvels from the Fair."

"We could do the same thing back home," Julius said.

"Nah," Bryce said. "There'd be too much competition in New York."

"And Taos is ripe for such a venture," Sharp said.

"Plus they have beautiful mountains for Mo to paint and Indians for me to meet," Bryce said.

Mo turned to Julius. "This is destiny. There was a reason we carted everything we owned here with us."

Julius cocked his head toward Bryce. "Yeah, a failure on his part."

"No, so we wouldn't need to go back for anything. We came to St. Louis ready for Taos and didn't even know it."

"Well, we are half way there," Julius said.

Bryce grinned like a child given a cookie. "This will be fun."

Mo looked at Julius. "What do you say? Partners?"

"Hell, yeah! Edison's lab was a long shot at best. Mr. Sharp, tell us everything you know about Taos."

CHAPTER 44

The next morning Julius awoke with second thoughts. Had he really decided over a couple of beers to start his life over in the wilderness? Even though he could see the merits of being the first to offer the latest inventions, and even with Sharp's assurances that Taos was the place to do it, wouldn't it make more sense to return to New York first? That's where all the major sheet music and book publishers were headquartered. Many of the inventions they'd want to stock originated across the Hudson, in New Jersey and Western New York.

"So what?" Bryce said. "I've got to go back to get my stuff. While I'm there, I'll see the publishers and manufacturers and get accounts for us set up. No reason for all three of us to go. You and Mo continue west to Taos and rent a building. I'll start shipping goods before I even leave New York."

Julius shook his head. "Bryce, we've been friends a long time, and you're an entertaining guy, with a good heart. But I'm sorry to say, you're unreliable as hell. Every time I trust you to take care of something important, I end up feeling like Oscar Wilde just gave me proctology exam."

"What are you saying?"

"You know what I'm saying. You've told us repeatedly you would talk to your father, and you haven't. Mo and I had to give up our apartment and tote our belongings out here like immigrants. Now you've left it so we can never go home."

"No one said you can't ever go home."

"Then why don't you do what you promised three weeks ago and telephone your father right now?"

"Because some things are better explained in person. Besides, long distance is expensive. Why waste money on a long distance telephone call that could be used to stock our store?"

"We can go over to AT&T and call for free."

"Julius, we're moving to Taos. Why do we care about New York City problems? We'll be living so far west that Bridget's people will never find us."

"Let me point out that I have a job I'll have to quit. You and Mo don't."

"You're right," Mo said, "But you were planning to leave the University to work for another lab."

"Yeah, but you and Bryce want this much more than I do. He's enamored with Indians, and you want to paint the light. But I just want to be part of everything this Fair has shown us is coming."

"You will. We all will. That's the point you're overlooking. Our emporium is going to bring the wonders of the Fair to the Western territories. Where's the fun in telling New Yorkers about electric lights and telephones? They've already seen them. But New Mexico? You'll be Prometheus, bringing fire to mankind."

"And the latest literature," Mo said.

"And ragtime," Bryce said.

"What about my interests?"

"You'll be the wizard of invention, demonstrating the wonders we'll be bringing the people there," Bryce said. "And you love to read. You'll have a job where you sit around all day reading books."

He was almost convinced. It did sound enticing. But there was also the question of money. "It sure doesn't seem like we have enough to open a store. We ought to go home and raise more capital."

"Julius is right," Mo said. "If we go back, I can sell my paintings."

Bryce took money from every pocket he had and laid it on the bed. "Here, take it all, everything I have. Rent us a place and get it set up."

"Oh, we can't do that," Julius said.

"Sure you can. Take it for our store. I'll just buy my train ticket and keep a half eagle for drinks on the ride home. You guys take the rest with you. I'll get more money from the bank when I get home."

"Home," Julius said, chewing his lip.

Bryce scooped up the money from the bed. "Let's go right now and buy some things to sell in our emporium."

The Palace of Manufacturers seemed like a logical place to start. Contained in its fourteen acres were nine hundred companies. One side exhibited heating, ventilation, building, and hardware supplies. Not the type of goods they were looking for. The other side was filled with companies who made carpets, silk, laces, porcelains, ceramics, ladies' gowns, furniture, stained glass, and bronze statuary. Again, not exactly what they had in mind, though Mo took down the address of the stained glass manufacturer.

Sharp had told them that Taos had become the place of choice for men who had prospered from recent gold strikes in nearby Glen-Woody and Red River. The influx of new wealth was one of the reasons he thought art would thrive there. Stained glass lamps might sell.

"I don't think we'll find what we're looking for here," Julius said. "Let's try the Palace of Varied Industries. It's just across the plaza."

They proceeded through exhibits of the second palace, but they, too, didn't fit what they had in mind for their emporium. What was different, though, was that here the exhibits were working factories producing goods on the spot. One exhibitor made shoes, another, hats. A machine manufactured envelopes before their very eyes.

Julius paused to study a machine weaving a picture of Festival Hall and the cascades from numerous spools of colored silk thread. "Mo, look at this. The picture you wanted to paint, done as a silk tapestry."

Mo watched it develop as the loom shuttle flew back and forth. "I admit, it's finely done."

Julius walked behind it to study the mechanism and discovered the automation was driven by a moving roll of paper with holes. "Look Bryce, doesn't this remind you of that player piano?"

However, this wasn't the only company with the same idea. The next exhibitor was weaving four-inch-wide silk scarfs with a picture of Washington at the top and the musical notation and lyrics of "The Star-Spangled Banner" beneath him.

Another exhibit had a machine making suspenders with the words "Souvenir of the Louisiana Purchase Exposition St. Louis 1904" woven into them. But they passed. No longer wide-eyed tourists goggling over the latest marvel, they had transformed into eagle-eyed businessmen, hunting for the very items that would appeal to their as yet unknown customer. Aiming for a wealthier clientele, they meant to avoid gimcracks and trinkets, seeking instead items of taste and distinction.

"Think of what my mother's friends would buy," Bryce said.

Julius was hoping for customers who were a little more forward thinking than Mrs. Holloway.

So determined were they, they skipped lunch and pressed on, surviving on food samples. There was a lot of the Fair to cover and only two days left to make purchases. He suggested they return to the Palace of Liberal Arts, where they had seen music boxes and Gramophones. The main problem there was prices. Just as he had suspected that morning, they didn't have enough money, even with Bryce's largess.

Mo had a different take on the situation. "Our problem is, none of us know anything about business. But isn't a universal business rule that you buy at wholesale and sell at retail? Everything sold at the Fair is priced higher than elsewhere."

"What do you suggest?" Bryce said.

"Tomorrow is Friday. We should go into St. Louis and locate a distributor who wholesales books and music, and purchase enough stock to start our store. You understand music and can decide what will sell. Julius and I are well read and will choose a good selection of books."

Bryce nodded. "Scott Joplin lives here. They must stock all his tunes."

"What about new inventions?" Julius said. "Our emporium is supposed to sell those too. We're only going to find those here."

"Saturday, we'll go through the exhibits again, even the Pike," Mo said, "but instead of buying anything, we'll find names and addresses of the manufacturers. When Bryce returns to New York, he can locate them and negotiate favorable terms for us. Let's stop for the day and return to the inn where we can eat for free."

"That's a sound plan," Julius said. "I'd like a juicy steak."

CHAPTER 45

"Are either of you superstitious about starting our new venture on Friday the thirteenth?" Mo said at breakfast.

"Not me," Bryce said.

Julian shook his head. Mo knew him well enough to know he wasn't.

"Well, it's settled then. Let's catch the streetcar into St. Louis."

Finding a wholesaler wasn't as easy as they expected. St. Louis was now the fourth largest city in the United States, and they had no idea where to begin. Bryce suggested they ask at a music store for the name and address of their local supplier. But the proprietor was tight-lipped.

Then Julius saw the man was wary they were going to set up a competing business. "No sir, we're leaving for New Mexico Sunday. Give us the address and we'll be out of your hair."

The man eyed the cut of their suits and their fashionable city shoes. "Sorry, you don't look like cowboys."

"We're not. We're just moving there to open a store."

"Ah-ha, I knew it. You *are* setting up business."

"In New Mexico."

"If that were true, you'd already have your goods and wouldn't be poking around here asking about my suppliers."

Bryce perused the racks of sheet music. "Let's go. He doesn't carry the kind of songs we'd want to sell, anyway."

They were not far from the Hotel Jefferson, and Bryce suggested he ask the concierge for directions to the wholesale district. That was fine with Julius, but the way he remembered it, the check-in clerk there was none too pleased with Bryce. Maybe he'd do better with the concierge. "Mo and I'll wait for you in the hotel café. I recall they serve really good coffee here."

They were seated, and a waitress came to take their order.

"Do you know Emily Stroud?" Julius said.

"She works in the main restaurant."

Julius slipped a nickel into her palm. "I'd appreciate it if you'd let her know three gentlemen from New York are at your table."

Her eyes shifted between them. "There's only two of you."

"Our partner is joining us. Bring an extra coffee for him, too, please."

She pocketed the nickel and sashayed away.

Bryce joined them while she was gone.

"We ordered you a coffee. Any luck?"

"Best. The concierge telephoned the newspaper and asked who the book and magazine jobbers were. Then he telephoned them and told them to expect us."

"I'm surprised he was so helpful," Julius said.

"Why wouldn't he? Everyone at this hotel finds me charming."

The waitress arrived carrying their coffees on a tray, with Emily following.

"This is a surprise," Emily said.

"We're in town on business, and I thought I'd stop in to say hello."

The waitress served their coffee, set cream and sugar on the table between them, and then hovered.

"Thank you," Julius said.

"Yes. Thank you, Susie," Emily said. "You can go now."

Susie, looking peeved, walked over and leaned against the wall, just within earshot, watching them.

Mo and Bryce both said hello, and Emily returned their greetings. Then she subtly grazed the back of Julius's hand with her fingertip.

"Did you get the message I left?" he said.

Emily smiled. "We're not really supposed to get telephone calls at work, but it was my first, so they let it slide. Very strange, though, what was it you were doing?"

"Damnedest thing you ever heard of—a telephone without wires. You could walk anywhere in the building and stay connected. Mo tried it too."

"I did," Mo said.

"Your message said you were leaving Sunday."

"That's the plan."

She stuck out her lower lip. "That's the only day I'm off."

"I know." Too bad she hadn't made more of their time together last week.

Mo and Bryce finished their coffee. Susie sprang away from the wall and dashed to their table. "Refill, gentlemen?"

Bryce stood. "No, thank you, we're expected elsewhere. Just the bill, please."

Susie handed him a slip of paper, and Bryce paid her.

"Julius, Bryce and I'll meet you in the lobby," Mo said and left with Bryce.

Julius rose, and Emily put herself between him and Susie, leaning as close as one dared in a public establishment. "Perhaps my girlfriends will want to visit the Pike tonight."

"I can't say if we'll make it there tonight. It depends how long this business in town takes."

She pouted.

"I believe we plan to go there Saturday."

She brightened.

"But we won't be staying out late. We have to pack that night."

"What time is your train departing? Maybe I could see you off at the station Sunday."

"I don't know. We haven't purchased our tickets yet." Oh damn, that's right. They better stop by Union Station today.

"Did you ever find those men I told you about?"

Susie tapped Emily on the shoulder. "You better go. The maître d' is going to come looking for you."

Julius shook Emily's hand. "Lovely of you to take time for us, Miss Stroud."

She blushed. "Thank you for thinking of me."

The restaurant maître d' appeared in the doorway and scowled.

Emily stepped away from Julius and smiled. "Perhaps not our last goodbye. I'll ask the girls about Saturday night."

Susie cleared the dishes. As soon as Emily was out of earshot, she said, "I've no previous engagement for Saturday night."

"Is that so?" Julius understood her meaning, but at the moment he had all the women he could juggle. "You've just met my partners. They presently have no engagements for Saturday. Ask Emily if you can come with her."

"I don't think she'd like that." Susie picked up the dishes and left.

Four hours later they were the proud owners of several crates of assorted modern literature and what Bryce considered a decent selection of sheet music. Everything would be delivered to Union Station and held for their departure. The money hadn't stretched as far as he'd hoped. Still, the prices were far less than at the Fair and left a little margin for them to turn a profit.

"Mo, don't worry," Bryce said. "First thing when I get to New York, I'll set up accounts for us to buy directly from the publishing houses."

By then it was getting late and businesses were beginning to close. Bryce was in a good mood. "Friends, we've accomplished something great today."

Mo nodded. "It's a good start. I'm sure we'll know better what to order once we're actually set up in Taos and get to know the people."

"Just let me know what they want," Bryce said, "and I'll ship it ahead or bring it with me when I come out."

"Speaking of which," Julius said, "we need to go to Union Station and buy our train tickets."

"Today?" Bryce said. "The station is clear across town. I want to get back to the Fair and have some fun on the Pike. We've only two nights left. We can buy tickets tomorrow."

"Bryce has a point," Mo said.

"We're already in town. Why have to come back in tomorrow?"

"We won't," Mo said. "We can buy train tickets at the Fair in the Palace of Transportation."

"You read that in your guide book?"

"As a matter fact I did, but we also saw where they were selling them when we visited that palace."

They walked to the trolley stop and boarded. When it crossed the Delmar Avenue line, where they had to transfer, Julius said, "You guys go ahead. I'll meet you back at the inn later. I'm going to call on Catherine. I don't want to leave St. Louis without saying goodbye."

"Catherine?" Bryce said.

"The Fairy Soap goddess."

Bryce grinned. "Oh, her. Have fun."

"Isn't she working today?" Mo said.

"She should be home by the time I get there."

The bell clanged, and the trolley started moving. Mo and Bryce jumped off and waved farewell to Julius. They caught the Delmar Avenue streetcar and rode it to the fairgrounds. The line ended at the Lindell Street entrance, which was on the opposite side of the grounds from their hotel and near the Pike. Bryce thought that was perfect, but Mo convinced him to return to the Inside Inn for supper.

Mo was right, of course. And they could refill their flasks from a bottle in their room instead of buying drinks on the Pike later that night.

He and Mo entered the inn lobby and immediately encountered the Jones sisters, accompanied by the uncrowned heads of Europe. Bryce tried to walk past them unnoticed, but Rose called out, "Oh, Mo."

Mo stopped and tipped his hat. "Evening ladies."

Bryce couldn't pretend he hadn't seen them. He was stuck. He removed his hat and smiled, hoping a pleasant countenance hid his resentment of the down-market marquesses who were with them. Stuffy looking nobs in tails. The sisters wore gowns. No doubt on their way to a fancy dinner somewhere. Lily acknowledged him with a nod, but did not introduce the men.

He didn't give a damn. They could keep chasing titles. His family was already among the upper-upper set, and he decided long ago that wasn't the class of people he wanted to spend his time with. If that was who Lily and her sisters wanted to be with, he wasn't missing anything.

"Excuse me for a minute." Rose stepped away from her sisters and their gentlemen companions and approached Bryce and Mo. "Good evening. Going to dinner?"

"Yes, then to the Pike." Bryce liked this sister. Maybe he should have chosen her on the train. Oh, wait. The women had done the choosing. Standing between Lily and Violet, Rose's light paled, but when seen apart from them, she was every bit as luminescent. In fact, he now realized it was she who had managed their dalliance with the sisters during the trip. She, who had boldly paraded around the Pullman car in her dressing gown and kept the porter distracted.

She smiled at Mo. "I received your telephone message. What was that about?"

"Oh, that. We were given the chance to try a telephone that required no wires. And you were the person at the Fair I most wanted to call."

She gave Mo a look that Bryce recognized. When a Broadway chorus girl looked at him that way, he knew he was going to bed her. Of course, Mo already had on the train. So . . . was she implying she'd step out on those lords huddled across the room with her sisters? Well, all three sisters had admitted they were free thinking women when he'd met them.

"Rose," Lily called out.

"Coming." She squeezed Mo's hand. "Sorry, duty calls. Thank you for thinking of me the other day." She spun around and rejoined her party.

Bryce slapped Mo on the back. "Forget them. Let's get a bite to eat and head over to the Pike."

CHAPTER 46

Saturday morning Rose lay in bed staring at the ceiling. Violet was sleeping next to her, lying on her side and breathing into Rose's neck.

A great weight had lifted. Lily and Violet had both landed lords and were making plans for their men to visit Florham Park and meet their parents. Mother might think her middle child had failed, but from Rose's point of view, she'd succeeded. No foreign customs or social pecking order to adjust to. Also, she'd be free to visit Mo in New York once they were home. Maybe finish that painting they'd started last Sunday.

Thursday night, Henry of Gloucester had served as her dinner date. With the pressure of having to marry gone, she'd relaxed with him and even agreed to his accompanying her to the Fair Friday. She would have preferred to go with Mo and his friends, but there'd been no point bringing that up with Lily.

Henry was nice enough, a handsome accessory to hang on her arm with a clear understanding that nothing romantic was going to happen between them. And unlike her college boy, she wasn't paying by the hour. They strolled along flowered walkways between the palaces and entered those she had yet to visit. Along the way, they passed gondoliers staring forlornly at their boats resting like beached whales on the bottom of the drained lagoons. Henry reminisced merrily about when they'd gone for a boat ride with her sisters, Sir Guy, and Lord Bath. As she remembered it, old Lord Bath's main contribution was to repeat frequently, "Quite so, quite so."

According to Henry, he'd seen much more of the Fair than she had. On his arm, she learned how he achieved this. They would walk into a palace which had 800 or 900 exhibits and saunter down a single aisle, stopping to admire this and that as they proceeded. Then he was ready to leave, claiming he had finished that palace even though there were numerous aisles begging to be explored.

But today would be different. No more Henry. Violet's viscount had informed her he had to go to Chicago on business, but he would definitely come to New Jersey before returning to England. That meant that, like Rose, Violet was on her own today. No reason to hire a guide or take Henry along—she and her sister could chaperone each other. Lily had a date with her earl, so she'd surely relent. Their first days at the Fair, Lily deemed three unescorted sisters proper. It followed that two should seem equally so. Rose considered the logic infallible.

She reached over and pushed a lock of Violet's hair behind her ear, not exactly to wake her, but wishing that she would, so that they could lie in bed whispering plans for their day. What would they do on their last day at the Fair? What exhibits they would see? The model city? They hadn't been there. She wouldn't mind going up in the Observation Wheel once more. Perhaps the lagoons were repaired, fountains flowing again. That would be a fine view from on high.

Oh, she shouldn't forget the Pike. After all, there were only so many exhibits of sewing machines and violins a girl could stomach, but the attractions on the Pike were experiential, making you believe you were riding a hot-air balloon or submerged under the sea. She started counting on her fingers the Pike attractions they'd seen, and it was far fewer than the total number. They should definitely reserve at least part of their day for the Pike.

She brushed the tip of Violet's nose with her finger, but Violet just turned over.

They'd also missed the Philippine village, though she'd heard a lot of talk about it. From what people said, it seemed perverse, yet provocative. Tiny brown people living in grass houses ran around completely naked in the middle of the fourth largest city in America while tourists stared. She didn't object to nudity. She'd seen her share of naked men, but treating them like a human zoo seemed . . . un-American.

Rose rolled on her side, threw her arm across her little sister, and gave her a hug. But Violet still didn't wake.

Oh well, nothing for it. May as well get up and go downstairs. Possibly she'd run across the New Yorkers eating breakfast in the restaurant. Lily wouldn't approve, but Lily was still asleep.

She tucked the covers around Violet and slipped into the bathroom to wash and dress.

Downstairs, the restaurant was full of families impatient to go to the Fair, but none of them were her three New Yorkers. Either they'd already eaten and left or hadn't gotten up yet. She drank a coffee, ate a pastry, and returned to her room.

* * *

Later that morning, Julius stretched and sat up on the edge of the bed. "What time is it?"

Mo leaned out the bathroom door, half shaved, razor in his hand. "Not sure."

"But not early?"

"No. Bryce and I stayed until they closed the Pike and then ran into Messieurs Latour and Valois, who invited us to join them for drinks. We got back here late and slept in this morning."

"So Bryce is still sleeping?"

"No, he's up—where he gets the energy, I'll never know. He went downstairs to get the hotel bill, so we'd know how much fair merchandise we can buy to take with us."

"I thought we were just going to get company names to order from later. We still haven't bought our train tickets, and we need money to live on in New Mexico until we get our store up and running."

Mo shook his head. "Well, look at you. I'm usually the one reminding everyone to watch our spending."

"Are we rushing into this half-cocked? I've never lived anywhere but New York."

"None of us have. But this is our chance. We'll never be this young again."

"Or foolish."

"It's not foolish. It's destiny. There is a light on a distant mountain calling us."

Julius laughed. "You switching from painting to poetry?"

The door flung open and Bryce burst in. He dropped the hotel bill on the table and rushed to his suitcase, where he began rummaging through its contents. Mo went back into the bathroom to finish shaving.

Julius stood, stretched again, and wandered to the table where he picked up the bill. He dropped it like a hot coal. "Jeez, Bryce, two-hundred and fifty dollars?"

"Two-hundred and fifty-two, actually."

Mo joined them. "What are you talking about?"

"The bill for the inn. Where are we going to get that kind of money?"

"Don't panic," Bryce said. "I have a bank draft. I'll cash it, and we'll have enough."

"How are you going to do that? Banks are closed on Saturday."

"I'll talk to Mr. Statler."

"He's in the hospital, remember?"

"I'll take it to the interim manager, then." Bryce pulled an envelope from the suitcase. "Found it." Bryce snatched the bill off the table and ran out the door.

Julius shook his head. "Typical Bryce. I had no idea this place was costing us that much."

"We should have guessed. In Bryce's strata of society, one does not ask the price. You gotta figure, one of the largest suites, meals included, and tickets to the Fair. We were naïve to expect it to be cheap."

"You're right. We just follow the guy along, never asking what we owe."

"Don't be too harsh on Bryce. We were living in a tent—"

"His fault."

"Right. Then we get kicked out, and about to live on the street—"

"Again, his doing."

"Yeah, but he pulled the rabbit out of the hat—"

"Pulled some strings, you mean."

"True, but we've lived pretty comfy the last two weeks. Now, he's downstairs paying our entire bill. I don't think we have the right to complain."

"Okay, sure. But is that the way we're going to run our emporium? What happens when he cuts the Holloway family strings and we're way the hell out west without a way home?"

"Do I have to remind you we no longer have a home in New York, anyway?"

"Again, that's on Bryce. We trusted he was taking care of a situation and we're the ones ended up out. Bryce is entertaining as hell, but are we really ready to start a business with him?"

"According to Sharp, Taos is ripe for an emporium offering eastern culture and bringing the latest innovations. We are the guys they're waiting for. They just haven't met us yet. And Bryce, for all his faults, wins over a lot of people. We've been friends our whole lives. Don't back out on me."

He wasn't backing out. But he was the only one of them who'd have to give up a paying job. And a decision like this would shoot his chances of working for Edison or Tesla all to hell. He was the one with the most to lose, and he didn't like starting empty handed. "I'm only suggesting that instead of traipsing off to a strange land with a piddling couple of crates of books and sheet music, we return with Bryce, save up some money, and all of us go to Taos together when we're ready."

Mo made a face. "It'll cost us more than it'd save. We'd end up buying twice as many train tickets, plus rent for a new apartment in New York. That feels like a giant step backward. We have an opportunity to bring something important to the people of Taos and to receive whatever inspiration that place offers."

"And you trust Bryce not to screw up?"

"You and I can accomplish anything we put our hearts into, and that more than makes up for Bryce's screw-ups."

"So we just take a leap of faith?"

"Call it that, or fate, or destiny, whatever you like."

Okay, Mo had convinced him. But they'd buy the train tickets before anything else. He could easily see them stranded here in St. Louis because of Bryce's screw-ups.

He walked into the bathroom. "You done in here?"

"All yours." Mo left to dress.

Julius looked into the mirror, rubbed the stubble on his cheeks, and filled the basin with water. It had been a late night, but he was glad he'd gone to see Catherine. She was surprised by his unexpected visit, and he'd finally met her mother, who was the nicest woman and a wonderful cook. She'd quickly put an extra place setting on the table and invited him for dinner.

He swirled his shaving brush in the mug, filling it with foam, and thought of Catherine, the soap fairy. She'd been discretely affectionate throughout the evening whenever opportunity afforded. Although her mother's presence put a damper on any real intimacy, Catherine was delighted he'd treated her like more than a one-night-stand, and he felt the visit had given their brief relationship a good conclusion. One never knew if some future trip east, he'd have a layover in St. Louis.

She'd offered to see him off at the station Sunday, just as Emily had. He'd given her the same excuse—they hadn't bought their tickets and didn't know what time they were leaving. Well, that was still true.

Bryce returned. "You're not dressed yet? Time's wasting." He had a hand full of cash and a cocky smile. "Inn bill is paid and we've money to spend."

"On train tickets," Julius said, buttoning his shirt.

"Right," Mo said. "We'll go to the Palace of Transportation on our way to the Pike."

The railroad ticket offices were located in the east wing of the palace. Bryce, of course, booked a first class Pullman sleeper back to New York, but Mo and Julius opted for coach so they'd have more money left when they got to Taos. The agent handed them their tickets and Bryce his change.

Bryce gave the money to Julius. "Here, you and Mo go ahead. I'll catch up with you later."

"I thought we were going to—"

"We are. But first I want to talk with some Pueblo Indians about Taos. They've only lived there a thousand years. They might know a thing or two." With a quick wave, he was off.

Julius looked at Mo. "I guess it's up to us."

Mo nodded. "Always is."

They exited the west end of the Palace of the Transportation and came out not far from the Observation Wheel. Julius watched it revolve and was tempted. But no, this was their final opportunity to find items for their emporium. If they finished early, there'd be time to take one last ride. He also wanted to stop at the Palace of Electricity to see if Edison was there. Of course, there was no point asking for a job in his Camden lab. He'd already committed to New Mexico. Still, it'd be nice to say he'd met the great man.

CHAPTER 47

Julius and Mo turned right on University Way and entered the Pike between the Galveston Flood and Battle Abbey attractions. They'd seen neither, but it was too late to do so now. They needed to finish shopping and get back to the inn. They hadn't even started packing, and they had a morning train.

They proceeded along the mile-long Pike, stopping at each concession, looking over goods and discussing which merchandise might sell best in Taos. They didn't buy much. Not that there weren't plenty of interesting and exotic items, but as Mo kept pointing out, everything was priced for the tourist. If they paid these prices, they wouldn't make a nickel.

They were still empty-handed the next time they saw Bryce. Or rather heard him. They had just exited China, when exuberant yelling in front of the Great Siberian Railway caught their attention.

Passersby had stopped and were regarding from a safe distance two fools throwing their arms skyward while crying, "Wahoo!"

"This is a perfect example of why it's a bad idea to give liquor to Indians," said a tight-faced woman standing next to Julius.

"I agree," her husband said. "And that white man with him is no saint. It's three o'clock in the afternoon, for goodness' sake."

"Looks like Bryce found his Indian friend," Mo said.

Julius nodded. "Shall we go see what they're up to, or ignore them and keep shopping?"

A woman in a white blouse and gray skirt stormed out of the child care building across the road. "Shush that wailing right now. There are babies sleeping inside." She motioned for two Jefferson Guards at the other end of the Pike to come to her aid.

"Well," Mo said, "it's either see what they're up to or bail Bryce out of the pokey."

In three long strides, Julius was between Bryce and Jesse. "Hello, boys." He threw his arm around each man's shoulder and said, "What say we take a ride on this attraction?" He steered them into the entrance of the Great Siberian Railway.

Inside a replica of the Moscow train station were four full-size Pullman cars coupled behind a locomotive. Posters advertised a ride through Russian countryside with stops at various villages where passengers could disembark, mingle with the Russian people and, Julius presumed, buy souvenirs.

He was too late. The Jefferson Guards arrived, and after a few brief words, the woman from the child care facility pointed them out. In seconds, the guards were at their side. "What's this about, yelling war cries and frightening babies?"

"'Wahoo' is an expression of joy, not a war cry," Bryce said. He didn't sound particularly slurred.

A guard confronted Jesse. "Why are you out on the Pike? Go back where you belong."

Jesse sneered. "I can't. Your people stole it."

"He's with us," Bryce said.

"Not any longer. We're taking him back to his people."

"No," Bryce said. "He's not a prisoner. I told you, he's with me."

The guard looked at Bryce. "That lady says you were part of it too."

Julius stepped in. "Look, mister—"

"That's Sargent."

"Sorry, Sargent, we were just about to take him on this ride. That'll get him out of everyone's hair."

"You fellows can go, but this Indian's coming back to the stockade with us."

"He's Pueblo, not Apache," Bryce said.

"Can't tell the difference myself," the guard said. "But okay, we'll take him to New Mexico instead."

Jesse hobbled into the road outside the attraction, flapped his crutches, and cawed like a bird.

The two Jefferson Guards lifted him under his arm pits and carried him away. He continued to caw as they went.

"Bryce," Mo said, "did Jesse ever tell you why he makes those bird calls?"

"Sure. That's Jesse flying above the mundane troubles below."

Julius lightly slapped Bryce on the back of his head. "What the hell were you yelling for?"

"The pure joy of being. Life deserves a good 'wahoo' once in a while, something the Indians understand.."

"Shit, you're as crazy as Jesse."

"I'll take that as a compliment. You know there is a simplistic authenticity to the Native's world."

"As long as you don't mind a bunch of old, white guys running your life," Julius said.

"They can do that on Park Avenue, too," Bryce said.

"Hardly."

"Since we're standing in the entrance of this Siberian ride," Mo said, "do you want to get on it or continue down the Pike?"

Julius shrugged. "I only ducked in here to get Bryce away from the guards. I figure we're going to be stuck on a train most of next week. No reason to ride one today."

"Good point," Mo said.

Just then the doors opened, and the attraction disgorged the previous group of riders. Among them were Violet and Rose, without their lords or their sister, Lily.

"Hello," Rose said. "I'd hoped we'd run into you. Today's our last day at the Fair."

"Ours, too," Mo said.

"Oh? I wonder if we'll be on the same train again."

"Not a chance."

"How do you know?" she said. "I haven't told you which train we're taking."

The exiting crowd kept jostling them, making conversation impossible.

"Let's all go someplace where we can talk," Mo said. "Perhaps a cup of tea in China?"

Violet and Rose both shook their heads. "No, not China," Rose said.

"How about a cold drink?" Julius said. "The Irish Village is right over there."

"I don't even want to think of the Irish," Bryce said.

"I wasn't bringing up *those* Irish," Julius said. "I was suggesting we get a beer."

Bryce pulled him aside. "The Irish pavilion? That's a likely place for Sullivan to sup." Bryce turned to the sisters. "How does Paris sound?"

Violet broke into a smile. "Ooo-la-la."

Bryce paid everyone's admission to the French attraction. Inside, they had their choice of two restaurants. Julius thought the ladies would be more comfortable at the café, because the Cabaret had dancing girls, but Rose pointed to the poster for the Champagne Dancers and led the group there straight away.

Julius glanced at Mo, who shrugged and grinned.

Once they were seated, Bryce ordered a bottle of wine for the table and told the waiter they'd eat later. Julius asked for a beer.

"Have you seen the Floral Clock they installed yesterday?" Violet said.

"No, we spent Friday in the city," Julius said.

"Well, you'll be amazed. It's the most marvelous thing! The dial is a hundred feet across, and the numerals are fifteen feet high and made entirely of flowers. The whole clock is covered in foliage."

Rose nodded. "The minute hand is seventy-four feet long and moves five feet every minute."

"Imagine that," Julius said.

Violet laid her hand on his arm. "Oh, Julius, you'll be fascinated by the mechanics of it. At the top of the dial is a building that houses the mechanism. When the minute hand reaches twelve, the doors fly open and you can see its workings. To the left of the building is a five thousand pound bell that, when it strikes, can be heard throughout the fairgrounds. On the building's right side is a giant hour-glass holding a hundred pounds of sand that runs through it every hour. With the first strike of the bell, the immense hour-glass flips over and the sand starts running back."

"The whole thing operates on compressed air," Rose said.

Violet beamed. "And nearby is a revolving globe that shows the current time in every location on earth."

"At night the whole clock is illuminated," Rose said. "We saw it last night, there must have been a thousand lights."

Julius was impressed. Not only with the idea of the clock, which sounded amazing, but with the way the sisters had paid attention to the mechanics of it.

"That does sound like something," Mo said. "We'll look for it tonight on our way back to the inn."

"Where's Lily?" Bryce said.

"She and the Earl of Thornborough are seeing the Fair without us today," Violet said.

Bryce looked like he'd swallowed a piece of cork from the wine. He quickly recovered and put on a happy disposition. "So, she accomplished her mission. I take it you two didn't fare as well."

"No, we each got what we wanted," Rose said. "Violet has a viscount she even likes, and Lily agreed to allow me to remain single for as long as I desire."

Mo's eyebrows shot up. "She said that?"

Rose smiled. "Lily finally understands that two titled aristocrats are enough. So, I'm free as ever. Maybe when we get home, I can come into the city and you can show me around."

Mo sighed. "Would that I could, but we won't be there. Julius and I are leaving for Taos, New Mexico in the morning."

Rose frowned. "I'm free, but not that free. Lily would never let me go to New Mexico. When are you coming back?"

"We're not," Mo said.

"What? Ever?"

"Well, I don't know about forever," Julius said, "but not before we've become inconsequential to certain parties in New York."

"What does that mean?"

Bryce cleared his throat. "Don't despair. I'm returning home to put things in order before joining Julius and Mo. If your parents will let you visit Manhattan, I'll happily take you to a Broadway show and a nightclub afterwards."

Julius saw her face light up at Bryce's offer. Interesting.

The band struck up a tune, and the stage filled with leggy dancers in ruffled skirts.

Julius patted Rose's hand and said over the music, "Don't pin your hat on Bryce's promises. He's a fun companion, but about as dependable as milkweed in a gale."

Rose nodded and turned her chair for a better view of the show. She watched the dancers lift their skirts and kick their legs, showing everybody in the room practically everything. Rose imagined what it must feel like to be on exhibition—every man's eyes reaching as far up her thigh as her high-kicks permitted. Leaning forward and shimmying until her breasts almost popped out of her dress. It reminded her of how she felt posing half-draped.

Bryce could introduce her to someone who hires dancers on Broadway.

She shook off the thoughts. It was a fantasy that could never come to pass. She was free, but not so free she could scandalize everybody in the family.

Mo put his arm around her shoulder and leaned close.

If they were back at the inn, she'd take him right now.

"Rose," he whispered, "I'm going to leave a package for you at the front desk. Be sure to collect it before you go to the station in the morning."

She tore her eyes from the performers and looked at him. "What did you say?"

"That painting we did? I'm giving it to you."

She was touched, and loved that he wanted her to have it as a keepsake. But what would Violet and Lily say? Of course, it didn't have a face. Still, how could she explain why he'd give her a painting of a half-naked woman?

He met her eyes and, as if reading her thought, said, "Tell your sisters it's a study I did of one of the works in the Palace of Arts. There are so many, they'll never know."

She glanced around to see if anyone was watching. All were steadfastly focused on the show, which was reaching its most risqué. She edged closer, quickly kissed him, then sat back and looked to see if anyone noticed. No one had. Mo dropped his arm from around her shoulder. She fumbled for his hand under the table and pulled it into her lap.

How sad that he was going so far, so soon.

She raised her voice over the music. "We're not leaving until Monday."

Bryce turned around. "What did you say?"

"I was telling Mo, our train isn't until Monday. Maybe he and Julius could wait and go to New Mexico then."

Julius leaned into the conversation. "Can't. Bryce tried to get the hotel to extend our stay, but no luck. We have to check out on Sunday."

"It's rude to talk during the performance," Violet said. "Train schedules can keep until the show is over."

"Sorry, Violet," Mo said.

Everyone in their party turned their attention back to the pretty women shaking their shoulders and swiveling their hips. Rose squeezed Mo's hand. If she couldn't be up there dancing, she could at least experience it vicariously.

CHAPTER 48

Bird and Finn had finished their shepherd's pie and were having a second pint of beer at the Irish Village restaurant after another day of fruitless searching. They'd shown the ragged clipping to every waitress, without a glint of recognition. It seemed pointless to keep asking at places they'd already been, but Irish food reminded them of home, and the beer was good.

A colleen who greeted visitors at the door came to their table. "May I have another look at that photo?"

Bird fished it out of his pocket and unfolded it for her.

She pointed to Bryce. "Aye, him. He's on the Pike with an Indian, creating a real row. Everybody's talking about it. They had to call the Jefferson Guard."

Finn leaped to his feet and kissed her cheek. "We got 'em, Bird." He tossed money on the table. "Some of that's for our bill, the rest is for you. Stop lagging, Bird. Let's go."

They rushed out into the throng of tourists crowding the mile-long Pike and frantically scanned the crowd. Failing to spot their quarry straight away, Finn began to ask the barkers in front of various attractions if they'd heard about the melee or seen the men involved. Several directed him toward the child care nursery.

A woman in a white blouse and gray skirt stood in front of the nursery building with her arms folded across her chest. She scowled at the boxers when they approached. Bird reached into his jacket for the photo, and she drew back into the doorway. Certainly none of the babies in her care had sprung from the loins of a giant with a nose like that.

Finn stepped between them. "Relax, sister. We heard there was some sort of ruckus."

"Keep your voices down. I just got my charges settled."

He took the clipping from Bird and showed it to her. "Were these the men?"

She pointed to the same one the colleen had. "Just that one, him and a wild Indian, wailing some kind of war chant. Woke every baby in the place." She patted her hair, making sure her bun was still tightly wound. "Can you imagine what a disaster that was, trying to settle a whole room of screaming infants? God only gave me two hands."

"Our sympathies, ma'am. Did you see where the rascals went?"

"Guards took them." She pointed toward the Pike entrance. "That way. Some place in the fairgrounds where they keep prisoners, I would imagine."

He tipped his hat. "Thank you, ma'am. Bird, if we hurry, we can catch them."

Finn and Bird trotted down the Pike like two boxers in training. Baffled tourists parted to let them pass. They made a right turn into the fairgrounds and picked up their pace until they spotted the blue caps of two Jefferson Guard. Finn grabbed Bird's arm and slowed him down. "Don't get too close. The Guard has our names on a list somewhere. We don't want to tangle with them again. We just want to get our man. Let's hang back and see where they take them."

Bird, a little less fit than in his heyday, breathed heavily, his nose whistling like a tea kettle.

"Breathe through your mouth, Bird. They're going to hear us."

Drawing nearer, it became apparent that the guards only had one man between them, a runt at that.

"Where's the other one?" Bird said.

"Whisper. I don't know. That must be the Indian. Maybe they let white men go."

"Indian's not the one we want. Wouldn't be good for Bridget."

"He's not, but he's the best clue we've got. So, we follow them to wherever they're taking him. Soon as the guards leave, we question him."

They tailed them to the Indian compound where the guards left Jesse. As soon as the guards were gone, Finn and Bird snuck inside. "He shouldn't be difficult to spot, he was using a crutch."

"Poor fellow," Bird said. "Did you ever break a bone?"

"No, but that's not important right now."

"I had my ribs broke a few times. Hurts bad, even to take a deep breath."

"Keep your mind on our business and your eyes open. He can't have gone far on one leg."

"Who can't?" Jesse appeared out of the dark.

Finn jumped. "What are you, a ghost? Where did you come from?"

"Who are you, and why are you following me?"

"You saw that?"

"Yes. I knew you were behind us the whole time. Those guards lack awareness of their surroundings. My people do not. Now, what do you want?"

"Not you," Bird said. "We want name of man you were with."

"What man?" Jesse said.

"Man on Pike. New York man," Bird said.

"I'm not telling you that. I'm not saying anything."

Finn doubled up his fists. "I bet you will."

"Yeah? You going to make me?"

"We are," Finn said. "This is Goliath McGuigan, heavyweight champion, and I'm twice as fast and hit twice as hard." Finn threw a series of fast jabs in the air to show he meant business.

Jesse stepped out of reach and swung his crutch at Finn, cracking him in the shin.

Finn grabbed his shin and Bird lunged for the Indian.

Jesse hopped back on one leg until he could get his crutch back under his arm. "Help! We're under attack from white men!"

Twenty men straggled out of their quarters to see what Jesse was carrying on about. Women peeked out their doorways.

Jesse pointed to the boxers. "Don't be cowards. Surround them."

The tribe did just that. "You men don't belong here after dark," one of them said.

While the tribal leaders wrangled with the white men, Jesse slipped out of the compound and headed toward the Inside Inn.

CHAPTER 49

When the dance show ended, Julius stood up and offered Violet his arm. She accepted. Mo and Rose preceded them out of the theater. Bryce held back, trying to talk to one of the dancing girls, but the manager separated them and ushered Bryce out.

They all met on the Pike outside the French Village. Julius felt a little sorry for Bryce. Three guys and two women was an awkward combination. If Emily would have shown up with her friends . . . but she hadn't. Of course, if she had, Rose and Violet wouldn't be with them now.

As if the ratio of men to women wasn't uneven enough, Prince Axel of Denmark and a party of men came down the Pike toward them. "Hello there." He tipped his hat to Rose and Violet. His companions did the same. He offered his hand to Julius. "Good evening, sir. We met last week at the Rodin exhibit."

Julius shook his hand and Axel introduced the rest of his party.

Once everyone had met everyone, Violet said, "I'm surprised you're still here."

"Had to be, the Olympic Games, you know. Didn't I tell you? I'm on the International Olympic Committee."

"Is that right?" Julius took a step back. *Sullivan's committee.*

"No," Violet said, "I don't think you ever did."

"Yes, and my companions are also on the committee. We're celebrating tonight. We held our first Olympic event today, an interscholastic track competition. We're on our way to meet the head of the games, James Sullivan. Please join us."

Uh-oh. Julius's mind raced for a way to duck out.

"The Olympics," Violet said, "imagine that."

"Sorry," Julius said. "Some other time perhaps, we need to get the ladies back to—"

"No, we don't have to go yet," Violet said.

Think, think, think. "Won't Lily be wondering what happened to you?"

"Lily won't mind," Violet said. "She's busy with Edward."

Julius caught Mo's eye and gave a quick jerk of his head toward the exit. "Violet, Mo and I haven't started packing yet, and we're booked on tomorrow's train."

Axel waved his hand at someone farther down the Pike. "Oh, there's Sullivan coming our way now."

Julius tugged Mo's jacket. Bryce, who'd caught on to what was happening, had already started in the opposite direction and had a step or two lead on them.

"Rose, dear," Mo said. "If you and Violet want to stay a while longer, I'm sure Prince Axel will see you both safely back to the inn."

Rose, still holding firmly onto Mo, reached out and grabbed Julius's arm. "You two are *not* leaving us. Tell Bryce to get back here, too."

Julius was shocked by Rose's assertiveness but did as he was told. "Bryce."

Bryce looked back but continued to move downstream.

Julius shook his head. "Can't leave yet."

Bryce stutter-stepped, one step toward the group, one more away, clearly undecided, but leaning toward fleeing.

"Come back, you big chicken."

Bryce hung his head and returned.

By then, Sullivan had reached them. He shook hands all around as Axel made introductions. A fit, athletic man, he gripped Julius in his island-sized paw, but didn't linger and moved on to the next man—the very model of efficiency. Sullivan was likely a good twenty years older than them, with a large black mustache, but silver hair.

Violet looked flushed and flustered. Julius recalled that last week she'd been squired by Lord Bath. Maybe she preferred really old men.

"Mr. Sullivan," she said, "I understand you're from New York City?"

"I am. And you, young lady?"

"Florham Park, New Jersey. But my friends here are New Yorkers. Perhaps you share mutual acquaintances."

Sullivan turned on them. "Is that right? Which athletic club do you belong to?"

"We don't," Mo said.

"You should." Sullivan pounded his chest with his fists. "Does wonders. Start while you're young. Twenty years from now, you'll thank me."

"Well," Bryce said, "we considered joining the International Order of Hoo Hoos."

Sullivan made a face. "Never heard of it. Come see me when we get home and I'll get you signed up someplace reputable."

"Oh, Bryce is fit," Violet said. "He was in the army with Roosevelt."

Julius tried to think of a gentlemanly way to shut Violet up.

Sullivan stepped close to Bryce and studied his face. "What did you say your name was?"

"B-Bryce."

"Holloway," Violet said.

"Holloway?" Sullivan broke into a broad smile that tipped the ends of his mustache upward. "Your father's in the State Senate?"

"You know him?" Julius said.

"Not personally, but I know of him. Good man."

Julius breathed a sigh of relief and grabbed Sullivan's hand. "Well, it was an honor to meet you, but we need to go. We were just leaving when you arrived."

Sullivan kept his grip and wouldn't let loose. "Wait. Not so fast, laddie."

Julius swallowed a lump the size of a meatball.

Sullivan reached into his coat pocket with his other hand. "Let me give all of you tickets for the pre-Olympic events."

"That's very generous of you, sir, but I'm afraid we're leaving tomorrow." He wiggled his hand free of Sullivan's.

"First thing in the morning," Mo said.

Violet spoke up. "They're going to New—"

Bryce stepped on her foot, evidently less worried about being gentlemanly.

"Ow!"

"Sorry, Violet," Bryce said.

Sullivan frowned. "Well, it's a shame you're leaving just when the athletic events are starting."

Violet looked puzzled. Julius took her arm. "Are you all right?"

"Yes, just surprised. Bryce stepped right on me."

Julius shrugged. "He's not usually that clumsy. Probably in a hurry to pack. Are you and Rose walking back to the inn with us or staying out with the Olympic Committee?"

Bryce leaned into his ear. "We can't leave the Jones sisters with Sullivan. They know too much."

He was right. While Julius puzzled what to do about it, Rose took Mo's arm. "We're coming with you. Violet, it's time to go."

Another round of handshakes and pleasant goodbyes, and then they left the Pike. Violet insisted they make a side trip to see the Floral Clock. Julius admitted she'd been right. It must have had a thousand lights, and the mechanism was ingenious.

They watched the clock strike the hour, then started across the fairgrounds toward the inn. Rose wanted to pause at a balustrade and stand with Mo, admiring the reflection of the lighted palaces in the now-restored lagoons. Julius and Violet stood a little farther away, giving Rose some privacy.

Bryce sidled up to him. "You notice, Sullivan had no idea who we were? Maybe our Irish problem isn't as bad as we thought."

"What are you guys talking about?" Violet said.

Bryce waved his hand dismissively. "Oh, the humdrum details of life."

"Right. Mo, what are Bryce and Julius talking about?"

Mo and Rose rejoined them. "Sorry, Violet, I didn't hear. Rose and I were . . . saying goodbye."

Julius, a head taller than Violet, gave Mo a conspiratorial wink. "Bryce just pointed out that Sullivan had obviously never heard of us."

"No," Mo said, "but when he finds out who we are, he'll know what we look like."

"Why would he care?" Violet said. "You're not famous or anything."

"Bryce's dad apparently is," Rose said.

"Violet, trust me, just leave it at that." Julius patted her shoulder. "And we've still got to pack." He took her arm and started toward the inn. The others followed.

Behind him, Mo said, "Rose, don't be sad that we're going west in the morning. It's a good thing."

Julius looked back at them. "Amen to that."

CHAPTER 50

When they reached the inn, Bryce said goodnight to Violet and Rose and turned to Mo and Julius, "I'm going to check on Jesse."

"Don't be gone long," Julius said. "We have an early train, and you haven't packed."

Bryce waved him off. "I need to make sure he's all right, that's all."

Julius and Mo escorted the ladies as far as the stairway. "Do you want us to walk you to your room?" Mo said.

Rose snuggled against his chest. "I'd love it, but Lily's probably there."

"I can't find the words . . ." Mo nodded toward reception. "Don't forget your painting. I'll leave it at the desk when we check out."

She turned her face up, as if to kiss him, but the lobby was full of people. "Write me when you get to New Mexico."

Violet shook both men's hands and pulled her sister's arm. "Lily's probably worried."

The women dashed up the stairs.

Julius watched them go and sighed. They had to make it through one more day. "Nightcap?"

"I thought you wanted to pack."

"I'd pack better with a beer in me."

As they passed a lobby window, a crow called from behind the drapes. Julius wheeled. "Mo, some damn bird got in here."

"Meet me outside," a voice whispered.

"Jesse?" Julius said.

"Shhhh. Outside. Two minutes."

They walked out the door and heard a bird caw from a nearby shrub.

"Jesse, what are you doing at the hotel?" Mo said.

"I came to warn Bryce."

"He's not here," Julius said. "He left to find you."

"No! I hope they don't find him first."

"Who?"

"Two Irish boxers, one the size of a mountain."

"How do you know about them?"

"They attacked the pueblo, tried to make me talk. But the only thing I gave them was a bloody battle." Jess began swinging his crutch wildly, acting out an exaggerated battle in which he was the hero. "If the tribe hadn't come outside and restrained me, I might be in the hoosegow this very minute for killing a white man."

A bellman spied Jesse's antics and came running over. "Stop or I'll call the Guard. You don't belong here. Go back to your stockade and quit threating our guests."

"He wasn't menacing us," Julius said. "He was telling us a story."

"Well, Indians aren't permitted on hotel property." He shooed Jesse like a stray dog. "Away with you."

Jesse backed toward the road. "Tell Bryce I never gave up your names." He hobbled a few steps farther, then flapped his crutches and cawed at the bellman.

"Shit," Julius said. "I hope Bryce is being careful."

Mo shook his head. "When have we ever known Bryce to be careful? At least our pursuers still don't know who we are."

"So Jesse says."

"You still want that beer?" Mo said.

"Why do you have to ask?"

* * *

A while later Bryce returned.

"Did you see Jesse?" Julius said.

Bryce shook his head. "I spoke to the Pueblos. The Guard brought Jesse there, then later some men came for him but left without him. None of the tribe knew where he was, or if they did, they wouldn't say."

"That's because he was here looking for you," Mo said.

"He was?"

"Yes," Mo said. "He gave us a message for you, said two Irish boxers tried to bully our names out of him."

"Swears he didn't tell them a thing," Julius said. "But these are probably the same two that Emily warned me about. Let's find them and explain that we did nothing to Bridget that she hadn't already done."

"Are you crazy?" Bryce said. "From their description, I don't think they came here to reason with us. Let my father do the explaining while we're at a safe distance."

"Jesse says there are only two of them," Julius said.

Mo shook his head. "Not a good idea. Jesse says one of them is a Goliath."

Julius snorted. "To a little fellow like Jesse, everyone is a giant. Bryce was a Rough Rider. He and I can take the big one and that just leaves one for you."

"That's a bad idea," Bryce said. "What if these guys are championship boxers? We're lovers, not fighters. What chance would we have against two professionals?"

Mo nodded. "Bryce is right. We've got enough goods to start the emporium, and we're this close to being on a train to where they'll never find us."

CHAPTER 51

Mo checked the room to make sure that they hadn't forgotten anything. Bryce was standing at the window, looking wistfully across the lawn toward the fairgrounds. Last night Mo had wrapped the painting of Rose in a copy of the *St. Louis Dispatch,* tied it with string, and left it for her at the front desk. While he was there, he asked the clerk to order them a wagon and team to transport their trunks to Union Station. Bellboys had come earlier this morning and carried the trunks away. Now all that remained was their hand luggage.

Bryce turned from the window. "I think I'm going to change my ticket."

"What?"

"I'll leave on Monday instead."

"Why in the world would you do that?"

"I still haven't found Scott Joplin. Be a shame to leave without meeting him."

"I thought that's where you went last Sunday."

"I . . . er . . . Did I say that? Well, I misspoke. Besides, another day here won't hurt."

Mo shook his head. Bryce hadn't worried about not meeting Joplin until he learned the Jones sisters were taking the Monday train. That probably wasn't a coincidence. "But where will you sleep tonight? There aren't any hotel rooms. We checked everywhere."

"Oh, I'm sure I can find something. It'd be nice to say that I met the man and heard him play in person."

Julius, tying his tie, whirled around. "Have you forgotten two Irishmen are scouring the Fair looking for us?"

"I won't be at the Fair, will I? I'll be in the city."

It seemed foolish, but Mo had known him long enough to accept that Bryce was going to do whatever Bryce was going to do. "Don't leave us dangling in New Mexico trying to start a store with a box of books and a couple crates of sheet music. Get home and get stuff ordered."

"Don't worry. I will. Seriously, what difference does a day make?"

Mo checked his watch. "Time to go, fellows. The Atchison, Topeka and Santa Fe Railway waits for no man."

At the station, they puzzled their way through fifteen train platforms until they located their train.

Bryce was exuberant. "The Atchison, Topeka and Santa Fe. Just the name sounds like an adventure, doesn't it?"

To Mo, it sounded like an interurban trolley line. "Julius, you find our car while I make sure our crates of goods arrived and are onboard."

Mo located the baggage car and checked that their trunks and the crates were properly tagged. He accepted a receipt from the baggage handler, verified the count, and nodded.

Mo spotted Julius and Bryce lingering on the platform near the coach-class cars. Boarding passengers swirled around them like dandelion seeds in a summer breeze. Some appeared to be businessmen or salesmen getting an early jump on the upcoming week, but there were many families, too. Mothers and daughters carried shopping bags loaded with World's Fair souvenirs, while fathers herded boisterous boys in knickers aboard. The excitement of the Fair persisted even as people were leaving.

Mo felt it, too. They had been part of something truly grand.

As Mo reached his friends, Julius threw his arm across Bryce's shoulder. "Don't get sidetracked. We're depending on you."

Bryce raised his right palm. "Give me a Bible and I'll swear on it. As soon as I get home, I'll set up everything. I'm as excited to see Taos as you are."

The engineer gave two short blasts of his whistle, and the conductor yelled, "All aboard."

Mo and Julius shook Bryce's hand and climbed the steps.

"See you in New Mexico," Bryce shouted at their backs.

They found a pair of empty seats and set their suitcases on an overhead rack. The decision to ride in coach meant they'd arrive with money to live on until their emporium opened.

Emporium. That had a nice ring to it. They'd bring New York's metropolitan culture, the latest literature, and the newest music. Plus the many wonders they'd seen at the Fair. The citizens of Taos had no idea what was coming to them.

And the mysterious light of the mountains. He could hardly wait to see it. He'd had a chance to study some of the impressionist's techniques up close and had learned a lot. Now he had the chance to apply it.

The train started forward with a jerk. Outside, Bryce, still on the platform, took off his hat and waved it in the air. Mo and Julius waved back. Bryce's vivacity was infectious. And why shouldn't they feel some excitement? Their adventure began here, now. As their railcar cleared the shed and morning sunlight flooded in the windows, Mo vowed he'd never forget this moment.

Chapter 52

Sunday morning Finn and Bird finally got a break. They'd awakened early, caught the omnibus taking folks to church, and slipped the driver something to drop them at the fairgrounds entrance near the Inside Inn.

"Fair's closed on Sunday," he said.

Finn nodded. "We know—just looking for somebody staying at the inn."

He and Bird snuck past the guard and made a beeline to the pueblo, intending to wait for the man they were seeking. But they were distinctly unwelcome and asked to move along.

Not far up the road was the Utah exhibit. From there, they had a direct eye line to the hotel entrance. Bird had gone to use the restroom when one of the bellmen from the Inside Inn scurried across the road.

"Are you still paying for information regarding those men in the newspaper picture?" the man said.

Finn snapped to attention. "You know something?"

"I might. What's it worth to you?"

Finn took out a silver dollar, flipped it in the air, and caught it. "Tell me. If it's helpful, this is yours."

"I know where they're going to be until noon."

Finn nodded and tossed the kid the dollar. "That'll do. Tell me."

"At Union Station. They just checked out and are headed there by horse-drawn wagon. I overheard them say their train left at twelve. If you hurry, you can catch them."

"No need to race them to the depot," Finn said. "We know their destination. All we got to do is catch the noon train to New York. Thanks, son."

Finn jogged into the lavatory building and found the men's room. "Bird, you in here?"

"Yeah."

"Button your fly, we got to get back to camp and get our stuff. The scoundrels we've been chasing are on their way home. All we have to do is get on the same train and wire your cousin's husband to meet us at the station. We'll walk them right off the train and into his waiting arms."

There wasn't time to waste waiting for the camp omnibus to return, so the boxers hired a hack to drive them to camp for their baggage, then dash to the depot. With the aid of a good driver and fast horses they made it to Union Station, bought tickets, and boarded the twelve o'clock train to New York with seconds to spare.

As soon as the train got under way, they searched the entire train twice, including first class where they were told they weren't supposed to be.

* * *

Bryce saw his friends off and went to change his ticket to Monday.

"No problem," the clerk said, and booked him on another Pullman.

After checking his suitcase, Bryce stepped out of the station onto busy Market Street and paused. He hadn't considered how to go about finding a black piano player in St. Louis. He went back inside and found a Negro porter.

"Yes, suh, how can I help you?"

"Do you live in St. Louis?"

"All my life."

"Can you tell me where Scott Joplin lives?"

"No, suh."

"I'm talking about the famous ragtime composer."

"I know that man's music, but I don't know him from St. Peter his self."

"Oh, I thought . . ."

"Expect you thought every black folk know every other black folk. Well, suh, there's 35,000 of us live here. I can't know 'em all."

Bryce chewed his lip.

A man with bushy eyebrows, wearing a railway uniform, shouted across the lobby, "Joe! You helping that man?"

"I'm trying, suh, but I can't do him no good."

"Well, then leave him be. Others are waiting."

The porter touched the brim of his cap and left.

Dejected, Bryce shambled back outside, spring gone from his step. Casting about for a direction, he watched couples in their Sunday best strolling home from church in no particular hurry. Suddenly, he realized they were all whites. St. Louis, like all cities in America, was segregated. He only needed to ask where the black community was. Joplin couldn't live anywhere else.

The streetcar driver looked at him like he was crazy. "The Ville, that's their area."

"Then that's where I'm going."

Bryce changed lines several times and managed to wind up in the Ville. Now what? Just knock on doors and ask, he guessed. The Ville was bounded by St. Louis Avenue on the north, Taylor on the west, and Easton on the south. He started wandering the streets, but they were empty. The Ville was replete with black churches that apparently did not let out as early as white ones did. Finally, he located an old wino who said, "He don't live in the Ville, he live over on Delmar Boulevard—number 2658."

"Where's that?"

"Say, you got ten cents? I just need ten cents more to get a bottle of vino."

Bryce fished a dime out of his pocket and handed it to him.

The man pocketed it, and, giving him a toothless grin, pointed southeast. "Walk three miles that way."

"Is there a streetcar that goes there?"

"You want to go down Taylor to Delmar. There you can catch one that runs the length of Delmar."

Bryce followed the wino's directions but had a long wait for the trolley. Finally, he reached Joplin's address. It was a nice two-story brick duplex with arched windows and arched doorways trimmed in white.

He knocked, and bounced on the balls of his feet. He knocked again. No answer. A third time, same result. Guess he wasn't home. In his mind, Joplin didn't seem like the church type, but who knew?

Bryce turned to leave when the latch clicked and the door hinges squeaked. An elderly black man looked him up and down.

This couldn't be right. Scott Joplin was only a dozen years older than Bryce. Had he knocked on the wrong door? He checked the number. No, this was Joplin's place. Probably the old man was his father.

"What you want?"

Bryce put on his most winning smile. "I was hoping to meet your son. I'm a pianist myself, and a great admirer of his."

"My son?"

"Scott Joplin. Isn't this his house?"

The man coughed up a wad of phlegm and spit on the lawn. "Used to be. Ain't no more. He couldn't pay his bills. Moved out last year."

Couldn't pay his bills? "Do you know where I can find him?"

"He plays most often in the area they call Chestnut Valley, over near Union Station."

Shit! That's where he'd started from. This day wasn't working out.

"I gotta go sit down, now." The old man closed the door, leaving Bryce on the street.

No point going there. Nightclubs were closed on Sunday. He'd never be able to say he met Joplin.

* * *

Unfortunately, Julius and Mo's train didn't go straight to New Mexico. First, it'd go to Kansas City, where they'd change to another which would take them into Colorado and finally, south into New Mexico It dawned on Mo they'd be on various trains for about a week.

Julius struck up a conversation with a family seated across the aisle. They hailed from Iowa and were returning home after spending two weeks at the Fair.

"That's how long we were there," Julius said.

"Did you see the Iowa exhibit in the Agriculture Palace?"

Mo couldn't recall if they had or not, though he remembered grazing all the free food samples the palace offered.

"I'm sure we did," Julius said. "But there was so much to see. A fortnight wasn't really long enough."

"I agree," the man said. "Still, we all have to go home some time."

Not him and Julius. Mo tried to imagine a world without brick streets and paved sidewalks. Would all the houses in Taos resemble the New Mexico pavilion?

The man's son, a boy about age fourteen, stood, removed his suit coat, and tossed it on the overhead rack.

"Don't just throw it up there," his mother said. "Fold it and lay it properly."

"Yes, ma'am."

The boy sported a new pair of galluses with the words "Souvenir of the Louisiana Purchase Exposition St. Louis 1904" colorfully woven into the straps. Mo smiled, remembering the machine that made them. Should he have bought a pair?

No. Too crass. Their emporium would be more subtle.

After the man had seemingly addressed every aspect of Iowa life, Mo stood. "Julius, let's stretch our legs."

This train certainly wasn't an express. It stopped to let passengers on or off at every whistle-stop depot in Missouri. "Fifteen minutes," the conductor would shout at each stop. These fifteen minute increments quickly accumulated into hours wasted. Mo doubted if they'd crossed three counties yet. How wide was Missouri? He didn't know, but at this rate it was going to be a damn long train ride.

They tried to find the dining car, but learned the train didn't have one.

"What?" Julius said. "We're not going to eat?"

"Yes, just not now. The next town with a decent size depot, we'll run in and grab some sandwiches to go."

Julius nodded. "I can live on sandwiches. Also, maybe we can buy a pail of beer."

"I don't know if we can bring that on board."

"I can't see any reason we couldn't."

The plan worked. At a not too distant rail station, they found sandwiches and beer. But they didn't have a pail for the beer, nor would they have glasses to pour it into, so they settled for quart bottles.

"Four should be enough, don't you think?" Julius said. "That's two apiece."

More likely three for Julius and one for him, but Mo nodded. "Any more and it'd just get warm. We can probably do this all the way to New Mexico."

"You mean get on and off to buy victuals?"

"Sure."

After they ate, they took their beers to a parlor car where two men were drinking and discussing the lumber business.

"You think these guys are Hoo Hoos?" Julius said.

"Ask them. Tell them we've been to their exhibit at the Fair."

Julius did, but the men looked offended and turned their backs to him. Mo guessed that meant they weren't. The Hoo Hoos seemed like a more fun-loving bunch.

Leaving the lumbermen, they wandered the full length of passenger cars, but fortune didn't favor them. There weren't any single women traveling alone on this train, pretty or otherwise, just families and business men.

CHAPTER 53

Bryce glanced at the afternoon sky and realized he'd better start looking for a place to stay. A creature of habit, he headed for the Jefferson, but they were still fully booked. He prevailed on the clerk to telephone a few other hotels, but to no avail. St. Louis might as well post a "No Vacancy" sign at the city limit.

His stomach growled. The Jefferson did have an excellent restaurant and an inviting lobby. He'd eat a leisurely meal and then take a glass of brandy to a comfy chair in the lobby where he'd sleep until morning.

The food tasted good, and he stretched the evening out with several courses plus dessert. When he could dally no longer, he took his snifter, as planned, to the lobby and settled in.

He didn't sleep long. The lobby clock said it was only eight when the doorman rousted him. "Go to your room, sir. You can't sleep in the lobby. Creates a bad impression."

"What? Oh, sorry. Too much brandy at dinner. I must have fallen asleep."

"That you did, sir."

Bryce picked up the snifter and swallowed the last dram of liquid, trying to think of some way to stay put.

He handed the doorman the empty glass. "Give me a few minutes to clear my head."

The doorman accepted the glass. "Certainly, sir." But he didn't go away.

"I'll be fine. You can leave."

"I'm afraid I can't, sir. It's my job."

Bryce's eyes raced around the lobby. Wasn't there a guest somewhere this man could go help?

A lovely blond came from the back and headed toward the door. Shouldn't the doorman rush over to hold the door for her? Wasn't that his real job? She glanced over and gave a small wave. And recognition clicked.

"Emily? Emily Stoud?" He jumped to his feet and brushed past the doorman.

She paused mid-stride and waited for him.

He took her gloved hand and pressed it to his lips. "Bryce Holloway."

"I remember."

"We missed you at the Pike last night. Julius said you and your girlfriends were coming out."

"My roommates begged off, and a girl can't go out on her own."

"Roommates?"

"You've met them. The girls I was with the night we rode the chutes."

That's right. All cute and single, as he remembered. "Oh, I was just surprised you don't live at home. I don't think any of you mentioned it that night on the Pike."

"Yes, my girlfriends and I share a place. Is Julius with you?"

"No, he left on the twelve o'clock train."

She frowned.

"Don't make that face. I'm still in town." Bryce took her arm and walked her to the door.

The doorman opened the door for them. Bryce slipped him a nickel.

He touched his cap. "Thank you, sir."

"So, Emily, where can I take you?"

"Home."

Wow, that was easy.

She blushed. "I mean, I'm going home. I've got to work in the morning."

"Let me see you home. Do you live far?"

"It's just a streetcar ride away."

"Okay. Which line do we take?"

"It's kind of you to offer, but as I said, I have roommates."

"They'll probably be glad to see me again."

"More likely they're in their nightgowns."

Bryce stopped walking, faced her, put his finger under her chin and gently raised it up. He gazed into her bright blue eyes. "You said earlier a lady shouldn't be out alone. At least let me see you safely to your door."

She leaned in until their noses almost touched, and whispered breathlessly, "All right." She stepped back, slipped her hand into his arm, and resumed walking. "The trolley stop is up here."

Bryce patted her hand and then let his rest on hers. "By the way, why *are* you out tonight? You don't work on Sundays."

"I came in to pick up my pay envelope. Our rent is due on the fourteenth, that's today."

"Ah, one of those inflexible landlords?" Actually, he had no idea what he was talking about. He'd never had a landlord in his life. He was trying to avoid a lull in the conversation. He hated lulls. It was his opinion that people around him only stopped talking and laughing when they weren't having a good time.

She laughed. "No, he's all right. We always pay him on time, and he's quick to fix anything we ask."

The trolley came. They boarded and continued to chat. She slid ever closer in the seat, pressing her hip against his. Promising. But then, when they reached her stop, she stood and shook his hand. He held it and stood up with her.

"This is as far as I go," she said.

"I said I'd see you to your door."

She stepped off the trolley, and he followed her up the walk. At the door, she put in her key and turned around, leaning against his chest. "Thank you. I'm glad we ran into each other."

He lifted her head and met her lips with his. She wrapped her arms around him and pulled him into her. He felt her flow against him. Very promising.

In a flash, it ended. She separated slightly, gave him one tiny kiss, and said, "Goodnight."

The next thing he knew she was through the door and he was alone on the sidewalk. He stood there, he wasn't sure how long, a few minutes at least. That hadn't gone as expected. At first, he hoped she'd merely gone in to make some arrangement with her roommates for him to spend the night. But in his heart he knew better. There was a finality in that, "Goodnight," and her door wasn't opening again.

He'd be damned if he was going to knock and ask to be admitted.

Bryce returned to the trolley stop and waited. When it came, he took it to Union Station. He'd sleep there tonight. He had his ticket. They couldn't very well deny him the right to wait for his train.

* * *

"Next stop, Kansas City," the conductor shouted. "Passengers to Colorado, Albuquerque, and points south should disembark and proceed to track number three. All for Topeka, please stay with this train."

Mo tugged the conductor's sleeve. "How long will we have to eat?"

"Let me see your ticket."

Mo stood, retrieved his coat from the overhead shelf, and pulled out his ticket.

The conductor glanced at it. "Two hours. Try the Harvey House. You'll like it."

He'd never heard of it, but it was likely to be a welcome change from stale sandwiches and warm beer.

An attractive young woman, about nineteen years-old, greeted them at the door and invited them to sit anywhere. Her uniform, consisting of a starched, long-sleeve, high-collar white blouse, a skirt that hung near to the floor, opaque black stockings, and black shoes, seemed designed to diminish her feminine attributes. Any remaining hint of female physique was further concealed by a long stiff white apron that covered everything between her collarbone and kneecap. Her hair was restrained in a net and capped with a wide white ribbon.

Their waitress—in fact all the Harvey Girls—were dressed the same, their only ornamentation being their pretty, pink, virginal faces. But she was friendly, well-mannered, educated, and her service was first class.

The tables were set with fine china on Irish linen tablecloths. Mo placed his napkin on his lap and listened attentively as she described the thick steaks and side dishes served in sumptuous portions. She also explained the "blue-plate special," a daily low-priced complete meal served on a blue-patterned china plate for travelers on a budget.

Did he and Julius look poor? They were merely striving to be economical so there'd be a little left in their pockets when they reached Taos.

"I'll have that," Julius said.

Okay, Julius had just confirmed their meager bankroll. Mo shrugged. "Make it two."

It was nice to sit down to a hot meal. The first of many, as it turned out. The Atchison, Topeka and Santa Fe Railway had contracted for a string of Harvey House eating establishments to be operated along their routes approximately every 100 miles. Trains made regular "meal stops" at each. Passengers disembarked, entered the dining room, and in less than half an hour the entire complement of passengers were served and had finished eating. Most had time left to browse the stand of western curios conveniently for sale near the exit.

Harvey Houses were fastidiously clean, and the food was consistently good. At a meal stop farther along the line, Julius chatted up their waitress, "I'm surprised that your food is so fresh this far from civilization."

"We're proud of that. Harvey and the railway have a set of signals that forewarn the kitchen and dining room staffs so we can make the necessary preparations before you even arrive. The railroad also delivers fresh meat and produce to the eating houses daily."

"Well, it's very tasty." Julius winked at her. "And does the railway also deliver Harvey Girls?"

She didn't blush, she winked back. "It does."

"Really? How often?"

"Whenever one of us gets married."

"So, none of you are married?"

"No. A Harvey Girl must be single, between eighteen and thirty, attractive and intelligent."

"Well, you certainly fit that bill."

Now she blushed.

"Are you from around here?" Mo said.

She shook her head. "New Hampshire. Harvey House runs ads in Eastern and Midwestern newspapers. I answered the one in the *Concord Monitor*. The pay is more than I'd make in a shop, and room and board is included.

It seemed like the perfect opportunity to travel and have new experiences." She lowered her voice. "Far from home."

Mo raised his eyebrows. "I'm surprised your parents let you move away."

"Well, there was resistance, but my father asked around and Fred Harvey has a sterling reputation for protecting Harvey Girls' purity."

"That doesn't sound like much fun," Julius said.

"Even less than you'd imagine," she said. "We have a strict 10:00 p.m. curfew, and every location has a senior Harvey Girl who acts like a mother bear."

"Then why not spread your wings, now that you're out of the nest?"

"Can't. We sign a one-year contract. Leave and you forfeit half your pay."

"And no one ever does?" Julius said.

"All the time. Marriage is the most common reason."

"Seems like a heck of a bind."

"Not at all. I like meeting new people every day, and the men out here outnumber women five-to-one, so the odds of meeting the right man are higher than in New Hampshire."

Julius smiled. "If that's your goal."

"It is. But I'm not in any hurry."

Julius touched her hand where it rested on the edge of the table. She didn't pull away. "Neither are we. I think we have time for pie, don't we Mo?"

Mo glanced at the clock at the end of the room and nodded.

"What kind would you like?" she said.

"What do you recommend?"

"Cherry."

"Sounds perfect."

"Make that two," Mo said.

She left and returned with two large slices. Mo thought they must have been a quarter of the pie each.

An older Harvey Girl approached their table and asked their waitress to take over for the girl at the souvenir stand.

"Stop and see me on your way out," she said as she left for her new post.

Mo pushed his fork through the flaky crust and speared a cherry. He put it in his mouth and the delightful flavor burst across his taste buds. "This is really good!"

Julius had his mouth full and could only nod.

The conductor stood up from his seat at the counter and walked to the door. "Fifteen minutes, folks."

Night came, and they slept sitting up. Again. If you could call it sleeping. In the morning, Mo rethought their decision about not paying extra for a sleeper car. Ah, but they were young. They could sleep in their seats for a week. Julius had taken a sweater his mother had knitted and balled it up behind his head. "Give me something to use for a pillow and I can sleep anywhere."

Mo had a jersey in his suitcase. He'd try that tonight.

CHAPTER 54

The porter took Bryce's suitcase and led him to his seat on the Pullman. "Shall I unpack for you, sir?"

"No, don't bother, George, just put it away and I'll do it later."

It'd been a hell of a night, and if he'd learned anything, it was that benches in train stations were not created for sleeping. He never did get comfortable. And when he finally drifted off, a guard woke him, but when he showed his ticket and said he was waiting for his train, the man left him alone. The rest of the night was a fitful half sleep.

When people began pouring in, he checked his watch and saw that he had time for breakfast. He went to the station café where he'd eaten eggs, bacon, toast, coffee, and orange juice. It had given him just enough energy to make his way to the Pullman and hand his suitcase to the porter. But he had hours to wait and miles to go before they'd make up the beds.

He slumped down in his seat and took random catnaps, missing lunch, and barely making it to dinner. When he returned from the dining car, his bed had been made up and he was grateful.

Bryce slept soundly and woke feeling like his old self. After a hearty breakfast, he began a diligent search for the Jones sisters. He walked the entire length of the train—twice. Searched the parlor of every Pullman. He remembered Lily liked to breakfast late, so he double-checked the dining car to make sure they hadn't come after he left. Finally, he had to accept that the Joneses were not on his train. Had they misled him, or simply taken a different train?

He repaired to the bar car, where he made numerous friends over rounds of drinks he paid for. He talked and talked about the World's Fair, about New Mexico, regaled them with his plans for the emporium, and made them laugh. Under Bryce's leadership, joviality ruled.

Bryce continued to talk until there was no one left to talk to. Bemoaning the absence of the Jones sisters, he drank and drank until he could drink no more. Finally, he stumbled back to his Pullman car bed where he slept the night and into the following afternoon, despite George's reminders that he'd missed breakfast and lunch.

Finally, the porter pulled the curtains open. "Mr. Holloway? You got to get up so I can change the bed."

"George? Don't worry about changing my sheets. Listen, go to the dining car and bring me a coffee, will you?"

"I can't sir, it's closed."

Bryce rubbed his face with his hands. "I need a coffee pretty badly."

"They sell it inside the station. Now, you got to get up. I got to get this car ready for the next passengers."

"All right, I'm up."

The porter waited in the aisle with Bryce's suitcase. "You can change in the lavatory."

Bryce walked to the end of the car, noticing the rest of the passengers were gone.

In the lavatory, he shaved, put on clean clothes, and checked himself in the mirror.

He stepped from the car onto the platform and experienced a moment of shock. This wasn't Grand Central Station. "Where in the hell are we?"

A man in white spats stopped mid-stride. "Sir! There are women and children present. This is a public place, not some roadhouse."

Bryce turned and started back up the steps, but the conductor stopped him. "We're not ready to board yet."

"I must have gotten off too soon."

"No, this is the end of the line. The train turns around here and heads back to St. Louis."

"But this isn't New York."

"It certainly isn't. This is New Orleans."

"What? I'm supposed to be in New York City."

"What can I say, sir? Welcome to Louisiana."

"I must have boarded the wrong train in St. Louis."

The conductor held out his hand. "Let me see your ticket."

Bryce fished it from his coat pocket and gave it to him.

"No, you were definitely on the right train. Pullman tickets are issued for a specific car and seat number. This was the correct ticket for this train."

"But I paid for a sleeper to New York City. That damn fool clerk in St. Louis must have mixed it up when I changed my reservation from Sunday to Monday."

He handed the ticket back to Bryce. "There's no call for coarse language. Take this to the ticket counter inside the station. Explain what happened and ask the agent to wire St. Louis to confirm your story. If it was the railroad's mistake, he'll issue you a new ticket from here to New York City —no charge."

No charge? He certainly hoped so. It wasn't like he was asking to ride for free—he'd already paid—and what about the two days he'd wasted?

St. Louis confirmed that his original ticket had been for New York City. The New Orleans office managed to get him on a train leaving that night for Jacksonville, Florida. There, he would change to a different railway line and begin his journey northward. It wasn't ideal. He wouldn't arrive until Friday evening, but they booked him on Pullmans all the way. And he would get to see more of the country, which would make a good story someday.

Having slept the whole day, he wasn't the least bit tired on the trip to Jacksonville, but the rest of his car surely was. Once the beds were unfolded, and the curtains set up, he had two choices—lie awake to toss and turn or go elsewhere. He chose the club car.

The crowd there was thin. He settled next to a southern gentleman who sipped bourbon and spoke in slow, drawn-out syllables. Although he was an interesting conversationalist, the pace at which he expressed his ideas was maddening. Bryce could have rattled off a hundred words in the time it took his companion to complete a sentence. This gave Bryce time to worry about two or three other things and still be ready to pick up where the man left off.

One of those things was Bridget's family and the impending problem of telling his father.

When a longer than usual pause came to their present discussion, Bryce decided to change topic and practice on the man as if he were Father. But he had to be sure who he was talking to. "You're not Irish, are you?"

The man's eyes grew wide and his jowls quivered. "I am not, sir. Nor any member of my family, neither. Why, I consider those shiftless, potato-eating immigrants barely a cut above a black man." He swallowed the rest of his bourbon, as if to wash-away the taste of the words he'd just spoken and motioned for the barman to give them both refills.

So not Irish. Okay, he'd give it a try.

"I'd appreciate your opinion on a bit of a moral dilemma I'm facing."

"I'm at your service, sir."

Bryce proceeded to describe the false impression Bridget's family had about her innocence, and his reticence to ask his father to intervene.

"Bridget? She's not Irish, is she?"

"Let's say, for purposes of our discussion, that she's not."

He reached over and laid his chubby hand on Bryce's shoulder. "You're a grown man, son. Forget about asking your father. You know, the honorable thing to do is go to her family and straighten the situation out yourself. If you and your friends didn't cause her wrong, they're never going to believe it if you keep ducking out. No sir, when you get home, I want you to go right over there. Will you do that?"

Bryce nodded, but in his mind he knew he wouldn't go into that neighborhood with an entire squad of Rough Riders behind him. For if he did, he'd feel compelled to tell her father she had a right to make her own choices. If he had the guts of Captain William O'Neil, he'd take her to a suffragette meeting and say, "Be free." But he wouldn't do either of those things. Maybe he'd screw up the courage to tell his dad, or maybe he'd just set up the contracts with book and music publishers and get out of town.

CHAPTER 55

"New York City Central Terminal," the conductor said as he moved through the car.

Finn stood and stretched. "Come on, Bird. We're here."

Bird didn't move.

Finn kicked his shoe. "Get up. We're home."

Bird folded his arms and sulked. He'd been moping ever since they'd discovered the dandies weren't onboard. "I don't want to see him."

"Who?"

"John, Mary Elizabeth's husband."

"You got nothing to be ashamed of. We ran our asses off all over that fair." Finn tugged on Bird's arm, trying to leverage him into a standing position. It was rather like a rooster trying to move a bull.

Disembarking passengers crowded against him. "Move, ya mutt. Get off the train or get out of the aisle."

"Hear that, Bird? Real New Yorkers. We're home." Finn sat down across from him. "What are you going to do? You can't sit here all night."

The car emptied quickly. Porters came aboard and began cleaning, gathering abandoned newspapers, odd bits of debris, sweeping under the seats and down the aisles. "Sorry, sirs," said a black man, "You got to leave so as I can get this car ready for the next passengers."

Finn stood and handed Bird his hat. "You heard the man. He's got to clean where you're sitting."

Bird rose lethargically and slowly followed Finn off the train. Bridget's father, waiting on the platform, rushed over and pumped their hands. "Welcome back. When I didn't see you get off with the other passengers, I thought you'd missed a connection."

Bird wouldn't meet his eyes. He took off his hat and held it over his chest. "I'm . . . so sorry . . . I failed."

"That's all right."

"We . . . tried . . . hard."

"I'm sure you did."

"Bird ain't lying." Finn held his thumb and forefinger slightly apart. "Twice, we were *this* close to catching them."

John grabbed Bird by the shoulders. "Goliath, look at me."

Bird hesitated, but finally faced him.

"Forget it," John said. "It doesn't matter any more."

"We can still get those dandies," Finn said. "New York is a big city on a small island. Now they're on our turf, they can't hide forever."

"No. I have a new mission for you two."

"You'd trust us with another job?" Bird said.

"Yes. Bridget escaped the convent and is running around with a young fisherman somewhere in Brooklyn. Mary Elizabeth wants you to find them and get her wed."

Bird put on his hat, grabbed the handle of his suitcase, and solemnly nodded. "Get Bridget married. Got it."

CHAPTER 56

Once Bryce reached Jacksonville and changed to a northern line, he found himself amongst his parents' people—wealthy cousins of Vanderbilt, Carnegie, Flagler, and their ilk—fleeing the impending Florida heat for their summer houses in Saratoga and Newport. He no longer had to buy rounds of drinks to keep everyone entertained. They bought his.

Good thing, too. When he'd generously given Mo and Julius most of his money to take with them, he thought he'd be home by Wednesday. Now, according to the train schedule, it'd be Friday night before he arrived, and the banks would be closed until Monday. He hated that he'd have to ask his father for money, even though it'd just be a temporary loan.

However, a new crowd heading north meant he could tell his stories again. While they kept his glass filled, he rhapsodized about the World's Fair, the promise of his New Mexico emporium, the nobility of the Pueblo people, and praised the Indians' simple life.

"Tell us more about the Fair," said a lawyer from the recently merged borough of Brooklyn.

"The World's Fair is like a magical elixir. Those who taste of it are immediately awakened to a vision of what the new century holds in store. There are exhibits from everywhere in the world. Countries like China and Japan who have barely let a westerner past their docks, have brought their best refinements and shown us wonders we didn't know existed. Old European capitals have crated their great works of art and shipped them to St. Louis. Why, even the wealthiest among us would have to travel the globe for decades to see what can be viewed at the exposition in ten days."

"Sounds big."

"Larger than any previous world's fair, and I'll wager, larger than any will ever be again."

Hell, he was inspiring himself. When he wasn't entertaining, he was thinking of how he and his friends would bring the new world to the primitive west.

On the last day of his trip, five days of drinking finally caught up with him. After lunch, he returned to his seat and fell into a deep slumber.

In the waning hours of the afternoon, he became aware that he was dreaming. This had happened before—awareness that he was dreaming while actually doing it.

Jesse was talking to him, "The white man is not authentic. The white man has lost himself in the harnessing of the world. He dams a stream with a wheel and uses it to do the woman's work of grinding corn. The women of my tribe have ground corn with a stone for a thousand years. The tortillas from that corn are authentic food."

"I'll taste one as soon as I get there," Bryce said.

"The white man burns black rocks to make steam turn steel wheels on iron rails. The Indian riding bareback feels the horse's muscles beneath him, but the man on the train feels only his own butt."

Was Jesse suggesting he ride a horse all the way to New Mexico? He'd never ridden a horse in his life. When he needed to go somewhere, he just hailed a hansom.

"At the Fair," Jesse said. "I saw a white man connect a basket to a great bag of air, light a fire under it, and lift off the ground. Men say he is flying, but he does not feel wind on wings like the crow or the eagle. He's just riding in a basket, drinking champagne. His experience is inauthentic."

"How do I become authentic?" Bryce said.

"Leave the gray city of New York and come to the brown adobe of my pueblo, where the tribal grandfathers will help you find your authentic self."

"Will you be there?" Bryce asked.

"I will not, my friend. I am a bird. I will be flying above."

Bryce frowned.

"Come to the sacred mountain," Jesse said. "There you can touch the sunrise."

CHAPTER 57

By Friday afternoon, the flurry of activity in the Jones's Florham Park home had reached a crescendo. It had built steadily since Rose and her sisters returned from St. Louis three days earlier with news that Edward, Earl of Thornborough, would be coming to meet Lily's parents on Saturday. Fortescue, Violet's viscount and future marquess, would not be with him. He had to stop in Chicago on business.

One nobleman at a time was fine with Rose. She'd had more than enough of them both in St. Louis and was well-glad for once to have her mother take charge. And that's exactly what Mother had done. Devising strategy and applying tactics calculated to win over a foreign power.

Their first morning home, before they'd even unpacked, Mother had brought in extra maids to attend every detail of the mansion from top to bottom. By the time she and her sisters made it downstairs for a late breakfast, strangers were polishing the filigrees in the banisters and wood-work.

"It's nearly noon," Mrs. Jones said.

Rose yawned. "Then let's call this brunch."

Violet kissed her mother's cheek. "It was a very long train ride."

Rose and Lily both kissed their mother and took their seats. Several scratched-out drafts of guest lists littered the table.

Mrs. Jones held up a deckled-edge sheet of linen stationary containing a list of names. "Obviously, we start close to home—Dr. Ward and his wife, the

Hamilton Twomblys, and our other neighbors. But what about the Astors and the old Knickerbocker families? Will they leave Manhattan to meet an Earl? I think so."

"Perhaps a word from Mrs Twombly will encourage her Vanderbilt brothers and cousins to accept our invitation," Lily said.

Mrs. Jones nodded. "That would set the stage for the rest of New York to fall in line."

"On our trip, we met the son of a New York Senator named Holloway," Rose said. "I think Holloways are part of that set."

Lily kicked her under the table.

Mrs. Jones wrote "Holloway?" in the margin. "I'm going to ask Mrs. Coggeshall to come down for a few days and tutor us in the fine points of hosting English nobility."

Rose rolled her eyes. She'd dealt with Edward and Fortescue all last week. There wasn't any mystery to it. They both had impoverished estates and needed her father's money to restore them. They weren't about to abandon their prospective wives because they used the wrong fork.

The always steadfast Mrs. Coggeshall said she couldn't possibly leave her current charges, but she would be happy to advise via telephone. Mrs. Jones took full advantage of that and called her with questions several times over the next couple of days.

Hardwood floors were waxed and buffed to the point where the reflected sunlight when you opened the front door could practically blind you. While the temporary help worked on the house, Mother's trusted maid, Nan, and the kitchen staff assisted with planning menus and ordering champagne.

Their regular groundskeeper found his domain invaded by a half-dozen immigrant day-laborers with rakes and hoes and a nurseryman with a wagonload of potted flowers wanting to be transplanted. Mother spared no expense, and Father didn't mind. He'd been well-pleased with his investment in their foray to St. Louis and her sisters' successes. He didn't even mind that Rose hadn't managed to land an aristocrat of her own. As she'd rightly surmised, two titles were enough.

Friday morning, Rose finished unpacking and had her trunk put in storage. Hers was the last room to be cleaned, and Mother wanted everything put away before the earl arrived tomorrow. Rose didn't see why. It wasn't like Edward would have any reason to enter her room. She picked up the package she'd left for last and tore the newspaper wrapping from Mo's painting. A smile played at the corners of her mouth as she recalled that Sunday together.

She lifted a pedestrian watercolor of finches perched on a rose trellis off its hook and laid it in on her bed. In its place she hung Mo's painting. It didn't have a wire on the back, so she just balanced the frame of the canvas on the hook. She walked to the other side of her bed and admired it from a distance. How pleasant it will be to wake and see herself through Mo's sensual eyes.

Mother walked in. "Good, you're unpacked at last. I just got off the telephone with . . . Good Lord, where did you get that?"

"At the World's Fair."

"It's indecent."

Mother and Father owned a lot of art. He liked patriotic portrayals of the founding fathers. Her taste ran to birds, flowers, and still-lifes—hence the finches. But there weren't any nudes in their collection. Of course, she was draped, but the implications were obvious.

"It is not," Rose said. "It's very European. There's an entire palace full of paintings like these at the Fair. This is a study after one of them." That's what Mo told her to say. But Rose had to admit that even covered, he'd made her seem more erotic than if she'd been bare. And she liked it.

"The subject doesn't even have a proper face."

Good thing, too.

Mrs. Jones pressed her finger to her lip and studied the painting. "No face, just that scandalous pose—splayed like a hind of veal in a butcher's case."

Rose put her hand to her forehead. Only her mother would conjure an image like that.

Worry lines creased her mother's brow. "What will Lily's fellow think of us?"

"He won't think anything. As I say, this sort of thing is found in drawing rooms throughout Europe. Besides, what business would he have being in my room?"

"Oh, I don't know, he probably never will. But take it down and put the birds back up."

Rose took a stance, hands on hips. "Don't be a prude. Edward visited the same palaces we did. He probably saw a hundred pictures more revealing than this one."

"Not in my house, he didn't. Just because you don't want to become a countess, don't ruin your sisters' chances."

She wouldn't. Let them go their way and she'd go hers. She regretted not getting Bryce's telephone number, but it shouldn't be that difficult to obtain. Once Lily and Violet were married, she'd plan a weekend in Manhattan.

CHAPTER 58

Bryce opened one eye. A black man in a navy-blue coat with brass buttons leaned over him.

"Mr. Holloway, sir."

Bryce closed his eye and tried to find where his dream had left off. Jesse, asking him to come to New Mexico and eat . . . something.

"We've arrived in New York," the porter said. "You got to get up."

He felt a hangover on his periphery, but he hadn't drunk anything since lunch.

The porter stood in the aisle holding his suitcase. "This way, sir. Please."

Bryce stepped down onto the platform and made his way through the waiting room. An enormous cast-iron eagle with a thirteen-foot wingspan caught his eye. He'd missed it on the outbound trip. How? Now it seemed like a specter from his dream, a sign from Jesse.

He stumbled into the electric-lit twilight of the city and hailed a hack. He gave the driver his address and fell back asleep, hoping to recapture his conversation with Jesse. But home was only a short ride up Park Avenue and, too soon, the driver was shouting for him to wake.

"Sixty cents," the man said.

Bryce fished around in his pocket and found only three quarters. He handed them to the man. "Keep the change."

The driver pocketed the coins.

Bryce closed his eyes and wavered.

The doorman rushed outside, took Bryce's bag and held the door for him. Inside, he rang for the Holloway butler.

Jenkins arrived promptly. "Ah, yes. I'll take it from here." On the way upstairs, he said, "Did you have a good trip, sir?"

"Mix up with the trains. Saw the country. Took me five days to get home."

"Well, you're here now. Have you eaten supper?"

"No, thanks, I feel on the edge of a hangover. I'm going to take a bath and then sleep for a week."

"I'll fill the tub and turn down your bed."

After his bath, Bryce crawled between the luxurious sheets of his familiar bed while Jenkins started unpacking his bag.

Bryce didn't fall back asleep as quickly as he'd expected. He thought about how the Fair had brought together people from all over the world—primitive Filipinos, modernized American Indians, stuffy English dukes, and title-seeking sisters from New Jersey. Yet, what they had in common was that they were forever changed by it. Mo and Julius had already altered their lives, and he vowed that he would, too. Yes, soon he'd give up this luxury to seek his authentic self.

His authentic self. That was what Jesse was inviting him toward.

He yawned and adjusted his pillow. "Jenkins, turn off the light. Finish unpacking tomorrow."

* * *

The brakes squealed, and their train came to a halt.

"La Junta, Colorado," the conductor said. "There will be a one hour meal break. Passengers destined for Carson City and Denver will change trains here. Passengers continuing to points south should re-board this train when time is called."

After another blue plate special, this time pork chops, mashed potatoes, and canned corn, Mo and Julius resumed their journey. The tracks clung to the rim of a canyon where below a beautiful stream raced over a stony riverbed. The day was hot, and passengers opened the windows, sucking in smoke and coal soot. God, they were going to need baths before they could meet anybody.

Mo turned from the spectacular view below them. "Julius?"

"Yeah, Mo."

"I was thinking about all the Harvey Girls we've talked with."

Julius grinned. "I'll bet."

"No, not that way. I notice that the whole west is full of Easterners who've moved out here."

"Sure, okay. What's your point?"

Mo pulled worriedly on his mustache. "I wonder if what we're bringing to Taos might already be there."

"No, of course not. Take ragtime, for example. Has anyone we've met so far show any sign of knowing that ragtime's what's hot nowadays? And Bryce plays ragtime piano better than anyone."

"He's not modest about it, either."

"Nor should he be. As for art? I watched you study those paintings by Monet, Renoir, and Rubens at the World's Fair. I'll bet the people in Taos haven't, not even the artists."

"Julius, you're right. We heard the new gramophone, saw pictures move, and even talked on a wireless telephone. Nobody out here has done any of those things. If they haven't been to the World's Fair, they have no idea what wonders this new century is unfolding."

"Exactly!" Julius winked. "But three handsome guys from New York are about to show them."

Mo let go his worry and laughed. "Our emporium is going to be a great success."

"I have no doubt."

Ragtime Dudes in a Thin Place

The Good Times Continue . . .

During the stagecoach ride from the New Mexico train depot into Taos, Julius and Mo change their names to Jack and Morgan. They open their emporium as planned, promising Taos the metropolitan culture of New York and the latest wonders from the World's Fair. The problem—neither they nor Bryce know how to run a business. Free love? That they understand.

Ragtime is in, Victorians are out, and free love is on the rise everywhere. Soon, the handsome young New Yorkers meet freethinking women ready to tryout the mores of a new century.

With too little capital, their venture struggles until a leading member of Taos society begins holding teas for her inner circle at their store. Then, just as the business starts to thrive, the ladies turn the tea parties into a committee to bring a Protestant pastor to Catholic Taos. Instead, they are sent a recently ordained Universalist minister.

Calamities ensue. The Universalist's sermons don't go over well, and the religious conflict hurts the emporium's already teetering business. Meanwhile, the men lose a lucrative Gramophone deal, and while Morgan tries to fix that, they get shaken down by a brothel owner. Then Jack's landlady dies, leaving him responsible for her nearly grown daughters. Oh, and Bryce quits the emporium to join a peyote cult.

Yet even as the partners fail at transforming Taos, Taos transforms them. And by the time the emporium goes belly up, they are ready to start their lives over for a second time.

Winner of the Royal Palm Literary Award First Place

Richard Gartee is an award-winning novelist who has also authored seven college textbooks, six novels, five collections of poetry and a biography. If you enjoyed this book, then you will certainly enjoy the next two novels in the Ragtime Dudes series: *Ragtime Dudes in a Thin Place*, and *Ragtime Dudes Meet a Paris Flapper*, each of which won Royal Palm Literary Awards.

A complete list of his available titles, upcoming events, and forthcoming books is available at www.gartee.com where you can also sign up to receive updates on his newest publications as they become available.

Also, please take a moment to leave a short review on Amazon and/or other booksellers' websites. Reviews help to sell books, and sales help an author to keep writing. You can readily find links to online booksellers' websites by visiting www.gartee.com and clicking on the book cover image.

Acknowledgments

Thank you to fellow members of Writers Alliance of Gainesville who critiqued the book as I was writing it: Ken Campbell, Pat Caren, Allison Durham, and Bonnie Ogle; beta reader, Dick Gartee; my editor: Dave King; and proofreaders: Pat Caren and Cindy Elder.

The Louisiana Purchase Exposition, commonly referred to as the St. Louis World's Fair, was the largest in history and left behind an abundance of historical records I found helpful in writing this novel. In particular, was Lee Gaskins' wonderful website "At The Fair: The Grandness of the 1904 St. Louis World's Fair," the archives of the Missouri Historical Society Library, and Laura Merritt's diary detailing her visit to the Fair. I also frequently referenced the *Official guide to the Louisiana Purchase Exposition*, and an official map of the fairgrounds.

While my descriptions of the palaces, exhibits, and events of the Fair are accurate, I have taken liberty with the opening dates of one or two exhibits to fit my story timeline.

In addition to my fictional characters, a few historical persons appear in the book. Opening day speeches are drawn from published copies of the speakers' text, but the dialog of Prince Pu Lun, Prince Axel, Joseph Henry Sharp, and Olympics chair, John Sullivan, is the product of my imagination.

Additional instances where historical sources were incorporated into character dialog include the following:

Spanish-American war story was paraphrased from a letter Roosevelt wrote to his children and from two books: *Roosevelt, Theodore, The Rough Riders.* (New York: Charles Scribner's Sons, 1920, reprinted from 1902) and Jeffers, H. Paul, *Colonel Roosevelt: Theodore Roosevelt Goes to War, 1897-1898.* (New York: John Wiley & Sons, Inc., 1996)

Scene outside the opening day luncheon at the Palace of Varied Industries was adapted from *Pictorial History of the Louisiana Purchase Exposition and the World's Fair at St. Louis*, by Murat Halstead, 1904.

Conversation at the Concatenated Order of Hoo Hoo was adapted from *A History of Hoo-Hoo International* found on the website www.hoohoo.org.